STARDAT
MY NAME IS

I'm human and a citizen
Planets. Whoever finds thi
tion outpost or any official of the planet Bajor and let them know what happened . . . that I ventured into the wormhole by myself and was caught in some sort of storm, one that caused irreparable damage to my shuttle. In spite of my best efforts over the last several hours, I've been unable to restore power to this ship, and will soon succumb to hypothermia.

These are my last words, it seems. I wish I could leave behind some profound statement about life or death, but all I can think is that this isn't what I expected. It doesn't seem real. All my life, I've heard "adults" talk about how young people don't really understand that they're going to die someday, and I always thought I was exempt from that particular patronizing bit of wisdom, probably because I lost my mother so early. That, and how I grew up. Who my father is. My life has been anything but sheltered.

The war changed things for everyone, I know, but even before that, before I learned firsthand about mortal terror on the front line at Ajilon Prime, I thought I understood that death was never all that far away—that it could slip in and out of somebody's life without warning, taking, stealing, changing things. I knew, I understood, but I can see now, I didn't feel it. Because no matter how bad things got, he was with me. My father created the foundation of who I am, guided me. He was . . . reality. There was a way that things weren't real for me until I could tell him, could take or ignore his advice, could feel his love for me and know that I wasn't alone. The way I'm alone now, finally understanding that I'm going to die—this is real.

STAR TREK
DEEP SPACE NINE®

RISING SON

S. D. PERRY

Based upon STAR TREK®
created by Gene Roddenberry, and
STAR TREK: DEEP SPACE NINE®
created by Rick Berman & Michael Piller

POCKET BOOKS
New York London Toronto Sydney Singapore Idran

An *Original* Publication of POCKET BOOKS

POCKET BOOKS, a division of Simon & Schuster, Inc.
1230 Avenue of the Americas, New York, NY 10020

This book is published by Pocket Books, a division of Simon & Schuster, Inc., under exclusive license from Paramount Pictures.

ISBN: 0-7434-4838-3

First Pocket Books printing January 2003

10 9 8 7 6 5 4 3 2 1

For information regarding special discounts for bulk purchases, please contact Simon & Schuster Special Sales at 1-800-456-6798 or business@simonandschuster.com

Cover art by Cliff Nielsen

Printed in the U.S.A.

For Mÿk Olsen, my man

ACKNOWLEDGMENTS

This book would not have been possible without the creative input of Marco Palmieri and Paula Block.

I'd like to thank my friends and family for their patience and support—Steve and Dianne Perry, Dal and Rachel Perry, Gwen Herzstein, Curt and Joelle, Sera, Thad and Britta, Leslie and Paul, Doctors Goldmann and Cohen. Oh, and Tamara, of course.

I'd also like to thank Denise and Michael Okuda for their compilation and reference masterpieces—and Cirroc Lofton, who was a fine, fine Jake.

Self-realization is a comedown from salvation,
but it still gives us something to hope for.

—Mason Cooley

PROLOGUE

THERE HAD BEEN a crack in the humidity mesh that shielded the Arva nodes, which, if left unchecked, would almost certainly lead to fuel dilution. He'd had to set down, and as much as Tosk disliked dealing with the maintenance of the ship, the circumstances were ideal for such a necessity; he'd discovered as much almost immediately. Getting to the surface had been particularly difficult due to the spinning drift of ice that surrounded the small world, a minor excitement that the *ochshea* would appreciate . . . although the quad of Hunters was at least ten days behind, and he doubted that they would think to search for him here. The unnamed, uninhabited planet was one of eight within the star system closest to the Anomaly, and that alone was enough to deter traffic of all kinds, not just Hunted Tosk.

As the filters expelled their toxic moisture into the alien air, Tosk surveyed the desolate plain that surrounded him, a vast expanse of broken rock covered with blue-green algae. There was a scent that he associated with wet soil, not unpleasant. He knew from the readings he'd taken before landing that there were no mountains, no oceans, only the endless sea of water-colored stone beneath a distant gray sky. The lifeless waves formed rifts and caves, valleys and peaks. It was serene and lovely, and, like the deserts of home, a reminder of the infinite cycle—birth and train, Hunt and death, birth and train . . .

Tosk took a few short, deep breaths, puffing to fill the tiny sacs beneath his plated skin. The planetoid was visually appealing, but not environmentally suitable for Tosk; the atmosphere was too cool, and thick with moisture. The vast majority of the Tosk lived and trained in the second-sun hemisphere of their homeworld. Still, the planetoid would be useful to other Hunted, Tosk decided. Its position and lack of resources made it an unlikely hiding place.

I would not have set down, were it not essential, he thought, still gazing across the mute landscape. Of course, the Tosk rarely did anything that wasn't vital, except for what was vital to the excitement and continuation of the Hunt. *And in that, I have done well.*

It was a proud thought, and well deserved. He had successfully kept the Hunt moving and active for more than four months now. They'd been close several times, the Hunters, enough for him to actually see their jacketed faces on three separate occasions. Even if he went to his rebirth the next day, he had earned another positive mark for the Tosk of 67, his clan by genetic material, and would die with honor. Group 67 was already near the top of requested quarry. It was a distinction beyond measure to be so acclaimed.

Behind him, he heard the soft coughing sounds that signaled the end of the humidity expulsion. The sound was small and flat in the thick atmosphere, dying quickly, and Tosk turned toward the hatch a few steps away, ready to leave. He'd already planned to double back on his trail and engage the Hunters, at the clouded stretch he'd passed through only yesterday—

—and Tosk blinked, stopping. There was a flicker of light, a glint like reflected shine coming from the shadow beneath his ship's narrow bow. Had something fallen from the body of the ship when he'd landed? He walked toward the flicker, relieved that he'd seen it before leaving, whatever it was. Maintenance was uninteresting, but neither did he want to die of a loose panel seal during his Hunt.

Tosk crouched in front of the shining object, knees sliding to attest to the slickness of the omnipresent algae, and narrowed his eyes, still unable to identify the piece—a crystalline chunk of matter the size of a fist, of a luminous tint that seemed to shift between orange and red. It was attractive and Tosk reached for it without thinking, deeply compelled to touch the shimmering surface—

—and *crack*, a violent surge of energy threw him back and away. He landed hard on his side but barely felt it, as power coursed through his body, not painful but so strong that he couldn't move, could only experience. He flickered in and out of invisibility helplessly, felt his tendons and muscles rapidly flex and release, the contractions all-encompassing and beyond his control. He couldn't breathe, could barely see, and what he did see was impossible—even, leveled ground beneath him, a pathway, lined with colorful organic growths. Where there had been empty, open space stood a great wall that towered beyond his unsteady sight, two of them, joined, the corner of a structure. There was a sound like high, lonely wind, but the environment's fundamental emptiness was gone; he wasn't alone, and neither was the single building, and all of it appeared and disappeared as quickly as his vision fluctuated, strobing like light, faster, his ears and mind filling with the sound of rushing air—

—and then it was over all at once, as though it had never happened. Tosk was himself again, he and the ship alone in the silent sea of damp, dusky stone. More confused than alarmed—there had been no pain, no physical damage—he sat up, breathing deeply. He looked to the red object that had inspired the strange experience and saw that it was gone, an ashy smudge where it had been.

Tosk got to his feet, checking the rudimentary proximity sensor on his sleeve, and saw what he knew he'd see—no structures within range. He had not dreamed it; Tosk didn't dream, nor were they equipped to hallucinate. The crystal had created the encounter, to what purpose he did not know.

Nor do I care, he assured himself. He was uninjured and the ship was repaired. Tosk weren't engineered to be overly curious, either—there was the Hunt, the apex of all education and training, and he was Tosk, the Hunted, and this was his time. To spend even a moment of that time concerned with pursuits not related went against his very being.

Tosk felt a sudden urgency to be away. He boarded his small vessel without looking back, and found himself hurrying through the simple procedures that would lift him through the planetoid's atmosphere. Never had he felt such a desperate need to leave a place, to go . . . elsewhere.

The ice storms that had so troubled his descent were now merely an annoyance, an impediment to his progress. Tosk wove into the stuff, blasting himself clear when maneuvering became too difficult, his thoughts occupied with something else—although it wasn't until he was well away from the lonely planet that he perceived his preoccupation, realized that he had actually forgotten his plan to backtrack. The urgency that continued to grow in his conflicted mind wanted for something, something that was not the Hunt. Something he didn't know.

Riding aimlessly through the vast dark, he struggled to understand. The Hunt was all, it was what he was. And as the pressure to find this new, unknown thing grew, Tosk finally began to understand that something was horribly wrong.

I

. . . battles fall and fail, and there is a Time of waiting, the space between breaths as the land heals and its children retire from war. The Temple welcomes many home, the faithful and the Chosen.

A Herald, unforgotten but lost to time, a Seer of Visions to whom the Teacher Prophets sing, will return from the Temple at the end of this time to attend the birth of Hope, the Infant Avatar. The welcomed Herald shares a new understanding of the Temple with all the land's children. Conceived by lights of war, the alien Avatar opens its eyes upon a waxing tide of Awareness.

The journey to the land hides, but is difficult; prophecies are revealed and hidden. The first child, a son, enters the Temple alone. With the Herald, he returns, and soon after, the Avatar is born. A new breath is drawn and the land rejoices in change and clarity.

* * *

Something was wrong.

Jake knew it before he was entirely conscious. He groped for understanding, roaming his mind for how and why . . . and because he was scared, he thought of his father, and the simple, strong emotions drew him up through the dark.

"Dad?"

He opened his eyes at the sound of his own soft, scratchy voice, felt the numbing cold, saw his bag floating amid a frozen snow of empty food packets, like a symptom of sleep, a detail of some strange dream. He was floating, too, facing the single, outdated transporter at the back of the shuttle, muted red emergency lighting taking the sting out of the unlovely decor. Obviously, the *Venture*'s AG had gone out . . . but it was the deep chill that had tipped him to wake up, that immediately had him moving before he could think clearly. Cold was bad.

Jake turned clumsily and kicked off the port wall, aiming for the tiny vessel's decidedly dead-looking flight controls; there were no alarms sounding and even the console screen was blank, a blind eye. He arranged his thoughts on the way, ignoring the growing urge to panic even when he realized that he couldn't hear anything—not even the soft hum of the recyclers.

I was in the wormhole, waiting, about to give up and go back to the station . . . and everything started spinning, the prophecy was coming true, I thought, except I couldn't control the ship; I started to black out, and . . .

"And now I'm here," he muttered, grabbing the back of the pilot's seat and pulling himself down. Wherever *that* was. He tucked his feet under the chair, hooking his ankles under the manual height adjust, and tapped at the computer's old-fashioned console keys for a diagnostic.

Nothing happened. No light, no sound. He took a deep breath and went through the sequence to call up the shuttle's fail-safe backup system—and it failed, not even a glimmer of power. He did it again, slowly and carefully, the knot in his stomach tightening further as he understood it was a lost cause. Except for the emergency lights, which ran off an independent battery, there was nothing on the ship that was working.

Okay, okay, don't freak out . . . check the main conduit, it's got to be a blown relay, I can fix that. . . .

A darker thought intruded. *What if it's not?*

As far as anyone on the station knew, he had taken his newly acquired shuttle to Earth, to see his grandfather. He'd been too embarrassed to admit that he was following a scrap of prophetic text into the wormhole, hoping to bring his father home . . . though considering his current situation, finding Dad had just dropped a notch or two on his priority list. Nobody knew where Jake was, himself included, his fix-it skills were barely competent, and it was already cold enough for him to see his breath, a pale, ethereal mist hanging in front of the blank viewscreen. Where was he? How long had he been unconscious? And with the *Venture* completely dead, how much longer before he ran out of air, or hypothermia set in—

—or is this all part of the prophecy?

The thought stopped him, refocused his thinking. The torn bit of parchment that had brought him here stated clearly that the journey to the land would be difficult . . .

. . . but that I would enter the Temple alone and return with the "Herald" before *Kas has the baby.* Kas was still months from her due date; maybe this was all part of it, maybe the Prophets had him and he just had to wait awhile. . . .

"Knock it off," he told himself firmly. Daydreaming about salvation was as bad as straight-up panic; he knew better. He needed to check the conduit, and the relays, and about fifty other things. Anything else was a waste of time.

Jake pushed off from the chair to get his bag—there was a light panel in it he was going to need—reminding himself that he'd been in tight situations more times than he could count . . . definitely more than most men his age. Somehow, things always worked out. This would, too, because the alternative . . . there just wasn't one.

Jake set his jaw, clenching his teeth so they wouldn't chatter, carefully avoiding the feelings of fear and dread that had taken root in the shadows of his mind, that were beginning to grow in the powerful absence of light.

Stardate 53267.5. My name is Jacob Sisko; I'm human and a citizen of the United Federation of Planets. Whoever finds this, please contact any Federation outpost or any official of the planet Bajor and let them know what happened . . . that I ventured into the wormhole by myself and was caught in some sort of storm, one that caused severe damage to my shuttle. In spite of my best efforts over the last several hours, I've been unable to restore power to this ship, and will soon succumb to hypothermia.

These are my last words, it seems. I wish I could leave behind some profound statement about life or death, but all I can think is that this isn't what I expected. It doesn't seem real. All my life, I've heard "adults" talk about how young people don't really understand that they're going to die someday, and I always thought I was exempt from that particular patronizing bit of wisdom, probably because I lost my mother so early. That, and how I grew up. Who my father is. My life has been anything but sheltered.

The war changed things for everyone, I know, but even before that, before I learned firsthand about mortal terror on the front line at Ajilon Prime, I thought I understood that death was never all that far away—that it could slip in and out of somebody's life without warning, taking, stealing, changing things. I knew, I understood, but I can see now, I didn't feel *it. Because no matter how bad things got, he was with me. My father created the foundation of who I am. Guided me. He was . . . reality. There was a way that things weren't real for me until I could tell him, could take or ignore his advice, could feel his love for me and know that I wasn't alone. The way I'm alone now, finally understanding that I'm going to die—this is real.*

I thought I had let the need of a son for his father become the friendship of two men. I should have broken away earlier, perhaps, beyond just physical distance, beyond the surface. I should have sought my own way emotionally, looked inside of myself instead of to him . . . but so much of what I am is from *him. It was too easy to ask instead of search, made all the easier because of his strength and certainty, even when he didn't know the answers. He has this way of making it okay, that the answers weren't always there, that things would unfold as they should. Maybe I should have done a lot of things different. Except . . . isn't it better that I had that time with him, now that he's gone? That we were still so close, now that it's over? My life . . .*

Tell them it was hypothermia. There are worse ways. Already I'm getting sleepy and my fingers are cold, very cold; I can barely feel them; I don't know if I'm making sense anymore and I want to cry but I can't. Tell Kas I'm sorry and that I love her, that she has become to me what I would have wanted with my mother, and I'm sorry I won't be there for her and the baby. Tell Nog I said to look out for her, he's my best friend and I love him, too. I just wanted to find Dad so bad, I thought I could accept it but then I started to hope and I had to come. But he's not here and I'm alone its so cold. I was wrong and Tell them I'm sorry I died. When he comess home, tell him I couldn't move on, I tried but wasn't strong enouggh I miss himand love himm There was so much I wanted to be he always said I could be anythingg my father

"I've got you. You're going to be all right, I've got you."

The low voice, soft, warm, strong hands lifting him, cradling. Someone on an intercom, a woman, was talking about something, but all Jake cared about was that deep, loving voice.

He felt tears threaten, tears of love and joy, an ache in his throat that hurt worse than the cold, but then he slipped back into the dark, lulled into sleep by the same feelings that had woken him not so long ago. His father held him; he was safe.

2

"HEY. Hey, human."

Jake stirred, frowning, trying to keep hold of the well-heated, pleasantly embracing dark.

A smell like dirty teeth washed across his face in a humid cloud, accompanied by the same insistent, low-pitched voice.

"Hey, wake up. Human boy."

It was the odor as much as the insistent verbal prodding. Jake cracked open one eye and found himself looking at a dog, one with dark brown eyes and a narrow muzzle, its head streamlined and sleek. He'd seen them back on Earth, played with them in the holosuites when he was younger.

"Finally!" the dog said, rolling its eyes, and Jake blearily realized it wasn't a dog. No ears he could see, no lolling tongue, and there was a narrow line of soft-looking, floppy spines running down its back, a shade darker than its fur, which was forest green.

Dogs don't talk, either, he thought randomly, trying to focus.

The alien leaned toward him, baring its narrow teeth slightly in a curling sneer. "Listen, if anyone asks, I had nothing to do with this."

Jake opened both eyes, backing away from the creature on his elbows until he came up against a wall, confused and very lost. He was on a low bunk in a small and dimly lit room, a ship's cabin from the layout. There were a few rumpled blankets thrown over him, but he was naked underneath.

"Easy, calm down," the alien said, backing up a step and raising its hands—paws?—palms open. Four long fingers and a small opposable thumb on each, also furred, its lean body curving and canine as it sat back on its haunches; definitely male. It wore a plain, rather nondescript collar but nothing else.

"Damn translators," it muttered to itself, then it, *he* bared his teeth again, his tone exaggeratedly friendly and overly loud. "Ah, I mean you no harm. I'm your friend. *Frieeend.*"

Funny, under other circumstances. Jake relaxed a little, recognizing that the fierce expression was probably the dog alien's version of a smile, but he still pulled the blankets up to cover his bare chest, uncomfortably vulnerable. "Right, same here. Friend."

The alien laughed, a pleasant chuckling in the back of his throat. "Sorry. I thought . . . anyway, you'll say you woke up on your own, right? I've got half a Klon paeg riding on it."

Before Jake could ask the first of several questions their conversation had already inspired, a deep, feminine voice spilled into the room from a speaker on the far wall. *"You know how I feel about cheating, Pif. Not only do you now owe me another half paeg, one more time and you're banned for a full cycle."*

"Pif" looked stricken, though his tone was placating. "Hey, Facity, listen, you know I didn't mean—"

"I know exactly what you meant," the woman, Facity, said. She didn't sound particularly upset . . . and her voice seemed familiar, somehow, as if from a dream.

"How's our guest?" she asked. *"Should I send Glessin down?"*

Pif raised a brow muscle in Jake's direction. Jake nodded uncertainly, opening his mouth to say that he felt all right, but Pif was already answering.

"Apex, top shape," Pif said. "Happy human."

"Good," Facity said. *"Why don't you invite him up to the bridge, Pif? Make him feel welcome, and I might forget to beat you."*

Jake relaxed further. Alien they might be, but he knew friendly banter when he heard it. They reminded him of Quark and Odo. Kind of.

"No problem," Pif said, and sighed, nodding at Jake. "First officer. I swear that woman has a built-in monitor . . . I'm Pifko Gaber. Welcome to the *Even Odds.*"

"Jake Sisko," Jake said, trying to remember what had happened and drawing a blank. There was the wormhole, and then . . . nothing. He felt tired and a little achy, his fingers felt tingly, but he was fine otherwise. "Thanks . . . though I'm not sure . . . where are my . . ."

"Oh, right." Pifko dropped onto all fours and padded around to the foot of the bunk. He picked up a stack of clothing, Jake's boots on top, and hopped nimbly back to Jake's side on his hind legs. "Here, get dressed. These are Dez's, yours are being cleaned. We found your shuttle late this afternoon, total meltdown, and you were about the same. Glessin said you might be confused when you woke up, though he thought you'd probably sleep through the night . . ."

Pifko shook his head, stepping aside as Jake sat up to dress. ". . . which Facity bet on—me and her and a few of the crew, we have these ongoing wagers? I can't believe I took her up on this one. She's Wadi, you know."

Jake paused with the loose shirt half over his head; he knew that name. "Wadi . . ."

"They bet on *everything,* you have no idea," Pifko said. "Anyway, Dez—he's the *Even's* captain, he found you—had us bring your transport on board, and here you are."

Still feeling only half awake, Jake tabbed his boots while the talkative Pifko went back to the rather complicated history of his ongoing wager game. The Wadi . . . Jake remembered them now. They had been among the first Gamma Quadrant visitors through the wormhole, a culture that seemed to live for games and gambling . . . though thanks to one of Quark's rigged dabo tables, the diplomatic contact hadn't been renewed. Jake thought it had been a mutual decision, by the Wadi and the Federation, but he couldn't remember the exact circumstances, or much about the species; their visit had been seven years ago, and while he'd had the definite impression that his father hadn't thought much of them, he'd never said why. They weren't part of the Dominion, at least, he knew that much.

Pifko isn't Wadi, though. They're humanoid. What kind of ship was this? Maybe a freighter . . . was he in the Gamma Quadrant? Jake was dazed, not sure what he should be thinking, not sure what he should be doing. Pifko was oblivious.

". . . so I told her a full paeg *owed* equals a week of watch shifts, unless you're willing to double up on points—"

Jake nodded absently, rolling up his sleeves as he stood. The clothes were simple, an off-white, woven shirt and dark pants, the top loose through the chest and shoulders. As though he'd stepped into his father's clothes.

Dad. Jake remembered hearing his father's voice on the shuttle, remembered thinking that he was safe. A dream, maybe. Or maybe this Captain Dez.

Sitting on his hind legs, Pifko's head came just to Jake's hip. The doglike alien fell silent as he sidled backward, craning his neck to look up at Jake. A slender, possibly prehensile tail curled around his back feet.

"I'm sorry to interrupt, Mr. Gaber—"

"Pifko," he broke in, baring his teeth. "Or Pif, most everyone calls me Pif. *Ga* is a region on my home planet, where I'm from, and *ber* means one of seven born. My mother was Ga*ba,* one of six, my sire, Ga*bek,* one of four."

Interesting, though Jake was starting to wonder if his new friend was capable of being quiet. "Pif—are we in the Gamma Quadrant?"

"Gamma—? Oh, right. Your people are from the other side of the Anomaly." Pifko cocked his head to one side, his inquisitive expression making him look more like a canine than ever. Jake saw that he had ears, after all, but they were laid flat against the side of his skull. "That *is* where you're from, right?"

Anomaly. Gamma Quadrant nomenclature for the wormhole. Jake hesitated, thinking about the recent attack on DS9. He'd been preoccupied with the prophecy when he'd left for the wormhole, but not deaf or blind; even with popular consensus being that the strike on the station had been an isolated event, a few rogue Jem'Hadar hoping to cause trouble, there'd still been serious concern over renewed hostilities between the quadrants. Last he'd heard, the Allies were sending a fleet to check things out, and though the general hope at the station had been that Kira would send them peacefully packing, there was a chance that things could go from bad to worse. *And as far as I know, right now I'm the only person in the Gamma Quadrant who knows what the Federation and friends are thinking. . . .*

On the other hand, was there any reason not to tell his rescuers where he was from? If they had his ship, they probably already knew, anyway. Even if there had been a "meltdown," all they had to do was open the backup files in the computer's storage boards and look at navigation. The possibility that he might be in personal danger was seeming more remote by the moment . . . and in any case, his point of origin seemed like pretty useless information.

"Yes," he answered finally, hoping he wasn't making a mistake. "I went in looking for something, and there was a kind of energy storm inside . . . and I guess my shuttle was thrown clear."

"I thought no one was traveling through these days. What were you looking for?" Pif asked casually, dropping out of his sit and walking toward the door. "Did you find it?"

If Pif cared, he was hiding it well.

"I wasn't . . . It's a long story," Jake said, looking around the small cabin as he stepped after Pifko. His shoulder bag was on the floor next to a sliding panel door, which presumably led to toilet and shower facilities. He scooped it up and did a one handed inventory, making certain that the prophecy was still safely wrapped inside. If Pifko was offended by the implication, it didn't show.

"Maybe later, then. You ready to meet the captain?" Pif asked, as Jake slung his bag. Jake nodded, but suddenly suspected that he might be lying. In the last week or so, his entire life had been one long, strange dream, from a doubtful prophecy at B'hala, to DS9, to a crazy decision based on hope and longing that didn't seem to be working out. That had, in fact, almost killed him. He was tired and sore and hungry, and suddenly dependent on people he didn't know. On the whole, he wasn't sure he'd ever felt less ready for anything.

Pif kept up a steady stream of mostly trivial chatter as they made their way to the ship's bridge. Jake tried asking a few questions, about the *Even Odds*'s purpose and where they were headed, but after a few transparent diversions by Pifko, he gave it up. Either the garrulous alien didn't know, or he wasn't supposed to tell—though he was agreeably harmless enough about it that Jake wasn't worried. He figured that he'd get his answers when they reached the bridge. Besides, it allowed him to get a look at the *Even Odds.*

He found himself memorizing details as they walked, taking it all in with the journalist's eye he had developed while working for the FNS. "Inconsistent" would be a fitting adjective, he decided. The few corridors they passed through were large but unevenly lit, some sections of each gloomy hall entirely empty, others nearly overwhelmed by dented storage lockers and half-empty equipment carts. He guessed they were on a freighter, only because he couldn't imagine what else it might be—not military, definitely, and it didn't have the organized feel of a science vessel . . .

. . . *or the sterility.* Cluttered though she was, the *Even Odds* didn't seem unclean—the air as flat and odorless as any other ship's—but it was still a far cry from sanitary. If he *were* writing an article, "well-used" would definitely make the edit—

Jake blinked, slowing down. There, to the left, what seemed to be an open control panel slot, a small square window set into the bulkhead—he'd seen a flash of silver movement, a brief, liquid shadow fleeting past the open space. He stared at the empty hole, waiting, but whatever it was, it was gone. He hesitated a beat longer, then jogged the few steps to catch up to Pif, who had continued to walk and talk.

Some kind of diagnostic mechanism? A trick of the light? A loose pet? Jake waited for an opening to ask about the metallic shadow, but there was none to be had; Pif talked almost as fast as Morn when he was on a roll, scarcely stopping to breathe. Jake sighed inwardly after a moment and filed the silvery glimpse away under things to ask about later.

They turned a corner, Pifko going on about a humanoid his sister's mate had once dated (he'd even hopefully mentioned the woman's name, as though Jake might know her) when Jake stopped in his tracks, staring. In the space of a few steps, the *Even Odds*'s architecture had changed.

"This is Cardassian," Jake said, stepping to the bulkhead wall, recognizing the simple, functional materials and arced construction of the support beams that lined the new section of corridor. They could have just stepped onto DS9, maybe one of the lower levels.

Pifko cocked his head to one side. "Oh? Interesting.

Anyway, Sfeila didn't want children, and Ptasme did, so his choice ended up being simple, really—"

Jake had stopped following, forcing Pifko to break off his brightly wandering story and turn back.

"The rest of the ship doesn't look Cardassian," Jake said, lightly touching a support. He felt an unexpected pang of homesickness at the cool, smooth texture beneath his fingers, remembering the time that he and Nog had tried to carve their initials into such a beam, down on one of the maintenance levels. Nog had managed a single, ashy line with an engraving light before Odo had just happened to wander by, scaring them both into renouncing vandalism until death. That seemed like a million years ago. . . .

"The rest of the ship's *not* Cardassian," Pifko answered. "This area got patched some years ago with salvage, before I signed on, anyway. That was three years ago. You'll have to ask Prees about who else pitched in on design . . . though she'll be guessing, whatever she tells you. She's Karemman, Prees . . . kind of the main engineer if you don't count Srral. The *Even*'s been around, I'll say that much."

Jake noted the names, oddly relieved that he'd met a few Karemma on DS9, hanging around Quark's. It made the alien ship feel less intimidating, to know at least one of the species aboard. "Who's Srral?"

"You mean *what's* Srral. You'll see," Pifko said. "But you really should meet Facity first, and the captain. Come on, we're almost there."

Jake trailed Pifko around another corner, noting that the architecture had changed back to generically well-used as the canine alien stepped into an open lift tube, asking for the bridge after the door had closed behind them. The trip took only a few seconds, barely enough time for Jake to straighten his shoulders before the door to the bridge slid open. He hoped he at least looked prepared for whatever was coming next.

Pifko had gone back to chatting about his siblings, apparently a favorite topic, and continued to talk as he stepped out in front of Jake, leading him into a large, well-lit ship's bridge, a semicircular room with a sunken floor. The walls of the upper "balcony" were lined with equipment, more sophisticated than anything he'd seen so far on the *Even*, but as he took in the three humanoids who watched him exit the lift, the ship's technology immediately ceased to be of interest.

Jake did his best not to stiffen as his heart started to race. A scantily clad woman sat at a control console against one wall, her blue and purple facial tattoos and plaited hair describing her as Wadi; a well-built man with gray skin and light eyes stood in the lowered center of the bridge, his muscular arms folded, his gaze intense and focused. And next to him, a Cardassian male, tall and unsmiling, staring at Jake and holding what looked like a weapon in one steady, scarred hand.

Facity Sleedow sat by communications, watching Dez and Glessin as they waited for the boy. Neither man spoke, though the bridge was far from silent—the engineers were in Three Bay, looking over the boy's shuttle (Jake, Dez said his name was Jake-something, from the other side of the Anomaly) and debating the merits of molded alloy fabrication. Facity studied Dez as she half listened to the open com, as curious about his reaction to their new passenger's arrival as she was about the young man himself.

Since beaming back to the *Even* with the near-frozen boy in his arms, Dez had been uncharacteristically introspective. No joking, no millionth recount of the time he'd been lost in the ice caves on Preth without his boots—which she'd fully expected, he dragged that story out when the mere *concept* of cold came up; even Srral's questions hadn't raised a smile, and the engineer's usually mistaken assumptions and guesses concerning humanoids never failed to crack Dez up. No, something had happened, she'd wager her last commission on it; he'd returned from the shuttle and disappeared into his quarters for much of the evening, mumbling something about research, and had spent his little time since on the bridge staring off into space. Even now, the captain stood by Glessin with his arms folded, his expression stern in thoughtfulness. Facity expected as much from Allo Glessin, he'd lived a hard life already and wasn't genetically prone to easy good humor besides . . . but Zin Dezavrim? The man was the very definition of carefree. Something had taken hold of his mind, and was unwilling to let go.

The artifact he found in the boy's bag, perhaps? Probably not. Dez had said the writing was old but not particularly valuable—religious, and in very poor shape—and though he'd been known to understate worth while working an angle, he'd left it with the boy . . . and if Dez defined carefree, he epitomized opportunistic.

Whatever the reason for Dez's mood, she could wonder later. The bridge's main door slid open and Pif stepped out, chatting away about something or other, followed closely by the young man. He was tall for a human, almost as tall as she was, and though he glanced around the bridge warily, his stance suggesting a sudden readiness for action, there was a sincerity in his brown face that gave him away—not a fighter, and probably much too nice to be traveling on the *Even Odds*. He seemed to focus on Glessin, nervously eyeing the medical bioreader in the Cardassian's hand; maybe he didn't like doctors, a lot of people didn't. Though a lot of people didn't like Cardassians, either, at least around the Anomaly. The *Even Odds* mostly worked the systems surrounding it, and the civilians, the farmers and traders living on the worlds their ship passed, were still trembling from the cold Dominion shadow that had fallen over them during the Quadrant War. A shadow that had included the faces of the Dominion, the Vorta and Jem'Hadar, and the names of their allies, including the Breen and the Cardassians. With the signing of the peace treaty, the shadow had retreated, but fear and mistrust would surely linger throughout the area for years to come, probably toward all strangers.

Facity lowered the volume on the engineering discussion and stood, wistfully wondering if the boy knew how to play dom-jot. It *was* an Alpha Quadrant game, but from the innocent look of him, she wouldn't bet on it.

As usual, Pifko didn't seem to be planning on shutting up. ". . . and here we are! Jake, ah, Sisko?" Pifko asked, continuing on without waiting for confirmation, "this is Captain Dezavrim, everyone calls him Dez, and this is Allo Glessin, our resident medic." Pif raised his eyebrows, grinning. "We call him Allo Glessin, though we could probably come up with something more descriptive, if we put some thought into it."

Jake seemed to relax somewhat as Pif made the introductions, but Facity decided to step in before he got carried away with "descriptives," fully aware that she was better at breaking Pif's stride than anyone else on board. Pifko had a lot of saving graces, but keeping his mouth closed wasn't one of them—creating one of the games she regularly played with herself, how-quickly-could-she-shut-Pifko-down. She wasn't feeling particularly playful at the moment, but all that practice came in handy for occasions such as these.

"Pif, thank you for escorting our guest to the bridge," she said, smiling widely. "You know, as long as you're here, why don't you let Glessin take a look at that sore spot you were telling me about, you know, the one on your belly, right next to your—"

"Actually, that's all better now," Pif interrupted anxiously, glancing at the Cardassian medic and quickly looking away. Pifko disliked being touched by non-mammalians, either by instinct or preference, she didn't know. "And I'm supposed to be looking through those inventory lists, for, ah, our next excursion, remember?" Pif grinned nervously at Jake Sisko, backing toward the door and nodding his farewells. "I'll see you later, I'm sure . . . Captain, Glessin . . . Facity."

She hid a grin at the edge he put on her name, turning her attention to the three men in front of her. Dez also smiled a little at Pif's hasty retreat, and she could see the further calming effect the interplay had on their visitor.

"So, Jake Sisko," Facity said, making sure she had his full attention, hiding another smile as Jake's gaze stuttered across her buxom form. The way she looked and dressed often had a strong effect on humanoids, Wadi and alien alike, though she was impressed with his determination not to focus on any of her more enticing parts. "What brings you out this way?"

"This is our first officer, Facity Sleedow," Dez said, actually stepping in front of her. He had on what she thought of as his meet-the-leader suit, his voice full and rich with command, his demeanor expansive and cordial . . . toward Jake, anyway. "And since Pifko already made the rest of the introductions, why don't we let Glessin look you over, and then you and I can go get something to eat? You must be hungry, and I'm sure we can dig up something fit for human consumption around here. We can stop by your shuttle, too."

Jake nodded. The human looked tired, but competent to be on his feet. "All right. Thank you."

Glessin aimed his bioreader and stepped forward, asking Jake how he was feeling, but Facity wasn't listening. She grabbed Dez's arm and pulled him away, not bothering to hide her annoyance.

"What are you up to?" she asked, keeping her voice low and directed. "And why did you cut me off?"

Dez met her gaze evenly, his own light eyes as far away as they'd been since finding Jake Sisko. "I'm not up to anything . . . but since you asked, has it occurred to you that he might not feel like telling you his life story?"

Facity opened her mouth to tell him exactly what was occurring to her—and then closed it again. This had the ring of something personal, and though she wasn't one to be stepped over lightly, Dez's defensiveness was as uncharacteristic as his previous silent reflection.

She decided to let it go, for the moment. "It has now," she answered casually. "And since it appears I'm not invited to hear it, perhaps I can join you later? For dessert?"

Backing off was definitely the way to play it, and reminding him of one of her prime attributes didn't hurt, either. Dez's jaw loosened, a small, familiar smile edging across his face. "Always."

That was the Dez she knew . . . though he was going to owe her some kind of explanation if he wanted something sweet after dinner. What they had sexually wasn't terribly serious, off and on for a year or two, but they'd been business partners for almost six. He knew better than to think he could pull rank and then expect open arms.

"Good," she said, smiling in turn. "I'll come find you after my shift. Maybe by then we can give Mr. Sisko a tour, see what he can tell us about the Wa." A small joke, an Alphie certainly wouldn't know anything about the *Even*'s unusual architectural additions, but keeping things agreeable with Dez now meant he'd be more likely to keep her in confidences later. She didn't state the obvious for the same reason—that there was a much greater chance they'd have to confine the boy, keep him locked up and in the dark until they had a chance to get rid of him. In that case, the best they could hope for was that he was innocuous, a random, harmless traveler. At worst, he could be the enemy . . . though she doubted it, and from Dez's strange protectiveness, she thought he doubted it, too.

Glessin cleared his throat before approaching, his expression as unreadable as usual. "I'm not an expert on humans, but he appears to be fine . . . hydration's good, and the tissue damage was minor, like I said. His fingers have healed completely."

"Wonderful," Dez said, turning to Jake and grinning broadly. "Let's go. I can introduce you to some of the crew along the way. Thanks, Glessin. Facity, I'll see you later."

The boy smiled neutrally at both of them before following the captain to the lift. There was something in Dez's voice that she wasn't able to place until after the door had closed behind them, carrying them off into the *Even*'s shadowy depths. Glessin wandered over to a console to add to his file of biological trivia, but Facity stayed put, gazing at the closed door, more perplexed than ever. It was a tone she knew only from their most intimate moments, when he spoke of his childhood . . . a kind of tenderness, for lack of a better word, hopeful and somehow careful, as though it were too precious to be challenged. For whatever reason, Dez *wanted* to like Jake, and she could only hope that the boy was worth the captain's trust. In their line of work, unnecessary risks could prove costly. They certainly had in the past.

No point evaluating without more information, there was no payoff. Facity determined to let it go for now, remembering that Feg and his brother had proposed a bet on the upcoming trip to Drang, one she needed to take them up on. Both Ferengi insisted that there'd be bloodshed, and though it appeared to be an even bet, she felt somewhat obligated to wager against it. She *was* first officer, after all; there was morale to consider.

"Glessin, I need to go by accounting—would you stay up here for a few minutes, watch things?"

Absorbed in his medical files, the Cardassian nodded, not even looking up from his console. The *Even*'s crew was fairly extraordinary at the moment, all but the new archeologist tested and trusted, and the *Even* herself was outfitted for facility—except for Srral, any one of the crew could captain the ship alone, at least for brief periods, and even Srral could do it as long as there was someone else around to explain a slightly less alien perspective than its own. It was an unusual, incredible ship, with a crew almost like family . . . assuming one had an extremely diverse upbringing, and a few dubious relatives.

More like family than most of us have ever known, anyway, she thought, feeling a surge of protectiveness for what the *Even Odds* was about. Love wasn't a word that came to mind when she thought about someone like Glessin, or Prees, or the majority of the *Even*'s crew . . . but everyone on board gave enough of a damn to offer at least a minimum of consideration and respect to their shipmates. It was no great leap for her to understand why a new face was a bit disturbing, even one as naive as the boy's.

Having already forgotten her decision not to concern herself with Dez and Jake Sisko, Facity walked slowly to the lift, wondering if Jake would still be around when the *Even* finally made it to Drang . . . and curious, whether the boy was to play some part in their unusual family, as Dez seemed to want, or turn out to be just another outsider, along for a ride that he couldn't possibly have anticipated. At the moment, Facity wouldn't bet either way.

3

AS THE LIFT door closed on the bridge, Jake saw the Wadi first officer staring after them, her expression wary. He wasn't sure what to make of her—what she was wearing would make a dabo girl blush—or Allo Glessin, though both had seemed nice enough.

Not dangerous, anyway. Glessin's handheld medical reader had thrown him for a moment, as had seeing a Cardassian on the bridge. What was a Cardassian medic doing out here, anyway? There was a story there, he was sure. It seemed entirely incongruous, and initially very unnerving—from that cool, expressionless stare to the heavy scars on his hands . . . Glessin's manner, though, had been politely neutral. And watching all of them interact had lessened Jake's anxiety considerably. It was strange, being on a ship where no one wore a uniform, where "orders" seemed as casual as requests, and again, Jake wondered what the *Even Odds*'s purpose was . . . though he'd already decided to let the captain lead the conversation. It seemed prudent, until he had a better idea of his exact circumstances.

Like Nog used to say—if you don't know what's going on, keep your ears open and your mouth shut. If it wasn't one of the Ferengi Rules of Acquisition, it should be. *Though I should make up my own list of rules . . . top of the list, don't go chasing prophecies without backup.* With every passing moment, the realization of how lucky he was to be alive grew stronger; Glessin said he'd been moments from freezing to death.

"Deck C," Captain Dez told the lift, his voice pleasantly deep and commanding, and Jake was struck anew by how much he sounded like Dad. It was no wonder he had imagined being rescued by his father; they even had similar builds, though physically the resemblance stopped there. The captain's body and facial features were basically human, but his skin was light gray and highly textured, rippled like corrugated matter. The flesh was thicker and darker at the top and back of his head, giving the appearance of hair, and his eyes were the color of a ripe peach—as close as they were in the lift, Jake could see that there were no pupils, only a grouped scattering of darker orange flecks at the center of each eye.

Captain Dez tapped at a com piece on his shoulder. "Prees, it's Dez—I'm bringing our new passenger to see his shuttle. Is Stessie around?"

A soft, girlish voice answered as the lift hummed to a halt. "Lema's here, says . . . Stess is actually headed down already, I think. Do you want Stessie, too?"

"No, I'm sure two will be more than enough. We'll be there in a minute." The captain tapped out and turned an infectious smile toward Jake, who was wondering if

Stess and Stessie were the same person; more names for his mental list.

Dez ushered Jake out of the lift with a sweep of his hand. They stepped into a corridor that was better lit than the ones Pifko had led him through earlier, the cool air scented with a light, oily tang of industrial lubricants.

"We're on C Deck, maintenance are on C and D," the captain said. "Quarters and living facilities are on B—that's where you woke up—and bridge is A. It's a basic enough layout, except . . . except there are some irregularities. I'll have Pif give you a tour tomorrow morning, after you've had some rest. I ask that you don't go wandering before that, not on your own. It's not safe."

Not safe?

His expression must have shown his unease. The captain smiled, shaking his head slightly. "It's nothing to concern yourself with, I assure you. Once you've had a chance to look around, you'll understand. So . . . do you have any questions?"

Where to start? "Ah, how many people are on board? Captain," Jake added.

"Just Dez, really," he said, still smiling. "Capacity is sixty, our current crew is sixteen. We've had as few as seven and as many as thirty-eight. Since she's capable of complete auto on code activation, one person could run her. I keep her in top-of-the-line, new upgrades as soon as they're available on the market." The last was delivered with a distinct note of pride.

"So you're . . . explorers?" Jake asked, his best guess.

Dez hesitated. "No. I'd say . . . Let's stop for a moment, all right?"

"Sure."

Dez leaned against one bulkhead wall, his expression

turning serious. "First, let me make clear that this is all in the strictest confidence. Anything you want to tell me stops with us, all right? And I'd appreciate the same courtesy. . . ." He grinned suddenly. "If Facity knew what I was about to tell you, she'd have my head. She worries too much about company secrets getting out, so to speak . . . so it might be better to play the innocent a while longer, until I have a chance to fill her in, all right?"

In spite of the nervousness that his prelude had brought up, Jake found himself smiling back. Dez came off as very sincere, very likable. "Deal."

Dez's smile faded, and he took a deep breath before continuing, as though nervous himself. "With your shuttle's computer down, there was no way to ascertain your identity, and . . . I read the document you're carrying, Jake. The translation was on the padd you were holding, when I found you . . . and so were your, ah, personal notes. I ran the contents of your padd through our translators. I know why you went into the Anomaly, and . . . and what you were hoping to accomplish."

Remembering, Jake felt himself flush. His last words. It was hazy, but he thought that he'd been crying at the end, could remember feeling deeply sorry for the impact that his impending death would have on his family and friends. *And everything about Dad. . . .*

"I just wanted to let you know that I respect your decision, and your privacy," Dez quickly continued. "There was a time that I . . . I understand why you went into the Anomaly, and see no reason that *your* reason needs to be popular knowledge. As far as this crew is concerned, you were traveling, you hit a storm."

Jake nodded mutely, not sure what to say. He felt

awkward, but Dez's understanding was almost a relief . . . and Jake realized suddenly that the captain was the first person who actually *knew.* He hadn't even told Nog about the prophecy.

"When we got back, I found your name in our library," Dez went on. "Or your father's name, I suppose I should say. For business reasons, I make a point of keeping our political files as current as possible, and his role in the Quadrant War is well documented. Considering, I felt I should tell you that the *Even* is, we're not exactly . . . we're wanted by the Dominion, for what we do. Wanted by a few other organizations, as well."

Jake was surprised. "Wanted . . . as in—"

"As in, there's a bounty out on us," Dez said. "We're . . . retrievers, I suppose you could say, we're in the retrieval business. We do salvage—a lot of that, particularly since the end of the war—courier security, an occasional mining excursion . . . but mostly we hunt down historical artifacts and other items of value that have been lost, or stolen, and we . . . once we find them, depending on the circumstances, we generally return them to the rightful owners. We're freelance, and we've crossed the Dominion and its allies on more than one occasion, and probably will again. They've stayed to themselves since they signed that treaty with your Federation, kept to their own space, but we don't know how long that will last. And if we run into them and they find out who you are, there could be trouble. . . ."

Dez cut himself off with a shake of his head. "Who am I kidding? You landed on a ship looking for trouble. We're fortune hunters, we have more than our share of enemies because we're good at what we do. And since you're going to be with us for a while, I thought it would be best to let you know up front."

What? "I, ah . . . actually, I was hoping to get back to the Alpha Quadrant as soon as possible," Jake said, hoping he didn't sound as desperate as he suddenly felt.

Dez shook his head, his orange gaze sympathetic. "Your shuttle is beyond repair. Whatever happened in the Anomaly, it caused a complete system failure and lock."

"If it's . . . I'm more than happy to pay for any work, or if you have a runabout I could borrow . . ." Jake began, but Dez was still shaking his head.

" 'Beyond repair' is literal," he said. "And we only have one dropship, and that's about to be refitted, there's no way I can spare it. I'd take you back myself, but we're at least three months from the Anomaly, even taking a direct route at our best speed. A nonstop flight isn't an option, in any event—as it happens, we're going in that direction, but we have business along the way that can't wait."

Jake blinked, still not sure he'd heard right. "Three *months?*"

"Whatever happened to you in the Anomaly, it threw your ship almost a hundred parsecs in an instant, which probably explains why your energy reserves were depleted. And why your ship is in the state it's in."

At Jake's stricken expression, Dez clapped one warm hand down on his shoulder. "Don't worry, Jake. We were planning to head to Ee after the Drang mission is complete, once we've met with the, ah, clients, perhaps dropped by a few salvage sites. Ee is an open marketplace between us and the Anomaly. I know you can find transport there. The main port has several sellers."

Ee. He'd never heard of it, but it sounded promising.

Jake nodded, swallowing his upset. "Okay. How long before you make it to Ee?"

Dez smiled. "Shouldn't be more than four months. Five, at the most."

His heart seemed to stop beating. He'd told everyone at the station that he'd be gone a few weeks, at the outside. Eventually someone would check with his grandfather, and they'd all think he'd disappeared, maybe even died. Jake wanted to protest, wanted to tell the captain that he had to go home, that Kas was due to have a *baby* in just five months . . .

. . . and in another week *she'll probably call Earth to check in, if Nog doesn't first.* How would he ever explain? Kas and his grandfather, Nog . . . they'd be sick with worry, and all because of his stupid pride. He'd been afraid of being embarrassed for his basically unfounded belief in the prophecy, afraid they'd stop him from venturing into the wormhole alone . . . afraid most of all that he'd see the pity in their faces, hear the unspoken indulgence in their voices as they told him that they understood, that his father would be back someday, that it was all right to grieve . . .

As if sensing his upset, Dez squeezed his shoulder, his expression softening. "Enough worrying over what can't be helped, eh? Come on, let me introduce you to a few more strangers."

Jake forced a smile and nodded, hanging on to the thin hope that the shuttle wasn't as bad off as Dez seemed to think, suddenly feeling much too young to be where he was.

Dez kept silent as he led Jake on toward the maintenance bay, respectful of the boy's struggle to maintain his composure. He wanted his father, and he wanted to go home, and neither was available at the moment, which put him in a difficult place.

And add on that he is what he is. . . .

There were a vast lot of cultural differences in the universe, but Dez believed that with little exception, young humanoid males were a species all their own. It was hard enough to know so very much but have lived for only so long . . . and even harder to accept comfort in the face of disappointment, when you wanted so badly to protest the unfairness of life but knew that you had to accept what was, that there was no other choice.

It's amazing that any of us survive. Luck played a part, certainly . . . though Dez felt it also took a certain spirit. Jake was young, according to the files, but clearly had the heart of an adventurer. He'd stolen away from the comfort of home to seek his father and his fortune, alone. . . .

Dez smiled inwardly, chiding himself again for the ongoing comparisons. Jake Sisko was probably as bravely hopeful and naive as the Zin Dezavrim of twenty years past, but the circumstances *were* different. Dez had hardly known his own father growing up, and Jake didn't appear to be concerned with fortune. Still, it was impossible not to feel a connection, of sorts . . . or some of the pain. Finding Jake's honest, pathetic, beautiful last words, apologizing for not being what he thought he was supposed to be, what he thought his father wanted . . .

Dez shook it off as they reached the Three Bay door. Memories of his own chaotic, misspent, heartfelt youth had been interfering with his concentration all day. Bad enough that he'd already told Jake the truth, about their semi-outlaw existence. His instincts told him unequivocally that the boy wasn't a rival spy or thief, but trying to explain his decision to the first officer wasn't going to be easy, particularly considering what had happened the last time they'd taken on a seemingly harmless passenger, several years before. He'd been pretty sure of his instincts then, too, as the lovely Facity would surely remind him. . . .

. . . Ancient history, to dust with all that. The boy needs to know that he's not alone. The young Dez could have used an inkling of such comfort, and he'd actually found *his* father, and on far less than the narrow hope of a religious divination.

Dez nodded encouragingly at Jake and then pressed the door panel to Three Bay, noting from the feelings of curiosity that edged through his mind that Stess had already arrived. He'd have to talk to her about that; she'd been careless as of late, and while he didn't mind, he knew that it drove a few of the other crew members to distraction. Glessin particularly disliked feeling Stessie's random projections, though Dez knew she was more careful around the solitary Cardassian. Stessie was nothing if not respectful.

The door slid aside and they walked into the cavernous bay, their steps echoing as they headed for Jake's ruined shuttle at the far side. Neither Prees nor Lema was in sight, probably inside—the shuttle's entrance faced away from their approach—though Stess was standing near the diagnostic control console at the small vessel's bow. Dez could feel her interest in Jake, and wondered if the young human picked up on it as well. Humans were certainly capable, but Stessie was a subtle creature; if you didn't know what to look for, you might not notice. Stess was the most interactive fifth of Stessie, probably because she was the only part that spoke, though the other four could all project to some degree.

As they drew closer, Dez tried to see Stess the way Jake was seeing her, and realized that he probably hadn't even noticed her yet . . . or recognized her as a sentient being, anyway. Like all of Stessie, Stess was barely a meter tall, an armless cluster of purplish fungal growths atop a trio of low, stocky legs.

Probably thinks you're a plant, Dez thought deliberately, mentally picturing her in the *Even*'s greenhouse, and felt her response, a kind of sarcastic good humor. It seemed that Jake felt it, too.

"Is someone . . . is there an empath on board?" Jake asked, just as Stess stepped out to meet them. Still watching her through Jake's eyes, Dez smiled, seeing how peculiarly graceful she was, as if for the first time. She seemed to roll smoothly toward them on her padded feet, the uppermost part of her soft, misshapen body gently undulating to keep balance. It almost seemed as though she were dancing.

"Not an empath, exactly," she said, her voice soft and hollow, the unusual creaking, moaning sounds of her language formed by shifting air pockets beneath her external sensory bulbs. Translators didn't do it justice. "I can read some imagery-based thought, but reciprocal emotional empathy is only possible within my own species."

Dez grinned. "You make sure we feel you, though. I picked you up out in the hall, Stess. This flirting of yours simply must stop."

"My passion for you is too deep," Stess said, and Dez felt another flush of projected sarcastic humor.

"She's joking," Dez clarified to Jake, who seemed thoroughly captivated, a wide grin on his boyish face.

With no visual cues to be read on the rounded, fleshy surface of her body, and no verbal nuances in her language, Stess's wit came from saying one thing and projecting another. The effect was mesmerizing.

"Jake, this is Stess," Dez said, giving some thought to his next words. Friagloims were extremely rare outside their homeworld, and Stessie took some explaining. "Stess is one-fifth of Arislelemakinstess, a quinteth Friagloim whom we call Stessie . . . though all you have to remember is that she's basically a walking multipart mushroom, and Stess here is the one that talks."

"Dez is the one who is funny," Stess responded, pushing a feeling of deliberate deceit, and Jake laughed.

"Stess, this is Jake Sisko," Dez said dryly.

"A pleasant occurrence," Stess said. "Arislekin are elsewhere, but I will introduce you to Lema. . . ."

As she spoke, Lema, physically nearly identical to Stess, moved out from and around the shuttle to join them, followed a beat later by Atterace Prees. The Karemman engineer looked tired but happy, her wide, hooked nose smudged with soot, a spanner in one slender hand. The shuttle was allegedly a lost cause, but Prees loved checking out anything new.

Dez let Stess make the introductions, first to the silent Lema, then to Prees. Dez was about to ask for a report when he realized that Srral hadn't spoken up yet.

"Where's Srral?"

"In the shuttle's computer system," Prees said, shaking her head. "We agreed it was blown, but then Srral *insisted* I run a conduit into the fiberpatch storage boards, just so it could see the layout, piece together the integral stats. . . ."

Prees banged on the shuttle's hull a few times with a

spanner and raised her pleasantly high-pitched voice, bouncing echoes around the bay. "Hear that, Srral? The captain wants to know where you are!"

Srral's androgynous voice, that of the *Even*'s computer, answered. *"I hear. I've returned from the shuttle 87336* Venture, *and am at this time primarily enmeshed in the secondary communication relay of Three Bay's external diagnostic console."*

Prees glanced at the side of Jake's shuttle, peering at the presumably Bajoran characters that spelled out its name. "*Venture,* huh? I wouldn't have guessed that," she muttered.

"I was told it used to be a Bajoran gambler's," Jake said.

"That explains the way it's decorated," Prees said, smiling crookedly, winning likewise from Jake. Dez remembered the gaudy clash that had assaulted his eyes upon beaming over and nodded, glad to know the boy wasn't responsible for the purple, gold, and green stripes that swirled around the cabin. Of course, Facity would probably love it, she was pure Wadi. As much as Dez tried to avoid gross generalizations, something about high-stakes gambling seemed to inspire risks of all kind, including a few in the realms of taste.

Dez walked over to the standing console at the front of the shuttle, motioning for Jake to join him. Srral was another unusual crew member, a living machine that lived in machines, but while its personal history was complicated, Dez figured that its nature was self-explanatory.

"Srral, come meet the shuttle's owner, Jake Sisko," he said, popping the top panel, exposing a network of unidentifiable circuitry. Even if he had known anything at all about diagnostic engineering, modifications to all of the *Even*'s major systems over the years had created a chaos of alien technical flotsam that Dez couldn't begin to guess at . . . which made Srral an extremely *valuable* unusual crew member.

"Yes, Dez," Srral said. As its voice emanated from the nearest speaker, its fluid, silvery form appeared, sliding up, around, and through the jungle of crystalline core sticks and silicon boards. *"Shall I extricate myself entirely?"*

"Unnecessary," Dez said, smiling at Jake's amazed expression, reflected dully in the partial puddle of Srral. "I just wanted Jake to have a face to go with the name."

"Jake has no face?" Srral *was* fascinating, but also as literal as your standard android.

Dez laughed, and Prees shot a dark look in his direction. Srral's limited emotional engineering didn't include embarrassment, so far as anyone knew, but Prees was extremely protective of the liquid alien.

"The captain's statement was unclear," Prees said smoothly. "He wants Jake Sisko to form visual memory imaging connected to your designation."

"I understand," Srral said.

"You were inside my shuttle's computer system?" Jake asked.

"I was," Srral answered. What little they could see of its body shimmered in communication, vibrating as its extensions streamed through the *Even*'s labyrinth of system connectors, manipulating the bits and bytes of its natural habitat.

"I think I saw you earlier, on my way to the bridge," Jake said. "Were you . . . do you travel through machinery?"

Prees picked up the conversation. "Srral hasn't met a

system yet that can't support it," she said, her tone somehow proud and shy at once. Dez used to tease Prees about having a crush on Srral, but had stopped when Facity had finally convinced him that she probably did.

Jake looked at Prees hopefully. "So, the *Venture*'s system is still viable?"

Prees didn't hesitate. "No. I've never seen anything like it, either. It's as if every relay in the entire network *liquefied.* Backups, too. The only thing that still works is your secondary lighting, and that's only because the connections are primary."

"The energy storm burned the system up?" Dez asked.

"Negative," Srral responded. *"Extreme heat would create composition change. There is none, nor are there internal indications of naturally occurring magnetic flash effection or psionic wave disruption, either of which might cause this level of network disorder."*

"So what was it?" Dez asked, turning to Prees. Srral was the internist; Prees handled a much wider range of cause and effect.

"A nonpareil incident, incalculable odds on that . . . or directed energy," she said. "I'd say weapon, but I've never heard of anything even close. . . ."

She flashed an uncertain smile in Jake's direction. "Angered any deities lately?"

"Maybe so," Jake said, mustering a fake smile. "Though, considering where it happened, a total freak occurrence can't be ruled out, either."

Dez could actually see the hope drain out of Jake's eyes, and decided it was time to move things along. Meeting some of the crew had provided a distraction, but it was late; the boy needed to eat and sleep before he'd be able to look at the situation with any real objectivity. He looked exhausted, and Dez reminded himself to give Pif a good kick later for waking him up. Figuratively speaking, of course.

"You're alive and well, that's the important thing," Dez said firmly. "And undoubtedly starving by now—why don't we leave all this for later, and go introduce you to something edible?"

Jake nodded unenthusiastically, though he managed to paste on a smile for Prees and Lemastess, muttering a polite word or two for having met them all. He certainly had better manners than Dez had kept at his age. . . .

. . . *Stop the comparisons. He's not you.*

Right. There was no reason at all to think that young Jake had gone looking for his father because he felt lonely or uncertain, coming of age, because he still looked in the mirror and saw his father standing behind him, tall and strong and sure, everything that he couldn't yet find in his own searching gaze. . . .

. . . *Enough!*

As they walked away from the broken shuttle, Dez found himself hoping that Facity might be willing to postpone their after-dinner date, realizing that he was feeling somewhat exhausted himself. Exhausted, but intrigued . . . wondering what it might have been like for him if he'd met a Zin Dezavrim when he was first starting out, someone who could have shown him even a few of the possibilities that were out there, just waiting to be touched and tasted and experienced by a willing young heart. Someone like his own father, if his own father had wanted the job. . . .

"How did you happen to come by that prophecy of yours?" he asked abruptly, and as Jake started to explain, Dez began to wake up, to see a number of new possibilities taking shape.

So, I've been rescued, and here I am, totally wiped out and still wide awake. I keep thinking about how far I am from home, and how long it'll take for me to get back. I'm thinking about a lot of things; it's been an interesting day, to say the least, and since I have absolutely no idea what else to do at the moment (Dez said I shouldn't go roaming until I get the tour, tomorrow morning) I thought I might as well write some of it down.

First thing, my grand journey into the Temple of the Prophets, to find Dad . . . I'm thinking "big mistake" might be the understatement of the century, and not just because the prophecy didn't turn out. What exactly happened to my shuttle? Maybe it was *some bizarre storm, maybe the Prophets saved my life by tossing me into the Gamma Quadrant, I don't know. . . . But I do know that if the* Even Odds *hadn't come along, I'd be Jake-on-a-stick by now. Which says what, exactly, about how important I am to the Prophets, to their so-called plan? Actually, how can I even ask myself that question? Dad is their Emissary, their Chosen, and it's been painfully clear throughout my life that how that affects me is of no import to them. Now that I think about it, maybe this* is *all for the best. . . . If I feel stupid and guilty now, for keeping it a secret from my friends, for jumping into it with both feet and very nearly dying for it, maybe I'll think twice next time before letting myself believe that the Prophets are watching out for my best interests. Does that seem bitter? Do I care? I want to go home. I know it's my fault that I'm here, I know I'm responsible for the decision, but it's about time I stop kidding myself. Maybe Dad didn't have a choice about having the Prophets in his life, but I do.*

*I'm incredibly lucky to be alive, and luckier yet that it was Dez and his people who found me. Over dinner (which was actually a pretty good seafood stew; after three days of basic carb-protein packs, I'm relieved to report that their replicators [*shifters, *in Gamma-speak] are restaurant-quality), after I told him about Kas, and how I really need to get back, he offered to drop out of warp and shoot a directed-channel message back toward the wormhole, just saying that I'm uninjured and accounted for . . . no ship identification, though, and no route plan (either they're really lawbreakers or they really think they are, I can't quite tell; so far, I haven't gotten the impression that Dez is any more crooked than Quark, which would make him just another entrepreneur of victimless crime . . . according to Quark, anyway). He said he's sorry he can't take me back, but they're going to be busy. Apparently Ee is only a few weeks away in a straight line; it will take them four or five months because of all of the stops they need to make along the way. He says that with the war having just ended, this is the* Even'*s one chance to "run salvage," that if they don't do it now, it won't be there later. . . .*

Not that I can or should complain. I'm grateful for the attempt to send word, though the chances of it being picked up are about one in a billion. Less, probably, no repeater hardware, no beacon signal, just a straight com; with no subspace relay on this side of the wormhole anymore, there'd actually have to be a ship on the Gamma side, listening for it. Still, it's all that can be done, and considering he knows practically nothing about me, it's nice of him to offer.

We talked some about the war, and though I didn't tell him what was happening at the station when I left—just to be on the safe side—I managed to get across that I didn't think it was the safest time to be near the wormhole. Dez seemed almost amused by my concern, in a friendly way. It's obvious that he's not worried. Apparently the Even Odds *managed to keep out of the Dominion's way when the Jem'Hadar were pushing into the sectors around the wormhole. It's easy to forget that not everyone was completely emmeshed in the fighting, that there were people just trying to make a living and hoping not to get involved.*

Contrary to what Dez said, this seems like a safe ship, with decent people—though in my current state, I feel a little overwhelmed by all of it . . . which is another reason to write, to keep all this straight. There are sixteen in the crew, including Dez. So far, I've met Pifko Gaber, Facity Sleedow, Allo Glessin, Attarace (sp?) Prees and Srral, and two-thirds of Stessie (who apparently counts as one crew member, not five). Dez mentioned that there are a pair of Ferengi on board, brothers named Feg and Triv, they handle finances (what else?). I was surprised to hear it . . . and to see a Cardassian, for that matter. How any of them ended up on a "retrieval" ship, I have no idea. Of the rest, I know there are at least two more Wadi or part Wadi . . . though I'm not exactly clear on what everyone does specifically, beyond the obvious (medic, engineering, etc.). Dez told me that it's taken him years to assemble the Even*'s current crew, but he didn't volunteer any job descriptions . . . except for a man named Coamis (Komes? Coemes?); he's apparently an archeologist of some kind. Dez wanted to know about the prophecy, and then had a lot of questions about the B'hala dig, about what I did there. He said* *that if I was interested in religious archeology, I should talk to Coamis. I told him I had ended up more interested in the geological aspects, actually, which Dez seemed to approve of wholeheartedly . . . my writing, too, now that I think of it. He was really curious, asked a lot about what I've worked on, what I like to read. . . . In fact, we spent most of dinner talking about me. So much for my reporter's instincts. It felt good, though, to lay out everything that's happened since Dad disappeared, particularly with what happened to Istani Reyla. That she was murdered right after giving me the prophecy. . . . Anyway, Dez said that worrying about that now would only make me crazy. He was very accepting, of everything. It sounded wild to* me, *chasing some ancient prophecy from a religion I don't even follow, but Dez seemed impressed, if anything. Said it showed initiative.*

I'm finally getting tired, guess I'll wrap up for now. Maybe tomorrow I can find out about this Drang place we're headed, see if there's a way I could take a ship from there. It's funny, part of me absolutely refuses to give up trying to find a way home before anyone figures out that I'm missing. . . . But there's another part that just wants to accept that the decision is out of my hands . . . or, rather, to accept that I've already made my decision and now have to live with the consequences. I don't know which will win out, in the end.

4

IT HAD BEEN late when Facity finally made it to Dez's quarters, and she'd been fully prepared to have it out over his earlier behavior on the bridge, but she never had a chance. The second she stepped through the door, he'd tackled her with a muttered "Sorry about before," and several long, healthy moments went by before an opportunity to talk came up again.

Afterward, Facity curled up against Dez's side, resting her head against his warm, heaving chest as they both caught their breath. Definitely a mutually satisfying arrangement, though she found herself mildly irritated that she'd lost her head of steam. As it were.

And if he ever steps on my toes like that again, in front of a stranger . . .

"Do that again and you're dead," she said mildly, tucking one mussed braid behind her ear, sure that he'd know exactly what she was talking about. Dez often came off as reckless, wild, and he was—but he also paid attention.

"I won't," he said, smiling but not indulging in the obvious joke. "Forgive me. It's just . . ."

He trailed off, but she didn't prompt him, curious though she was; he'd tell her when he figured out what he wanted to say. She'd discovered long ago—much to her frustration—that trying to drag it out of him only slowed things down. Exponentially.

That, and I'm more tired than I thought. She felt herself relaxing, enjoying the warm silence; postponing the conversation wouldn't be such a bad thing. She'd spent most of the morning running Drang probability scenarios, on screen and holo. Then there was the business with the boy's dead shuttle, followed by what had ended up being a full night arguing investment planning with Feg and Triv. A number of interesting new trade avenues had opened since the end of the quadrant conflict, but the Ferengi wanted to play it safe until the numbers were better established. *They really should take more risks, though. We have the capital, particularly after that coin-collection job, and what's the point of having wealth if we don't get to play with it? They need to relax, dream a little, spend a little . . .*

"He's Benjamin Sisko's son, did you know that?" Dez said finally, drawing her back up from a near-doze in which Feg had been wearing earrings and a crown.

Facity blinked. Benjamin Sisko . . . it sounded familiar. Federation? The *Even Odds* had been busy enough the last few years without getting caught up in the Quadrant War, but it was good business to know the players in such a consequential game. Most of Facity's knowledge of the Alpha Quadrant came from database swaps with cultures that had had direct dealings with those on the other side of the Anomaly: The Parada, the Argrathi, the Karemma . . . and of course, the *Even's* resident Alphies, Glessin and the Ferengi brothers.

"Isn't he . . . didn't he head up the Anomaly's Alphie station, Federation Nine?" she asked. "The one that the Cardassians built . . ."

"The same," Dez said, nodding. "Sisko was originally assigned to Deep Space 9 to oversee the Cardassian withdrawal from Bajor, the religious planet right near there . . . and he ended up playing a key part in the Bajoran religion, and in the war with the Dominion. A few months ago, Sisko disappeared. It appears that he either died or was whisked away by the Bajoran gods . . . noncorporeal life-forms who allegedly reside in the Anomaly."

Facity was fully awake. "And Jake went looking?"

"The text I told you about, that I found in his bag," Dez said. "It's a prophecy, about the son of a religious figure going into the wormhole and coming back out with one of the gods' chosen. The wording's ambiguous enough, you can see how he got the idea. . . ."

Facity laughed. "Makes it easy to see why there's not more of a market for prophetic religious text."

Dez wasn't smiling. "We've chased artifacts on a lot less. And he was trying to find his father."

"Who apparently doesn't want be found, wouldn't you say?" Facity asked, suddenly feeling a lot better about what had happened on the bridge. Dez had just been trying to save Jake the embarrassment of telling the story, of having to explain himself. "Poor kid . . . though how old is he? Just matured, I'll wager?"

Dez seemed to tense slightly. "So?"

"So, was his father kidnapped by these gods, or what? If he chose to go off and live with them, he can probably choose to go home, too." Facity shrugged. "It doesn't sound like he needs rescuing . . . and Jake's certainly old enough to be on his own, don't you think?" She grinned suddenly. "I wish someone had kidnapped my father when I was his age. It would have saved me all kinds of grief."

Dez didn't answer, and he was definitely tense, she could feel it coming off him in waves. Facity pushed herself up and wrapped the coverlet to her chest, not sure what she'd said, if anything, to bring about the sudden coolness of his gaze.

"What?" she asked.

Dez stared at her another beat, then sighed, seeming to deflate slightly. "I told him what we do," he said simply.

It was her turn to stare. She could feel the muscles in her jaw go tight, could feel a hot flush creeping up the back of her neck.

"You can't be serious," she said, her voice surprisingly mild to her own ears. "Have you forgotten what happened last time?"

"That was years ago, Fac," Dez said, looking away.

"When you met that helpless, pretty little thing, who just needed a ride to the next port, she said, to get away from her boyfriend?"

Dez shifted uncomfortably. "There's no way this kid staged anything, he didn't even have a distress beacon—"

"I risked my *life* to get that dagger, and next thing I know, you're telling Miss Vash-the-wide-eyed all about your glorious new find—"

"—and the next day she disappeared along with the knife," Dez said, sighing. "I was wrong, I shouldn't have trusted her. But the circumstances really are different here—if you just talk to him, Facity . . . I don't think he could lie with a straight face if his life depended on it."

"Talk to him, right," Facity snapped. "That'll make me forget that we *agreed*, Dez, we agreed that nobody on this ship talks without both of us signing off on it. You *promised* me."

Arms tightly folded, thoroughly irate, she waited for his retort, expecting him to fight, *wanting* him to fight, so she could fight back . . . and as the seconds stretched, his gaze distant, not seeing her at all, she felt her anger met by confusion. What *was* it, anyway, why was Jake Sisko so damned important?

"I'm sorry," he said finally, his voice soft. "But I want to help him. When I was . . . my father . . ."

With those two unguarded words, her anger collapsed. Dez rarely mentioned his family, his unusually mixed parentage—he didn't even identify with a single species, let alone relative, and had he ever talked about his father with his defenses down? No. No, she would have remembered.

He shook his head suddenly, his voice turning firm, his pale eyes flashing with resolve. "Look, I apologize, all right? I should have talked to you first, but it's done now. I'll bet you a thousand paegs that I'm right about him. And if I'm wrong . . . if I'm wrong, *you* get to be captain."

From self-righteous ire to dismay at the small hint of a very old wound, her emotions weren't sure what to do with his final pronouncement. It surprised her into laughing, and after a few seconds, Dez started to smile.

"Captain, huh?" she said, and laughed again, the tension in the room going, gone. "That seems fair."

"We have a deal, then," Dez said, reaching for her, and with barely a token resistance, she let herself be pulled back down to meet him, wondering if he would ever stop surprising her.

Jake had just stepped out of his cabin's tiny bathing cubicle when Pifko Gaber signaled at the door, bearing Jake's own clean clothes and a wide, canine grin. Pif, it seemed, was a morning person. Jake wasn't so much, but was glad to see the chatty alien; while he felt a lot more like himself than he had the day before, he was still disoriented, and there'd be no question of his having to carry the conversation.

"Dez said to give you the full tour," Pif said happily, pacing while Jake quickly got dressed, "then head up to the bridge. I hope you didn't mind, I was ducking your questions yesterday, I wasn't sure what was appropriate to tell you . . . orders, you know. Espionage paranoia and all that."

Pif smiled winningly, marching ahead of Jake as they stepped out of the cabin. "I could have told them, though, I knew you were all right. Let's get breakfast."

They set out for the mess hall, Pifko giving Jake an extended version of what Dez told him yesterday along the way, spouting facts and statistics so quickly that Jake could barely keep up—four main decks, bridge at the top, maintenance and cargo down below, quarters and living in between. The ship was 150 meters long, 120 wide, 60 high, and its mass was roughly 300,000, empty. It carried a minimum armament, and had a high shield capacity, a couple of general-purpose labs, and exceptional data-storage capacity in all of its systems. It was all very functional, although there were three holo-suites on B Deck (*actuality-web rooms,* Pif called them, but from the description, Jake assumed they were essentially the same), two small ones for personal use and a much larger one for training and mission practice runs.

"Did Dez tell you anything about who built her, or the C-D subdeck, or the Wa?" Pif asked, as they walked into the bright, spacious dining hall. Jake saw two Ferengi sitting with another humanoid alien at the far corner, a rather intimidating one—it was bald, dark green, and built like a Klingon. A big, frowning Klingon. All three looked up at Jake and Pifko's entrance, the non-Ferengi raising one massive green hand in what Jake hoped was a welcoming wave. It looked big enough—and scary enough—to eat the flanking Ferengi as hors d'oeuvres.

"Uh, no," Jake said, as Pif waved back. "What's the Wa?"

"We don't know," Pif said, and, before Jake could ask, "Come on, you should meet everyone."

"Everyone" was Feg and Triv, the *Even Odds*'s financial team, and Brad-ahk'la, a female gemologist from a planet Jake had never heard of, in a system he'd never heard of. Pifko explained that Brad, as she preferred to be called, also acted as ship's security when it was required.

"Not that it's generally necessary," Pif said over breakfast, smiling at the impressive Brad. "One look at her and problems generally disappear, if they're smart."

Brad had actually blushed a shade darker, insisting—in a voice like gravel being crushed—that on her planet, she was considered petite.

Feg and Triv, it turned out, had ventured into the Gamma Quadrant shortly after Quark's early negotiations with the Dosi and the Karemma, looking to see the universe and exploit new markets. Feg was definitely the more assertive of the two, though Triv seemed to agree with his brother on just about everything. They'd met Facity on a freelance consulting job and been most impressed with her "assets," as a toothily grinning Feg put it, though her financial acumen had impressed them even more. After looking over the *Even*'s books, they'd promptly lobbied the first officer for permanent positions. Since Facity had apparently grown tired of dealing with investments herself, they'd gotten the job . . . salary, benefits, *and* a percentage of sales, Feg had informed Jake proudly.

Because they planned to stay with the *Even Odds* until they reached an undisclosed financial goal, and the ship had never ventured into the Alpha Quadrant, they were excited for any news of Ferenginar; it had been years, Feg said, since they'd heard a word. Jake's announcement that Rom was the new Grand Nagus was met with blank looks, followed by a slowly dawning distaste. They both remembered Quark from their stop at DS9 on their way to the wormhole—"the loudmouth with the bar," as Feg put it—and they also remembered the loudmouth's clumsy, lobeless brother who had spilled a snail juice on Triv's new jacket. Though tempted, Jake decided not to volunteer his personal connection to Rom; while neither brother was unfriendly, they were stereotypical Ferengi . . . which meant he'd end up drowned in sycophancy the second they knew he had the connection.

Pif sat impatiently throughout the conversation, which lasted most of breakfast. As soon as Jake had pushed his plate aside, Pif was on his feet, hurrying the rest of them through the pleasantries of having met. Once they were out in the hall, his reason came clear.

"Brad's great, and Triv is all right, I suppose, but *Feg,*" Pif said, shaking his head. "Impossible to get a word in, once he gets started. I mean, I've been known to be a bit loquacious myself, but I wouldn't say I talk *too* much, would you?"

Jake shook his head. "I'm—"

"*Exactly,* and we *are* supposed to get to the bridge sometime this century," Pif said. "It's not as though we have all day. So . . . what were we talking about before? Oh, let's head for the subdeck, the Wa starts there anyway. . . . Did I mention I have siblings?"

Jake sighed inwardly as they started toward the ship's stern, Pif listing family members as they walked. There was definitely some humor to the situation, but what was he supposed to do if he had a question?

"I could have been a tour guide, you know, two of my siblings are," Pif was saying. "When my litter took the PPs—that's prospect-propensity testing?—the counselor told my parents that we were all highly extroverted multitaskers, good with people, good organizers . . . fast, too, we got that from my mother's side. Not that it takes speed to be a tour guide, obviously, but my sister Jirro is a runner for our local parliament, an eyes-only courier? She made it to first line, too, that's fast. Anyway, there was this one time, she had to give a parliament tour for a friend of hers who was sick—"

"What's the name of your planet, anyway?" Jake interrupted, not sure how else to stem the tide of Pifko. The information was all interesting, but so random that it was hard to put in any context.

"Aarru," Pifko said, the sound emanating from deep in his throat, a very doglike, gentle bay that ended in a brief whine. "In the Buof system. I say it's the Buof, anyway, but that's only what the Aarruris call it."

Being interrupted didn't seem to bother him, Jake noted, and he couldn't help thinking that it might be a familiar occurrence in Pif's family. Trying to imagine seven extroverted little Pifkos growing up together, all competing for attention . . . it hurt his ears.

On the other hand, I bet they were cute. He thought it was a safe guess that Aarruri children looked something like puppies. With raised-back spines.

Before Pif had a chance to get back to his story, they came to a stop at a dead-end lift. Pif pointed out the corridor code on the wall, an alien alphanumeric.

"Remember that symbol. This is the only lift on B that always goes directly to the subdeck," Pif said, "though depending on the day, there's another one farther aft that might take you there."

Jake nodded. DS9 had a number of diagnostic programs that were scheduled to run automatically. "You mean it's on some kind of automatic timetable?"

"No, which is why you should never take the aft route if you're in a hurry," Pif said. "It's not the lift that changes, it's the location of the Wa."

Okay, that's *confusing.* "You're telling me that there's a part of the ship that *moves?*"

Pif nodded, steering him onto the lift as he answered. "The subdeck is always in the same place, and the Wa is mostly confined to the subdeck, but it spills over in spots. And it migrates, we don't know the exact pattern. Every time Prees thinks she's got it pinned down, it pops up somewhere else." At Jake's expression, Pif grinned. "Didn't I tell you that the *Even*'s been around? C-D subdeck," he ordered the lift.

"The ship was built by an unknown species, approximately two hundred years ago, we think," Pif said, as the lift began to move. "She's passed through so many hands since her inception, she's probably barely recognizable from the original, but the builders were extremely advanced technologically; according to Prees she's been through a dozen major design overhauls, at least. Some of the systems have been added to by ten different species, something like that, but somehow, they all work together. With each addition, the ship adapts. She makes herself compatible."

Remembering how Chief O'Brien had struggled constantly with DS9's three conflicting technologies—Bajoran, Cardassian, Federation—Jake was impressed . . . and a little uneasy. Was he saying that the ship was alive?

"Fac has been able to trace it back about half of her life, but even with that, there are gaps in her history—periods where no one knows where she was," Pif continued. "Dez has had her for, ah, ten years, I think. Anyway, one of the few original parts left of the ship is the subdeck, and the Wa, which both go to show . . ."

The lift hummed to a stop, and as the doors opened, Pif's grin widened. ". . . that clearly, the original builders were very alien aliens. Oh, very important—*don't touch anything*. Can't stress that highly enough. And stay close."

The lift had opened up into what appeared to be a vast white tunnel of varying circumference, the material of its construction unfamiliar. The air was cool, and smelled faintly like wet organic fabric. Soft white light came from no source that Jake could spot, evenly lighting the randomly swirled, soft patches of pallid color that decorated the tunnel room. There were dozens, perhaps hundreds. Some of the pastel smudges seemed to hang in the air, three-dimensional, others dripped and melted down the rounded walls, pooling at the floor; the sizes ranged from a handspan across to two and three meters. The colors and tunnel extended to either side of the open lift as far as Jake could see.

Pif stepped out in front of him and stopped, waiting. After one long, unblinking second, Jake followed. Instead of turning left or right, Pif walked straight ahead, and the plain white tunnel wall that had seemed to be only a few meters in front of the lift, that should have stopped them, continued to hang the same distance away. Jake started counting paces, five, ten . . . he glanced left and then right, and saw that the infinite tunnel was starting to look more like a very large room, *like we're stretching it out. What* is *this place?*

Finally, Pif stopped and turned around, still smiling. "That's about right. Look back the way we came—see that red cross?"

Jake nodded, vaguely noting that Pif's voice sounded flat and muted, as though he were hearing it over a cheap com. They now stood in a very large, somewhat rounded chamber, still white and decorated with soft color swirls, still entirely strange, and there was a bright smear of two-dimensional red about ten meters behind them, ambiguously X-shaped. It was no bigger than Pifko.

"That's the lift. If you ever get lost down here, that's the way out. The color changes sometimes, but the shape is always the same."

Jake nodded again, speechless, his brain too busy trying to figure out what they were standing in to wonder why the lift was so disproportionately close, or how the color might change. It was like they were floating in a still white space . . . but no, that wasn't right. The floor beneath his feet *felt* like floor, even if it looked as white and ethereal as the rest of the bizarre chamber. More like they were in thick fog . . . except that wasn't right, either. The color swatches were pale but unobscured. He couldn't see a ceiling, only white, couldn't clearly make out walls anymore, but there was a definite sense that they were inside a room.

"What is this place?" Jake asked.

"We're in the Wa, on the C-D subdeck—which doesn't actually take up any space, by the way," Pif said. "The external dimensions of the *Even* haven't ever changed, which means this is some kind of dimensional-shift subspace deck, or something. Honestly, I don't know anything about the physics of it. Anyway. Check this out."

The closest blot of color was only a few meters from them, a very wan, amorphous purple approximately the size and shape of a human head. Pifko stepped toward it, motioning for Jake to follow. When they were close enough for Pif to touch it, he reached out his front right hand—

—and they were somewhere else, a small, square room that smelled like burning lemons, that was darker and warmer and empty—except in front of them hovered a tiny black sphere that seemed to be hissing. The sibilance was steady, soft, the fist-sized ball bobbing gently in the warm air.

"Oh, good. I like this one," Pif said, watching the sphere, obviously perfectly relaxed.

The feeling wasn't catching. "Pif, what's going on? What happened to the Wa?" *And what happened to the exit, 'cause I'm* definitely *lost—*

"This *is* the Wa," Pif answered, his gaze still fixed on the floating, hissing orb. "It's a bunch of rooms and environments where different things happen . . . though there are some that are just *there,* too. We don't know if it has a real name. Dez called it the *Wa* after a festival on the planet where he grew up, some kind of riotous, one-night-every-ten-seasons sort of celebration? The kind where everyone gets altered and ends up fighting or fornicating with one or more strangers, you know. Seems like every other planet in the universe has something like it."

Jake nodded, recalling the Mardi Gras on Earth, stories from his grandfather's great-grandfather. Once upon a time, it had been a less-than-wholesome affair.

"Anyway, each of those colors out there does something different," Pif said. "Some of them you have to wave your hand at, some you can just get close to—wait, here it comes. Stay where you are."

The hissing of the tiny ball began to grow higher in pitch, and the ball itself began to spin in place, quickly picking up speed. The sound and movement continued to accelerate, to climb—and all at once the ball stopped spinning and changed shape, dozens of small black rays protruding from every side, turning it into a tiny symbolic sun. At the same instant, the hissing became a clear, melodic tone, the sound hanging in the air like the hollow note of a metallic chime . . . and as the note faded, the small sun absorbed its black beams, returning to its original spherical shape. After a few seconds, it began to hiss again.

"Isn't that neat?" Pifko marveled. "There's another one just like this one, only made out of white light. I think it's a little bigger, too."

Jake nodded uncertainly, still not sure if it was okay to move. "Yeah, but . . . what does it do? I mean, what's its purpose?"

denly *woof,* there's a liquid control panel in front of you, or a whistling rock, or one of the dark faces. Maybe they *are* still here. Maybe they're trying to tell us something. . . ."

Pif's voice returned to lively normality, so abruptly that Jake started. "Anyway, it's a thought. Want to look at another one? This is the good part of the tour, the rest of the ship is mostly just a ship, you know?"

"Sure," Jake said eagerly, and was delighted when Pif let him pick the next one, which turned out to be an alien garden where the flowers spat seeds at each other. The one after that was a room full of important-looking console equipment, with handles and dials that pulsed; that one, they quickly backed away from, next choosing a perfectly blank, cold corridor dotted with pinkish pockets of warm air that smelled a lot like *raktajino.* In the next two hours they visited fourteen separate environments, carefully avoiding the gray splotches and anything that looked mechanical . . . and in that entire time, Jake didn't stop once to think about going home.

As soon as Pif and Jake stepped onto the bridge, Dez asked for Facity to call a meeting. It was early for lunch, but he had her set it in the conference room closest to the dining hall, in case it ran long. Not that he expected it; except for introducing Jake to the crew members he hadn't yet met, it was just going to be a standard mission-kickoff meeting, prep work for Drang. He wanted to announce that they'd be starting daily conferences, some update and delegation . . . most jobs, they didn't go daily until three or four days before, but Drang was big, the most important assignment in years . . . with the potential to be one of the most important ever.

As Facity's husky voice spilled out over the shipwide, Dez set aside the stat reader he'd been reviewing and walked over to where Pif was showing Jake the library access codes. Jake's gaze was bright and awake, his posture better . . . he seemed well rested, and much more relaxed.

"Good morning," Dez said. "How was the tour?"

"Oh, fine," Pif answered cheerfully, looking up from the console. "We spent all of it in the Wa, of course, but I'm sure you expected as much, since that's really the most interesting part—"

"Pif," Dez interrupted, his smile turning clenched, "would you do me a favor and run ahead to the meeting, make sure that Feg didn't forget to bring his current Drang estimates?" Which Feg surely had, since Dez hadn't asked the Ferengi to bring the list.

Pif's eyes lit up; asking him to run anywhere was a sure motivator. "No problem," he asked, then added hopefully, "And if he *did* forget, I could go get it . . . ?"

Dez nodded, finding a real smile. Pif was tiring at times, but so easy to please that it was hard not to like him. "Good idea. If he forgot, it'll still be on the conference table before anyone has a chance to sit down."

"I'm your man," Pif said, obviously delighted with the small praise. "See you later, Jake."

Pif trotted to the lift, leaving Jake and Dez alone. Facity stayed sitting at communications, intently watching whatever was on her screen, clearly not wanting to intrude. It seemed she'd decided that Jake Sisko was his personal growth project for the year, and didn't want to interfere. Dez felt a surge of affection for her. She was a good first officer and a good woman, undoubtedly better than he deserved.

"How are you?" Dez asked. "Settling in all right?"

Jake's smile was hesitant. "Everything's great . . ."

". . . but?"

Jake squared his shoulders, meeting his gaze levelly. "But I'm still wondering if there's some way I can get back to the Alpha Quadrant sooner than four months from now. This place you're headed, Drang—is there a chance I could get a ship there, or access to a repeater beacon?"

Dez looked into his eyes, saw the hopeful determination, and wished he could say yes, that he could offer the help Jake wanted. . . .

. . . though maybe this is best. Once he knows it's hopeless, he can focus on other things.

"Walk me to this meeting, and I'll tell you what I know about Drang," Dez said, sighing, tossing Facity a wave as they headed for the lift. She would participate from the bridge; as automatic as the *Even Odds* was, leaving a bridge unmanned was bad policy.

"In all of the systems closest to the Anomaly, there's been a lot of chaos over the last seven years," Dez began, stepping onto the lift, "and during the Quadrant War, things got worse. The Dominion never formally annexed the region, but they did establish a strong military presence here while the conflict lasted."

Jake nodded, recalling that some critics of the Federation's policies toward the Gamma Quadrant labored under the misconception that the wormhole opened into Dominion space. They tended to forget that it was nearly a year after the wormhole was discovered that Alpha Quadrant explorers first started hearing *rumors* of the Dominion. The Jem'Hadar didn't begin to encroach on the sectors near the wormhole until much later.

"They did a good job of upsetting the balance of power among a number of star systems around here," Dez went on. "A lot of nonaligned worlds got hurt by the changing political landscape. Dominion-friendly cultures took liberties they might not otherwise have been able to get away with. Basically, the situation made a lot of nice people look the other way, and gave a lot of opportunistic people the chance to make money or take power."

"It was pretty much the same on the Alpha side," Jake said, as the lift carried them toward the conference room. "My father always said that war brings out the worst in the worst of people."

Dez nodded. "I agree . . . and the Drang epitomize that sentiment. Drang is the name of the planet and its people. They're deliberately isolated, territorial, and very, very aggressive."

The lift had come to a stop and they walked off, Dez leading them toward the conference room.

"Think big, tough, bipedal reptiles, nasty temperament," he continued. "Anyway, the Drang took advantage of the increasing political and economic uncertainty in these parts. They've used the last five years of general confusion to stage a series of successful raids on a number of planets, stealing everything they could get their claws on—weapons, ration supplies, various types of currency, anything that could be valuable to somebody, somewhere . . . and they've ended up with hundreds of precious cultural and historical artifacts in the process."

"So . . . they're selling them?" Jake asked.

"As far as we can tell, no," Dez said. "They seem perfectly happy just to *have* them, although we suspect that they're still looking for markets. On the other hand,

Neane, she's our head researcher, she'll be at the meeting—she came across a rather obscure field report on the Drang, in a science survey file dated a century or so ago, that suggested their behavior might reflect some kind of religious conviction. The report said the Drang believed that the end of the universe would come after a massive interstellar war, and that the species with the most . . . well, *stuff,* is the one that the gods will favor with salvation. That's the basic idea, anyway."

Jake smiled a little. "Or, they could just be bad guys."

Dez smiled back, stopping. They were almost to the conference room. "Right. In any case, they finally stole the wrong artifact from people smart enough to hire us, and that's why we're going there . . ."

Glancing over Jake's shoulder, he lowered his voice slightly. ". . . and why you won't be able to find transport," he finished. "I'm sorry, Jake."

Brad, Neane, and one part of Stessie—Aris, he thought, though he wasn't close enough to be positive—had just come around the corner at Jake's back, the three females pausing when they saw Jake and Dez. Dez could feel Aris's sudden interest, and Brad's whisper to the smiling Neane was clearly not about the meeting. It was a small ship; a new face on board was no minor event.

Jake was obviously disappointed with the news, but visibly faring much better with it than he had the night before. "It's okay. Really. I hope you know how grateful I am already, for all you've done." He sighed, smiled resignedly. "And I also hope you'll let me *do* something as long as I'm here. I'd hate to just take up space."

Dez had been waiting for just such a declaration. As Brad, Neane, and Aris filed into the conference room, he and Jake started after them—and thinking about what would come next, Dez found himself hit with a particular kind of excitement he'd first known at Jake's age, a thrill that he'd spent most of his adult life working to recreate . . . he could still remember that time so clearly, leaving home to meet new people, to see new places, adventure, romance, intrigue . . . danger. Above all, that sense that anything was possible, that there were no certainties.

I didn't know to appreciate the magic of it then, I was too busy trying to survive. I didn't know that it would pass. There'd been no one to help him, to tell him that he was only young once, that those feelings needed to be treasured.

It didn't have to be that way for Jake.

"Actually, I was thinking you might be interested in helping out with this Drang situation," he said, smiling widely as they followed the others into the meeting, reading in Jake's gaze exactly what he hoped to see. That glitter of excitement suggested that there'd be no room for dwelling on false prophecies or broken ships, for worrying about who he was supposed to be, what he should be feeling or thinking. And if he could get Jake involved *enough,* maybe there'd be no time for hurting, either, over a father who'd left his son behind.

5

FEG *HAD* FORGOTTEN the estimate list—and since he'd left it in the accounting office and not in his and Triv's private rooms, the Ferengi agreed to let Pifko run for it . . . and Coamis agreed to keep time. Pif was elated. He liked to run, but running for a reason . . . he *loved* running for a reason, and being on the clock made it even better. Just because it was instinctual, genetic heritage, that didn't make it any less enjoyable.

Of course, Pif made it back to the conference room before the majority of the crew had even shown up. The entire trip, dashing to the office, tucking the Ferengi padd under his collar and tearing back, took less than two minutes. Even at a brisk run, any of the ship's humanoids would have taken a minimum of six to cross and recross an entire deck. He knew, he'd bet Coamis once, had even let Coamis pick the long-legged Facity to run it. Sure enough, Pif took less than half the time, as wagered. Of all the things he was good at, he was best at running.

Now, estimate list placed neatly on the table, Pif sprawled on the raised bench at the table's end reserved for himself and Stessie and caught his breath, waiting for the crew to finish assembling. When Dez and Jake showed, Dez called Coamis over to meet the human, and stood by while the two younger men talked quietly and the last crew members straggled in. There were several low conversations going on, creating a soft sound backdrop that was pleasing to the ear. Pif lounged, watching the curious glances at Dez, noting the interest in Jake from the handful who hadn't yet met him.

"I gave him the ship's tour this morning," Pif told Lema, sitting next to him. "He's a nice young man, quiet, not too pushy . . . I really feel that Dez has finally started to appreciate my interpersonal skills, my way with people. The best tour guides in the quadrant are Aarruris, you know."

Lema exuded a nondescript pleasantness, the Friagloim equivalent of polite bemusement, effectively killing a promising conversation. Strange species, Friagloim. Pif liked Stess—everyone liked Stess—but the rest of Stessie was sometimes hard to talk to. More than once, Pif had received the distinct impression that Stessie wasn't truly interested in what he was saying, though he supposed it was possible he was reading her wrong. Probable, even . . . Aarruris had excellent senses and were certainly a compassionate species, but were not known for any sort of empathic ability.

Prees, as usual, was the last to arrive, and as she hurried into the room, Dez sent Coamis back to his seat, then moved to stand at the head of the table with Jake at his side. Prees muttered an apology as she sat down, pushing wayward strands of blond hair away from her long, thickly lined face. The engineer was always elbow deep in something or other, always showing up late, smudged and mussed. Pif thought she was beautiful. Sadly, she seemed to have a thing for the Appliance Worm (as Pif privately thought of Srral), a nonstarter relationship if ever there was one.

Dez nodded at the screen cube on the table, acknowledging that Facity was tuned in, and then cleared his throat. The room quieted and stilled.

"Srral, you with us?" Dez asked. "I'd like to get started."

Srral's sexless voice spilled out of the wall comm. *"I'm here, Dez."*

The captain nodded. "Good. Before we get into ship's business, I'd like to formally introduce our guest—this is Jake Sisko, from the Alpha Quadrant. Jake will be traveling with us for a while. So . . ."

Dez nodded at Glessin, directly to his left, who stayed sitting. The Cardassian nodded back, no trace of warmth in his face. Glessin had never been anything but polite to Pif, to anyone on board, but Pif felt wary around him and knew that some of the others did, too. He was extremely . . . *controlled;* it was hard to fathom that he and Pif were of an age, just old enough to look back over ten years of adult life. Glessin seemed much, much older. Pif knew that the Cardassian had been involved in some sort of Dominion conflict years earlier, before the Quadrant War, but it wasn't something he ever talked about. Though for that matter, there wasn't *anything* he ever talked about, or at least not to Pif.

"You remember Allo Glessin, our medic," Dez said. "Glessin is also quite proficient in recognizing and dealing with biological artifacts, living and dead. . . ."

Pif sat up straighter. It seemed that Dez was going to give out job accounts along with the introductions. Pif wasn't shocked, he'd witnessed the captain's friendliness toward the boy, though he was startled, and could tell that he wasn't the only one. They'd had passengers before, of course, consultants, people they'd been hired to escort, the occasional random traveler—but for any of those people, "medic" would have been description enough. It seemed that the captain had decided Jake was trustworthy, and on very short notice.

". . . and next to him are our art researchers and appraisers, Fajgin and Itriuma. Fajgin specializes in paint, sculpture, and forcefield, while Itriuma's expertise runs to mixed media." The mated Wadi couple both touched their triangled fingers to their foreheads, a traditional Wadi greeting. Smiling, Jake did the same, earning nods and glances of approval from several others at the table. As Pifko had already ascertained—and well before anyone else on the *Even* —the boy had manners.

"Feg and Triv, I believe you met this morning," Dez continued. "Next to Triv is Aslylgof, weapons and historical weapons research."

Aslylgof nodded at Jake, his thick, graying beard briefly creasing with a smile. Aslylgof was part human, Pif thought, though he wasn't positive; like Glessin, Aslylgof mostly kept to himself . . . though while Glessin was distant and removed, in Aslylgof's case, Pif suspected it was because the pudgy humanoid thought more of his own company than anyone else's. His expertise was unmatched, which was probably why his rather pretentious personality was generally tolerated. He *looked* human, except for the lack of ears and eyelids. And he had those bone patches on his arms and legs. . . . Actually, now that Pif thought about it, maybe he didn't look all that human. The beard covered a lot.

"—and you met Stess and Lema last night . . . here are Aris, Le, and Kin. Stessie works recon and communications during retrievals, and usually takes point. She's also . . . she's a defense expert, I suppose one might say; she's certainly defended me on more than one occasion."

All of Stessie shifted happily along the bench, radiating pleasure . . . as did Pif, because it was his turn.

"Pifko, besides being the *Even Odds*'s best tour guide, is our all-around thrill-seeking risk taker and general athlete. If something dangerous needs to be done, Pif not only *wants* to do it, he'll get it done faster than anyone else."

Pif couldn't help it. His tail wagged, two quick thumps against Lema's velvety side. Flushing, he tucked it, ignoring the soft laughter of his crewmates. They all thought it was "cute," which clashed with his carefully maintained, witty but easygoing demeanor.

"Ha ha," he muttered, but with no real malice. If he was cute, he was cute.

"Brad-ahk'la is our jewelry appraiser specializing in rare stones," Dez went on. "And also handles ship security, when the need arises."

Jake smiled at the immense Brad. "We also met earlier, hello."

"Hello," Brad rumbled, and Pif swore he could see the deep green of a blush on her chiseled cheeks. He sighed, surprised she didn't giggle. Brad was still a young woman, and could be extremely girly at times.

"And next to Brad is our archeologist, whom you've met . . ." Coamis, who was part Wadi, part unknown-to-Pif, nodded rather seriously at Jake. The crew was still getting used to the new archeologist; he'd only been aboard for five or six months, taking over for the well-liked YimMa, who had retired last year. Pif liked Coamis all right, but also thought he could stand to relax a bit. His sense of humor, while inoffensive, didn't extend to cover himself.

". . . and Pri'ak, who works with Srral and Prees in engineering . . ."

The short, squat Merdosian tapped his nose, smiling with see-through teeth. Jake politely tapped his nose in turn.

". . . Prees, our chief engineer . . . and finally Neane Tee, our general data researcher. Everyone has their specialty, but if you want to find out about anything anywhere, talk to Neane."

Neane, a middle-aged Hissidolan, had spent a year in the Alpha Quadrant right before the big conflict, coming to work on the *Even* soon after. She stood and extended her far right hand. Jake reached out with his right and they clasped hands for a second, then let go. Presumably an Alpha thing; Pif had seen hand touching before, but never so brief.

"So, if no one objects, I've asked Jake to join our meeting today . . . and our future Drang discussions, as well," Dez said, taking his seat at the head of the table. He motioned for Jake to take the chair next to his, where Facity usually sat. "As I said, he'll be with us for a while, and has graciously volunteered to take on the responsibilities of a crew member. Jake has some background in geology and archeology; he recently spent some time on a field expedition, uncovering and cataloguing religious artifacts, so . . . so, if things work out over the next two weeks, maybe we'll be able to persuade him to join the Drang crew."

The announcement was met with silence and stares. Two weeks before Drang, and Dez wanted someone new—not just new, but an outsider—on the team? Pif looked around at the others, saw the same uncertain surprise that he felt, saw the Ferengi brothers frowning, saw that Aslylgof and Facity were both about to speak up—

—and Jake beat them to it. "Well, that's *if* things work out, and everyone agrees," he said, shooting his own startled look at Dez before turning his appealing half smile outward. "I mean, I'm perfectly willing to do whatever I can, but you're the experts."

The statement was sincere, not an effort at flattery, and everyone in the room knew it, could feel it. Pif sensed the sudden Dez-inspired tension dissipate, or at least dwindle considerably . . . and thought that the human's estimation had just gone up, because he had stated what they were all thinking, in a way that wasn't challenging to Dez's authority. Dez was their captain and friend, the *Even Odds* was his ship, but he had made less than sound resolutions in the past, on more than one occasion. No one expected him to be perfect; he was a fortune hunter like the rest of them, and there was a certain reckless streak that went with the territory . . . but it did mean that his sudden "inspired" decisions sometimes deserved some extra consideration.

Like the Veltan Sex Idol run last year, when he decided to pilot that land hopper himself, instead of waiting for Facity, and crashed it into the dropship. We barely escaped. Or the time he tried cleaning those antique Akada chairs with chemical water, melted off the top layer of finish and lost the client . . . those chairs took eight days of negotiation, cost almost a hundred paegs and not a few favors. There's that story about the girl he was trying to impress with the Tirges dagger . . .

or that fake codebreaker key he bought . . . Pif could think of a half-dozen more without really thinking. Everyone on board made mistakes, but Dez was famous for his, because . . . well, because he was captain. And fortunately for all of them, his successes far out numbered his missteps.

On the cube, Facity was smiling slightly, and though her response was ostensibly to Jake's comment, it was plainly aimed at Dez. "I'm sure we'll all keep that in mind; we can walk that path when we come to it. For now, let's concentrate on preparation, there's still a lot to do before we get there . . ." Her smile widened into sarcasm. ". . . and I know you've all been working like beings deranged to be ready for this meeting."

Pif smiled, along with several of the others. The researchers had been researching; the rest of them had taken a few days off, officially recovering from the last job, which had been yet another uncomplicated salvage. (Since the end of the war, it felt like they'd done about a hundred million of them. Five, at least.) Pif, for one, had been lounging heavily for almost a week straight.

"Neane, you have the current inventory comp?" Facity asked.

The researcher nodded, picking up a reader as the crew refocused, shifting their attention to what they were all hoping would be an extremely lucrative mission. They had been hired to retrieve only one item, the Yaron Oracle, which had been taken only three months before—but with as much as the Drang had stolen over the last several years, there were hundreds of pieces the *Even* could profit from during the core retrieval. Assuming they could find them. The actual tunnel maps they had to work with were collectives, pieced together from a number of sources, some unsubstantiated. The retrieval team wouldn't know how accurate they were until they actually got there.

As Neane read off the updated list, Pif found his attention wandering back to Dez's new protégé and to Dez himself, both listening intently . . . and Pif saw the look that Dez had on his face when he glanced at the human boy, a look that no one else caught, and suddenly understood things a little differently. It had been only a few years since Pif had seen the same look on his own sire's face, proud and hopeful, when he'd told him about being hired to run.

Pif decided it was sweet, and then wondered if he could get anyone to bet as to whether or not Jake would end up on the Drang retrieval team. That look was inside information; Jake might not know it yet, but it had taken less than a day for him to become a crew member of the *Even Odds.*

Day 2, night. I'm tired but don't feel like sleeping yet, my brain is too full. After two-plus months of B'hala, quietly whisking dust off of kejelious fragments, I think I'm on sensory overload.

So much has happened in the last twenty-six hours, I feel . . . contradictory, I guess. I know there's a better word, but it's not coming to me . . . conflicted. A duality. Everything is hyperreal, but it's still hard for me to believe that this is my life right now, if that makes sense. I mean, I got a tour of the Even *today, which was amazing—part of the ship, the Wa, is like nothing I've ever even heard of before—and I sat in on a covert mission plan meeting, and visited the main lab, where they've got this incredible living artifact collection, things I could hardly believe . . . and I felt* there, *I felt whole in each moment . . . but I also kept having to think, "This is actually happening to me, this is my experience." I kept thinking that, and everything still felt so strange, so unreal. . . . I don't know, I don't even know if I'm making sense. Maybe this weird reality/unreality conflict is because I'm not supposed to be here at all, or maybe it's because I'm in the Gamma Quadrant—not just away from home but very, very* far *away. Anyway, I feel . . . I feel uncertain.*

Now that that's all cleared up (!), I asked Dez about Drang, and no luck. The way he describes it, we're headed to a planet of aggressive, fanatical xenophobes—to steal from them, no less (though I think I like Dez's word better, they're retrieving*). I still want to go home, but . . . for now, at least, I'm stuck here.*

Not that I'm saying that's such a terrible thing. Beyond that whole lucky-to-be-alive thing, I'm incredibly grateful I didn't get picked up by a rogue Jem'Hadar ship or something . . . and past that, the Even Odds*'s crew is interesting, intelligent, and generally friendly (okay, I barely know them, I'm talking about first impressions), not to mention unique. I met the rest of the crew at the mission meeting, and there was a kind of group lunch afterward—and everyone I talked to was just so different, culturally and physiologically. It was like a Wa of species. For instance, Pri'ak (or Priock, and I should just give up on worrying about spelling right now) is from the planet Merdosa, where there's a superstition about a liar's tongue turning colors . . . so Merdosians have clear teeth implanted, early in childhood. Pri'ak says it's one of those beliefs with no real basis in fact, but it's become a kind of cultural habit, so everyone does it. Neane Tee, she's a Hissidolan—apparently,* *only the females have four arms; the males have six, and are only about half as tall. Pifko's people are born in litters of up to fourteen, though between two and eight is considered average—and on Stessie's homeworld, each individual has three, four, or five parts, no more or less.*

Srral is really unusual. It's the creation of an extremely technologically advanced people called the Himh (this I found out from Prees, by the way; Srral wasn't around for lunch). Srral and its kind are an engineered species, designed to live and work inside these vast, complex network systems that cover much of the surface of the Himh world. The species doesn't have a name (I guess they just call themselves "Himh workers") but Srral named itself, after a sound it said it liked, of superheated plasma flow heard through a single thickness of conduit wall. Crazy, eh? Anyway, they were invented not only to effect repairs, but to improve on whatever they found . . . and since the Himh gave them free will—they made them to be assistants, not servants—a few of them, like Srral, decided to leave the homeworld to look for new challenges. Apparently, it wandered around for some time before ending up on the Even Odds, *purely by accident; it was in one of Dez's system upgrades, a trifiltered sensor array console. After it had been introduced to the ship—which Prees says is internally very curious—it decided to stay.*

Fascinating stuff . . . and this is going a sound really stupid, but I feel kind of guilty *for enjoying myself so much today, for being so interested. Shouldn't I be trying harder to get home? DS9, my home. That looks wrong now, how's that for strange—but where* do *I live? I had my own quarters on the station (well, with Nog), but it's not like I planned to settle down there. Then I was at B'hala, but that was definitely temporary, just a job . . . and now there's a room for me in Kas's new house . . . I know I'm welcome, I* know *that, but is that home now? Will it ever feel like home to me, even if Dad finally does come back?*

Maybe I should look at what's happening now as an opportunity to expand my boundaries, be out in the universe . . . be around some people who don't care that my father is the *Benjamin Sisko of the Federation, the Emissary, the one who transcended the linear plane. It's clear from Dez's attitude, at the mission conference and at lunch afterward, that he wants me working as part of the* Even'*s crew, for as long as I'm here—not just doing research or data entry, either. He wants me to be a full participant.*

Jake Sisko, fortune hunter. That's about the silliest thing I've ever written, just looking at it makes me want to laugh, but . . . okay, it's kind of exciting, too. What's wrong with that? I'm stuck here anyway, why shouldn't I learn a new skill or two, do something interesting with these next weeks? At least I won't have to sit around wondering what to do next, now that I can do anything. . . .

Enough. I'm going to bed. Tomorrow, I'm going to pretend that I belong here.

"From the beginning," Facity said, and sat back to listen and watch, already aware that he was as prepared as any of them. Eight days. It had been only eight days since they'd picked him up, and he was ready.

"We drop behind the second moon and establish orbit, timing the rotation so Drang can't pick us up on a standard pulse survey," Jake began, sitting back in his own chair. Dez would be meeting them in a few minutes, but for now, it was just the two of them, the post-breakfast dining hall otherwise deserted. The mission team was off in one of the web rooms, looking over a visual identification register that Neane had come up with—holos of the more valuable items they might happen across while looking for the Yaron Oracle. The rest of the crew was taking a tour of the dropship, checking out Prees's superior refit.

"Why the second moon?" Facity asked, reaching for her cup of currant juice.

Jake didn't hesitate. "The first probably has an observation relay, the third and fourth are too far out." At Facity's nod, he continued. "The dropship team loads up—Dez, Pif, Brad, Stessie, Coamis, and Glessin will be hitting the tunnels, and you, Fajgin, and Srral will stay on the ship; you'll pilot, Srral will run the transporters, Fajgin helps move team members and inventory on and off the pad. Everyone else stays aboard the *Even*—Neane will have command, and—"

"Why is Glessin on the team?" Facity interrupted.

"In case anyone on the team sees one of Giani'aga's boxes," Jake said promptly. "Even the small ones are worth a fortune. There may be as many as seven of them on Drang, but they're a popular forgery, so there are bound to be some fakes, too. Glessin can tell the difference."

"Which is . . ." Not something he actually needed to know, but she liked to see if he'd been paying attention.

"He said the balance is different, and the colors . . . but basically, the real ones are alive," Jake said, smiling. "They respire. The fakes just blow air."

Facity smiled back, impressed as usual. This was the third time in as many days that she'd subjected him to one of her impromptu quizzes, and she had yet to watch him fumble an answer. "Go on."

Jake gazed up at the ceiling, frowning in concentration. "Let's see . . . everyone left on the *Even* stands by to hit Drang orbit as soon as the final objective is met, or to rendezvous with the dropship itself in case of an emergency. Prees pilots, Aslylgof is on tactical, Pri'ak stays in engineering . . . Triv is on communications . . ." Jake broke into a grin. He was obviously thrilled to be able to include himself in the plan. ". . . and Itriuma and I stay in the transporter room to unload and sort whatever you send us when we get close enough. Feg keeps the inventory list."

Good boy. "How do I get us to Drang without being caught?" Facity asked.

"You go in over and through the magnetic fields in the southern hemisphere and head west, skirting the ocean line," Jake said. "It'll be the middle of the night where the vaults are, and an unlikely area to be monitored for invasion anyway, since the big decoy vault and tunnels are about seven hundred klicks to the north and west. There's also a good chance the dropship will be confused with local traffic, because of the size. You'll stay at the edge of transporter range for the easternmost tunnel boundary, set up a holding pattern, and send Stessie in first. She incapacitates the watch guard—at that hour, probably no more than three Drang—and disables surveillance, if there is any. She then splits up and moves out along the three main tunnels. Stess stays put at the transporter meet point—the TMP—transmitting Stessie's information back to the dropship."

Jake's recital was probably as helpful to her, to look for flaws, as to test him, but she'd already gone over it so many times that it was difficult to actually *hear* it anymore. It was a good plan, though. Simple. Facity had been on infinitely more complicated runs, had dealt with everything from humidity-pressure alarms to holodecoys over shadow-trigger pit traps, and though she tried never to assume anything, Drang really did look easy.

The security was ridiculously unsophisticated for several reasons—first and foremost, because the Drang placed an absurd amount of faith in their aggressive reputation and their brute strength. They didn't even use energy weapons, preferring clubs or their own bare hands, believing that no one would dare infiltrate their underground stores. To be fair, no one had, but there *had* been a war on. Second, they thought that using a decoy vault was brilliant, apparently not realizing that they weren't the first to think of it . . . or, for that matter, that two or more decoys might be even better. They might be ill-tempered, but they weren't the smartest lizards walking, no question. Third and not least, they didn't really differentiate between having things and having nice things; to them, a priceless Bienwon'ata lamp or bottle of alpha-currant nectar was as valuable as a crate of souvenir resin beads . . . and they protected it all accordingly.

They'll do better after us, though. This would probably be the *Even*'s only crack at Drang, so they had to be at their best . . .

. . . *and* is *Jake really ready?* She thought so. She *hoped* so.

Keep asking him questions, find out.

"When does the team beam over?"

"As soon as Stessie locates the room with the Yaron Oracle, or any of the articles that were taken with it," Jake said, "which shouldn't take too long. According to the maps, there are between eight and ten storage rooms off each of the three main tunnels, plus a couple of smaller connecting tunnels, but since the Drang aren't worried about preservation, everything we're looking for should be sitting out. The Oracle's remains are in a heavy carved wooden egg, stained dark blue, about a meter tall. The Yaron robes, jewelry, and candleholders are all dark blue, too."

Facity nodded slowly as he spoke, her mind wandering off target again, thinking how much she'd come to like the young human in such a short period . . . how much everyone on board was coming to like him. There were plenty of reasons why, but if she had to put it down to a single attribute, it was that he didn't try to be what he wasn't. There was a minimum of facade to Jake, and while that was a rarity in the retrieval business, it certainly wasn't a flaw. Besides that, he had a quick mind and a warm sense of humor, he was definitely too honest for his own good . . .

. . . and let's not forget, he's got the reflexes of—well, of a young man. For retrievers, good reflexes could mean the difference between life and death, literally.

She'd learned just how precise he was the day before yesterday, when she'd challenged him to a game of dom-jot in one of the web rooms. He'd absolutely slayed the table. He could've won a bundle, too, except he'd actually informed her ahead of time exactly how proficient he was. She'd thought he was flirting, at first, showing off, but no . . . and that was another area where he'd shown maturity and restraint, always ignoring her deliberate dress code, his gaze rarely straying from her face. Facity liked sexy clothes, always had, and early on, she'd also come to appreciate the reaction factor. It applied to everyone, too, all sexes, races, and species—the way people responded to what she was wearing or not wearing told her something about them. Jealousy, lust, indifference, respect, contempt . . . whatever the reaction, she usually walked away knowing more about someone upon meeting them than whatever assumption they'd walked away with regarding her. And young Jake Sisko, whose blushing inclinations were clear—female humanoids, no question—was a gentleman. He worked at not looking sometimes, but he was determined.

Jake was watching her, patiently waiting for the next prompt.

"The team goes over . . ." she started.

". . . and tags the Oracle, and the dropship beams it out," Jake picked up. "Then the team splits into pairs—Pif and Brad will take the long west tunnel, the one with rooms farthest from the TMP. Coamis and Glessin take another one, Stess and Dez handle the third. Stessie—except for Stess—will be keeping watch, posted at every likely Drang transport area she can cover, in case any of them decide to drop in unexpectedly.

"As long as they remain undetected, each team will collect inventory, stack it up and put transporter tags around it, then signal Srral to beam it out. At ten minutes after going in, regardless of security status, they fall back to the TMP and are removed."

"And then . . ."

Jake nodded his chin at her. "You'll signal to the *Even,* a few seemingly random clicks on an open channel, then head back out the way you came in. We hop out of hiding, pick you up as soon as you leave the atmosphere . . . and with any luck, the *Even* hits warp before the Drang even realize we were there."

Smiling confidently, Jake reached for his own cup of juice, a citrus concoction. "We rendezvous with the Yaron three days later. And start figuring out what belongs where from the rest of the yield."

"Oh, really?" Facity asked, arching one brow at his quick finish. "And what happens if something goes wrong? What happens if the Drang catch wind of what is happening before the team is finished?"

Dez answered, walking through the entryway. "Everybody grabs whatever they can carry and runs for the TMP."

He sauntered to the table, grinning at Facity's annoyed expression.

"Thank you, Captain," she said, and rolled her eyes for Jake's benefit. "Aren't we lucky, to have such a brave and masterful leader?"

Jake laughed. Dez sat down, his bright gaze fixed expectantly on Facity . . . who sighed, and then nodded slightly. Dez had agreed to let her make the final decision, but had there been any question? Not after watching him play dom-jot.

"It's fine with me," she said. "I don't think you'll get much argument from the crew, either."

Dez's expression remained calm, but she could see the light in his eyes go even brighter. "You're sure . . ."

Facity nodded again, pleased at the warmth and animation in her lover's face as he turned to a curious Jake. Dez hadn't said anything else about his own father since that first night, but watching him with the young human, talking and listening, showing him elements of the *Even*'s code system . . . for the first time in all their years together, Dez had started to seem . . . content. He was almost always happy, but she'd never seen him so content.

"I want you on the tunnel team, Jake," Dez said bluntly, "with me. We still have four days to go, but I don't see the point in waiting to see if you can be more capable somehow. Stess is good but she moves slow, I'd end up doing all the marking . . . anyway, it makes more sense for her to stay at the TMP and keep watch while I go hunting with someone else, and I want you. Are you interested?"

Jake hesitated. "I—" And grinned, a beautifully unself-conscious expression of excitement. "I'm interested."

That takes care of that, Facity thought, smiling, hoping hoping *hoping* that nothing would go wrong on Drang, suddenly wishing that her earlier meeting with Feg and Triv had gone differently. It meant nothing, the Ferengi were famous for sticking to their deals, the witnessed ones, anyway . . . but she had hoped that they would have at least tried to back out of their bet with her, that there would be bloodshed on Drang. Unfortunately, they were holding firm . . . and maybe it was because the job looked so very effortless, but she was starting to worry that they might actually have a chance of winning.

6

For the Drang time zone they were planning to hit, the early hours of the morning corresponded to the *Even Odds*'s midafternoon . . . which meant that the team had a chance to digest a light meal as they mentally and physically prepared for the raid. Even if he had been hungry—and he was, in fact, slightly nauseated—Glessin's training made it nearly impossible to imagine eating, dulling his senses with food. Nor did he participate in the anxious, excited chatter that echoed through the frigid air of the dropship's bay as the crew got ready. Suited and outwardly poised, Glessin stood aside and watched, working to maintain his internal focus by observing the others.

He could see almost everyone—the entire crew was present except for Neane, who had the bridge. Srral was present, too, but had already gone inside the specialized transport, presumably to check relays or some such; as Glessin watched, Prees also entered the dropship, carrying a spare tool kit, her shoulders anxiously hunched.

After four years of working with her, Glessin knew that Prees worried overmuch on missions; she was a fine engineer, and when it came to emergency repair—*if* it came to emergency repair—Srral was even better. Still, Glessin had never known an engineer to relax when his or her work was about to be tested.

The Karemman had to step past Dez and Facity, talking in low tones near the ship's cabin door, smiling at one another in the private way that only committed bedmates did. The captain and first officer were excited, Glessin could see it in the intensity with which they spoke, but they were still much calmer than any of the others, their anticipation almost a casual thing. Although he didn't understand their lighthearted take on imminent danger, Glessin respected it. For most Cardassians, peril was a very serious business.

Against the bay wall nearby, the Wadi art appraisers were rapidly reading lists at Jake and Coamis, both young men paying half attention as they nervously checked and rechecked their gear belts, grinning too much, too quick to laugh at their own fumbling fingers. The half-Wadi archeologist was the newest crew member; he had only been aboard the *Even* for five months . . . which explained why he was almost as apprehensive as the human boy, Sisko's son.

Glessin's gaze settled on the human for a beat. Strange, how small the universe could sometimes be. Glessin had trained with a medic who had been positioned at Terok Nor, which the Federation had so cleverly renamed "Nine" when they'd sent Sisko there to represent their interests, some seven years ago. Glessin had considered mentioning as much to the boy, but the information was useless and doubtless uninteresting to anyone but himself . . . and *interest* was probably too strong a word for what he felt, anyway.

While he expected as much of the happily reckless Dez, Glessin thought it rash of Facity to be allowing a novice to go to Drang. The young Sisko was an agreeable enough boy, certainly, and he seemed at least as prepared as some of the others, but he'd been training for only days, not weeks or months. Glessin supposed it didn't matter, in the end. They would survive and emerge victorious, or—or not.

There could be an ambush. They could be waiting for us.

Feeling a fresh wave of nausea at the absurd thought, Glessin swallowed heavily, ashamed at his stomach's discontent . . . but aware that it was the past, not the present that sat so uneasily.

The past. He could feel his focus slipping, turning inward. Before any and every mission, he was haunted by the specific circumstances that had led to his employment on the *Even Odds* . . . and it seemed that they would be no exception today.

There had been twenty in the fleet of Cardassian and Romulan warships that had sought to stop the Dominion almost five years ago, before the Founders had escalated their plans; that was also before the Federation had blundered in, he was fairly certain. It had been a strange alliance—the Obsidian Order and the Tal Shiar, Romulus's version of the same, both wary, untrusting intelligence agencies coming together in the hope of destroying the Founders' homeworld, stopping their particular madness.

Glessin remembered feeling deeply honored to have been tapped for the assignment. He'd been trained as a medic in his mandatory military days, but had spent the few years since his tour studying biology, interested in historical species design . . . and he'd been "fortunate" enough to receive individual instruction from a man who secretly worked for the Order. The Order, which needed a few combat medics to fill out their veteran-staffed cruisers, headed to the Orias system to covertly meet with Romulan allies. And though Glessin had never seen combat, his instructor had been willing to attest to the competence and loyalty of his favorite pupil.

I was so proud, so eager . . . I thanked him. I actually thanked him for referring me to a massacre.

Twenty ships, *D'deridex* warbirds and *Keldon* cruisers, cloaked and armed. They'd slipped through the wormhole, sailed through the dark Gamman seas, carrying oblivion to the unsuspecting Founders' planet. From the Orias system to the Omarion Nebula, Glessin had enjoyed the finest days of his life. He'd been young and unscarred, surrounded by the best soldiers and agents of his world, of any world, on his way to a victory that would reaffirm the Cardassian reputation for excellence and cunning. The rest of the *Danasket*'s crew had known it, too, the very air alive with emanations of unity and strength and the pleasure of anticipating triumph.

Twenty ships had surrounded the defenseless planet, dropped cloak and opened fire. Standing by in sickbay, making jokes about having to repair the sprained finger of a technician, perhaps the strained vocal cords of a happily shouting gul, Glessin and his colleagues had not known of the trick—that the planet was deserted. That somehow they had been lured into a trap. That for each of their twenty ships, there were seven-plus Jem'Hadar fighters about to attack.

We didn't know. And then the ship was rocking, alarms blaring for attention, and every deck started screaming that they had medical emergencies as the power destabilized and the flickering corridors began to fill with terrible, choking smoke. . . .

It had all happened fast, the ship taking hits within a minute of opening fire on the deserted world, most of the medical staff beamed out to emergencies in less time than that. Glessin had been ordered to stay behind, to treat casualties that walked or were helped into sickbay, but the *Danasket* had already been on the edge of total destruction; in the brief time between the first strike and the end, only a handful had made it, most carried in, and Glessin had done what pitiful little he could for them, unaware that it was pointless; everyone on the ship had been dying, they just hadn't known it.

Everyone but me.

The horrors of those final moments stayed with him, the imagery so vivid that when he remembered, he could sometimes taste the bitter smoke. He remembered the coarse, ongoing scream of the glinn whose legs had been severed below the knees, Glessin had not known how, remembered hearing the sound turn wet as the screamer's throat had filled with blood. He remembered looking up from a sucking chest wound a moment or so after the artificial gravity had cut out, seeing the bay defined in a million swirling droplets of blood rain. And of course he remembered the panicked, wild eyes of the wounded young soldier who had come in at the very end, who had waved a disruptor in his face, demanding that Glessin go with him to an escape pod; how could he forget? The soldier had died only moments after forcing Glessin into the tiny, damaged pod and ejecting them into space, somehow escaping the notice of the Dominion fleet . . . and it had been six days before a Merdosian salvage ship had found him drifting helpless amid the wreckage, traumatized and reeking of death, his hands scarred from trying to fix a dying air filter without tools. As far as he knew at that time, he had been the only survivor . . . not just of the *Danasket,* but of the entire doomed fleet.

The small, amiable Merdosian crew of the mostly mechanized salvage ship had been short a button pusher and had let him stay on, apparently not bothered that he avoided contact of any kind. He'd remained for almost a year, uninterested in going home, uninterested in anything . . . until he met Dez, who hadn't asked too many questions, who'd offered Glessin a job after hearing that he knew something about medicine. The *Even Odds* had been hit during an escape, it seemed, and though no one had been hurt, Dez had decided that he wanted a medic aboard, that the automated medbay wasn't enough. The *Even* had flagged the junk ship down to buy repair material . . . and besides coming away with a new medic, they had ended up buying and installing a Cardassian cruiser deck segment, from the engagement that had marked the end of Glessin's peace. Glessin walked through it almost every day. He wasn't sure if that represented some great irony, but at least it didn't bother him. It was framing and hull plating, nothing more.

Later, toward the end of the war, Glessin had heard a rumor that one of the Romulan organizers of the short-lived alliance had been working for the Founders . . . and Glessin discovered that he didn't care. It didn't change what had happened, to know how it had come about, it didn't take away the memories . . . or the scars.

He'd kept them, the scars on his hands, not because they were some symbolic reminder that he had survived, but because compared with what he carried around inside, they were nothing. Less than nothing. . . .

At the sound of shrill laughter, Glessin pushed away the possibility of any more memories, reflexively seeking the source as an escape—not far from the bay's entrance a grinning, confident Pif and his happy audience, the Ferengi brothers and Brad. Brad was still tittering heavily at whatever quip or story the bombastic Aarruri had come up with. He didn't begrudge them their excitement, or think them foolish; among the laughing, chattering crew, he was the one who didn't belong . . . though a very small part of Glessin suddenly wanted to know the joke, even if only to scoff, to enjoy the comfort of friends while there was time. He ignored it, forcing his attention back to his silent survey, determined to regain his focus. Besides, they were decent people, but they weren't really his friends. Much of his capacity for friendship had died at Omarion, five years before. Not self-pity, but a fact.

In an open space behind the dropship, Pri'ak and Aslylgof were painting Stessie, spraying her the same rock-shaded colors as the close-fitting suits the rest of the away team wore . . . except for Pifko, who was also painted. Glessin closed his eyes for a moment, feeling. . . . Stessie was obviously agitated, threads of eager apprehension escaping her, though Glessin could tell that she was working to rein it in. He knew it wasn't easy for her, but on days like today, he found it difficult to appreciate her efforts. The generally pleasant, buoyant feelings that the Friagloim radiated were distinctly alien to his inner landscape.

"Glessin?"

Facity. He'd been peripherally aware that she'd moved away from Dez, but hadn't realized she'd been approaching him. He found a smile for her, determined not to give her cause for concern. She was a kind woman and, except for Dez, the only *Even* crew member who had more than a vague idea of his history.

"Are we ready for all this?" she asked, her tone light, smiling back at him but her gaze careful, searching.

Glessin shook his head, matching her tone. "Are we ever?"

"Good point. Find your belt, we're going to drop in ten."

She lightly touched his arm and then walked away. Glessin took a single deep breath and let it out slowly, as focused as he was going to be, then went to get his equipment belt.

Jake couldn't believe it was actually happening, but as the dropship fell away from the *Even Odds*, his stomach confirmed it with an unpleasant lurch. Someone had flipped the AG on without calibrating it first.

"Sorry about that," Facity called back cheerfully, and was answered by groans and sour expressions. Brad loudly volunteered that she was going to be sick, winning another series of groans, but after a few low, grunting belches, she appeared to get it under control, for which Jake was deeply thankful; he was sitting next to her. Pif started kidding her about what she had for lunch, while Coamis and Fajgin got into a conversation about a statue they both wanted to find, stolen from the Gocibis two years earlier, all of the talk high and excited, the cabin flush with anticipatory glee.

Warm, too. Jake shifted uncomfortably in his bodysuit,

feeling crowded. The dropship was easily twice the size of Jake's transport, but the crew cabin was small, barely enough room for the team. Twelve seats, six to either side, hooked together and facing inward; counting each of Stessie's parts, there were twelve bodies. Except for the one empty copilot seat at the front, directly to Jake's right, that was it. There *had* been transport room for twenty, but Prees, Pri'ak, and Srral had spent the last ten days expanding the transporter area at the ship's stern, increasing the system's load capacity and creating some extra cargo space, for all the things they'd be taking from Drang. . . .

. . . *This is so incredible! If Nog could see me now. . . .* Jake looked down at his belt, at his retrieval gear—a hooded light, a transponder beacon and a clip of transport tags, even a small, almost silent nonlethal disruptor with three charges; it was small enough to hide in one hand. No padd to jot notes for a story, no "gear" for *observing,* he was suited and prepped, like the others. . . . *he'd be* insanely *jealous. Me, on a dropship with a team of fortune hunters, preparing to infiltrate the stores of alien thieves.* Jake wanted to laugh. It sounded like fiction, like the adventure books he always used to read—but he was ready, too, he could feel the adrenaline pumping through him and he knew the plan inside and out. They'd had three practice runs in the big actuality-web room, different tunnel configurations each time, and he had aced all of them.

Sitting directly across from Jake, Dez grinned at him, as if he sensed the burst of excitement. The look in his eyes was somehow casual and intense at once, the gaze of a man in his element, a leader who was enjoying himself immensely—and it was also achingly familiar, and just like that, Jake was nearly overwhelmed by thoughts of Dad. Except it wasn't thoughts, it was feeling, a mix of longing and nostalgia, warmth and love and . . . and something else.

He wouldn't approve of this.

The thought was sharp, clear, and Jake knew that the something else was anger. He instantly, reflexively felt guilty . . . but a small, sullen part of himself wasn't so quick to dismiss it.

Since he's not here, and he can't exactly be reached for comment, his approval can't be verified one way or the other, can it? And let's not forget that you wouldn't be here at all if he hadn't gone off to fulfill his grand destiny.

That's not fair, he answered himself, disturbed, he thought he'd been through all this already, but the petulant inner voice had fallen silent. It *wasn't* fair, either—his father was a person, he had a right to a life beyond fatherhood . . . and Jake was grown, it wasn't like he'd left behind a struggling adolescent. . . .

But he did leave. Maybe he had no choice, maybe they just took him, but if he did *have some say . . . if they* had *invited him, would he have turned them down? Would it have made a difference for me if he'd talked to me about it first, asked what I wanted?*

That led to questions Jake was afraid to consider. Over the years, he'd seen time and again how desperately important the Prophets were to his father . . . sometimes all-important. He still remembered the brutal "touch" of the Prophets, when they had altered Dad's mind to show him B'hala, among other things. Dad had begun having visions, important visions that had started to tear up his brain. Jake remembered begging his father to have the surgery that would save his life . . . but would also take away the visions, his connection to the Prophets, and a supposed understanding of the vast mosaic their influence encompassed. His father had weighed his son's—and Kas's—tears and pleas against the visions, and chosen. That had been three years ago, but Jake remembered it as clearly as if it had been yesterday; Dad had chosen the visions. Jake had ordered the surgery when the visions had finally put him in a coma, and Dad had survived, all had been well . . . but he hadn't picked Jake, and that was something he would never forget, if he lived to be a thousand. . . .

"Jake—you still with us?"

Jake blinked, saw that Dez was watching him curiously. The cabin was still full of talk, but Dez had somehow managed to keep his voice low, directed . . . and open, always open, inviting him to respond however he wanted—to take it as a light question or as an opportunity to unburden himself. There was no judgment in Dez's expression, no self-righteousness, not a threat of criticism. As usual.

Jake was suddenly very, very glad that Dez had decided to take him in, to *encourage* him in. Dez was great; he'd gone out of his way to make Jake feel welcome and accepted, for no other reason that Jake could see except that he felt like it. They'd had dinner together almost every night since he'd come aboard, Dez telling funny and interesting stories about the retrieval business, listening to Jake's stories about growing up on the station . . . and if Jake needed any further proof that Dez wanted to be his friend, he'd invited Jake along on the adventure a lifetime.

Feeling a surge of exhiliration, of good feelings toward Dez, Jake nodded, putting his other thoughts aside. It wasn't the time, anyway. "Yeah, I'm still here."

Dez smiled, looking down at the clock patch on the back of his hand. "Good, because we're about to hit atmosphere."

Even as he said the last word, there was a sound like rushing water outside, getting louder, and Jake felt the AG dip, felt the ship vibrating madly for just a second as the system adjusted. Brad shifted queasily, and across the cabin, Glessin closed his eyes, Pif scowling as the sound became obnoxiously loud—and then it was gone entirely, the ship running smoothly once more, presumably skimming down through the planet's night sky. The cabin didn't have any windows or viewscreens.

"We're in, I'm cutting the grav," Facity called, and an instant later, Jake felt the heavier pull of Drang. It wasn't too bad—they'd used it in the actuality-web room runs—but he could definitely tell the difference.

At least they breathe a class-M oxy mix. . . .

Brad sighed, smiling. "Better."

"Like home, huh?" Jake asked.

She shook her massive head. "No, but it's a quarter atmosphere closer," she rumbled. "What was it where you came from?"

Jake was still trying to remember the numbers for gravitational constants he'd learned in Keiko O'Brien's class years ago when Srral's soft voice spilled out of the flight control console, presumably directed at Facity. Sitting closest to the front of the ship, Jake could hear it clearly.

"The ship's long-range sensors are receiving an unexpected energy signature from near our target," Srral said.

Dez had heard it, too. "Facity?" He asked loudly.

"I see it," she said. "It looks like a transporter system, but . . . no, that's over here. And this is much smaller. Whatever it is, it's not turned on, we're just getting a read on its power source."

Dez unstrapped himself and stood, stepping past Jake into the open cockpit. The rest of the team was listening now, the cabin silent except for the hum of the engines.

Jake frowned, waiting anxiously. Facity and Dez had both made it clear that if the circumstances weren't as they'd expected, they'd pull out and go back to the *Even,* no question. It was funny—he'd been so nervous about going, but now, faced with a possible abort, Jake wanted nothing more than to see the mission through.

From where he was sitting, he could just see Dez's shoulder, the captain leaning over the console as Facity pointed out the reading, talking in a low voice. Jake caught that whatever it was, it was to the north of the TMP. After what seemed like a long time, Jake saw Dez shrug.

"It's not an alarm system or a weapon, and it's definitely not shielding, that'd be turned on," Dez said, loudly enough for all of them to hear. "It's digging equipment, that's all. I wouldn't worry about it."

Jake's anxiety turned back to nervous anticipation. He smiled, looking at Brad . . . and saw that Brad, who was exceptionally easy to read, looked skeptical and unhappy. Jake glanced around, saw similar expressions on the faces of the others.

"I don't like it," Facity said. "If we knew what it was . . ."

"Fac, it's not turned *on,*" Dez said, sounding exasperated. He lowered his voice then, and they talked another moment before Jake heard Facity's doubtful acquiescence. Dez stepped back out a second later, smiling reassuringly at the team.

"The sensors picked up an unknown piece of equipment down in the tunnels, but it's not operating," he said, turning to sit back down. "Everything's fine, we continue as planned."

As Dez strapped back in, Jake saw Pif and Fajgin exchange a look. Brad still wore a dubious expression, and even Glessin's features seemed to have hardened somehow. Stessie, who had been emitting small flashes of excitement all day, suddenly stopped putting out anything at all, as though clamping down. Jake was surprised; he knew everyone liked Dez, and respected him . . . but it appeared that there was some trust issue he didn't know about.

It can't be too serious, though, no one's saying anything. It wasn't a particularly reassuring thought.

Dez picked up on some part of it. He held up his hands as if being harassed, looking around at the team. "It's not a weapon, and it's turned *off.* Anyone here want to cancel, speak up, I'm listening."

The glances exchanged this time were resigned, and no one spoke. Dez lowered his hands, smiling easily at them.

"Okay, then. Stessie, we're looking at six minutes—are you ready?"

Stess answered, still not giving off any feeling. "I will be in six minutes."

Dez nodded but didn't say anything else, settling back in his seat. He didn't appear to be bothered by the somewhat underwhelming vote of confidence . . . but he didn't seem quite as eager as before, either.

The vaguely uncomfortable silence lasted about ten

seconds, and then Pif spoke up, asking Stessie if the body paint was making her skin itch because it was *him*, and the moment was gone.

Jake wondered what it was, what past decision Dez had made that had inspired such caution, but he didn't wonder long . . . because then Stess was asking for help unbelting, bringing it back to Jake that it was almost time, that in just a few minutes Stessie would be beamed into the Drang tunnels to take out the guards.

This is really happening, he thought, unstrapping Le and helping her down from her seat, not thinking about his father, Kas, his unborn brother or sister, the station, not thinking about anyone or anything but what they were about to do. He had no idea that he was smiling, but he knew he felt good, better than he had in a long, long time.

By the time Dez had placed Stess's communication collar and the rest of the team had synchronized their time patches to hers, the dropship had reached transporter range. Stess told Dez she would need a moment and he assented, familiar with her habits. For her to be effective as point, she needed to achieve a unity of self. Arislelemakinstess gathered so that all her parts were touching, and closed her external senses.

Grow, I grow. See, I see. Feel, I feel. Hear, I hear. She repeated the mantra several times. Stess, as usual, tried to lead, but she kept at it until there was smooth continuity, until there was sameness.

After a moment, she carefully reopened her sensory bulbs, all of her parts in tune, projecting and receiving as one. She wanted to send Dez her feelings of readiness, but did not. When she was in complete unity, her projections were much stronger, and though she could also direct them better, there was always some emanation beyond her control . . . which meant that Glessin would be made uncomfortable, which she didn't want. He was an honest man who too often thought negative things about himself because of a bad time in his past, a terrible battle *(dead Cardassian soldier, room of blood rain),* she believed . . . but that seemed to be what he wanted, and she did not wish to interfere. Coamis didn't care for feeling what she felt, either, though for a different reason—he was simply uncomfortable with his own emotions, which made it difficult for him to be comfortable with another's. He tried to pretend indifference, even to himself, but some of his thought images were quite clear on the subject *(dish of spoiled fruit, feigning enthusiasm for an unwanted gift).*

Instead of sending, Stess told the captain that she was prepared, and then Arislelemakinstess started toward the back of the ship. Several of the others wished her well as she passed, audibly and in directed thought *(smiling faces, a chest of polished gems, a triumphantly howling Aarruri),* and she did her best not to project her thanks, letting Stess thank them verbally.

Past the cargo hold, she gathered herself tightly on the transporter pad, visual bulbs directed outward. Srral had moved into the system controls, and informed her that, as expected, there were three Drang guards at the TMP, grouped together. It had not picked up any other Drang in the tunnel system, though it admitted that there were a few sensory blind spots, almost certainly organic. Arislelemakinstess thanked Srral, and said she was ready for transportation, asking that it place her as close as possible to the southeastern corner of the open area. Srral said that it would. The conversation was painfully formal; because the engineered creature did not think or feel on a level that Arislelemakinstess understood—a mutual circumstance, no doubt—she was as verbally specific as possible whenever they interacted. Srral, of course, was rarely anything else.

Arislelemakinstess concentrated, collecting her thoughts. A second later, the ship disappeared around her . . . and then she was at the edge of a massive, shadowy cavern, unseen by the trio of tall reptilian beings some ten meters away, gathered near a freestanding control console. She'd transported into the shadows, and there were, in fact, loose piles of rock heaped at all sides of the rough-hewn cavern, some taller than she, very close to the shades of her body paint. She'd gotten lucky.

Although none of it was necessary—she'd been ready to hit them immediately—she was glad for the camouflage, and for the heedless guards. An instant strike would have been weak, wearing off quickly; she always preferred extra preparation time after transport, even if only a second or two. The change in environment—from cool and dry to hot and dry, in this instance—sometimes upset her carefully achieved balance, making her attack less potent.

She studied the guards a moment, their sloping brows, their open, toothy mouths. *I might be able to take an* hour *or two to prepare on this one. . . .*

The three Drang—males, from the clothing—were completely oblivious of her presence, deeply immersed in their conversation, spitting and hissing loudly around each guttural word. Her translator was switched off; it was entirely possible that they were discussing music or art, but from the lurching, monosyllabic growls and saliva-sucking gasps, she couldn't help but doubt it.

Time to get moving. She closed off most of her external sensory bulbs, this time leaving Stess's open. Stess focused on the trio, on their collective energy, opening herself toward them. She got a sense that the fat one on the left disliked the other two *(fist punching, fake smile, broken stick)*, but nothing else directly. . . .

. . . *I feel. I see.* Stess concentrated on all of Arislelemakinstess's internal self, pulling together feelings and thoughts, pictures and sounds, letting them build in intensity. It happened very quickly, the amplification; Friagloims needed all their parts operating together—either open, sending and receiving, or closed, joined internally—or there was a kind of psychic backlash, one that quickly became dangerous. Stess felt Arislelemakin struggling to maintain sensory withdrawal and used that pressure, too, adding it to the internal storm. *I hear. I grow.*

In the space of a few heart pulses, it was all Stess could do to maintain her share of sanity; it was time; she didn't want to kill, only stun them. She opened her pores wide and then closed them, aimed at the energy of the three guards—and *sent,* as hard and as focused as she could.

In mid-snarling-hiss, all three of them crumpled to the stone floor, hitting hard. Stess felt a flush of accomplishment. From the intensity of her projection—what Pif had once referred to as a "brain blast"—they wouldn't be waking up for at least a half hour.

Arislelemakin opened up once more and she spread out, looking around, Stess moving toward the guards and their console. The tunnel entrances all connected here, three yawning mouths that opened into the cavern they'd designated as the transporter meet point from the northwest and west . . . and there was a fourth, smaller mouth that led directly north. Arislelemâkinstess assumed it led to the surface, that it wasn't part of the storage facility. She *hoped* so; the maps that they'd based their plans on had shown only three tunnels, running vaguely parallel; the drop ship sensors had confirmed. There were supposed to be smaller tunnels running between the three, but none leading into the TMP cavern . . . and it was odd that the dropship hadn't picked it up.

I could cover each tunnel and still remain here.

She considered it only briefly before rejecting it. Stess was to remain at the TMP. Of the other four, two would take the west tunnel—it was purported to be longer than the others—and then a tunnel each for the other two. That was the plan, and she wasn't about to break from it without consulting Dez or Facity.

Fortunately, one of the guards had fallen close enough to the control console for her to climb on top of him, saving her from having to boost herself up. The control panel was almost exactly like the one the *Even*'s actuality-web room had come up with, based on uninspired Drang technology. She was incapable of pulling the optical network board, that was for someone else on the team, but she could lean into the main tunnel observation switches and turn them off, which she did. As soon as that was done, Arislelemakin separated and moved off to their respective tunnels.

Stess climbed down from the unconscious guard, checking the time patch applied to her front knee. It had been just under two minutes since she'd been transported from the dropship, about what she'd expected.

She felt herself spreading out farther, could see the

first rough cave rooms coming into sight, through both Kin and Arislema. It was time to call in. Stess used one of her aural bulbs to compress her collar's com and translator, thinking that if the rest of the job went as smoothly, they were going to walk away with not only the Yaron Oracle, but everything valuable that the Drang had ever stolen.

The team listened carefully, everyone keeping very still. Except for Facity and Srral, they had all gathered around the patch com, next to the transporter controls.

". . . B tunnel, room four . . . fabrics, embroidered linens, pillows, no value . . . a set of silver daggers, origin unknown . . . three racks of glassine or crystal bottles with liquid, definitely liquor, possibly Serk . . ." Stess's soft, nearly expressionless voice was translated directly through the com; it was strange, hearing her talk without the normal backdrop of creaks and moans, but not strange enough to divert Dez's attention from what she was telling them.

That we could retire off of this one.

". . . and there's a table of sculptured pieces. Small, clay and metal . . . some are carved stone. Several of them look Gocibi, but I'm not certain."

Dez glanced at Coamis and Glessin, saw both men concentrating, memorizing. B tunnel was theirs. A was Brad and Pif's, C was Dez and Jake's. So far, Stessie had spotted a number of extremely valuable items in the rooms off each tunnel.

"A tunnel, room three . . . there are paintings and wall hangings, stacked, I can't tell . . . there, there it is," Stess said, no change in inflection but Dez saw the entire team

tensing. *"The Yaron Oracle, it's sitting on the floor next to some of the candleholders."*

"Keep looking, we're on the way," Dez said, grinning widely as the team quickly assembled on the transporter pad, all of them grinning, too. Even Glessin wore a small smile. It was impossible not to, with what was waiting for them in the tunnels.

A full tube of VihnAKAn scissor pearls . . . the v'Xaji glass, still intact . . . a collection of pre-blight Teplan system folk art . . . And Stessie was not even halfway through the scout.

Dez glanced at his chrono patch as Srral started the transporters. Only eight minutes since she had gone in, too. Things could not be going better.

The ship melted away and then they were there, in a large, roughly rounded chamber littered with rock and shadow. There was Stess, looking remarkably like a rock herself, standing near the downed guards. Dez noted absently that it was overly warm, the air artificially heated to keep the cold-blooded Drang guards happy. Bad for the artifacts, though at least it was dry, too.

"Everybody check time, and get in position," Dez said, and pointed at A tunnel. "Pif, mark it and get back here."

The team moved, Pifko gone before Dez could blink, everyone else stepping to the mouths of their assigned tunnels. The idea was for each team to make the most of their limited time, searching the rooms that Stessie hadn't yet reached, marking off the most valuable items that she'd already seen along the way. It wasn't as organized as a room-by-room, but there was no way they were going to be able to mark every worthwhile piece; the very best would have to do.

Dez had already decided to disregard the north tunnel, which hadn't been on the maps; he figured that the Drang had finally gotten tired of transporting in and out, and had hacked out a surface entrance. The drop-ship sensors hadn't been able to see much of it, but they hadn't been able to pick up parts of the other tunnels, either—it seemed that the Drang underground was full of sensor jam, as Facity liked to call it, a kind of dense, naturally occurring clay that messed with density measurements. The stores were clear, at least. In any case, they had more than enough to look through without worrying about scouting and marking a fourth tunnel.

Dez walked quickly to a standing control console, the only piece of equipment in the chamber, and yanked all of the optical and communication boards. The tunnel switches were already off, but it never hurt to play it safe. He dropped the thin plates on the back of one snoring Drang.

"Nice work, Stess," he said, smiling down at her, and was about to ask if Stessie had spotted anything T-Rogoran—T-Rogoran items were suddenly in demand, another postwar jumper—when Pif rocketed back into the room. He was going fast enough that he had to run halfway around the chamber before he could stop.

"Marked," he said, his eyes bright.

"Good, let's get started," Dez said, and touched his com button as he walked toward Jake, waiting at their tunnel's entrance. "The Oracle is locked, take it out."

He glanced back at the others, saw Pif and Brad stepping into A, while Coamis and Glessin had already disappeared. Stess had propped herself against a real rock to keep watch and wait; if Dez wasn't looking for her, he wouldn't have noticed her at all.

He turned back, satisfied that his team was on top of things, and grinned, almost laughed out loud; the eager, frightened, delighted look on Jake's face was priceless. It was the face that every fortune hunter had but kept hidden, and it did his heart good to see Jake wearing it.

Together, they stepped into the shadowy corridor and started walking, Dez wondering if they should skip the first room entirely, remembering that Lema had seen those pearls in the second—

—and suddenly, Facity's tight voice was spilling out of his com, the tone hitting him before the words, clenching his gut. Her tone said it was bad. When he heard what she had to say, it got worse.

"Dez, that signature we picked up—it was a scrambler," she said, talking fast. *"It must have been set to trigger if we tried to transport anything out; Srral says it went on just as we tried for the Oracle—*I can't get you out, *do you copy?"*

"Okay, okay," Dez said, thinking fast, not taking the time to kick himself, aware that he'd have to, later—he'd forgotten about the "turned off" power sig about a minute after Facity had pointed it out. If the Drang had set up a scrambler to keep them there . . .

. . . then somebody will be coming to meet us, as soon as they see it's turned on. They wouldn't have much time; he had to make some quick decisions.

"Can we get to it?" he asked, looking at Jake. Jake's eyes were wide with alarm.

"It's about a hundred twenty meters due north of the TMP," Facity said. *"I'd bet money it's through that fourth tunnel, but the sensors won't back it up, they say there's no tunnel at all between you and the scrambler."*

Sensor jam. "All right. I'll take care of it, we're just going to have to—"

"They're coming," Facity interrupted, the panic in her voice barely controlled. *"Full run, twenty, twenty-five Drang . . . from the north, Dez, through the fourth tunnel. They'll be there in a minute, maybe less."*

The time to decide had run out.

7

Dez barely hesitated. He double-tapped his com button for an open line, plucking it from the front of his suit as he spoke, his tone quick and sure.

"Mission abort—company's coming and we can't transport out right now," he said, and paused. Jake saw that he was adjusting his com button into an earpiece. Pif had shown Jake how to do it only yesterday . . . along with a few tips on aiming the disruptor, Jake remembered, feeling sick. He reached for his own com with suddenly clumsy fingers.

"Find a good room in which to hide, now, and switch to ears-only when I say 'go,' " Dez continued, as he slipped the communicator into his ear canal, pinching the tiny directional pickup over the flap of cartilage at the front of his ear. "There's a transport scrambler on in the north tunnel. Jake and I are going to knock it out—"

—we are?

"—but it may take a few minutes; *stay down,* it looks

like there are going to be five to ten Drang for each tunnel, so don't start a fight . . . but stand ready to throw some diversion noise when I say, and Stess, I may need a mood—anxiety, bloodlust, some kind of a physical motivator. Everyone listen for your name or team before direction, I'll be as specific as possible.

"I want everyone to give Facity your location and status updates at two-minute intervals, if you can—actually, no, scratch that," Dez went on, reminding Jake that there wasn't a plan, that in spite of how it sounded, he was making it up as he went along. "Keep quiet, update at discretion. Srral, do your best to keep the beacons locked. Ground team, when Facity or Srral say they can transport, get somewhere they can read your beacon. . . . The TMP is ideal, no sensor jam, but we may not be able to clear it. Most of the storerooms are good. And let me repeat—this mission is an abort, don't risk yourself marking. Say check if you copy, A tunnel."

"Check," Pif said, his voice high and taut.

"B tunnel."

"Check," Glessin said. Jake thought there was an almost resigned note in his voice, as though he'd been expecting this.

"Stessie?"

They were actually close enough to the main cavern to just lean back in and ask her, but Jake suspected that Dez didn't want to waste a single second. Jake didn't, either. He suddenly noticed that the air was much too warm, that he was sweating.

"Check," Stess said softly.

"Stess, can you adjust the com collar alone?" Dez asked. "I'll need to talk to you."

"I can adjust it."

"Good," Dez said. "And good luck, everyone. If you don't hear from me within ten minutes, Facity, you're in charge, coordinate with Glessin for a second run at the scrambler. Now . . . *go.*"

Jake had just managed to fit the communicator in his ear. Dez lightly placed one hand on his shoulder and steered him down the tunnel at a jog, directed toward an opening ahead on the right, room one. Jake remembered Stess saying that there were a lot of crates in the first room, with what appeared to be dishes inside. That seemed like forever ago, listening to Stess list off items, safely standing around on the dropship. Safe and totally unaware that in a matter of moments, they were going to be trapped, about to be overrun by the famously angry Drang. To think he'd been *impatient.*

How do we know when it's safe to get to the scrambler? How are we supposed to clear the TMP? He had about a hundred questions and was afraid to ask any of them—because even as they stepped into the first Drang storeroom, Jake realized he could hear them coming. It was distant, but he could hear them, sounding like—there was nothing he could equate it with, nothing like it. It sounded like a large group of reptilian aliens running through a tunnel, getting closer.

The cavelike room they jogged into was big, not as big as the main cavern but large, about the size of the *Even Odds*'s bridge. There were boxes and crates everywhere, stacked five and six high. Most were average-size storage containers, cubic meters, and of the open ones Jake could see, they were, in fact, full of dishes. He saw a number of vases and urns, too.

Dez put one finger over the com's pickup, talking low

and fast. "We're going to stay in here until at least some of the Drang get past us, then we're going back to that tunnel."

Jake's mouth was dry, his voice sticky. "Won't some of them stay in the main cavern?"

"Yes," Dez said, seeming much too calm. "Which is why we're going to create a diversion. Right now, though, we hide. See if there's room in any of the big boxes."

Most of the oversized crates were at the back of the cave, many of them standing open. With the hissing, thundering echoes of the approaching Drang getting louder, Dez pointed Jake toward a less obvious choice, a long, low storage unit that Jake had to crouch-walk into. A quick look with the hooded light showed some stacked plates and cups in the back, a spilled basket of ornamental trinkets, nothing useful like a rack of phaser rifles. Dez crouched next to the opening, easing the side panel closed after Jake had crawled inside.

"Stay here until I say, and *don't move,*" Dez whispered just before closing the panel entirely, and then he was gone. Jake thought he heard a wooden creak a few seconds later, and then all he could hear was his own ragged breathing and the pounding of blood in his ears. That, and the oncoming Drang horde. Facity had said twenty or twenty-five, but it was starting to sound more like twenty-five hundred.

This is bad, this is so bad, Jake thought randomly, holding one hand out to balance, his feet already hurting. It was a nightmare, literally, hiding in the dark, knowing that the monsters were coming, hoping that they wouldn't find you. How had Dez seemed so confident, so certain that everything was going to turn out?

Back on the ship, the way the crew looked at him after

Facity pointed out the scrambler's signal . . . Had something like this actually happened *before,* was that why they'd all seemed vaguely skeptical of his decision to continue? Jake tried to reassure himself with the thought—the crew was willing to follow him for this mission, which suggested that if he'd messed up before, he must have fixed it—but mostly he just wished someone had warned him. It probably wouldn't have made any difference, but at the moment, he was willing to pretend that the information would have led to the safe, sane choice of staying behind. He'd been on the *Even* less than two weeks, what had he been thinking?

He could actually pick individual footsteps out of the clamoring noise, now, could hear individual voices—deep, snarling voices that hissed and slurped. It sounded like they had reached the TMP cavern, and he felt a stab of fear for Stess, alone and in the open. The camouflage was very good, but the idea of being right out there like that, having to hold perfectly still—

It was either the thought of forced immobility or the heavy gravity or both; Jake shifted ever so slightly and was suddenly unbalanced, unable to stay on the balls of his feet. He toppled backward, clutching his knees as he fell to make himself as small as possible, terrified that he was going to send one of those stacks of dishes crashing over—and subsequently bring the entire Drang mob into the room—

OUCH!

—but except for a piercing internal scream, he made no sound at all, a barely discernible *fump.* He rolled onto his side as quickly as he dared, reaching over to scrabble at whatever it was that he had crushed into the small of his back, his jaw clenched—and flashed back to baby-sitting for Vilix'pran's offspring one night on the station, remembered clearly the exquisite pain of stepping barefoot on one of the children's small toy pieces, something hard and rounded with torture-inducing ridges.

This was apparently the exact same toy, perhaps a little bigger. Terrific. A little warm-up pain before his probable death. It would be laughable, but he was much, much too scared to laugh. Jake slowly, carefully rolled forward into a half-kneeling position, the offending item still in hand, wanting to be ready to move when Dez said—and heard the growling, grinding voice of a Drang booming into the room, filtered through his translator implant.

"We look here!"

Jake froze. He could hear others out in the tunnel, their sibilant breathing and angry voices reverberating . . . and then two sets of ponderous, heavy footsteps stomped into the room. He heard a box being kicked aside, heard glass break. They sounded so close, it seemed impossible that they were still coming closer, but the sounds were getting louder.

Jake closed his eyes, trying to be invisible like in hide-and-find, *I'm not here, can't see me.*

The Drang hissed and snarled as they crashed through the crates, coming even closer . . . and because Jake suddenly thought of how terrible it would be if he had to cough or sneeze, he felt a tickle in the back of his throat.

No, that's too stupid, I can't, his mind moaned, but of course, that made his throat tickle worse. *Stop it, don't think about it, think about anything but having to cough!*

That did no good whatsoever, and one of the Drang had to be less than a meter away, he could feel the vibration of its massive tread through the bottom of the crate.

There was another bright shatter of sound just as close, more glass breaking, and now he thought he might have to sneeze, too.

Jake grabbed the toy piece tightly in both hands, desperate for any kind of distraction. What was it? It was small, about half the size of his clenched fist, and seemed solid. He stroked it with his jittery fingertips, felt a few bands of smoothness through the raised parts, thinking that its bony edges and overall shape reminded him of the oysters his grandfather served in his restaurant. *Why didn't I go to Earth like I told Kas I was going to, I could be there now, sweating in his kitchen instead of waiting to die inside this crate—*

"Not here!" a Drang shouted, its voice so close and loud that for a split second Jake thought it was yelling at *him.*

The second Drang snarled back from across the room. "I stay, guard! Go see else!"

There was a hissed, mumbled reply—and incredibly, the Drang that had been right on top of him stomped away, its footsteps receding, kicking another crate, then gone.

Jake clutched the oyster toy to his chest, letting himself breathe. Beautiful, wonderful oyster toy, he didn't have to cough or sneeze anymore . . . but what were they going to do about the Drang guard? Jake could hear it breathing somewhere in the room, the wet, gasping sound very clear now that the tunnel had apparently cleared somewhat; he could still hear echoes of the rest, but they seemed farther away, the sound sparser. He and Dez had the muffled disruptors, but if the guard saw either of them coming he (or she, Jake supposed) could call for help, and they only had three charges apiece—

"*Jake, knock,*" Dez whispered in his ear, the simple request explaining the plan.

Jake didn't hesitate. He raised his right hand and thumped his fist solidly against the top of the box . . . and heard a sudden, slurping gasp from the guard. Footsteps stomped toward him, closer—and there was a creak, and a soft burst of disruptor sound, high-pitched and clear but not very loud. Not as loud as Dez's grunt of exertion that immediately followed.

Jake didn't wait to be told that he could come out. He tucked the lucky oyster toy in his boot and sidled out of the box, staying low; he was blocked from the cave's entrance by several rows of crates, as long as he didn't stand up. Dez was crouched a few meters to his right, still lowering the unconscious guard to the ground. He finally dropped the obviously heavy Drang the last half meter, shooting a crooked smile at Jake.

"Fun, huh?" he said, obviously not meaning it.

"No," Jake replied, and he definitely meant it . . . and then they were both grinning, Jake unable to help himself. No, this was definitely not fun, they could *die,* but he grinned anyway, giddy that they weren't dead yet.

Dez crouch-walked over to Jake, still smiling. "Fair enough. You're doing great—just hang on, we'll be out of this in no time."

"Yeah, but what now?" Jake whispered.

Dez didn't answer, touched his earpiece. "Stess, one for yes, two for no—are there Drang in the TMP room?"

There was a hesitation, then a single, soft *thump.*

"Stess, more than five?"

Thump.

"Stess, more than ten?"

Thump. Thump.

"Stess, do you see any weapons that we didn't expect?"

Clubs and bare hands, Jake remembered. The Drang had access to energy weapons, but only used them when absolutely necessary. They took great pride in their brute physical strength.

Thump. Thump.

That's a relief, Jake thought, then, *kind of.*

"Stand by," Dez said, and touched his earpiece again. He looked at Jake, frowning slightly as he studied him for a few beats . . . then he smiled again.

"We're going to sneak past the Drang, and run up the north tunnel, and bash that scrambler," Dez said. "And then we're going to beam out. Answer me seriously . . . are you up for this, or do you want to stay here?"

"I want to stay here," Jake said immediately. "But . . . I'm up for it."

Dez nodded slowly, his eyes bright and warm and proud, and though Jake knew he was being an idiot, knew that he wasn't ready by any stretch of the imagination, he also knew that seeing Dez look at him like that made him feel incredibly, supremely brave. Dez believed he could do it; who was to say he couldn't?

Dez tapped his earpiece again and started talking.

Pif and Brad were hiding together in a room that no one had come to check yet, the sixth in the long A tunnel . . . though Pif could hear the Drang outside, shouting and pounding and spitting their way closer. He'd had to bite his tongue a number of times to keep from making cracks about the subtleties of the Drang language, well aware that when Brad was nervous, she often giggled—and in all fairness, it could be a very subtle, very complex language, just not easily translated.

Right. Talk Drang smart.

They had crawled under a veritable mountain of sheer gossamer fabric to hide, reams and reams of the stuff in two equally hideous shades of brown, piled twice as high as Brad standing, its base taking up nearly half the room. Crouched beneath the gauzy peak, they listened silently as Dez asked Stess about the TMP, and Stess thumped back. Pif thought he had a pretty good idea of what Dez meant to do, and thought also that while he was sorry that the profitable mission extras had fallen through, and nervous about all of them getting safely out of the tunnels, he couldn't wait to take part in the diversion. He hoped Dez would ask for volunteers, *he has to, he needs me for this one.* He would, of course he would.

"Stand by," Dez told Stess, and Pif smiled widely at Brad.

"I think he's going to ask me to run," Pif whispered.

"Good. Be quiet," Brad whispered back.

"They can't hear us, they're still too far away."

Brad glowered at him. *"I* can hear you. Hush."

Pif couldn't resist. "Can you hear the Drang? 'I no see!' What do you think that means?"

Brad clapped one giant hand over her mouth. Her shoulders heaved and shook, creating a small fabric-quake. Pif grinned, but then saw the helpless, frightened look in her eyes and was instantly sorry. He rubbed the top of his head and muzzle against her arm soothingly, and after a few seconds, she relaxed.

Just in time, too. *"Ground team, listen up,"* Dez said, his voice soft but perfectly in command. *"Jake and I need to go through the TMP without being seen. I need a loud noise in the distance, and I need the Drang blocking the north tunnel to want to go investigate. Stess, can you get them agitated, maybe frustrated that they're standing guard, not looking?"*

Thump.

"Good, get started . . . and once they hear the noise, give them a push, whatever you think will work. It doesn't have to be for long, just so we can get past."

Thump.

Pif couldn't wait another second. "Dez, I can make the noise," he whispered. "A good running howl, I can get them all chasing me. I know where the connecting tunnels are, too. I want to volunteer."

He could hear a smile in Dez's voice. *"I thought you might, Pif. You're our man . . . but I also want everyone who can to help even things out. Everyone got that? As soon as Pif gets going, if you can take one or more of the Drang out of commission without bringing them all down on you, do it. If you can't, you can't, don't be reckless; we'll leave that to Pif."*

Pif grinned, ignoring the urge to wag his tail.

"Stess, tap three times when you think the Drang are pumped up enough to act. Pif, wait for it, or wait as long as you can. Facity, anything to add?"

"No," she said tersely. *"It's a plan."*

Dez paused. When he spoke again, Pif didn't know if it was for the team's benefit or the first officer's. *"We're practically home already. See you on the drop-ship. Out."*

Pif turned to look at Brad. He could still hear the Drang shouting out in the tunnel, closer now but not so close that he was afraid to risk whispering.

"They'll probably see me leave, so don't come out until after I'm gone a minute or two," he said. "They might come in looking for more of me."

Brad smiled slightly. "There aren't any more of you," she whispered back.

Though he couldn't be sure—Brad was prone to taking things too literally, and responding likewise—Pif decided to take that as a compliment rather than a statement of the obvious. He smiled back at her and started to wriggle out backward from beneath the mound of shifting fabric, stretching his front legs as he went; *time to teach these mental giants how to run.*

Pif's heart was beating strongly and soundly in his chest, his breathing was even, he was primed . . . and exceedingly happy. He was going to run, he was going to make some noise and go streaking past a large number of big lizards while he did it, big lizards that would be trying to get him. He knew that it was possible for him to get hurt, even killed; all it would take would be for one Drang to bring his or her club down at exactly the right instant while he was running past and *wham,* no more Pif. And the thought didn't bother him a bit, because although he knew it was *possible,* he didn't believe it was going to happen.

Because I'm faster than they are, faster than anyone down here. I'd bet a million paegs that I'm faster than anybody on this whole planet. Pif didn't believe in false modesty, he thought it was a waste of time, and though he knew some of his self-observations weren't necessarily the absolute truth, he also knew that this one was. Aarruris were born runners, and his mother's side of the family had been champion at it, and he was ready.

Once out from beneath the fabric mountain, he stuck to the edge of the room where the shadows were heavier, padding slowly toward the entrance. It gave him further opportunity to stretch, and he also started to get a better sense of where the approaching Drang were, exactly. "Directly outside" wouldn't be a bad interpretation of the facts; in another ten, perhaps twenty seconds, at least two of them would be walking into the room, coming in from his left. If Stess didn't signal soon . . .

Thump. Thump. Th—

Pif aimed himself right, opened his mouth wide, and took off, howling death and destruction.

As soon as Dez told her to get started, Stess, alone and holding very still against a rock at the east side of the TMP cavern, felt an almost overwhelming relief. Physically, she'd been fine; Friagloims were known for their ability to stand immobile for long periods, a leftover evolutionary tactic to avoid motion-sensing predators. But mentally and emotionally, she'd been feeling more and more desperate to do something, to do *anything*. Deliberately projecting negative feelings went against Arislelemakinstess's nature, but with such deserving recipients, she thought she could manage. Besides which, she only had to build on what was already there.

Watching and listening to the eight Drang standing around, occasionally nudging one of their fallen comrades as they hissed out their respective hopes for violence . . . that was unpleasant, and made her dislike them. But the mental imagery that went along with it, what every one of those Drang wanted . . . smashed alien heads, broken bodies, grinning Drang faces splattered with blood . . .

Stess opened herself up, let her bad feelings stain the already oppressive atmosphere. It wasn't hard to produce unhappy restlessness—Arislelemakin, spread out in the tunnels and having to edge back toward the TMP centimeter by centimeter, was feeling an abundance of it—but it took some work to find a desire to commit violence. It was the team's best chance, plainly the strongest Drang motivator, but she couldn't simply steal it from the Drang; she had to nurture violent feelings of her own, of which there were very few . . . though considering what the Drang meant to do to them made it easier. No one on the *Even* had really understood the danger presented by the reptilian species, thinking them slow and stupid with anger, which was true—but they were also merciless and eager to destroy, and she and the others had been foolish to underestimate them.

Stess sent the feelings out, adding to what the Drang were already feeling, the anger, the discontent with standing still, the desire to be smashing something. She had to design her projected feelings to match those of the Drang as closely as possible, keeping them brief and intense . . . and had to ignore a sense of accomplishment as all eight of them began to fidget after only a moment or so. One, two, three of them were feigning blows with their weapons, swinging at air or slapping their own open palms with heavy clubs; two others began to pace, one of them walking back and forth directly in front of her, unaware that one of the alien heads he so wanted to crush was barely a meter away.

It was unlikely to get much better. Having tucked the communication collar beneath her sensory bulbs, she only had to nudge the transmitter with one of her vocal muscles, tap-tap-tap—

—and at seemingly the same instant, a rough, high-pitched scream came bounding into the cavern, loud and startling and seemingly unending, *aaarrrroooorooorooroo—*

—and Stess pushed, *alien, kill Drang, get it, go!*

The effect was exactly what Dez had hoped for, what Stess had wanted. One of the Drang stayed where she was, snarling at the others to stop; the rest ignored her and ran, weapons high, four of them into the A tunnel, three into B.

Aris saw Pif go running by near the west end of A tunnel, a flash of howling gray fur . . . and seconds later, Lema, near the narrower of the two connecting tunnels between A and B, saw the same thing. The Drang that were following were so far behind that they might as well have been standing still.

As the TMP cavern's bloodthirsty Drang disappeared, their excited cries all but drowning out Pif's echoing howl, Dez stepped out of the shadows at the C-tunnel entrance and took aim at the one remaining Drang. She didn't even see him coming, still cursing after the deserters, demanding their return. If any of the departing Drang heard the muted blast of the tiny disruptor, they didn't return to investigate.

Stess felt great satisfaction with Dez's plan and her part in it, rotating an optical bulb to watch Jake and Dez dash across to the north tunnel. Satisfaction and no small fear—because soon enough, even with each part of her participating, urging them on, the mob chasing Pif was going to get tired of running in circles. Then they were going to get organized, and when that happened, it was going to be over for all of them.

Stess repositioned herself and settled in to wait, hoping that she wouldn't have to wait long.

After Dez outlined the plan, Glessin quickly moved from his hiding place to the clump of pillows where

Coamis hid, leaning down to whisper to the frightened half-Wadi.

"Stay there. When Facity says the transporters are working, tell her where you are."

Coamis stammered out an affirmative and Glessin moved to the cave room's entrance, standing to one side, half shielded from the tunnel by a shelving unit. He watched and waited for an opportunity, sure that Pifko would have the Drang running amok in short order.

Even as he thought it, two Drang hurried by, not even looking in his direction. He held very still, listening to the hisses and snarls that filled the tunnel with echoes, thinking about Coamis. Assuming they survived, he would have to tell Facity and Dez to keep him on the ship from now on. Glessin didn't blame him for his inability to cope . . . or, rather, his unawareness of that inability. It was the first mission the young archeologist had been on in which something had gone wrong, and probably the first time in his life that he'd ever been so tested. Some things just couldn't be prepared for.

Glessin had known from the moment that Dez had called the abort that Coamis was going to be useless. It wasn't that he didn't want to help, it was that the young archeologist was half paralyzed with fear, and that made his every move a liability.

To begin, Coamis had been unable to choose a place to hide. He and Glessin had slipped into the fourth room along B tunnel, the one where Stessie had seen the possible Gocibis; they'd been near it already, having decided while still on the dropship that if the Drang actually had the statue of Hyrcham the Swib, they had a duty to retrieve it. The statue alone was worth twenty Yaron Oracles.

After a quick assessment of the room, Glessin had seen that it held a multitude of subtle hiding places, spots the Drang probably wouldn't think to search—crouched in the darkness beneath the wine racks, perhaps, or tucked between the giant spools of embroidery threads and fabric, perhaps acting as a base for some of the stacks and stacks of feather-stuffed pillows . . . and Coamis had immediately run for the tall standing cabinet in the back of the room and climbed inside, easily the most obvious place to look. Worse, he hadn't wanted to come out; Glessin had spent precious seconds convincing the young half-Wadi that it was a poor choice, then more time watching the hysterical Coamis flail around the room, rejecting every good spot he came across.

Glessin didn't have much of a temper, but with the Drang bearing down on them and Coamis working his way into a blind panic, he'd been on the verge of losing what there was of it. He'd finally just grabbed the boy and shoved him behind a mound of pillows, throwing more on top. He'd barely managed to hide himself—in the wine-rack shadows—before a Drang had stormed into the room, followed by a second. They had knocked over a table or two, broken a few bottles, and ripped the cabinet door off of Coamis's first hiding place before storming back out, joining the shouting throng out in the tunnel. It seemed they were in some kind of a frenzy for alien blood, which Glessin was glad to see; *frenzied* was generally the same as *careless.*

Dez had been clear about the crew not taking risks, but after the searchers had gone, Glessin had decided that it wasn't exactly an order, after all. He further decided that if the Drang came back, he would kill as many as he could, and then they would probably kill him, and the universe would be less one battle-scarred Cardassian. He had left his spot just long enough to better arm himself—there was a set of daggers he borrowed from, cheaply made but quieter than the disruptors—and to take a brief look at the sculptures and statues still standing after the Drang's violent search. There were a few pieces that had looked Gocibi, but no Swib.

At least we got the Oracle marked, Glessin thought, and was starting to wonder if he had time to try marking a few other items when Pif began to howl. Almost immediately afterward, he heard the raised, eager shouts of more Drang feeding into the tunnels, each gasping creature surely stoked into a maniacal, murderous rage by Stess's gentle touch. Dez had his shortcomings, obviously, he and the rest of the ground crew were standing witness to one of them, but he could also pull a working plan out of thin air like no other—

—rooroOROOOroo—

The Aarruri flashed by at a full run, gone before Glessin realized he'd been that close; the tunnel acoustics were definitely throwing him off. A few beats later, the start of a lumbering, seething, snarling Drang mob passed by, three, five, seven of them, sticks and clubs raised, their bulbous, glittering gazes apparently oblivious of everything but the pursuit; none of them even glanced toward the storeroom.

Glessin shook his head slightly as the last of the mob passed, astounded. They were making so much noise, too, it was tempting to just step out and fire the disruptor at one of them, to see if the others would stop—

He suddenly understood that they wouldn't, not if he chose the right one. With a quick glance to either side,

Glessin stepped out from around the shelf and halfway into the tunnel, turning east. The slowest runner was less than three meters away, a short, growling male holding a studded mace. Glessin pointed the disruptor and fired, immediately stepping back into his half shelter, where he waited, counting slowly to five.

No surprised exclamations, no alarm raised, no returning Drang. Glessin shot a glance back out and saw the short Drang facedown on the tunnel floor, completely alone. He had to fight a brief urge to step out and move the fallen male to one side so he wouldn't be trampled the next time Pif came through . . . because he had no doubt that the unfortunate Drang's comrades would stomp right over him.

Glessin shook his head again, wondering how these creatures had managed to amass such a fortune . . . though he knew, of course. Violent people often got what they wanted. It was the way of the universe.

Already, he could hear Pif rounding through the tunnels, leading the Drang back in his direction. He decided he would shoot one more from where he was, then try moving to another room. Coamis would be fine as long as he stayed down, and he didn't want a pile of bodies too close to where he was standing; even the Drang would eventually get suspicious.

And eventually they'll stop running, too. And then they'd realize it would be just as easy to block the tunnels off and search each one thoroughly, one by one. Glessin hoped that Dez and Jake knew what they were doing . . . and that they were getting close to doing it.

Dez knew he was in good physical condition, but between the Drang gravity and the heat, running up the north tunnel made him realize that good was not great. Jake ran easily at his side, as calm as he had been throughout their misadventure. Dez continued to be impressed; he'd followed instructions, asked only relevant questions, even made a joke when Dez had asked him about staying behind. And he was in better shape than Dez, at least in terms of stamina, simply by virtue of being half his age, give or take.

He was made for this, Dez thought randomly, then went back to concentrating on not collapsing. All around them, the echoes of Pif's ongoing howls of alarm and the splutters and hisses of the Drang had merged into a distorted confusion of sound, rising from behind like a hot wind.

It was a hard run. Unlike the other tunnels, which were basically level and curved gently back and forth, the north tunnel was a series of sudden turns, each short stretch angled sharply upward. The floor wasn't as smooth, either, the footing uneven. It didn't help that it felt like they had been running forever and might continue to—it was incredibly difficult to tell how far they'd gone, each turn seeming to wind back on itself. Dez thought they were getting close, but he was also starting to think that the device was 120 meters directly above the TMP. As they reached another sharp corner, he supposed he should just be thankful that the Drang hadn't thought to post any guards along the way—

"*There,*" Jake panted, around the corner first, and Dez felt relief wash over him, *finally,* as he stumbled forward to see for himself. The scrambler was seated into the rock just before the tunnel cornered back out of sight, facing south. It looked so innocuous, the long, blinking, boxy unit, small, probably light enough for two men to carry.

Should only take one to break it, though, Dez thought, tucking his disruptor in his belt as they jogged toward it. He didn't recognize the design, didn't care; the big plan was to find the activation switch, turn it off, and smash it with a rock. With as many Drang as there were in the tunnels, he didn't want to use his last disruptor shot, and besides, it wasn't necessary. As long as the Drang couldn't fix it for three or four minutes, the team would be safe.

"Find a rock," Dez said, spotting the big switch at the bottom right and reaching for it—

—and they both heard the sudden hiss coming from just around the corner, heard the urgent, angry cry.

"Send more now!"

Damn!

He grabbed at his disruptor, saw that Jake already had his out and was stepping away from the wall, into the curve of the blind corner. Jake's gaze was determined, his stance unsteady but his hands still as he pointed the disruptor and fired.

His own disruptor in hand, Dez grabbed the rock wall and swung around to see, just as the lone Drang hit the floor. It was another mistake to add to today's list, not checking for a guard at the scrambler, and something else for him to feel bad about later; the Drang's message was clear. Reinforcements would be coming. They had to get out, now.

Jake was staring at the fallen guard, the small weapon still extended, wearing a look of mild surprise.

"I didn't think about it," he said.

Dez scooped up a rock near Jake's feet. "That works,

too," he said, turning back to the scrambler. He flipped the switch, and as the panel lights blinked out, he brought the chunk of rock down, hard, and again. The thin alloy crumpled, the switch breaking off and dropping to the tunnel floor.

Scramble that, he thought, tossing the rock aside, turning a triumphant smile toward Jake—and then he heard them, heard thundering steps, Drang voices echoing down at them from somewhere ahead, raised in an excited fury. They must have been standing by at the entrance, just waiting to be told that the alien threat required an additional team of skull crushers.

Dez grabbed Jake's arm and pulled, Jake hardly needing the encouragement; the look on his face said he was ready to run again, to run faster.

"Don't wait for me," Dez said, and then they were both pounding the tunnel floor, heading back the way they'd come, Jake a few paces ahead.

Dez thought he heard Facity as they rounded the second corner down, but the sound was bad, just a few broken syllables. Dez slapped his earpiece, watching Jake run the few paces between turns and neatly take the next corner, leaning away from the outer curve. Dez was right behind him.

"Facity, repeat!"

"—working—"

It was all he got, and he had to hope there wasn't a negative preceding it—and that the ground team could hear her, and was getting out. It had to be the sensor jam, if there was enough of it, communications could get garbled, *I should have thought of that, too, this whole mission has been a disaster—*

—but the Oracle egg's marked and you're going to make it, you're almost there—

Even as he ran for his life, his eternal optimism wouldn't shut up; it wasn't the first time he'd noticed, and with any luck, it wouldn't be the last. Dez half smiled, too otherwise engaged to do better, and attempted to put on more speed. As fast as they were running, he could still hear the Drang behind them getting louder—but suddenly, he couldn't hear Pif anymore. The constant, raspy howl had disappeared from the din below, the din that they were fast approaching, and was replaced by a sudden roar of sound, a united cry of outrage . . . or victory.

No, he thought, answering a flicker of doubt. Facity had taken him out, that was all, that had to be all.

Jake was only just in sight now on each corner, Dez catching a bare glimpse each time he turned. Good, that was good, if Pif had been beamed out, that meant the rest of the team was already gone, except maybe part of Stessie, less likely to be discovered—when Jake hit the TMP cavern, Srral could lock on him first. Dez wanted to be last, Facity knew him well enough to know that, she would beam out accordingly.

His body heavy, his diaphragms desperate for air, his muscles hot and shaking, Dez stumbled on, recognizing a broken light bar, *near the bottom now, passed that going up* . . . They were losing the Drang behind them, he was sure of it, but it was costing him. From now on, he was going to work out in heavier gravity, eat better, stop drinking as much . . . and as long as he was going to improve his habits, he was also going to listen when Facity said she didn't like something from now on, really give it some thought—

—and turning another corner, he heard the sound of a disruptor blast, heard Drang expletives and snarls, saw that the light was different, that Jake was entirely out of sight. They'd made it to the TMP . . . and if anything had happened to Jake . . .

There was another blast as Dez ran the last stretch, somehow finding the strength to run faster, *I talked him into it, he wouldn't be here if I hadn't pushed—*

Dez hit the last corner and burst into the cavern, saw no Jake, saw seven or eight Drang bodies strewn about, saw a dozen more turning toward him, furious, slack, eager jaws drooling, clubs raised, talons reaching—

—and then it all melted away like a fever dream, and there was the team, looking tired and sweaty, Pif was lying on the floor, sides heaving, and there was a nice, cool dropship all around him.

"Everyone here?" Dez gasped, and saw nods, some smiles. "Did we get the Oracle?" More nods, a few fingers pointing behind him.

Good enough. Dez collapsed onto the transporter pad, leaning back on his elbows—and saw that Jake was right next to him, lying out flat and breathing deep.

"That was awful," Jake panted.

"I love this job," Dez panted back, and smiled, and so did Jake.

"Dez and Jake Sisko have been transported," Srral said. *"Neither appears injured."*

Facity let out a breath she hadn't realized she'd been holding, felt herself sag in her chair, worn out. It had been only eleven minutes since the team had gone in, eleven, but as she'd learned long ago, sitting helplessly by created an eternity all its own.

She tapped the return-flight controls and asked Srral to take over as pilot, wanting to see for herself that Dez was all right. She knew he was, knew because Dez was one of the luckiest people alive—he should have been killed ten times over just since she'd known him—but she also wanted for him to see her, to make sure he understood just how lucky he was.

Lucky I don't boot him upside the head, for making me worry like that, she thought briskly, striding through the small, empty passenger cabin to the transporter room. The door between the two was open, the disheveled team members standing and leaning against equipment, sitting on the empty crates that had been packed to store some of the Drang fortune. Facity looked them over, relieved to see that no one had been hurt. All of them looked wide-eyed and dazed, excessively tired for the brief period they'd been gone—except Stessie, of course, and even she seemed slightly faded.

Dez was still on the transporter pad, just sitting up, his runneled face dripping with sweat. Jake looked about the same, his movements slow and exhausted, though she saw that their other runner, Pif, was drinking from a water tube and chatting easily with Brad, fatigued but evidently recuperating well from his mad dash through the tunnels. By comparison, Coamis looked terrible—he seemed especially pale, strangely irritable, not interacting with any of the others—but before she could ask, Glessin caught her eye. He glanced at Coamis and then shook his head very slightly.

He froze, Facity realized. She'd seen the symptoms before, and felt the standard mix of emotions that came with the knowledge—concern, disappointment, surrender to the way things sometimes played out. She'd have to ask Glessin about it later, see if there was any chance or if they were going to have to start looking for another archeologist.

Dez was grinning at her, his gaze sparkling with good humor, the same look he always wore when he'd survived another mission, successful or not . . . and as was so often the case, she felt a flash of irritation with him, for his obvious joy at almost dying. She understood the love of the game, absolutely, but did he have to be so damned ecstatic about it?

I was worried, she thought, and wanted to say it, but knew it would have to wait. Their relationship wasn't a secret, but it wasn't something either of them flaunted, either.

Instead, she smiled, crossing her arms and gazing around at the rest of the team.

"Anybody bring me anything?" she asked lightly.

Almost immediately, she was sorry she'd said it; the high mood of the room dropped a few notches, as it sank in for the team that they had risked their lives for the Yaron Oracle, nothing more. Worse, she saw the slight frowns, the flickers of irritation in Dez's direction. It hadn't been his fault, not really, she could have aborted the mission and hadn't . . . but he was the captain, and the responsibility stopped with him, and they all knew it.

Glessin held up a shining, slightly curved dagger. "I got this," he said, handing it over. "But only as a keepsake, I'm afraid."

She examined the blade, and nodded. A decent knife, but no value beyond the intrinsic. "I appreciate the thought," she said, and then put on a bright smile for the others. "As long as someone brought me something, I'm happy. And don't forget, we got the Oracle. The Yaron are giving us three-fifty."

Wan smiles and nods. It was a good take, but it wasn't untold riches, either.

Jake was holding out something he'd fished from his boot. "Here, you can have this," he said. "Sorry, it's a little damp."

Facity reached for it, Brad and Glessin leaning in, Dez sitting up a little straighter, Pif rising to sit. Even Coamis turned to look. It was small, a rounded, flat object with textured stripes . . . pretty, in a way, though it was damp, and awfully warm. . . .

Glessin's voice, when he spoke, was oddly flat, a little strangled.

"It's one of the boxes," he said.

Facity stared down at her open hand, her skin suddenly flushed, her mouth dry. "What?"

"One of his last," Glessin said. "Giani'aga was going smaller right before he died. I read about them, but only saw a picture once . . . and that's one of them. He made forty-seven boxes just over twice that size, his life's work, that's what we were looking for down there. Any one of those is worth nine hundred, easy, and that's a low estimate."

"And this one?" Facity asked, her voice almost a whisper. She felt her palm getting warm, saw the tiny box shiver, though that might have been her shaking hand.

Glessin shook his head. "There are only three. Priceless."

For a long second, no one moved, no one seemed to breathe—and then they were all howling, shouting and laughing, Jake saying something about toy-stirs with a stunned expression as the team surrounded him, pounding his back, ruffling his hair. Dez looked on with something akin to love, and Facity carefully, gently handed the living box over to Glessin, terrified she would drop it when she went to give the young human the big, wet kiss that he so rightly deserved.

8

Day 16, late afternoon. I meant to write immediately after Drang, to record the experience so I wouldn't forget anything, but I haven't gotten around to it, it's been a busy couple of days . . . well, sleeping and eating and having everyone congratulate me and thank me a thousand times over, which I totally don't deserve. I keep telling them that it was a complete fluke, my finding the Giani'aga box (and a painful one, at that)—and it's like they know that, but they're just so pleased, they have to say something anyway. Feg has already started putting out feelers, to see what the market is, though Dez said it'll probably be weeks before we find a buyer. I have to admit, I don't exactly hate all the hoopla—not only do I now feel accepted by everyone in the crew, I'm suddenly very popular. We're doing a salvage job day after tomorrow, which in this case just involves poking through an abandoned Dominion settlement, looking for assorted ship parts (it's terrifying, how many "unofficial" outposts they had in the Idran system), and everyone keeps making jokes about wanting to partner with me.

I didn't sit down to write about Drang today, either, and I'm realizing only now that I don't have any desire to do so in the immediate future. Maybe because writing down a bunch of details to have for later, to look back over . . . it's not being there. It will make a good story, I think, and maybe I'll write it that way someday, for somebody else to read, but I don't need to write it down for me, not here. I know what happened, I know that it was exciting and scary and intense, and while I can document those feelings, I can't capture them . . . and I don't particularly want to try. It's like Dez was saying yesterday, about living those moments to live them. He said the experience itself is what counts—that, and having a good story to tell when you've been drinking (!).

I guess I'm writing right now because I'm feeling . . . dissatisfied, maybe, and maybe that's dumb. The Even rendezvoused with the Yaron ship Glimnis today, to return the Oracle. It's strange, I kind of expected the whole crew to turn out, to present the egg and the other stuff, but it was just Facity, Dez, Feg, and me. There wasn't an announcement or anything, either, I only ended up going because I was on the bridge when the Glimnis hailed. Anyway, they seemed like nice people, the three men who came aboard, kind of tall and greenish, soft-spoken—and they were elated to get the Oracle back, positively overwhelmed. Two of them cried.

It's just . . . I think I wrote before, about how the Yaron are a religious culture, how they believe that the millennia-old ashes of their supreme being are in the egg—or, rather, the remains of Her physical embodiment on

Yaron—and that's why they wanted it back so badly; it symbolizes their entire faith. I knew that much before Drang, and I thought it was kind of . . . well, heroic that the Even Odds *would be helping them out. I can see now that I had this little story going in my head, about the desperate Yaron needing help, and us returning the Oracle in this big ceremony after having an exciting adventure. . . . The adventure part didn't turn out the way I expected, but the rest was kind of fixed in my mind.*

Except . . . Dez told me on the way to meet them that when the Drang stole the Oracle a few months ago, the Yaron were struck by a kind of planetwide insomnia. He said the entire society has been unable to function, a total shutdown—and that they'll probably have to deal with a lot of aftermath from that, probably famine in some areas over the next year, and longer-term, drug-dependency issues arising from so many people having to be tranquilized for so long . . . and that there have been literally thousands of suicides. None of those details were in the little unconscious story I'd constructed . . . I guess because they weren't fun *details, if that makes any sense. And then when we gave it to them . . .*

For how important the Oracle is, the money is nothing to them, right? They *certainly thought so—they were happy to pay us, they* wanted *to pay us . . . so why do I keep thinking about Feg counting that money after they were gone, and feeling bad about it? The Yaron were looking for someone to hire, it wasn't like they expected strangers to risk their lives for nothing. . . . They sent ships to every port they knew of, with money, to find help—that's how the* Even *heard about it, a call from a contact at one of those ports. And this is what the* Even *does, this is the retrieval business. The crew didn't come together to perform acts of altruism, they hired on for excitement and money (at least most of them—Glessin I'm not sure about).*

Maybe my uneasiness with all this is because I'm an "Alphie," as Facity says, and a Starfleet brat besides. The GQ doesn't have a Federation, there's no Starfleet to come to the rescue when someone is being oppressed, or whatever. I grew up with such clearly defined beliefs about right and wrong, such a solid, black and white morality . . . but do I really think that the Even'*s crew is immoral somehow, because they accept money for the work they're doing? I think that would make me kind of condescending, actually. I mean, look at someone like Stessie, who doesn't really care about the money at all—she left home because she wanted to travel, to have an adventure. Pif, too, he likes the money, but he'd probably do this for free. . . .*

Maybe I should stop trying to apply my own morals to this, maybe that's the problem. Or . . . not even my own morals, but the morals I grew up with. Maybe I need to reexamine what I was taught. It's sad that the Yaron were victimized by the Drang, but they asked us—the Even Odds, *I mean—to do a job, to bring them the Oracle in exchange for three hundred and fifty Klon paegs (there's no direct exchange, but that's something like 80 or 90 bars of gold-pressed latinum, from what I can tell). We did, and they paid us, and maybe I should stop being so puritanical about it.*

Okay, I feel better. I should probably go, I wanted to try and talk to Coamis again before hooking up with Dez for dinner. Over dinner last night, Dez and I were talking about Drang, and he kept saying how calm I was (?!), and I ended up telling him about what happened on

Ajilon Prime. It's weird, it wasn't as hard to talk about as I thought it would be . . . maybe because Dez isn't Starfleet. When it happened, the only people I could really interact with about it were soldiers themselves. Anyway, I told him about running instead of fighting, and he told me about Coamis. I've kind of wondered why he hasn't been around. . . . Dez asked me not to talk about it to anyone else, said that Coamis has already decided to leave the Even *when we finally get to Ee. Dez and Fac offered to let him stay on as a researcher, I guess, but he turned them down. Anyway, I'm not going to go ask him about it, or just walk up and start talking about Ajilon. . . . I just thought it might help if he had some company. We're still eight to twelve weeks from Ee without the big stops, and that's a long time to feel like you're all alone. . . .*

Gotta run.

About two weeks after Drang, something strange happened in the Wa . . . corresponding with something very strange that apparently happened everywhere else in the known universe. Facity, who'd always had a love for mysteries and stories of the bizarre, took a special interest in the event . . . and because she took the time to look up a few things, she ended up winning big.

She heard about the Wa from Prees, of course, who spent more time on the C-D subdeck than anyone else on the ship. It seemed that the engineer had gone down for one of her regular explorations, and discovered that all of the colors had turned a murky gray, the color to avoid. There was no telling how long it had been that way, exactly; it had been days since anyone had gone to visit, the crew busy between salvage sorting and bidding for the contract to find the Ahswidus cup. Facity had asked Prees to leave it alone for a while, and set about solving the minor mystery.

On a vague hunch that it might have something to do with the *Even*'s location, Facity had tuned in to subspace communications—and had ended up spending several hours listening, followed by another hour digging through the library. By the time lunch rolled around, she'd picked up enough information to offer up a truly interesting wager. Considering that the *Even*'s crew members had been known to bet on what one another had eaten for breakfast, Facity thought she might get some serious money involved on this one.

At lunch, she laid out the situation to an intrigued crew, from the Wa going gray to the reports she'd heard flying around subspace. All of her betting mates were present—the Ferengi, her fellow Wadi and Coamis, Pif, and Pri'ak. Dez, Jake, Neane, and Brad were also there, though of the four, only Dez gambled, and he already knew better than to bet with her. Or, rather, against her.

"So, these doors have opened up everywhere?" Pif asked.

Facity nodded. "Since yesterday. A whole network of interspatial gateways, and people and ships either are wandering into them by accident, or they're being sucked in. Instant transport. It's a mess out there."

"Do you know if any of them open into the Alpha Quadrant?" Jake asked.

Facity hesitated. Jake's voice was full of hope and optimism, and she hated to squash it. "None of the ones nearby," she admitted. "The comms I picked up described a few Gamma places I've heard of, and the words 'galaxy's edge' came up more than once. But no mention of the Alpha Quadrant. Sorry, Jake."

Jake looked away, obviously disappointed.

"Why did the Wa turn gray?" Dez asked, frowning.

Facity shrugged. "Sympathetic vibrations, maybe. The Wa is a series of doors, opening up to places that aren't necessarily entirely on board this ship."

"Doors, I see," Dez asked, smiling. "Scientific reasoning, huh?"

"To dust with you," she said mildly. "You have no imagination."

"It's the Q," Feg announced, and Triv nodded. "Has to be."

Pif was also nodding, as were both art appraisers. Jake seemed surprised. "You know about Q?"

"They're kind of hard to miss," Pif answered. "I'm with Feg. It's just the kind of thing they'd do to bother people."

Neane was shaking her head. "I disagree. It's not their style. Too . . ."

"Mechanical," Facity said, and Neane nodded.

"Who do you think it is?" Jake asked, addressing their head researcher. Facity was also curious about what she would say. She already thought she knew who was responsible, but Neane would know more of the possibilities. The Hissidolan had probably forgotten more trivia about the universe and its peoples than Facity would ever learn.

"There are a number of species that come to mind," Neane said thoughtfully, "who have the power to create such an event. Metrons, Organians, BiaMertis, Twelfthray, Q . . . the real question is, what's the motivation?

With the exception of Q, life-forms that advanced don't generally have any interest in complicating the lives of lesser beings."

Facity smiled to herself. Neane was overlooking the obvious. *It's not the power, it's the technology.*

"It could be an accident," Pri'ak said. "It *sounds* like an accident, or maybe a side effect . . ."

Facity had noted that the engineering tech had a piece of food stuck to the back of his front teeth. While he was talking, she caught his gaze and picked at her own teeth with a fingernail. Nodding gratefully, Pri'ak trailed off and started working at the food bit with his tongue, creating a much bigger spectacle.

" 'With the exception of Q,' " Feg said. "Because it *is* Q."

"Want to bet?" Facity asked.

"Why?" Coamis asked, sitting slightly apart from the others. "Who do you think it is?"

She was glad to have perked the half-Wadi's interest—had been glad, in fact, to see him at lunch, talking with Jake. It was the first time in two weeks she'd seen him at all outside of mandatory meetings.

Doesn't mean I won't take his money. . . .

"I think it's the Iconians," she answered, stating it strongly, wearing an expression of absolute certainty.

Neane nodded, her eyes lighting up. "Oh, I—"

"Right, Iconians," Feg sneered, cutting her off. "They're an Alpha species. And haven't they been dead for about a million years?"

Facity nodded slowly. "Yes . . . but they created a kind of gate system just like this, I read about it," she said, fairly certain that Feg and Triv would already know about the "dead" gates. She was counting on it, to influence their decision. Iconian gateways weren't uncommon, they just didn't work.

Though it looks like they're working now. . . .

Of the twenty-plus reports she'd heard about sudden appearances and disappearances, she'd cross-referenced two of them to survey files that documented actual gate sites in the area. It wasn't much, but it was enough for her to bet on.

Facity let a trickle of doubt enter her voice before reaffirming her belief. "And no one *knows* that they're dead . . . it's the Iconians."

Played perfectly. Overly sure, but still ever so slightly doubtful. She only hoped that her intuition wasn't playing *her* wrong. A couple of the subspace reports had mentioned the Iconian possibility, but no one had proof of anything.

"It might not be the Q, but I'd bet a half paeg that it's not the Iconians, either," Feg said.

"Me, too," Triv said.

Facity smiled nervously. "I don't know . . . honestly, I'd hate to take your money . . ."

Pif pounced. "I'm in for a half paeg."

A second later, so was Coamis. Facity hesitated and blustered and hesitated again, and within a few minutes, she was up to six full paegs—four from the Ferengi, one each from Pif and Coamis. Having never heard of the Iconians, Fajgin and Itriuma wisely opted out, as did Pri'ak.

"So, we have a deal?" Feg pushed, showing as many teeth as possible.

Here's the best part.

"I don't know," Facity said, shaking her head. "I'd feel a lot better about this if you'd go look up the Iconians first, maybe listen to some of those reports. I'm pretty sure I'm right about this."

Dez was smiling. "I'd listen to her, boys."

Feg grinned impossibly wider at her. "You're trying to back out?"

"I . . . no, it's a deal," Facity said, sighing, much to the delight of everyone involved. There was a Wadi saying, that there was no tool more powerful than the truth; still, it never failed to amaze her, how well it worked as a diversionary tactic.

From there, the conversation wandered toward other unusual occurrences, to tales of other mysterious civilizations and legends from home. They stayed in the dining hall until late into the afternoon, exchanging stories, speculating on the strange. Dez told a few of the famous retrieval myths to Jake—the lost planet of the Eav-oq, known only by the few rare crystals that had recorded their culture, that melted at a touch; the tombs of Luw, where the dead supposedly told accurate fortunes, for the price of a day inside a living body. He even dredged up the one about the alien race of females who wept gems and flowers. Pri'ak told the haunting Merdosian myth of the Five Kings, forever searching the night for their stolen crowns, occasionally willing to take unwary children instead. Neane told the legend of the Ascendants, among others, the mythical crusaders who had once destroyed entire planets for what they considered sacrilege, and even Feg and Triv got into the spirit of things, recounting the numerous myths involving the demon contracts.

Facity enjoyed herself immensely. It wasn't an exciting day, but she knew that the impromptu experience would stay with her . . . specifically because it was unplanned and unimportant, but it was time spent really enjoying some of the people in her life. It was one of those rare days that just happened, that allowed her to feel the fortune of being alive, and to revel in a few shivers over the unknown.

Two days later, it was over, the gates closed, and the Wa returned to its normal state. Two days after that, the *Even* caught a report that some group claiming to be the Iconians were haggling to sell the gateway technology. Facity was actually disappointed that the whole thing hadn't lasted longer, that the *Even* hadn't gotten involved somehow . . . but the event had led to a full, wonderful afternoon of storytelling, and hours of interesting reading afterward, from downloaded subspace-communications reports . . . not to mention six Klon paegs. For a truly good day and six Klon paegs, she was willing to be a little disappointed.

Day 59, night. A lot has happened. . . . I don't want to catch up on everything, though. Today was bad, it was a bad surprise, and I don't really want to talk about it, but I have to get it out, at least part of it.

Since I've been aboard, we've stopped at four abandoned Dominion outposts to run salvage—one offline temp station and three surface settlements—and I went along on two of the surface ones. It was strange, both those times, walking through those desolate places, looking for stuff, but all things considered, I wasn't disturbed; they were just empty buildings, random locations. Even knowing that second time that the land once belonged to somebody else, that the Jem'Hadar had forced relocation on the original owners . . . I mean, of course I thought it was bad, but I also reminded myself what Dez said—the Jem'Hadar are back inside the Do-

minion now, those people can come back, and most of them aren't interested in ship parts or surplus fuel tanks. Taking that stuff doesn't hurt anybody, I told myself, I told myself that I was sure I could make myself feel terrible, thinking about all of the people the war displaced, but what good would it do? Dez's right, he's right, but I'm getting sidetracked, that's not the point.

Today, this evening, we reached a planet without a name, one on the seemingly endless list of places to check for salvage. Dez said that the planet had been colonized five or six years ago, and that the Jem'Hadar had taken it over, and that was all he knew about it. The team was me, Facity, Dez, Pif, and Brad, a basic three-point salvage survey—ops, maintenance, and quarters. First, check out the designated ops building, see how thorough they were, pulling out—did they get all of the secondary optical and communication boards, were the sensor line patches yanked? . . . It's mostly small stuff that they might have forgotten, but it adds up. Second, look over any maintenance areas, particularly where they might have kept transport shuttles or land hoppers; that's where the best salvage comes from and also where weapons were usually kept, near the transports. Third, living quarters—but only if there's evidence that Dominion allies were present, beyond the Founders' direct subjects. Most of these outposts were strictly Jem'Hadar and Vorta, neither species likely to keep personal valuables. But allied Gamma species might, like the Bwada, or the Hunters.

Easy, common sense. So we beamed down, evening for us, afternoon on the planet . . . which felt as lonely and empty as any place I've been in my life. It was beautiful, too; we'd transported down to a wide, slightly elevated clearing a few dozen meters from the settlement buildings, and the air was clean and sweet, and there were tall grasses everywhere, and mountains in the distance. Facity pointed out that the clearing had once been a farmer's field—that we were, in fact, standing at the edge of a whole run of fields. The grasses were tall, we could only see a few bare lines here and there, but Facity said that from the Even, *you could see a clear grid pattern of irrigation trenches. She said that someone put a lot of work into it, and I remember thinking, "What a shame," but I was also excited to be on another salvage run, hoping to find something valuable. Once, years before the war, Dez found a glove stuffed with jewels on a salvage run. Two years ago, the* Even *found a shuttle that was being repaired, left behind during an emergency evac. Prees fixed it in less than an hour. Pif once came across a secret cache of premium bloodwine. Most of the rest of the crew is bored by them, but this was only my third salvage, and I was hoping to find something valuable. Too bad about the farmers, right?*

We did the survey. There were five buildings in the small compound, all knocked-together Dominion prefab, no more than a couple of years old . . . and it didn't take long to see that there was nothing left. Brad, Dez, and I checked out ops, and they'd stripped out everything, down to the light panel connectors. We went back outside to wait for Pif and Fac, they were looking at maintenance, and I was disappointed, but it was such a nice afternoon, I felt pretty good. So quiet, such a lovely, quiet place. Dez was saying we should invite the rest of the crew down for the fresh air, and I couldn't tell if he was joking, and then Pif and Facity came walking up—and she was wearing two Bajoran earrings. They were bent and dented but still pretty, the damaged chains still shining.

"Look what I found behind the maintenance bay," she said, pulling her hair back so we could see, and then I knew where we were.

Everyone started asking if I was okay, it must have shown on my face, and I don't remember if I said anything or not, then. I had Facity show me where she'd found the earrings—there were pieces of twenty or thirty of them in the gap between the industrial incinerator and where the feeding belt had been, the pieces smashed into the dirt—and then I walked back to the field, and got on my knees, and saw the untended katterpod beans that had been grown over. There was kava in the next field over, also overrun by the wild grass.

New Bajor had just been starting out when the Dominion had decided to attack, only a few hundred colonists, I think. I remember that it happened when I was actually in the Gamma Quadrant, that ill-fated science survey project with Nog, and Quark, and Dad. It was the first time any of us saw a Jem'Hadar, I remember. When we got back to the station, we found out that the Dominion had made their first overt acts of war against the Alpha Quadrant, blowing up several ships on "their" side of the wormhole—and wiping out New Bajor, killing every last unarmed colonist. People were mourning, and talking about war, and getting ready to fight or run—for me, it was the event that signaled the beginning of those long, bad years.

I told most of that to Dez, sitting in the overgrown bean field, with the wind blowing ripples in the grass, and the mild afternoon sun shining down. I told him it made me feel sick to be there, and so we left—and though he wanted to talk about it, I could see that he wanted to help, I came straight back here and took a long shower instead. I didn't tell him that I felt sick because I suddenly wanted—I want—to go home, I want to see the people I grew up with. The people I spent the war depending on, and caring about. And I didn't, couldn't *tell him that I felt horrible about what we were doing. Like I said, I can see that he's right, mentally, logically, I know that there's nothing wrong with salvaging—but facts aside, that's not how I feel, not right now. Even if we're only taking from the Dominion, even if the people were only relocated, not slaughtered like the innocents of New Bajor, we're still making money from the aftermath of pain. He doesn't care, he just doesn't understand.*

I'll feel better tomorrow, I'm sure I'll be able to put things back into perspective; but right now I just want to go home, I want to be with people I know, who know what's right. Who know me.

Dez sat and waited for everyone to arrive in the conference room, occasionally shooting warning looks at Feg and Triv, who were grinning much too widely. Neither of them had *chula* eyes, as Facity liked to say, a Wadi game that sometimes required keeping one's luck from showing in one's expression. When Jake walked in, both of the Ferengi brothers were practically jumping out of their seats, making Dez wish he hadn't called for a full assembly. Still, the secret had to hold for only another few minutes.

As soon as Feg had let him know, Dez had called the gathering himself, then asked Srral to watch the bridge. He didn't even tell Facity what the sudden meeting was about when they met in the hall outside, vaguely suggesting that he had more information about their next job, the treasure hunt on Hw17. It was childish, he supposed, but he wanted everyone to be as happily surprised as he had been by Feg's report.

The crew straggled in, singly and in pairs, taking their traditionally assigned places. Jake and Coamis came in together, talking about the web-room program they'd just left, some dig or another. In the almost six weeks since Drang, the young men had spent a number of hours in the web rooms. Coamis had been informally teaching Jake about some of the more famous archeological expeditions in the Gamma Quadrant, and how to recognize the style of artifact from each . . . and Jake had been teaching Coamis and some of the other interested crew members how to play *baseball,* a game from Jake's planet. Dez didn't care much for it himself, too active, but he liked watching . . . and liked that Jake was feeling so at ease with the crew, and they with him. Coamis was even reconsidering his decision to leave when they reached Ee, having started to fit in better. Dez knew it was in no small part due to Jake's influence; Coamis might not stay on, but Jake belonged on the *Even.*

If he'd just stop talking about going home. . . . He did a lot of that, wondering aloud what his father's wife, Kasidy, would say about something, or his friend Nog, or the serial being, Dax. Well. There was still plenty of time for Jake to change his own mind, too, and today's meeting would help forward the notion—if not in Jake's mind, then certainly in the minds of the crew, whose influence would surely help. After Jake's unhappy, homesick reaction a week ago to the planet where those colonists had died, Dez wanted him to know that he had friends here, too, good friends. Jake had withdrawn a bit since then, hadn't seemed quite as talkative . . . but Dez was sure it was temporary.

Although she was last, as expected, Prees didn't keep them waiting for too long. She and Pri'ak had finished inventorying the latest equipment salvage the night before, from a damaged freighter they'd come across two days back, abandoned by the Dominion.

Not that we need *to be picking up scraps for a while,* Dez thought, standing up as Prees took her chair. They would anyway, of course; the *Even*'s crew had happened across too many profitable extras that way to just give it up, particularly in the weeks since the end of the conflict—cases of contraband supplies and weapons, forgotten or misplaced, equipment upgrade possibles . . . scavenging parts wasn't glamorous, but it was a mainstay of the retrieval business.

Dez smiled at his crew, wanting to tell them immediately, also wanting to draw it out. He opted for something in between.

"As you know, we don't have anything big scheduled before we reach Ee," Dez said. "We still have two Dominion posts to look at, down from five—Thijmen's team got to the others, it seems—and there's the hunt for the jettisoned cargo on Hw17, in a few weeks . . . and if we're lucky, we'll get the contracts that we're currently bidding on." The Ahswidus cup had gone to another rival team, but one of Off-Zel's vases was being sought by a private collector named Toff, and the Rodulans were trying to get back several of their early basotiles. Both were offering good money to the crew who could come through for them.

Dez smiled directly at Jake, sitting next to Coamis. "But even if those fall through, even if we don't make another half paeg, dirak, or sto in the coming months, I know we'll have a fine time hunting . . . and I'm certain it will help ease our minds, having the two thousand, seven hundred and fifty paegs that our new friend Jake Sisko has brought in for us."

Shocked expressions . . . and dawning grins, all around the table.

"The offer on the box came in today, from a collector who will be meeting us on Ee," Dez said, and nodded at Feg. "I'm sure our accountants will be happy to provide the details, upon request. And since I have no other ship's business that even comes close to being as important . . . meeting adjourned."

Immediately, the entire room was up and moving, questions being fired at Feg and Triv, Jake being heartily congratulated . . . and while he seemed to be enjoying the warm attention, he didn't seem as happy as Dez had expected. Something was missing from Jake's smile, which was broad but not beaming. Dez had hoped that making such a strong financial contribution to the ship—making his new friends so happy—might make him feel better about missing the old ones.

Maybe it wasn't homesickness that had been troubling him. Dez felt a flash of frustration, watching Jake's not-wide-enough smile as Triv chatted away at him. What was it? He'd worked so hard to make Jake comfortable on the *Even,* and for the most part, Jake seemed content. A few times in the past two months, he'd noticed some discomfort here and there . . . maybe . . . Dez frowned, thinking. Remembering the Yaron.

Glessin and Aslylgof both departed soon after, but everyone else stayed around for the next little while, talking about the offer, speculating on what they might use their share for, recounting their own experiences on Drang. Dez kept an eye on Jake, paying close attention to the young man's reactions to what was being said . . . and as the spontaneous party started to break up, Dez decided that his developing theory on Jake's discontent was correct.

I think I know how to fix it, too. He should have seen it coming. As he'd told Jake early on, people primarily got into the retrieval business for two reasons, money and excitement. He'd known all along that Jake didn't care about the money, and had assumed that the excitement would be enough to sustain his interest. It hadn't occurred to Dez that the financial aspect might actually be offensive to Jake in some way, but the more he thought about it, the more it made sense. It was a little disheartening, that Jake hadn't felt free to express his disdain . . .

. . . but he didn't want to hurt my feelings, either.

"Jake, may I have a moment?"

Jake nodded, then turned back to the wrap-up of a conversation with Stess, who was just leaving. Dez had noted before how well Stessie and Jake got along, and now it was further evidence to back up his theory. With the exception of Srral, Stessie was probably the least materialistic member of the crew.

Stess left, and Jake wandered back in Dez's direction, smiling . . . but a reserved smile, not as entirely open as it had been even a week before. Now that Dez was looking for it, he could see that Jake's attitude *had* changed, had become just a little bit cautious. It hurt to see . . . and it was exasperating, too, but he was already committed to making it better. Besides, it wasn't Jake's fault that he'd been raised with the high "virtue" of contempt for earning a paeg.

Brad and Pri'ak were still in the room, but deeply immersed in conversation. Dez walked Jake to one corner of the room, deciding to play it mostly straight.

"I've been thinking, about those last Dominion outposts," Dez said, and immediately saw his suspicion confirmed in Jake's honest gaze. He quickly went on, using his frustration with Jake's implanted morality to ease the small deception.

"Maybe we should just skip over them entirely," he said. "The other day, what you told me about New Bajor . . . it puts a different spin on things, sometimes, to see them through someone else's perspective." That was certainly true.

Jake was surprised . . . and hopeful, but trying not to show it. It made Dez's heart feel warm, seeing Jake work not to offend him.

"Oh, I don't know . . . I mean, you do work as a salvage ship sometimes," Jake said. "There's nothing wrong with taking stuff no one else wants. . . ."

Dez nodded, stepping carefully now. He didn't want to lie; he wasn't a liar. "That's true—but we don't need it, we're not exactly destitute right now, thanks to you. And when you told me about what happened back on that planet . . ." He smiled, shrugging, putting a hand on Jake's shoulder. ". . . suddenly, digging around in the ashes for a few paegs just doesn't seem all that great."

It was the right move. He could actually see Jake relax, see his smile become wide and genuine again. He hadn't even realized how much the last few days had altered Jake until now, seeing the open good humor return to his young face.

They made plans to have dinner together, and then Jake was off, his head high, proud once again to be on the *Even Odds.* Dez felt a slight twinge of conscience, but it was a mild one. He hadn't lied about anything. With as much money as the Giani'aga box was going to bring in, they didn't need the salvage . . . and if Jake believed that they were going to disregard the last outposts because Dez felt bad about the war, what was wrong with that, what was wrong with Jake thinking that he was a good man? He *was* a good man, and Jake needed to feel like they were doing "ethical" work to be comfortable, and Dez had no problem with that.

As long as I don't make a habit of it. He wouldn't have to. Jake would loosen up after a while, once he realized that he wasn't going to be judged for daring to relax. *I'm not his father, after all.*

From the stories Jake told, Benjamin Sisko had been a brave and thoughtful man . . . but also a smugly judgmental one, always defining right and wrong for the boy, narrowing his perspective, making Jake into his own image. It hadn't been fair . . . but Jake wasn't a child anymore, and could draw his own conclusions. It would just take a little time.

Dez smiled to himself, thinking of how happy the rest of the crew was going to be, dropping the last two salvages. Thinking of how good it felt, to be showing Jake something of life—and to be making a safe home for him, too, a place he could belong.

Day 71, night. The Giani'aga box sold today, for 7500 Klon paegs (I'll do the latinum exchange math later, thank you), though that's not why I'm writing. Just had dinner with Dez, and got back here, and read my last couple of entries—and I felt a need to put something after them, to soften them somehow, particularly after the talk we just had. Dez continues to surprise me, and I keep surprising myself, too . . . but I think I'm finally starting to understand both of us a little better.

For weeks now, I've been building up to a self-righteous snit over certain financial aspects of the retrieval business, and I can see now that I've been way too quick to jump to conclusions, to make assumptions about how important the money is. Today, after the announcement about the box being sold, Dez pulled me aside and told me that he didn't feel right about profiting off the war anymore. He wants to skip the last couple of Dominion sites(!), because of last week—it was like he suddenly realized how terrible it was, to understand we were at the site of a slaughter, looking for leftovers. I knew he was a strong, solid person, and all this time, I've been struggling to come around to his point of view, but I've felt so awkward about it . . . and it turns out, he's been feeling awkward with his *viewpoint. I know it's stupid, I mean, there are a lot of people in the universe who don't feel the way I do about money, who actually care deeply about it (all of Ferenginar, for example), but I feel so much better, anyway, to hear him say it's not so all-important. He really only sees it as a means to an end—he didn't say it outright, I think he's even a little shy about it (it's so unfortune-hunter-like), but over dinner he implied that as the business continues to grow financially, someday he'll be able to help people like the Yaron for free.*

We could have talked about this weeks ago, if I'd actually made the effort to look past his wishful reasoning. Over dinner, he told me that he's just gotten so used to needing the salvage, struggling to keep the Even *running . . . but it's only because he loves the retrieval part so much. He loves the excitement, the thrill . . . all those clichés, about feeling truly alive . . . it's true, I know that now, looking back at Drang. My entire focus was on the situation we were in; I wasn't worrying about trivial matters, my mind wasn't wandering, I didn't care about anything beyond what was happening in the moment, in the second. Of course Dez loves it, and I'm embarrassed now, thinking of how sanctimonious I've been over him trying to support himself and the crew.*

The crew of the Even Odds, *my friends. Dez hasn't asked outright, but I know he wants me to stay, and part of me wants to. So much time has passed, it's weird . . . there was Drang, right after I got here, and all of a sudden, I've been on board for over two months. I've had some great times, too, it's going to be really sad when this is over; I feel as close to Pif or Stessie or Facity, as I do—no, scratch that, I feel closer to them that to most of the people back home. Not Nog or Kas, obviously, but thinking about going back to face the Bajoran masses . . . it's going to be rough. I've felt truly welcomed here, as* me, *Jake, and for once in my life, not because of my accidental relationship to Dad.*

In a few weeks, we'll have the hunt on Hw17 . . . and a few weeks after that, we'll be at Ee, and I'll be able to buy transport home. It turns out that passing on the last Dominion salvages doesn't save us any time, they were on the way to Hw17, but I suddenly don't mind, so much. Dez's been such a good friend to me. I only hope that in the weeks remaining, I can be as good a friend to him.

9

MUCH TO PIF'S annoyance, he was teamed with Aslylgof for the Hw17 job. Even Glessin would have been better than Aslylgof, because Glessin didn't talk as much—and when he *did* talk, it wasn't to demonstrate how much he knew—but Glessin wasn't even on the team, and Pif was stuck.

"The planet Hw17 is not inhabited, as such, though there is clear evidence that various spacefaring cultures have settled on the surface for short periods," Aslylgof said, settling his equipment belt over his wide hips. "No one is sure why it hasn't been permanently colonized, although it seems likely that the consistently cold temperatures, combined with the poor exposure to light, make it an agriculturally unproductive environment. . . ."

All I wanted to know is whether or not the locals are alien friendly, Pif thought, gritting his teeth at Aslylgof, hoping it looked like a smile. After a moment, he stopped hoping, and a moment after that, he stopped bothering to grit. Aslylgof just kept talking. While the team—Stessie, Pif, Itriuma, Brad, Aslylgof, Jake, and Dez—was assembling in the transporter room, gearing up, Pif had made the horrible mistake of asking a simple, casual question, and Aslylgof had taken it upon himself to answer.

Pif shot a helpless look at Dez, pulling on his boots, who shrugged, smiling.

". . . thick ice and snow, which will actually prove favorable to our hunt," Aslylgof continued, and held up his AD light. "Against the backdrop of frozen precipitation, the distinctive red color of the engaged alloy-density illuminator should stand out clearly. . . ."

Itriuma was standing nearby, adjusting her nose filter and yawning; it was early. Pif sidled close enough to her to whisper out of one side of his mouth.

"Why are we doing this again?" Pif asked. Oblivious, Aslylgof kept talking, explaining what Pif and everyone else in the room already knew.

"Ask *him,*" she whispered back, and quickly stepped away before she got caught in Aslylgof's line of sight.

He'd probably try to tell me, too. As if it hadn't been a near-constant topic of conversation on the *Even,* since Srral had first intercepted the report. A month ago, a rival retrieval team—the ship's name escaped Pif, something like *My'lta*—had jettisoned its extremely valuable cargo over Hw17 while being chased by authorities. The crew had been arrested—larceny, of course—and the cargo was still missing; said authorities, of a cold-blooded species called Horgin, had yet to mount their own retrieval expedition. It appeared that the *My'lta*'s cargo compartment had split open on the way down, and though the Horgin had found their own piece—the entirely uninteresting Horgin Thas—they'd decided to return home before searching the rough ice fields for the rest, needing to properly outfit themselves for the weather. In the "scrambled" report they'd sent home, they suggested that they'd taken measures to protect the site zone . . . as it turned out, a laughably ineffectual satellite forcefield that Facity had tapped out of commission with one shot.

Besides the Thas, which the crew had been arrested for stealing, the *Even*'s researchers had figured out that the *My'lta* had been carrying a number of exceptional pieces—art, jewels, weapons, a little of everything. It was a top haul, and because of Srral's exceptional ability with filtering reports, it seemed that only the *Even* knew about the jettison. Well, and the Horgin, who were still a week away from their return.

Pif had to admit, he'd been looking forward to this one in spite of the cold, and was glad to be included on the first search team. It was going to be a real treasure hunt, looking for containment boxes large and small in a jagged ice field. Facity would lead the second team down when Dez's group returned . . . assuming they didn't find everything on the first pass.

Pif felt a rush of excitement at the thought. He had double-sprayed his coat with thermal oil, and Aarruris had good eyesight; he was going to find twice as much as anyone else, *me and my "partner"; he may be dull, but with those unblinking eyes, he's going to do well. Assuming he can keep quiet long enough to see past his own breath.*

". . . but I disagree," Aslylgof said firmly. "Don't you?"

"Yes, of course," Pif said, not bothering to replay the conversation. Whatever it was, he didn't want to start an argument, certainly prolonging the conversation. Aslylgof had been making more of an effort lately, probably tired of not being asked to play Jake's *baseball,* but Pif was pretty sure everyone preferred Aslylgof the silent elitist. Still, he was trying, and no one had the heart to ignore him entirely.

"Everyone ready?" Dez called.

Pif looked around, saw nods and uncomfortable smiles from the decidedly overdressed group. Except for the equipment, he and Stessie had both gotten off with foot treads and oil; Friagloims did well in any temperature, and though Aarruris didn't like cold, they were naturally suited for it. The rest of the team wore bulky environment suits, gloves, and head covers. Excepting Stessie, they'd all be wearing nose filters, too. The air would be toxic if they had to breathe it for an extended period, something about the particulate count.

"Let's filter up and go," Dez said. "Remember to stay in sight of your partner at all times, and watch yourselves and each other for signs of overexposure. Don't forget, we've got days to look for everything, we don't have to get it all this minute."

Right. Everyone was grinning; Dez's responsible act didn't fool anyone, he wanted to grab it all up as much as anyone else. Only Jake seemed dutifully sincere, though that was one of the endearing things about the young human, how respectful he was of Dez as captain, how earnestly he took everything. It was no wonder Dez had such an obvious soft spot for the boy . . . but then, they all liked him. Feg and Triv had tried offering up a bet that Jake would leave within a day of the *Even*'s arrival at Ee, and while everyone was hoping that the Ferengi were wrong, no one had been interested in playing. No one wanted to contemplate losing Jake.

The team stepped up to the transporter pad, Aslylgof moving to stand next to Pif, smiling, apparently quite happy that Pif had agreed with whatever it was he'd agreed with. The weapons researcher immediately started telling Pif how it would be best for them to stay in sight of one another, and to watch each other for signs that they were getting too much exposure—as though Pif had somehow missed hearing Dez say it, only seconds before. Pif smiled back, sighing inwardly, reminding himself that it was going to be dark down below, the footing treacherous; perhaps, if he was lucky, Aslylgof would fall down and break his mouth.

They were on the *Even,* and then they were standing together in the near-dark, in a still, silent cold. It was the middle of the day on Hw17, as bright as it got, the light similar to that of late dusk on Bajor. It was freezing, but not intolerable. Jake remembered going ice fishing with his father once, a holodeck program . . . had it been on the *Saratoga?* He thought it was about the same temperature.

Brad and Dez immediately started setting up the portable lighting units that would mark the transporter site, while Jake and the others got a look at their hunting grounds, what little they could see of them. Between the darkness and the strangely thick air, everything seemed blurred and vague, like the setting of a dream.

Jake searched for an analogy and quickly found one—an ocean at twilight, storming, frozen into angular blocks. They had transported to the top of one of the frozen swells, could see the outlines of other swells all around them, dark valleys in between. As jagged and rough as the frozen terrain appeared, Jake knew they wouldn't stand a chance trying to struggle through—

—except we can always jump, if we have to.

He took an experimental step, lifting up on his toes, and smiled at the pleasantly buoyant sensation. As on Drang, the difference wasn't huge, but he could definitely feel the lower gravity. It was going to make climbing those broken chunks of ice about a thousand percent easier.

The other team members were also making tentative movements, orienting themselves, trying to balance. Stessie let out a burst of unrestrained giddiness, and everyone laughed, even Aslylgof. The shared sound of laughter seemed very small in the vast silence. Jake thought it was a lonely sound, but comforting, too.

"Let's take some readings," Dez said, still adjusting the guide lights. "See if we can get a direction or two. Aslylgof, Stessie?"

In the hope of narrowing the hunt's scope, Arislelemakin was wearing directional sensors, and Aslylgof carried a reader. The *Even*'s sensors had been woefully inadequate to the task, mainly because of the density of the atmosphere, but also because of the cargo itself. It was apparently common practice for GQ traders and retrieval teams to store their valuables in sensor-repellent containment boxes, made of a composite alloy that actually tuned itself to its surroundings, to some extent. Of course, if one knew what to look for, they could be spotted . . . but that was where Hw17's thick atmosphere came in. From the *Even,* Srral had been able to pick up two of the larger pieces of the actual cargo hold, but nothing smaller than two meters across.

Stess stayed where she was, near Jake, while the rest of her started walking, somehow managing to look graceful as she bent and wobbled out over the dark ice. Aslylgof tapped at the reader's controls, frowning, as Stessie got farther apart.

Jake felt another flush of happiness from Stessie, and smiled at Stess. "Having fun?"

"Yes," she said, projecting a sense of simple well-being. "I love experiencing new environments. More than anything else, I believe."

Jake nodded, watching as Lema—or Le, he still had trouble telling Lema and Le apart—disappeared into the frigid darkness directly in front of them. "I know what you mean. When I was younger, I didn't appreciate it quite as much, but—"

"Wait," Aslylgof interrupted, still frowning. "I think I'm getting—"

CHOOOMM!

The darkness strobed into brightness, the harsh landscape illuminated for an instant in an explosion of light and thunder, and of shock, mental, emotional, and physical. Jake cried out, his voice lost among the voices of the others as they all crumpled in pain, blinded, the blast still ringing across the freezing emptiness.

What remained of Arislelemakinstess understood almost immediately what had happened, or at least sooner than the other members of the team. Having stepped on the hidden explosive directly, Lema didn't feel anything, dying instantly . . . and Kin died only a few seconds after the explosion, her small form ripped apart by slivers of ice. The pain was mercifully brief.

Even as Arislestess collapsed, she did what she could

to clamp down on her feelings of shock and trauma, numbly realizing that she'd projected them outward when Lema had triggered the blast; she felt it reflected back at her now by the others on the team, curled into poses of agony, not yet understanding that they hadn't been wounded. Le and Aris had both fallen out among the boulders of ice, were immersed in shock, but at least there was no more physical pain.

Everything seemed distant, strange and limited. Arislestess vainly tried to see through the blind places, couldn't find part of herself, didn't understand why she tried; she knew that Kin and Lema were gone, knew it but tried again, and again.

Stop I have to stop. If she kept trying to extend through the missing parts, she would create a buildup of emotion that much faster, creating an overload.

Stess rotated her opticals, searching, saw Jake's face close to her own, his expression of pain fading, becoming a deep, fearful concern *(a bleeding man, his gaze patient for death).* Jake understood, she thought. Hadn't she explained her physiology to him, soon after Drang?

The others were moving now, asking, trying to understand as they came to their feet, and Jake was talking fast, and Pif and Brad and Itriuma had run off into the dark. Le and then Aris were lifted from the cold ground, were being carried back, and Dez was gently picking Stess up, cradling her, shouting for transport as soon as the others were found.

"There's only us," Stess said, feeling some of the fear slip through in spite of her efforts. How long would she have, before her consciousness turned inward? She'd heard of a quad once going for three days after losing half of himself, but that had broken every standard.

Hours, she could count on only hours of sanity, and each of those getting progressively worse. "Lema and Kin are gone."

"You're going to be okay," Dez said miserably, and Stess didn't answer, aware that he knew better. The Horgin had protected the area better than any of them had foreseen; she had been killed.

10

THE MISSION was an abort, not that anyone cared much. Throughout the long day, everyone came to say goodbye, to sit with her for a little while, to say or do whatever it was they hoped would make it easier . . . more for themselves than for Stessie, Glessin thought, though he supposed that couldn't be helped. There was nothing that anyone could do for Stessie beyond what little he'd already done, putting her on a self-administered sedation line, trying to make her last hours comfortable.

Glessin spent most of the day standing in the corner of his small sickbay with a reader in hand, watching the monitors from a distance and trying not to intrude on the private farewells. Aris, Le, and Stess lay huddled together on the same bed, seeming to shrivel smaller with each hour that passed. She was no longer projecting clearly, though Glessin could still feel her, to some degree; mostly, she just seemed tired. The atmosphere of sadness that hung over the rooms came from the stream of visitors coming and going, trying to prepare themselves for the loss.

Almost everyone had questions for him after they saw her, wanting to know if anything could be done, and so he'd had to explain, again and again, mostly information that he'd learned from Stessie herself—Friagloims were psychologically fragile creatures, complicated, each part dependent on the others to maintain a healthy mind system through feedback and expression . . . and losing any one part meant that the mental and emotional connectors could no longer operate properly; health could not be maintained. So, although Arislestess wasn't physically injured, she wasn't a whole being anymore, either, and what was left of her would inevitably cease to function, probably within a day. The part that Glessin didn't tell them was that Stessie would lose her capacity for reason, first, that her sanity was already rapidly waning . . . and that she'd made her wishes regarding her death clear shortly after being brought in.

It was early evening when Dez finally left her, for the last time. He'd come and gone throughout the day, sometimes to talk with Stess, more often to stand and watch while someone else sat with her, his fists clenched in frustration, his eyes wounded and angry. Glessin had watched each of the crew struggle with the experience, and though he hadn't deliberately listened in, he'd been unable to avoid noticing what went on . . . nor could he help his interest in their different expressions of grief. There was Dez's self-directed anger, Neane and then Pri'ak's quiet prayers to different deities, Feg and Triv's uncomfortable formality. Aslylgof and Coamis had also been uncomfortable, their visits brief and unhappy, while Jake and Facity had both been surprisingly calm, each obviously sad but nurturing, too, working to put Stessie at ease. Prees and Srral had come together—at the same time, at least—Srral reciting a surprisingly touching poem it had once come across, about the peace of silence. Fajgìn and Itriuma had sung, a wordless Wadi lullaby. Pif had talked incessantly, recounting adventures they'd shared, but had been sincere and honest in his simple emotional statements, telling her more than once that he would miss her very much, that he wished she wouldn't die—whereas Brad had wept silently, copiously, seemingly dumbstruck by her own pain. Through it all, Stessie had somehow managed to be as pleasant and accommodating as always, acknowledging the wishes and sorrows, doing what she could to make it easier for each visitor. By the time Dez finally left, Glessin was exhausted for her.

After giving her a few moments of quiet, he walked to the bed, noting that she'd been steadily upping her dosage of sedatives over the last hour. While a natural physical death was still many hours away, it wouldn't be long, he suspected, before she asked for his help. The hypo gun was already prepared.

"How are you?" he asked, looking down at her, not sure if he should sit.

"Tired," Stess answered, her voice soft. "How are you?"

Glessin hadn't expected the question. "Fine. I'm . . . I'm well, thank you."

"Not dying, anyway," Stess said, and though it was weak, he could feel a pulse of good humor coming from her. "I believe I'm about ready to stop now."

Glessin nodded, turning away. "I'll get the hypo."

"I . . . actually, I was hoping you might sit with me for a moment," Stess said. "Though I'm afraid my self-control is limited . . . I hope you'll excuse any emotional indiscretion on my part."

Glessin was startled. "No, of course. I mean, don't concern yourself."

He sat on the low bench next to her, not sure what to say, what to do. He'd spent the last nine hours watching over her, observing the others, feeling . . . feeling like a medic with a patient, he supposed, and now that she'd asked him for a personal moment, he wasn't sure how he felt about it. About her.

I'm . . . sorry, he thought, and reached out to adjust the sedation line, wishing he could *tell* her that he was sorry—that she was dying, that he couldn't help her more, that he would be the last person she spent time with. It was such a selfish thought, though, he refused to consider saying it aloud. She deserved some peace in her final moments.

Tentatively, he reached out and placed his right hand on the top of Stess's head, resting it there, knowing that the warmth should be soothing; he'd seen Facity doing it earlier. All three Friagloim parts shifted—taking comfort from the action, he hoped—and he tried to relax into it, wishing it felt less contrived. He'd always felt so awkward around Stessie, but he'd also always known it was his problem, not hers . . . and he realized, thinking about it now, that she had been perhaps one of the kindest people he'd ever met. She had always worked to make everyone else comfortable, restricting her own nature, keeping her pleasant, curious, friendly emotions to herself so that people like him could maintain their selfish feelings of loneliness. It was unfair, it was dismal and unfair.

I should be the one dying, Glessin thought, knowing it was a ridiculously self-indulgent notion, embarrassed that he should be thinking of himself now, knowing that he meant it . . . and he suddenly felt a gentle warmth surrounding him, felt a soft, bittersweet longing, felt compassion. The feelings were mild but powerful, and growing stronger.

"Stessie, I . . . you're projecting," he said, and meant to pull his hand away, felt the first tinges of panic as her warmth pulsed over him . . . and then the panic was being washed aside, her feelings overwhelming his. He knew he should struggle against them but found that he couldn't, felt the emotions fold over him like warm water. Like an embrace. He'd never felt anything like it.

"Forgive me," Stess said, her weak voice far away, "but I want you to know the truth, Allo Glessin. I've always tried to respect your distance, but I've never understood it. It was so long ago, the battle that you carry with you."

How did she know? His hand was still resting on her head, and he couldn't move it, wasn't sure if he was trying. Her empathy, her compassion, was endless, filling him up, the sheer magnitude of the feelings keeping him still—he couldn't feel his body, couldn't feel anything except what she felt. There was such sadness, for herself and for him, such warmth.

"Only you think these bad things about yourself," she said. "Only you keep yourself apart. You're a good person. I see, I've always seen. I'm glad you're here with me now."

He'd known she was capable of so much power, that she could knock down enemies with her thoughts, but why was she doing this to him? Did she know what she was doing, did she understand what was happening? Of course she did, he could feel that she did, but how could he possibly deserve such . . . such absolution?

Her feelings continued to pulse through him, and

tears welled up in his eyes, his throat aching . . . and he suddenly realized that she was *accepting* him. He couldn't run from it, couldn't avoid it by telling himself that she was wrong, that it wasn't true, because he could feel the truth of it. She had seen inside, and she knew the broken core of him, and she still accepted him. He felt entirely exposed, vulnerable to her . . . and safe, he knew he was safe because the knowledge wasn't hidden. There was nothing secret, there was nothing dangerous in her embrace . . . except that it was starting to fade.

It was all he could do to speak. "Don't . . . don't hurt yourself," he whispered.

"It's time now," she said, and he could feel her becoming weaker, could feel his own emotions coming back . . . not just the ones he allowed himself, but feelings that he barely recognized, it had been so long. Sorrow and love and regret and gratitude, the gratitude stronger than all the rest.

Glessin stood and went to get the hypo. When he returned, he could feel how ready she was, could feel her exhaustion and her desire for sleep.

"Good-bye," she said. "Be well."

"Thank you," he said, weeping openly as he administered the hypo, and he could feel that she was happy in her last moment of life, knowing that she had helped him.

A few seconds later, she was gone, and the tears went with her. Glessin was himself again, and alone, more confused and uncertain and hopeful than he had been in years.

Dez was on his fifth Saurian brandy when somebody signaled at his door. It was late; Facity, probably. He'd told her that he wanted to be alone, but that had been three brandies ago. He'd been alone long enough, he decided, he was sick and tired of loneliness.

"Come in."

It wasn't Fac, it was Jake, looking tentative as he stepped inside. Dez was just drunk enough to be glad to see him, in spite of what he knew Jake must be thinking.

That I should feel responsible, that it's my fault.

Maybe not, he shouldn't, couldn't assume that. The look on Jake's face suggested only that he was unhappy. No surprise there; since Glessin's brief announcement shortly before dinner, the *Even* had been a very unhappy place.

"Jake! Come in, sit . . . have a drink," Dez said, gesturing at the open bottle on the table. He'd never seen Jake imbibe but offered anyway, hoping for company. "It's an Alpha import, Saurian. . . . There's another glass over on the shelf there."

"No, thanks," Jake said, walking to the chair opposite Dez's. He sat down, glancing around at the low-lit room, at the handsome pieces with which Dez had furnished his quarters—the antique Seerwagah clay furniture, the matching T'p urns, the Dosi birth-rite masks, the pre-Axwism Hissidolan pottery. Dez remembered that Jake had been by on only a few occasions, that they usually spent time together in the conference rooms or web rooms or dining hall.

We should spend more time here, Dez thought blearily, the thought immediately followed by a wave of sadness. Jake would be leaving before long. And why not? Why would he choose to stay on a ship where the captain couldn't keep his people safe?

It's not *my fault,* Dez told himself, not for the first time since the explosion. He wasn't any closer to accepting it. Stessie's death was a tragedy, and the blame had to rest somewhere.

"I just wanted . . . I thought I'd see how you were doing," Jake said.

Dez shrugged, took a swig from his glass. "Fine. I'm mostly drunk, I think. Can't get any better than that, considering."

Jake's forlorn expression invited something more substantial. Dez set his glass down and leaned back into the soft chair, studying Jake.

"I'm holding up," he said, and sighed. "How are you?"

Jake hesitated. "Worried," he said, after a beat. "When I saw you earlier in sickbay . . . Are you . . . Do you think this is your fault?"

Dez stared, not sure what to say. Even Facity hadn't been so direct. Jake fumbled on.

"Because it's not," he said. "There's no way you could have known. Everyone feels terrible about what happened, she was . . . I didn't know her as well as you did, but she was really special, I know that. It was a horrible accident, but it didn't happen because of you."

Dez reached for his glass, downed what was left in one choked swallow. What Jake was saying . . . he wanted it to be true, had been telling himself all night that it was, but he couldn't let himself off the hook as easily as that.

"I could have sent the dropship in for a closer look—" Dez began.

"—which wouldn't have made a difference," Jake interrupted, "and you know it, the mines were barely detectable from a meter away."

Jake leaned toward him, his expression compassionate, understanding.

"You told me yourself, the day I came aboard, that

your business is about trouble," he said softly. "Stessie knew that. When I talked to her earlier, she told me she didn't regret a thing, that she loved her time here. She didn't hold you accountable for her death, you know that."

"I'm the captain," Dez said firmly, shaking his head, still resisting. "I'm . . . I'm not going to turn away from my responsibility."

Jake nodded. "I know. Believe me, I know how important that is, I grew up knowing how important it is . . . but there are some things you can control, and some you can't. And if you hang on to feeling bad about the things you can't control, you're going to go crazy. You'll drive everyone else crazy, too."

From the look on his face, Dez suspected that Jake also knew something about that—watching his father agonize over some decision gone wrong, undoubtedly, Sisko perhaps even taking his frustration and anger out on the young Jake . . .

. . . not me. That'll never be me.

Dez opened his mouth to say as much, to tell Jake that he was right, to send him along his way—Jake's simple advice had been given, he should be able to feel good about it and go commiserate with the rest of the crew—and what came out surprised him, as completely as if he'd suddenly leapt up and started to sing.

"My father was a ship's captain," Dez said. He stared into his empty glass for a moment, then looked up, feeling strangely uncertain. Jake's expression was receptive and kind. Had he expected anything else?

"He ran freight, but he did some retrieval work, too," Dez said. "I know he did well for himself . . . but he turned away from his responsibilities, at least the ones that wouldn't pay off. His wife, and me. Left us on a mixed agricolony planet with nothing, when I was very small.

"My mother wasn't all that interested in child-rearing, either, but she stayed, at least," Dez said, remembering. "She used to tell me . . ."

. . . you're just like him, you don't care about anyone but yourself—

Dez shook it off, grasping for the thread of his original thought, the brandy hiding it, confusing him . . . and again he saw Jake's generous expression, and knew, suddenly knew why he'd brought his father up. It was his own subconscious mind, telling him that the time was right, to press Jake into making a decision.

Dez hadn't yet asked him to stay, well aware that Jake had always meant to return home once they reached Ee—but he'd also known for some weeks that he wasn't going to let Jake walk away without a fight. His own history didn't matter, it wasn't even interesting, let alone important; what was important was the look on Jake's face. Jake cared about him, he was a bright, good kid and Dez wasn't going to just let him go.

His father didn't deserve him, probably took him for granted all those years . . . and left him behind, off to visit his exalted gods, never caring that his son wanted or needed him, still *wants and needs him. . . .*

I *care. He belongs with me.* He had to make Jake understand, that was all . . . and didn't he know Jake well enough by now, to see how it could be done? He suddenly felt near soberness, ideas and angles unfolding, his instincts taking over.

"I was your age when I went looking for him," Dez said, letting his need form his words, letting it sculpt the truth. "I knew he was doing a regular run between a couple of industry worlds, and I worked my way across fifty light-years to see him . . . to show him, I think, that I was a man. That I was ready to be a part of his life, not as a son, but as his equal."

Jake was nodding slowly.

"I just wanted him to know that," Dez said, and he wasn't lying, wasn't, he was just elaborating on feelings he'd once had, finding in them what he knew Jake would respond to. "I wanted him to know that I was okay, that I was ready for this . . . this new phase of my life.

"It took nearly a year to get to him, working on freighters, hopping between ships, running salvage . . ." Dez smiled. "Amazing times. I learned a lot about myself, and I met a lot of interesting people. I didn't know, then, how that year would stay with me as one of the best times of my life. Back then, I didn't know that life was something that just happened, even when you were waiting for it to get started. I had this plan, you see—I believed I'd be happy when I finally got to see him, once this great wish of mine could be realized . . . that he'd look at me and be sorry that he went away."

Jake's gaze had gone distant, but he was paying close attention, Dez could tell by the swiftness of his nod, the eagerness of his acknowledgment.

"And one day, there it was," Dez said. "The moment I'd been working toward, that I'd wanted more than anything. The ship I was on docked at the same port as my father's ship, he was supposed to be meeting some client there . . . and I beamed down and I saw him, standing on this shuttlepad, tossing orders at his crew. . . ."

Dez smiled a little, remembering how hopeful he'd been, how he'd felt like he was going to explode, he'd been so excited—how he felt like his entire life had just been a prelude to that moment, the day he faced his father as a man. He'd known, absolutely, that everything was going to change because of it. Had he ever been so young, to believe that life actually worked that way?

"What happened?" Jake asked.

What happened is, he didn't remember me, Dez thought, studying Jake's honest, intent face. *And when he finally realized who I was, he clapped me on the back and insisted on buying me a drink. We got drunk together, my father and I, and at the end of the night, he wished me luck and said he hoped I'd find my way home all right . . . and when I told him I wanted to stay with him, perhaps take a job on his freighter, he made it painfully clear that he wasn't interested in being a father or even a friend to me. He felt guilty about leaving me, I could see that, but not guilty enough to try and make up for it . . . or maybe so guilty that he didn't want to try, didn't want to be reminded of his failure every time he looked at me. . . .*

That had been the last time Dez had seen his father. Two years later, when Dez had been smuggling contraband into a civil war zone outside the Xlidu Expanse, he'd heard that the elder Zin had been killed over a gambling debt. Some creditor had shot and killed him, and that was that. Dez's days of crying had been long over by then, though he remembered being annoyed that his father had died in debt, leaving nothing behind for his family to claim.

Dez paused for only a second, in that second remembering what had actually happened, the intense pain of that one drunken night, the months and years afterward learning how to bury that pain . . . and he also decided how it would play best for Jake.

"He was glad to see me," Dez said, determined to hang on to the truth as much as possible. "And he was sorry that he hadn't been much of a father to me . . . but he also made it clear that I was a grown man, who needed to stake out my own life. That I was too old to be following him around, trying to get him to figure out what I was supposed to do with my time."

Jake seemed uncertain. "But . . . but he was glad to see you. . . ."

"Yes, I think so," Dez said. "He was proud of me, too, that I'd grown up, that I was making my own decisions. . . . I think it pleased him to know that I had taken the initiative, to head out into the universe on my own. . . ." He smiled at Jake. "Isn't that what every parent wants for his children? To know that they're no longer dependent, that they can make their own decisions?"

Jake nodded, his gaze thoughtful. "Yeah, I guess so. That, and to know that they're happy."

Dez nodded. "Exactly. Wouldn't your own father . . . wouldn't he feel good knowing that you're with friends, having adventures and . . ."

. . . and almost dying?

Dez looked away, hit by a sudden wave of guilt. Stessie, poor Stessie. How good would Sisko feel knowing that Jake could have been killed, too? To dust with that, how did *Dez* feel?

And how do you feel about yourself now, a part of him murmured, *manipulating Jake like this, using the emotional chaos that Stessie's death has brought up?*

Dez ignored the thought, remembering that Stessie hadn't wanted Jake to leave, either. And had he ever lied to Jake? No, never. He only wanted what was best for him. Jake was bright but also woefully naive in so many ways, he needed to be around people who cared about him, who wouldn't desert him now that he was on his own, now that he needed real friends more than ever—

"Hey," Jake said gently, reaching out to touch Dez's arm. "I meant what I said before. You have to know, it wasn't your fault."

Dez blinked, realized that Jake had misread his guilt . . . and that it gave him an edge. Jake was so compassionate, he so wanted to make things better . . .

. . . so used the truth. It's the most powerful tool there is. A Wadi saying, one of Facity's favorites, and it would be the perfect final push. Jake had cared enough to come to him, to give him comforting advice over Stessie, and Dez had talked about his father, establishing even more common ground between them; a last tap, that was all it would take.

He smiled bleakly at Jake. "I'm going to miss her," he said.

Jake nodded. "Me, too."

"She didn't deserve to die like that," Dez said, and felt the liquid sting in his eyes, the truth working on him as well . . . and wasn't that why it was so effective? "Maybe there wasn't anything else I could have done, but . . . but it's hard not to think that. I . . . we all cared about her."

He looked at Jake, saw that the sensitive young man was also on the verge of tears . . . and let his own brim up, not fighting them, glad for the brandy that made them so accessible.

"I want you to stay with us, Jake," he said, absolutely sincere. "After Ee, we can take you back to your station, you can put things in order . . . and then you can come back here, with us. Not forever, but for a while. . . . We need you here, Jake. You're one of us, now, you belong with us."

Jake was blinking back tears, and Dez let his own spill over, reminding himself that Stessie was dead, it was terrible, a reason to cry, truly . . . and some good could come of it if he could convince Jake to stay.

"*I* need you," he said, looking into Jake's eyes, the words that Jake surely had wanted to hear from his father, that Dez had wanted so badly to hear from his own.

He immediately dropped his gaze, easing back. "Think about it, at least," he said, and sighed. "Now's probably not the best time to make a decision . . . but at least think about it, all right?"

He looked up, and saw exactly what he wanted to see—a struggle in Jake's wet gaze, over a choice that was no longer simple. He'd played it well, and it was going to pay off. If not tonight, then soon.

"I . . . I'll think about it," Jake said, standing.

Dez nodded, staying seated as Jake walked to the door, keeping his shoulders slumped in spite of the triumph he felt.

"Good night, Dez," Jake said, pausing for a second in the entry, and Dez nodded, offered another wan, grateful smile . . . which widened as soon as Jake was gone.

He's going to stay.

Dez poured himself another drink, silently toasting Stessie with it, feeling the sorrow come creeping back as he drank to his dead comrade . . . but it was easier to bear now, knowing that Jake wasn't lost to him, that his young ward was more likely than ever to become a permanent crew member.

"Thank you, Stessie," he said, raising his glass again, wishing her well in whatever afterlife she'd gone to, hoping she understood how much she'd be missed . . . and how something good had come from her death, after all.

Day 109, afternoon. We'll be at Ee in a week, and I've made my decision. It wasn't as hard as I thought it would be, though I've certainly taken my time with it. . . . It's strange, how it seems inevitable, now that I've actually decided to stay. In the three weeks since Stessie died, everyone has treated me like I'm one of the crew. After all we've been through together, from Drang to Hw17 . . . I feel at home here, now.

I told Dez this morning, and he's going to make an announcement tonight, I guess, though I think everyone already knows. Dez's elated. He's been trying so hard not to push, too, though I've felt a little manipulated at times . . . but it's only because he really wants me to stay. For all his dropped hints and semi-subtle plays, I saw his true face the night that Stessie died, I think, and it cleared up a lot—for one thing, why he's been so friendly to me, from the very beginning. His big life adventure started when he went looking for his father, too . . . and I think maybe he wants to do for me what his father didn't do for him. He's such a good guy, he comes off as self-centered sometimes, but he really cares about people.

Anyway, I think my staying on is the right thing, and it doesn't have to be forever, just for a while. I know Kas will understand, and even Nog, once he gets used to the idea. I belong here now, until Dad comes home . . . and even then I'll only be able to take a little time off to see him get settled, particularly considering that the Even *will be doing a lot more "charity" work from now on*

(Dez says I shouldn't talk about it too much, he wants to ease the crew into the program; I think he's worried that Feg and Triv will quit!). I may not be able to get away for long, but I know Dad will feel good about me helping people; he'll see that I'm making mature decisions, that I'm an adult, not just his son. Is it wrong of me, to want that? I hope not. I'm staying because I want to, not because of how my father might perceive it. He's living his own life, and so should I.

Everyone misses Stessie . . . I miss her a lot. It's been good to talk about it, to Pif and Fac, to Dez and Brad and everyone else . . . strangely enough, even Glessin has been making some effort to bring it up. He sat with me at lunch a couple of days ago, obviously uncomfortable, but apparently determined to say what was on his mind, even if it did take the better part of an hour for him to get it out—that Stessie had died bravely and well. It seems he's worked himself up to similar conversations with almost everyone on board. No one is sure why, or at least no one I've talked to about it, but I guess this is a first for him, trying to engage in conversation about anything, let alone something emotional. Good for him, I say. Pif is doubtful, but I think Pif has problems trusting non-mammalians (I'm fairly sure that Stessie was an exception).

It's so different from back on the station, losing someone close. Like after Jadzia died, Dad and I left for Earth, so I didn't get much of a chance to talk about her, and then Ezri was there. . . . I don't know, the circumstances were different, but I don't remember anyone asking me how I *felt about losing Jadzia. And it didn't even bother me. I think I was just so used to being Ben Sisko's son, to the people on DS9 . . . like an accessory or something. Dad was always the important one, he was the focus, if that makes any sense. It always meant so much to me that I was* his *focus. . . . Anyway, it's not like that here. I feel like I'm on equal footing, like these are* my *people.*

I guess now I have to decide what I want to specialize in. Dez is still pushing geology, just because I mentioned that that's what I liked about B'hala. Coamis has taught me a lot about GQ archeology, which is *interesting (except he's staying on, which kind of negates the need for that position) . . . and just about everyone else has offered to train me in their respective fields. Aslylgof makes a point of bringing up weapons every time he sees me (decent guy, but he and Morn should get together sometime, have a talk-off . . . I think I'd actually have to bet against Morn). Neane has shown me a few basic research skills . . . and Brad keeps telling me I'd look "lovely" in gems. She's been flirting with me, I think, though I kind of let it get around that I have a girlfriend, which is not exactly the truth. I haven't been serious about anyone since Mardah, but I don't want to hurt her feelings. She* is *nice . . . but appearance to the contrary, Brad's just too "girly" for me.*

I don't know what I want to do. I always assumed I would be writing by now, because that's what I know, it's what I've always wanted . . . but the Even *doesn't need a writer. Put that way, I guess no one really* needs *a writer . . . in any case, I don't have to decide right now. After Ee, maybe. From the stories I'm hearing, maybe I'll see something there that will inspire me. The way everyone talks about it, it sounds like this giant, planet-wide market, where you can buy anything that's ever existed, and meet every species in the universe. I'm sure they're exaggerating (especially Pif), but it really does seem like a big deal. I guess the Alpha-Gamma conflict put a damper on trade, but Dez says Ee's economy should be going full force by the time we get there. The* Even *hasn't been in about two years, so everyone's looking forward to it.*

Anyway, I should go. Facity wants to brush up on dom-jot before Ee, and I told her I'd be free this afternoon . . . plus Pif and Pri'ak were talking over breakfast about getting a ball game together later, and Neane was going to set aside some files for me to read, about the Rodulan basotiles. . . .

It's a busy existence, fortune hunting, but a good one. I'm not waiting for my life to get started, anymore, and I'm not observing it as it happens; I'm just going to enjoy what comes, and trust in my friends, and in myself.

11

"VESSEL *Even Odds,* noncom slash trade, number 2454al116-Ka, confirming orbit at coordinates provided," Fac said, hurriedly punching the accompanying codes through the board. The first landing party was waiting in the transporter room, as eager as she was to get to the surface. "Local time at . . . eighteen hours four."

"*Received,* Even Odds," a female's voice responded a few seconds later, sounding decidedly harried. It was no wonder, considering; there were over a dozen starships sitting just outside the main port, twice as many personal vessels. "*Welcome to Ee.*"

Facity nodded to Neane, reminded Srral to keep their transponders locked in, and was on the lift to the transporter room within seconds of the perfunctory welcome, adjusting her tri-band suit and imagining a hand-cooked meal.

Wadi food, too, a nice curis rib, basted espods, a glass of real wints . . . Last time they'd been to Ee, there'd been two sit-down restaurants featuring Wadi cuisine, among others. Maybe this time around, there would be a Wadi-only, she thought, stepping off the lift. She didn't see why not, the Wadi were surely responsible for half of Ee's casino business. . . .

. . . *May be a solid market there. If there's not one already, I should ask the brothers to look into financing one of the stalls.* It'd be a good long-term investment, to back a business on Ee. Retrieval was so hit-and-miss, it was difficult to look at long-term, but the *Even* had been doing well for some time. Besides, going into business was serious gambling.

She walked into the transporter room, smiling broadly at the looks she received from her crewmates, all waiting on or near the pad. Aslylgof, Brad, Pif, Pri'ak, Jake, Coamis, the Ferengi brothers, Fajgin and Itriuma—and Dez, especially Dez—wore varying expressions of surprise, ranging from mild to openmouthed. It was a new outfit.

"Let's hope it's not cold this evening," Dez said, cocking an eyebrow.

"We're coming back after dinner, Captain," Facity said, stepping up to the pad. "Or did you forget?"

Dez sighed heavily, shaking his head. They'd agreed to head back to the *Even* early, to let the rest of the crew enjoy the first night's leave to the fullest. Everyone had plans. Glessin, Neane, and Aslylgof all wanted to go to the library banks. Feg and Triv had been salivating for weeks over meeting with the big traders—including the Giani'aga box buyer, whom they were scheduled to meet with the following day—to talk about auctioning some of the doubles from the living artifact collection. Prees and Srral were planning to hit the equipment dealers, do some console-diving, Fajgin and Itriuma wanted to head to the *chula* hall, Brad wanted to shop . . . and, Facity suspected, meet up with a subspace date she'd been "secretly" corresponding with for months. She knew that Pif and Pri'ak had been dying to take Jake and Coamis on their first tavern hop. She also knew that Dez wanted to go with them, he was so excited about Jake staying . . . but somebody had to watch the ship, and she wasn't going to do it by herself.

Besides, it'll be romantic. She caught his eye, grinning, as Prees worked the transporter controls. When they returned, they'd send Neane, Srral, Prees, and Glessin down to the surface, leaving just the two of them on board. Dez grinned back—

—and then they were standing at the outer gate of the open-air market, breathing in the exotic smells of cuisine from a dozen worlds, bright colors and conversations and music all competing for attention. High above, the clear weather shield glimmered brightly between towers, defined by a grid of light lines that compensated for the fading day. From the lavender sparkling effect Facity could see in some of the unlit areas, the shield was also evaporating a light rain.

The outside market had something like four hundred vendors now, she had heard. The market, and the shallow, pleasantly scented chemical lake that bordered it to the south and west, formed the southernmost area of Ee's main port. The sprawl of outdoor food stands and small vendor shops behind the gate gave way to higher-quality restaurants and businesses to the north, municipal buildings—museums, the library, local government—to the northeast, and industrial fabricators and shipyards to the east. Throughout all of the roughly divided areas there were security checkpoints, taverns, and lodging houses, the quality of the latter two directly proportionate to the wealth of the businesses surrounding them.

It was as loud and enticing as always, Facity thought, smiling, looking over to see Jake's reaction, noting that the rest of the crew was doing the same. Jake seemed positively awestruck, his eyes wide and shining.

A detachment of smiling security people stepped forward, running handheld scanners over their team, reminding them of the rules, no weapons-fighting-theft-vandalism, no business conducted without proper licensing. Each of the crew received an official scan patch set for four days, dermed onto the back of either hand. Facity knew of a half-dozen places inside and out that sold "official" patches for the right price, but she had nothing against the government making a little money. Besides, they could afford to go it legitimate.

As the security folk hustled them off of the landing pad, Facity turned to catch Jake's reaction again, and saw him looking southeast, away from the gated city, a frown creasing his soft brown face as he studied the stretch of prefab huts and smudge fires that began several hundred meters away, that continued on for some indeterminate distance.

"Who are they?" he asked, watching the ragged figures that moved slowly through the unsheltered dusk.

"Beggars and parasites," Feg answered, scowling. "And obviously inadequate ones, at that. They're not even looking in our direction."

Facity smiled. "Maybe it's their day off, or—"

A sharp look from Dez, along with a glance at the still-frowning Jake, stopped her cold. Right, Jake. The kid had a soft spot for the poor, or people who were victims somehow. . . .

"—or maybe they're just waiting for work permits," she finished somewhat lamely. Jake didn't seem to notice, at least, and Dez visibly relaxed.

"Sure," Feg scoffed. "Permits to eat leftovers, so they don't have to work." A few of the others nodded. The rest looked impatient, obviously eager to go through the gates.

Dez glared at him. "That's not fair, Feg."

Feg frowned, looking confused. "I thought you were the one who always said that if they have enough energy to beg, they probably have enough—"

One of the security people, an Ee native from her coppery hair and black eyes, saved them.

"Don't concern yourself with those people," she said brightly. "They're just poor—new immigrants without resources, or the disabled, or the untrained. They're clean, though, and they won't bother you."

Jake didn't seem placated. "But . . . do they have food, access to medical supplies?"

The woman's well-trained PR smile didn't falter. "Of course."

"There, see?" Facity said quickly. "Everyone's fine."

She turned to Dez, her own smile overbright. "I'm starving. And I could definitely use a drink."

That got a response from the rest of the crew. They all started moving toward the main gates, carrying Jake along with them. Jake shot one last, troubled glance at the poverty-stricken community and then let himself be led away.

Facity and Dez brought up the rear, Facity slipping her arm around Dez's waist as they walked, noting his troubled expression as he watched Jake. She knew it bothered him, that Jake had such liberal notions about money . . . not because Dez didn't share those views, although he didn't, but because he'd led Jake to believe that they were of a like mind.

She suspected that Jake had agreed to stay on at least partly because of it, too . . . which was going to cause problems, sooner or later. She wasn't first officer on a community-services ship, she was a gambler, living to risk or ride from score to score. And the others in the crew, while not averse to the occasional good deed, weren't working to give things away, either. Jake was going to have to change his views . . . and she wasn't so sure that it was going to be as easy as Dez seemed to think.

Worries for another day; they'd reached the gate and the pleasures of Ee awaited. Facity put the unpleasant thoughts aside, adjusted one of the three narrow bands that made up her suit, and held out her hand to be scanned.

The team split up immediately, off to their own vices, Facity making Pif and Pri'ak promise to keep track of Jake and Coamis before jiggling off to her private dinner with Dez. Pif promptly lost track of the others in his group, wandering the open market for the next hour or three, enjoying himself immensely. He saw at least six species he'd never seen before, and ate a candied roast-bird dish that was delicious, served on a piece of metal foil with hot spiced vegetable paste, and bought a whistle that changed colors and a souvenir Ee shield tower made out of sugarfruit. There was a lot of gossip to be overheard, people talking about Sen Ennis, a local religion or something, about the alleged end to the Dominion expansion problem (was it true, that a Jem'Hadar ship had been seen only yesterday, just off the main port? Pif doubted it), about the Iconian gateways, that thing he'd been stupid enough to bet against Facity on. He ran into an Aarruri couple outside a leather shop, both from Ri, one of whose aunt's mates was from Ga (a Gabele, in fact), and they agreed to meet with him the next day for lunch, to fill him in on news from home. Pif had just started to wonder if he should be looking for Pri'ak and the two boys when he spotted them about to go into an alehouse, the first of the evening.

Pif trotted up to meet them, his vendor bag swinging from his neck. "Hey, one of you want to carry my stuff?"

Pri'ak looked irritated. "About time. We thought you'd been abducted, or something."

Pif shrugged. "You could have called."

"You know what the interference is like down here," Pri'ak said. "And I wasn't about to hit the emergency signal. Facity would kill us."

He was still frowning, but he took Pif's bag, tucking it into one pocket. "Anyway, we already ate, we were about to start without you."

Jake and Coamis both seemed unduly relieved to see him, which made Pif very happy. "How nice, that you were all so worried! The first round is on me. It's the least I can do."

The alehouse was small but clean, the servers polite, the prices fair, and Pif ended up buying the first two rounds . . . except that Jake barely touched his one drink, finally admitting that he'd never developed a taste for alcohol, synth or straight. Coamis, already flushed, immediately offered to finish his drink, while Pif exchanged a grin with Pri'ak. The Merdosian's clear teeth sparkled as brightly as his eyes.

"Think he'd like a spinewater?" Pri'ak asked.

"I think *I'd* like a spinewater," Pif said. "There's a place over by the shipyards that has over a hundred flavors."

"What's a spinewater?" Coamis said, setting Jake's empty glass back in front of him.

"Unscented liquor," Pri'ak answered. "Served in these tiny glasses, and you can get it flavored to taste like just about anything. It's not exactly a, ah, rough-customer drink, but it does the trick."

Jake looked hopeful as Pif paid the bill. "I'll buy the first round."

Once they'd resituated themselves at the Laughing This, apparently Ee's foremost spinewater establishment, Jake, in fact, bought the first three rounds. Over them, they toasted Stessie, and talked about Facity's wardrobe—respectfully, of course—and reminisced about childhood, and Drang, and first loves. The drinks were interesting, each of them daring to try flavors they'd never tasted, and the conversation was generally upbeat and pleasant, Pif saying a number of times how happy he was with the company, the others agreeing. Pri'ak bought the next round, another drink to Stessie, and Coamis bought two, toasting Jake's decision to stay on, as well as his own—and then it was Pif's turn again, but he suggested that they hop, tired of the way that all of the old women at the bar were staring at them. At least he thought they were old women, though he supposed it was possible that they were just very lined and unhappy. He said as much to the others, which for some reason induced Jake and Coamis to laugh so hard that they couldn't breathe for what seemed like a long time. That was when Pif realized that the two young men were already drunk . . . and he noticed, as they got up to leave, that his own legs were tending toward unsteady.

There was some disagreement once they left the This, over what sort of establishment they should take their business to next, but it was quickly resolved when Pri'ak mentioned that he liked nice women, and in fact knew of a place where some congregated. They all agreed that nice women were nice, and Coamis began singing a beautiful song about a girl with stars in her eyes, and they made their way to Pri'ak's spirits bar . . . where, sadly, there seemed to be very few women willing to look at them, let alone talk to them.

Pif didn't mind, by then, having decided that Jake, Coamis, and Pri'ak were the best friends an Aarruri ever had, even after Pri'ak ate his Ee tower souvenir. The night was young, and they were free men, they had money and song and another round on the way.

Jake was drunk, drunker than he ever had been in his life, and couldn't understand why he'd never done it before. Coamis couldn't, either. Jake had drunk wine before, of course, usually with dinner . . . and he told Coamis all about the incredible dinners his father had made, which impressed Coamis no end . . . and he'd had a few cocktails at Vic's, here and there . . . Jake had a lot to say about Vic's, like about the time Frankie Eyes tried to take it over, and how Vic Fontaine was a hologram but he was aware, too, and he also remembered the time he'd taken Kesha to Vic's when Nog had been staying there, and he and Nog had fought.

"I *love* Nog, though," Jake said, turning to Coamis once more, as he was closest. He was prepared to convince Coamis of the fact, if need be, but Coamis didn't seem to be entirely awake. His eyes were mostly open, but they kept flickering, like he was trying to watch a ball bouncing very quickly, somewhere past Jake's head. Watching his eyes flicker was making Jake feel a little queasy, actually.

"That, and the heat," Jake said. The bar they were in seemed very warm, and crowded, and loud. "Don't you think?"

Coamis nodded, and then put his head down, apparently needing to rest. A few seconds later, he started to drool.

"You're drunk," Jake said, grinning, but Coamis didn't respond. Mildly concerned, Jake decided he'd better inform the others, and leaned across the table toward them, but Pif and Pri'ak were talking with their heads together, oblivious. Jake couldn't tell what they were saying, but he heard the word "bet" and the word "sick," and decided he didn't want to know . . . mostly because the mere mention of the word *sick* had him thinking about the fried meat and salad he'd had some hours before, and how it was roiling around in his gut all sweaty and hot. . . .

Gah. He needed some water, or some fresh air or something. Jake looked around the bar, at the standing and sitting and leaning people of all shapes and colors, hoping that one of them would stand out as a drink server . . .

. . . and he saw a familiar face across the room. It took him a second to place it, but just seeing someone from home, from the station, made Jake forget all about his unhappy stomach. It was Chief O'Brien's friend, the one who had caused so much trouble all those years ago. . . .

Dad was so mad, what was his name, it can't be the same guy but the whole species goes by that name. . . .

"*Tosk*," he said, and at that, Pif and Pri'ak finally looked up, following Jake's gaze. The Tosk was by the door, his wide yellow eyes staring, scanning the crowd. The reptilian creature seemed tense, his movements quick and jerky.

"Where there's Tosk, there're Hunters," Pif said. "Last time we were here, a couple of 'em had just been detained for barging into someone's house, looking for Tosks, remember?"

"Those things are trouble," Pri'ak said, firmly but slowly. "I think they should be banned from public places, or someone's going to get seriously killed. Or injured."

Watching the Tosk, Jake numbly realized that the sentiment was a popular one. A number of people in the tavern were glaring at Tosk, the conversation level dropping a notch as the customers who knew about Tosk explained the species to those who didn't know. Jake remembered that Tosk's brief appearance at DS9 had set off yet another round of debate about the Prime Directive. The Tosk were hunted for sport, which was flat-out immoral as far as Jake was concerned, but the issue was complicated; they were an engineered species that wanted to be hunted, and were honored for it.

Not that he looks all that honored. . . .

The longer Jake watched, the more he became convinced that the Tosk was sick. He seemed deeply anxious, his eyes were glassy with fatigue, and his scales were cracked and faded. It didn't seem fair, the way everyone was staring, angry, talking about him as though he'd *asked* to be created for bloodsport, and not even noticing that he was ill. The bartender was speaking to the Tosk with a distinctly unfriendly air.

"I'm going to say hi," Jake said, determined, and pushed away from the table. It took a moment for gravity to work with him, but he managed. He'd forgotten he was so *tall.*

"How about you don't?" Pif asked.

Pri'ak was nodding, carefully enunciating his words. "Yes, I agree. You should leave him alone."

"No, I'm going," Jake said. "I need some air, anyway. I'll be careful."

Pri'ak said something else, but Jake was already walking, and that took most of his concentration. Unfortunately, Tosk was also walking, disappearing back through the tavern's door before Jake was halfway there, but Jake was resolute. He dodged a number of standing people, wheeling for balance as a drink server danced in front of him, and finally made it to and through the door, the cool night air so sweet and soft that he was glad for his persistence. His stomach seemed to settle almost immediately.

"Where'd you . . ." Jake mumbled, looking around, and thought he saw the Tosk stepping around the tavern's far corner, back into one of the still-busy Ee avenues.

Since his initial instinct had turned out so well, Jake decided to follow, at least for a little ways. Even if he couldn't find the Tosk, there was music in the air, and laughter, and interesting things to see.

That, and going back in there's going to make me throw up, Jake thought, and was already walking before he realized he'd made the decision.

Around the corner, and he was suddenly in the midst of a moving group of tall, strange-smelling furry people. He stepped aside, smiling apologetically as they sidled past, squinting ahead. Was that Tosk, already four shops away, ducking behind another building?

Jake hurried after him, nodding at a Merdosian family that was going in the opposite direction, *Pri'ak's peo-*

ple, good people, past a closed shoe store, an open kiosk that was handing out disgusting-looking, goopy black stew in disposable cups, a shop that was apparently selling antigrav halos. There were some small orange people walking past, and what looked like a monster Aarruri, only with six legs, and a smell like old fish—

—and then a hand slammed down on his shoulder and jerked him into a dark alley.

12

TOSK PULLED the male creature into the space between the buildings and pushed him against the wall, barely able to control his enthusiasm or his hope. He had followed Tosk from the tavern, it meant something, surely it meant something.

And there's a feeling . . . Yes, there was something about this one, he felt it, this one *knew* something.

"Will you tell me the new purpose?" Tosk asked eagerly.

The young male's eyes were wide and staring, his voice a stammer. "Wha—what?"

"The new purpose, Other than Hunt," Tosk said, gripping the male's shoulder tighter, too tight, he was wincing. Tosk let go with an effort, forcing himself to speak slower. "The new purpose. Do you know what it is?"

"I don't . . . I just wanted . . . no," the male said.

Tosk stared, searching his face for truth, and found it—in the bleary eyes, and the tavern smell. The young male was intoxicated, and entirely clueless as to why Tosk had suddenly grabbed him. He didn't know.

Tosk sagged, turning away, feeling the brief hope die. The young male stared, apparently not angry. That was too bad. Tosk wished that someone would kill him, but no longer believed he would be so fortunate . . . and he knew he would defend himself regardless of his wish, because there was the Hunt, and there was the Other. He was doomed.

"I apologize to you," he said. He was suddenly too tired to walk away, so he simply stood, waiting for the young male to do so. He was *tired;* Tosk needed only seventeen minutes of rest per rotation, and yet he was exhausted. Had he rested recently? He didn't remember. It didn't matter.

The young male didn't leave. It watched him a moment, finally speaking in a low, careful tone. "Are you sick?"

Tosk considered ignoring him, he'd ignored others who had asked . . . but remembered that he'd hurt the male, squeezing his shoulder hard enough to hurt him, and thought he might as well answer. For all that it mattered.

"I don't know."

The young male watched him another moment. "My name's Jake," he said. "Are you . . . are you being Hunted?"

Tosk looked at Jake, feeling a great distress at the question. Yes, he was being Hunted, and instead of fulfilling his duty and purpose, instead of proudly seeking his death with honor, he was wandering a populated world, asking strangers questions that they didn't understand. Questions that *he* didn't understand.

"Yes," he said.

Jake shook his head as though trying to clear it. "But . . . isn't that your only purpose, to be Hunted?"

"Yes," Tosk said again, and felt the great rift in his mind shift, felt it widen, felt the desperation hit him anew. "Yes, yes, but there is another! I don't know what it is, I have to find it, it's here, I believe it's here, but I don't know why and I can't find it!"

"Hey, calm down," Jake said, his voice soothing and low. "It's okay, you're okay, just, ah . . . just breathe, take a deep breath."

Tosk did as instructed, but nothing was resolved, he felt no calmer.

"If you don't know what this other purpose is . . ." Jake started, and then exhaled heavily. "Maybe you should start at the beginning. How . . . What made you decide that there was something besides the Hunt?"

Tosk stared at him, not sure whether or not he should answer. Tosk did not speak of the Hunt, that was the Hunter's privilege . . . except he'd already admitted that he was being Hunted, and Jake had not asked about the Hunt itself, Jake had asked him about the Other. In the four days since he'd come to Ee, since he'd just happened to "feel" that the purpose was here, of all places, no one had asked him to relate his story. He'd been ignored or shunned or asked to move on, and twice, beings had physically threatened him, but no one had asked him about the Other, or how he'd come to find a new purpose.

And there is nothing for me to lose.

It was the truth. Tosk looked into the young male's, Jake's, searching gaze and nodded once.

"I will tell you, Jake."

Jake smiled, and motioned toward a stack of crates

nearby. "Good. Though I've got to sit down, if you don't mind. I've had a bit to drink this evening."

Though Tosk didn't need to sit, he did the same as Jake, and because he was not sure where to begin, he began as Jake had asked.

"There was a crack in the humidity mesh over my ship's Arva nodes, and I had no choice but to set down . . ."

Jake slowly began to sober as the Tosk told his story, which was decidedly weird. It seemed he'd stopped on some random, uninhabited planet to fix his ship, and been zapped by a rock, and . . . as near as Jake could figure, he'd been implanted by a deeply felt need to find something, some specific but unnamed . . . thing. He'd spent the next fifteen weeks—which, Jake noted offhandedly, corresponded almost exactly to the time frame he'd been on board the *Even Odds*—just wandering, choosing his path seemingly at random. He'd been on Ee for the last few days, and seemed to feel that this unknown purpose was somewhere nearby, but he wasn't sure why he felt that way. He'd apparently worked his way across the entire main port, starting in the north, where he'd set his ship down, and was about to run out of places to look.

"What about the Hunt?" Jake asked, trying not to think about how desperately thirsty he was getting, or how his stomach had gone back to unsettled. They were sitting at the mouth of the alley, only a couple of meters from the passing parade of consumers, and a lot of them were carrying food—steaming cups and plates of alien cuisine, some of which smelled exceedingly toxic.

Tosk paused uncertainly, and Jake remembered that they weren't supposed to talk about it.

"I mean, don't say if you can't, but do you know if the Hunters are still after you?" He asked.

"They are," Tosk said.

"How do you know?"

Tosk seemed confused by the question. "Because . . . because I'm still alive."

Oh. "Well, have you thought about going home for help, or maybe asking the Hunters if they could . . ."

Tosk's shocked reaction made finishing the thought pointless.

"I am Tosk," he said, his eyes wide.

"Right," Jake said, suppressing a sigh. His head hurt, and he was already running out of ideas, either because he was still halfway to drunk or because there just weren't that many helpful suggestions to be had.

How do you find something without knowing what it is? Maybe Dez would have some ideas . . . though how would he feel about Jake bringing a Tosk back to the ship, let alone talking to one? Pif and Pri'ak hadn't been too "hip" to the idea, in Vic vernacular—

Tosk stood up suddenly, turning, and Jake realized that they had company—a slender humanoid female stood just a meter away, staring directly at Jake with an expression of confused and unhappy surprise.

"What are you *doing* here?" she asked, her voice thin and reedy. She was short, a meter and a half at most, and pale gray, with nose and brow ridges that accented very large black eyes, and long, straight white hair. She wore a simple, lightly padded bodysuit a shade darker than her skin. Jake had never seen her before.

"Excuse me?" he asked, also standing, wincing slightly at the disagreeable effect of sudden movement. "Have we met?"

The female blinked, once, twice, and then shook her head, looking at Tosk and then back at Jake again. "Why are you out in the open like this? It's not safe. If Tosk is being Hunted . . . Why are you talking to this human?"

She directed the last to Tosk, in a tone that was strangely parental, as though she were talking to wayward children rather than two complete strangers. Tosk looked helplessly at Jake, who looked helplessly back.

"Uh . . . we were having a private conversation . . ." Jake began.

"It's not safe out here like this," the female reiterated, ignoring the conspicuous hint. She seemed genuinely worried, and unusually protective. "Perhaps . . . why don't you come with me?"

"Who *are* you?" Jake asked, thoroughly mystified.

She stared at him a beat, and suddenly smiled, the expression transforming her, finally dating her—she was Jake's age, give or take a few years.

"I'm Wex," she said. "Forgive me, you must think it rude of me to intrude on your privacy like this . . . I've had dealings with Hunters and Tosk in the past, that's all. Really, though, it's not the best idea, to stand about in such a public venue. May I ask . . . why *are* you here? Is there a problem, something I might be able to help with?"

Automatically, Jake started to tell her that there was no problem—she was, after all, a stranger. But of course there was a problem, and he'd known Tosk for a whole ten minutes, they weren't exactly close friends . . . and since neither he nor Tosk knew what do about his dilemma, Jake thought that another opinion might not be such a bad idea.

That, and she seems honestly concerned. He had to take his own situation into account. Pif and Pri'ak and possibly Coamis were going to start getting worried soon, if they weren't already. Jake didn't want to walk away without helping, but it was looking like a bigger job than he'd anticipated, and if Wex really wanted to assist . . .

"Tosk, maybe Wex has some ideas," Jake said. "You've already talked to me . . ."

Tosk hesitated, then nodded his consent. Relieved, Jake introduced himself and Tosk to Wex and then gave her an abbreviated version of Tosk's story. Wex listened intently, asking a few thoughtful questions along the way . . . and at the end of the brief summary, she nodded firmly, decisively at both of them.

"I was right before. You should come with me."

"Why?" Jake asked.

"Because I'm on my way to see somebody who might be able to help," Wex said. "I came to Ee . . . it's a long story, but I'm here to see a sage, a wise woman with the power to heal. It's said that her very touch brings peace, that it can calm the wounded spirit. Stories like that make me curious, and it sounds as if your friend here could use some of that."

Jake nodded, inwardly wincing. Ee didn't exactly seem like an appropriate backdrop for such a person. "Is she . . . does it cost very much, because—"

Wex shook her head. "Oh, no. She's not even here. That is, I've just learned that she lives outside the main gate. It's only a short walk from here. I was on my way to see her when . . . when I saw you."

Jake smiled. "Lucky us. What do you say, Tosk, do you want to give this . . . sage a try?"

Tosk didn't sigh or shrug, but the look on his face expressed his feelings clearly enough. He was resigned, and Jake thought it was a few steps up from desperate, which was good. Tosk's gaze seemed less haunted, as well. Maybe sharing the burden had done something for him.

"Great," Jake said, smiling wider at Wex. "Let's go . . ."

The bar. ". . . or, actually, maybe you two should go on ahead, I could catch up with you."

Wex was frowning. "Why?"

"I should tell my friends what's going on, so they don't worry," Jake said.

"Your friends . . ." Wex said, her expression carefully neutral. ". . . all right. We'll come with you."

Jake suddenly realized that Wex probably thought he was trying to push Tosk off onto her, which he wasn't . . . but it didn't seem like a good idea to take Tosk back to the tavern, either, not after his earlier reception.

They were *pretty drunk, and she did say it wasn't far.* . . . If they really got worried, they could always use the emergency signal.

"Never mind," Jake said. "They can wait."

"I'd like to . . . maybe you can tell me how *you* ended up here, while we walk," Wex said, and smiled tentatively. "I mean, there aren't a lot of humans out this far."

Jake smiled back at her, still feeling the alcohol, thinking that she was kind of attractive, for a . . . for a female humanoid.

"Now, *that's* a long story," he said, and with Wex leading the way, they started walking.

Tosk didn't know how he felt it, but he felt it. Something was happening. The desperation and anxiety that had driven him for so long seemed to be lessening ever so slightly as they walked through the busy night avenues, as though . . . as though he were getting closer to what he needed. It seemed almost a chemical reaction, rather than an emotional one—and wasn't that how he'd come to Ee in the first place? He'd thought all of his decisions random since encountering the crystal, but if that were so, how had he made it across so many light-years, to end up where he now was? He had not analyzed his reactions, the reasons for his decisions, but he could see it now—there had been some small sensation of relief when he'd landed on Ee. And since, just thinking about leaving had caused the slightest increase in his distress, enough to keep him from withdrawing.

He considered telling Wex and Jake, walking in front of him, but they were conversing, explaining their own paths to Ee. Jake had come through the Anomaly, it seemed, and had been picked up by a salvage ship, and was now working for the ship. Wex, a Trelian, had been on a journey of self-enlightenment, a customary practice among her people, and had heard of the sage on some other planet. The sage, it seemed, had moved through at least two other communities before coming to Ee, and Wex wanted to meet her.

Tosk listened and walked, examining and reexamining his thoughts with each step, feeling for an awareness of the Other. He kept hoping that it would reveal itself, that his mind would open and have the knowledge of the new purpose, but as they reached the market gates, he still did not know. What he did know was that he felt . . . better. Still deeply anxious, still profoundly alarmed that the Hunt was not all, but better.

On the other side of the gate, Tosk could see the community of poor, of which Wex had spoken. It was far enough from the port's lit shield that much of it was cast in shadow, the darkness broken up by many small fires.

"Do you think it's safe?" Jake asked Wex, who nodded.

"I'm sure of it," she said.

The security people posted at the gate ignored them, once they realized where the trio wanted to go. With Wex still leading the way, they moved out from beneath the protective weather barrier and into the gloom, toward the tattered community. The temperature dropped a degree, then another as they moved away from the shield. Tosk reflexively puffed himself, realizing as he did that it was the first time in weeks he'd had a care about his personal comfort.

As they neared the first of the low, poorly made structures, heard the edges of soft conversation, the air scented with boiling meats and poverty, Jake paused, again addressing Wex.

"How do we find her?" he whispered.

Wex didn't answer him directly, instead loudly clearing her throat. Tosk saw a figure on the stoop of one shabby building stir, a shadow thickening as it leaned forward.

"Who is it?" An old man's voice, mild and unafraid.

"We're looking for the leader of the Sen Ennis," Wex said.

Tosk could hear a smile in the man's response. "Walk to the twelfth structure from this one, straight back, with the two lights in the window. Sulan lives next to it."

"Thank you," Wex said.

"Tell her that Umi says hello," the old man answered, his voice still smiling.

Wex began walking again, Jake and Tosk following, Tosk continuing to feel, with each step, that something was happening to him, to the planet, to reality. He wondered if he would have found this relief on his own, given more time, or if he would have blundered past it, mistaking and misreading the subtle difference. Surely, this Sulan would be able to tell him the new purpose, there was no other explanation for the steadily decreasing tension in his body, and in his mind.

"Nine . . . ten . . ." Jake was counting softly. Somewhere nearby, a child laughed, an innocent sound. Talking to Jake had been the right thing, Tosk realized. He'd felt something when he'd first touched the young human, but hadn't understood it then. Now he could see that talking to Jake had led to Wex, which would lead to Sulan.

There, the two lights in the window. They stepped past the small building, moving to the second, Wex approaching a cracked and dirty door. Jake smiled encouragingly at Tosk, but Tosk needed no encouragement as Wex knocked, he was desperate to meet Sulan. A second later, the door opened, and instantly, wonderfully, Tosk's mind shifted. Perspectives moved, and for the first time in weeks he was well, his mind sound and whole. The Hunt was all, and this was the Other, a second thing, he'd found it and now he could breathe again.

We have to go back, he thought, and was consumed by relief. That was the purpose, it was why he'd suffered. But . . . would she go with him?

The Other studied them for a few seconds, her tiny, lined face serious and searching and a little sad . . . and then she smiled warmly, radiantly peaceful, and stepped back from the door.

"Come in," the Other said. "I've been waiting."

For many weeks, Opaka Sulan had suspected that the Prophets would be sending for her soon. Throughout her seven years away from Bajor, there had been signs, dreams, and shadows. For a long time she had dreamed of struggle, of sacrifice, of her ancestors hiding in the dark . . . but for several months now, there had been better dreams. New life, and hopeful children reaching toward a rising sun . . . and something else she couldn't see, but knew was important and wonderful and different.

New hope, she dreamed of . . . and travel. When she heard the knock at her door, she had a feeling that it might be time . . . and when she opened the door and saw the Emissary's son, she knew that it was so. She didn't recognize the other two on the step, but knew that they, too, had come to take her away from Ee, and from the people who had been her family for the last seven years. She felt a fleeting sadness, but let it pass. She would go where and when They wished her, of course, as she always had.

"Come in, I've been waiting," she said, smiling, thinking of how amazing the Tapestry was, and her own place in Their weaving. She'd left Bajor and the Alpha Quadrant seven years earlier, knowing only that she wouldn't be returning with the Emissary and his crew . . . and now the Emissary's son had come to take her home.

The three filed past her into the sparse, open room where she received visitors. A slim, pale gray girl, Trelian, she thought—there was a Trelian family in the camp—with lucent eyes, only slightly taller than Opaka, her manner courteous and respectful. Jake Sisko, looking so grown . . . and puzzled, peering at her without recognition as he stepped inside. And the third, a reptilian being, tall and muscular, his pleasure at meeting her a palpable thing. From the relief in his eyes, she imagined that he had suffered to find her . . . and that he had something to tell her.

Just as in the dreams. In them, there were three beings who came to travel with her, faceless but familiar, bearing a message of great import . . . or a task to be done, she wasn't sure which. She went away with them, and though it wasn't clear what they did together, the dreams always ended with her at the monastery where she'd lived as Kai. She was going home, back to Bajor. At least, that was what she'd taken away from the dreams. She could be wrong, she supposed. The Prophets weren't always clear, but the challenge of interpreting Their meaning had always been her secret joy.

"Please, sit down," she said, motioning at the two plain benches that made up the main room's furnishings, choosing for herself the one padded chair across from them. "I hope you don't mind if I take the chair, but my back isn't what it used to be. . . ."

They all seemed reluctant to sit, but obeyed, all watching her intently as she sat back in her seat. She smiled, realizing that she was going to have to get things started.

"I'm Opaka Sulan," she said.

"Wex," said the Trelian. "And this is Jake, and this is Tosk. It's . . . it's very good to meet you."

"It's good to meet *you,*" she said, and saw that Jake was staring at her, his handsome young face a picture of surprise. Of course, they'd met only once, and he'd been a child.

"You . . . you're Kai Opaka!" He said.

"I was Kai," she said gently. "I've just been Opaka Sulan for some time now."

Jake was shaking his head. "But . . . you were stuck on that moon, years ago, where the runabout crashed."

Opaka nodded. Seven years earlier, she had died in

the crash of the *Yangtzee Kiang,* the craft shot down by the satellites that guarded the Gamma moon. Died, and been brought back to life by a miracle of science, only to discover that the miracle was environment-specific. Like the moon's prisoners, the bitterly warring tribes of the Ennis and Nol-Ennis, leaving the environment would have meant her death. For them, the miracle had been a curse . . .

. . . which was why the Prophets had me go to them, she thought, smiling inwardly; that, too, had been in a dream. A dream that had catalyzed her first journey away from Bajor to DS9, where she had, in turn, asked Jake's father to take her through the Celestial Temple and into the Gamma Quadrant, where they had crashed on the moon. The Prophets had given her such opportunities; she was truly blessed.

"You died there," Jake added, eyes still wide. "You couldn't leave, it would have killed you. How . . . *how?"*

"Will of the Prophets," Opaka said . . . and saw the slight tightening of the boy's mouth at her words, and understood a little more about him. Poor child. It must have been very difficult for him, growing up as the Emissary's son.

Wex seemed to have gathered something from Jake's surprised half-questions. "If I may ask . . . how did you leave this moon where you, ah, died?"

Opaka folded her hands in her lap, considering the question, remembering. In recent weeks, since the dreams had begun to shift, to tell her that she was soon to leave, she'd found herself reflecting over her time in the Gamma Quadrant more and more . . . from the first days on that moon to the release, to her traveling time, to where she was now. It wasn't an exciting story, stories of faith rarely were, but she thought it was an interesting story, of a brief span of years in an interesting life.

I have been so blessed, she thought again, and sat back in her chair, searching for a few words to answer Wex's question, remembering so much more.

13

"SULAN!"

Her name echoed through the cave garden, the eager shout much louder than was necessary. Opaka looked up from the patch of greens she was tending, smiling as the ever-excitable Misja came rushing in, preceded by his resounding cry. He had been a young man at the time of his clan's imprisonment and still looked like a child, scars or no.

"Sulan, are you here? Sulan!" Misja cast a single, wild stare around the enclosed garden and turned to run back out again.

Acts as a child, too. That he was at least a hundred years her senior made no difference. Opaka rose to her feet, brushing dirt from her knees.

"Yes, Misja. What is it?"

At the sound of her voice Misja spun toward her, as excited as she'd ever seen him. "There's—Zlangco was out walking at the east cliffs, and he saw a ship crash-land, right in front of him!"

Surely the satellites again. Opaka's hands reflexively went to her heart. "Oh, no."

Misja nodded, visibly calming now that he was able to deliver his important news. "He sent me to get you—there was an alien inside, it's alive but he says it's sick. You have to come, they're at Tadia's."

"Of course," she said, well aware that there was nothing she could do for a sick being that Tadia couldn't do better. Opaka also knew, however, that the Sen Ennis, the recently united tribe she had helped create, still depended heavily on her counsel. They didn't need it, but they believed they did . . . and until they believed otherwise, she was willing to continue counseling.

Together, she and Misja left the cave and started for Tadia's, her thatched home located at the outskirts of the newly appointed communal area—a series of caves and structures and open spaces where the Sen Ennis met to work together, that had once belonged to the Nol-Ennis. Tadia was the closest thing the united tribe had to a healer, in that she had studied plant medicine before the imprisonment; afterward, of course, there had been no need, but since the fighting had ended, she had taken it up once more, mostly because she could. There was finally time for more than mere survival.

In spite of the unhappy circumstances, Opaka took some enjoyment from the brief walk. The sun was shining, and there were a number of people out and working, smiling at one another and talking pleasantly as they sewed or dug for roots or sharpened tools. The scars were harder to see, when they smiled. The grim reminders of more than a century of battle were still apparent, too deeply etched by time to disappear so quickly, but were no longer so obvious as they once were.

It pleased Opaka to see the flourishing sense of community, still so new to the young tribe. It seemed the discovery of the alien crash had not yet spread. In the nearly four years since Opaka had come to the moon, there had been three other crashes, all considered to be events of importance. None had yielded any survivors.

Zlangco, once the leader of the Nol-Ennis, was standing outside of Tadia's home, apparently awaiting Opaka's arrival.

"It seems to be breathing all right, it just won't wake up," he said, in lieu of a greeting. "Shel-la has taken some people to look at the ship."

Opaka nodded, gratified that Zlangco had already contacted Golin Shel-la, the Ennis's leader, to include him in the event. It had been less than a year since the end of the fighting, and while she could feel the strength of both men's resolve to maintain peace, she also knew that a year was hardly an eternity. In their prolonged lives, it was barely a blink.

Excused, Misja ran off to spread the news, while Zlangco and Opaka went inside, moving to the bedchamber at the rear of the small home. Zlangco knocked once on the clay wall, and pushed the chamber's curtain aside, ushering Opaka inside.

Tadia and her mate, Korin, were sitting beside the floor pallet against the back wall, studying the alien; it seemed they had just managed to pry a face shield off, the thin rind of alloy still in Korin's hand.

How lovely it is, Opaka thought, and moved to join them, kneeling beside the pallet.

The semiconscious creature was very tall, perhaps half again Opaka's height, its body defined by a layer of fluid-looking armor, a silvery metal shell that closely matched the color of its pale face. Two arms, two legs . . . it had breasts, small but apparent, and Opaka assumed it was female—the face, too, had a feminine cast in spite of its alien nature, a roundness to the cheek and jaw.

The armor was cracked across the breastbone, a short, deep break . . . and a thin, cloudy fluid was leaking from beneath it. Opaka was about to suggest that they remove the armor when she noted the veinlike threads running through the edges of the crack, and how the armor surrounding it was discolored, a dusky matte gray. She realized that it wasn't armor at all, but an exoskeletal sheath, organic.

As Korin set the mask aside, the alien opened her eyes for a few seconds, blinking dazedly around the dusky room before lapsing back into semiconsciousness, rolling her head from side to side, tensing and flexing her limbs. Her large golden eyes were fluted at the outer edges, in a way that made them seem to be melting into her metallic skin, and as she tossed her head, she mumbled something unintelligible in a high, melodic language. She wasn't wearing a translator that Opaka could see, and since the Sen Ennis had no need for them—Opaka hadn't worn hers in years, having learned the Ennis-Nol-Ennis language soon after her arrival—the alien's words might have been lost to translation, rather than sickness.

"I'll get a translator," Zlangco said, then turned and left.

Except for the crack in her chest there were no other apparent wounds, and as Zlangco had noted, she seemed to be able to breathe the air well enough, taking in ragged breaths as she squirmed restlessly. She mumbled again, seeming to repeat what she'd said before, her tone delirious and desperate. It sounded like a plea.

Gently, Opaka stroked the alien's brow, noting that the smooth mercurial flesh was cool . . . and at Opaka's touch, the alien ceased her thrashing, breathing deeper, calming.

"Will she live?" Korin asked, in a near-whisper. "Or will she . . . become like us?"

Without thinking about it, Opaka reached over and traced the outer curve of the being's delicate left ear—and felt a powerful tingle in the tips of her fingers, felt the dilation of blood vessels in her own hands and face. The being's *pagh* was strong, almost violently so.

"She'll live," Opaka said.

Before Opaka had happened upon them, the Ennis and Nol-Ennis had been stranded on the moon by their homeworld, Tevlin-De, for at least a century, and had been fighting for well over a hundred years before that. The ruthless leaders of Tevlin-De had imprisoned the two warring factions on the distant moon as an example to other fighting tribes, a punishment for being unable to negotiate a peace—and had condemned them to immortality, inundating the harsh environment with artificial microbes that repaired even the most serious of wounds on a cellular level. Upon being stranded, the Ennis and Nol-Ennis had begun fighting an endless battle, dying and rising and dying again, cursed by their own hatreds to war without end. Made infertile by the microbes, trapped on the moon by the satellites, they had only their vengeance to live for, the original dispute so far in the past that neither side could remember why they had begun to fight in the first place.

When the *Yangtzee Kiang* had crashed, the Federation doctor, Bashir, had discovered that a person once repaired by the microbes would be unable to leave the environment . . . and so Opaka, led to the moon by the Prophets and then killed in the crash, had understood that she was meant to stay behind. She'd remained willingly, recognizing that the Ennis and Nol-Ennis needed her far more than Bajor; why else would the Prophets have sent her to them? And even if she had been physically able to leave with the Emissary and his crew, she wouldn't have turned her back to such deeply wounded people.

In the first year, she had learned the language, and talked and talked and talked. Back and forth between Zlangco and Shel-la, trying to reason with each, with their families, she had succeeded in little more than making herself known to both tribes. For much of that year, she'd been viewed with suspicion and disbelief, and even after she'd gained some level of trust, both leaders had insisted that she was wasting her time.

In the second year, she had added action to her voice, hoping to show them a better way by example. Opaka had spent hours meditating on the battlefields, allowing herself to be caught in the fighting. Both tribes had called her enemy, deciding she was with the other, and both had struck out in anger. The pain had been terrible, her deaths many . . . but slowly, slowly, some of the combatants had begun to listen when she went to their homes, intrigued, perhaps, by the stranger who refused to pick up arms, who died with the rest of them but held no spite.

So it had been, her long struggle to help the Ennis and Nol-Ennis, dutifully walking back and forth between the tribes each day, making small increments of progress and seemingly just as often watching the progress unravel. Only once had she faltered, had she found herself unsure of her purpose, and that had been early in the third year, when she had gone to the Emissary.

She'd dreamed/seen that he'd lost his way, that he was wandering his space station alone, unaware of his own identity; she'd asked him who he was, and he hadn't known. It had been an orb shadow, *his* shadow that she had seen, caused by his faltering from his path. Opaka had waked/returned afraid for Bajor. Not because of the Emissary—she'd known that self-doubt was to be his greatest burden, and was sure that he would regain his clarity—but because she'd sensed that something dark was on its way, something vast and consuming. Years later, she had learned of the Quadrant War, and known then why the Prophets had called upon her to visit the Emissary; They'd needed all of Their Chosen, then, supporting one another for the good of Bajor.

The day after she'd seen the Emissary, looking so changed, bearded, his hair gone, his eyes full of uncertainty, she'd wondered if the Prophets were telling her to return, somehow, telling her that she'd failed and was needed at home . . . and that very day, both Zlangco and Shel-la had agreed to lay down their arms for the first time. The truce had lasted only two days, but it had been the true beginning of the end, and she had taken it as a sign that she was where she was supposed to be.

Within a few months, there had been no more fighting, and more and more of the Ennis and Nol-Ennis had joined in her daily meditations as the weeks passed, searching for something to fill the black holes where the hatred had been for so long. Gradually, she stopped holding separate meetings, as much from her own exhaustion as for reasons of unity, and the Ennis and Nol-Ennis had begun coming together to meditate with her. Aware that neither tribe would be comfortable with gods alien to their culture, Opaka showed them ways to look to whatever greater essence they chose, to look within, to look to each other for the light of the eternal . . . and in so doing, she had discovered for herself a much richer understanding of her own boundaries, ways in which she'd limited herself by believing that there was only one true path to understanding the Prophets. It was a magical time for them all.

Starved for peace of spirit after so long and bitter a war, the tribes quickly adopted the meditations as lifestyle . . . and once they'd begun their spiritual searchings in earnest, the last of the tribal enmity had disappeared completely. At her own gentle suggestion, Zlangco and Shel-la had called to combine the tribes, to discard the last great barrier to unity, the separate names . . . and so the Sen Ennis tribe was born, barely a month before Raiq's ship landed.

It took over two weeks for the exoskeletal crack to heal, and in that time, Raiq acted as though in the grip of a fever. The tribespeople took turns watching her, bathing her with cool water, feeding her sips of water or gruel—and though she was rarely coherent, her ravings provided them with some information, through Zlangco's ancient translator pinned to the pillow. Her name was Raiq, and she believed she was dying, and her gods were not gracious ones. Again and again, she cried out for judgment, her gold eyes glazed with a fevered determination, insisting that her gods find her worthy before leaving her to burn. Opaka's presence seemed especially soothing to her, so Opaka sat with her as often as she could, calming her when she shouted, praying for her recovery when she was still.

The condition of Raiq's ship added to what little they knew, yet somehow made her all the more mysterious. It was an extremely advanced single-pilot vessel, equipped with systems that no one had ever seen, couldn't even begin to guess at . . . and it had not been shot down by the moon's advanced satellite "defense" system, as they had all assumed; everything seemed intact, and there was minimal blast damage on the hull. In fact, from the debris that was found scattered through the cliffs, it seemed that Raiq had been the victor. At least two and possibly three satellites had lost, opening a sizable hole in the network that had been designed to keep the tribes from being rescued. They could only assume that it had been her sickness that had forced her to land. Perhaps the crack in her exoskeleton had brought on an immediate illness, or perhaps the damage to her exoskeleton had been sustained elsewhere; it was a source of endless interest in the days following her arrival.

Except for the group healing meditation the day after Raiq's landing—for which the entire Sen Ennis tribe turned out—life went on as usual . . . or as it had been going, at least. Opaka had been on the moon almost four years, and so much had changed, she had yet to think of any time period as "usual."

After sixteen days, the feverlike trance broke. Korin came and found Opaka, leading the morning meditation outside the main cave garden. He waited until she spoke the final words, reminding the gathered Sen Ennis to reach for light in every deed, and then hurried to meet her, deferentially helping her to her feet as the assemblage broke up.

"She's awake," Korin said. "And she's asked to see our leader."

Opaka sighed inwardly. She was interested in Raiq, curious about her, but wasn't comfortable portraying herself as the leader of the Sen Ennis, regardless of what the Sen Ennis were determined to believe. She had helped them find peace, it would have been false humility to deny her own part—but neither did she deserve to be deified for it. It was a question that had plagued her from her earliest days as a vedek; why did people so often choose to revere the messenger, rather than the message?

"I'd think Zlangco or Shel-la would suffice," she said.

Korin quickly nodded his agreement, his gaze telling a different story. "They're with her now. Will you come?"

Resigned, Opaka smiled, answer enough, and they went to see Raiq.

She was sitting up when they arrived, her luminous gaze fixing on Opaka immediately, unwavering. Except for a faint discoloration across her chest, a fading bruise, the crack might never have been. Zlangco and Shel-la were in the room, both seeming unsettled even before Raiq addressed Opaka.

"I will see Opaka alone," Raiq said, and there was no question in her voice.

Opaka looked at the Sen Ennis leaders, waiting. They hesitated, glancing at one another, stood, and with nods at Raiq and Opaka, they left the room, taking Korin with them.

Opaka couldn't help a faint smile. For as hard as Zlangco and Shel-la still fought to maintain leadership, they were apparently more than ready to turn the demanding alien over to Opaka.

"You have been with me," Raiq said, even as the curtain swung closed. "You have saved my life. Sit."

Throughout her illness, Raiq had been desperate at times, driven, obsessed with being judged by her gods, afraid of dying unworthy. Her manner now was cool and imperious, her voice still melodic but much sharper, the tone of a being used to getting her way. Opaka suspected that Raiq had commanded her to sit to see how she would react, but she was uninterested in power games. She wanted to talk to Raiq, and so she sat.

"I'm glad that you've healed," she said. "We've been concerned."

"When I asked to see this moon's leader, they told me something of you, and how you've brought peace to this world," Raiq said, as though Opaka hadn't spoken. "Do you worship the True, the Unnamable? Is that how you control?"

Opaka studied Raiq, considering the question and what it implied. It wasn't a surprise, after listening to Raiq in her delirium, but still she felt a great sorrow for the creature, and a wariness for herself—for the Sen Ennis. She had lived most of her life surrounded by worshippers, and while the vast majority of Bajorans had led integrated lives, balancing their love of the Prophets with their secular duties, there were always those who went too far.

Her first question, too . . . of all the information we could share, who do you worship? Raiq was a zealot, and Opaka thought she'd best step lightly.

"I do not control," she said, finally. "I walk with the Prophets, the gods of my homeworld, and I came here to help these people heal themselves."

Raiq stared. "The True have eyes of fire. They see all, and judge the worthiness of those who seek the burning empty that is Their fortress, hidden among the stars. Do your prophets burn? Do your people seek their judgment?"

Opaka shook her head, speaking gently. "No. The Prophets guide and teach . . . but the people who live on *this* world know nothing of the Prophets. The Sen Ennis are only just learning the joys of faith, in themselves."

"These people don't worship?" Raiq asked, her fluted eyes narrowing. "You'd swear it?"

Opaka sighed. "The Sen Ennis don't worship."

"And these 'prophets' of your home," Raiq said. "Do they live in the stars? Do they see all?"

Opaka hesitated. The Celestial Temple *was* in the stars . . . and the Prophets were all-seeing, but something kept her from saying so.

"Raiq, why do you ask these questions?"

"Answer me," Raiq demanded, her face flushing with color. "Do your prophets have eyes of fire? *Will you die and be burned?"*

"No," Opaka said, relieved that she could answer those questions without hesitation. Raiq sat back, seemingly satisfied.

"I will trust you," she said, almost dismissively, and changed the topic without transition. "I will leave as soon as I've rested, but you and your people will be rewarded for saving the life of an Ascendant."

"An Ascendant," Opaka said, nodding, seeking more comfortable footing. "Where are you from?"

"Everywhere," Raiq said. "Our world is lost to time. I was born on the Quest, and will die on it, as my ancestors did before me."

"What do you quest?"

"The Fortress. I have traveled vast distances to seek the hidden home of the True, so that I might be judged and found worthy to burn in Their eyes. Then I will be all-seeing, as They are." Raiq sat forward again, her eyes shining. "They hide, just as They hide Their Names, but the Ascendants will find them."

Opaka nodded again, starting to understand. "So you wanted to know about my beliefs, and the beliefs of the Sen Ennis, to see if we worship the True."

"Only the Ascendants worship the True," Raiq said, her voice cold.

"But . . ." Opaka frowned, confused again. "Why, then, do you concern yourself with what others believe?"

Even as she asked, she understood, the question answered by what she already knew of Raiq.

"I am responsible to the True during my quest, to seek the destruction of those who falsely worship," Raiq said, confirming Opaka's suspicion. "So it has been for a thousand millennia. Long, long ago, the Ascendants were many, and we cleansed a hundred stars of heresy against the True. . . ." Raiq smiled, a thin, dreamy sliver of imagined glory. "The Unnamed saw us, then, painted in the blood of the false. Those who dared to name the True ran before us like frightened children. . . ."

Her smile faded, her cool attention turning back to Opaka. "There are fewer of us, now. We rely on technology rather than numbers to cleanse the stars we pass on our quest. But since you and yours don't shame the True, you have nothing to fear from the Ascendants . . ."

Raiq's expression softened slightly. ". . . and as I said before, you will be rewarded. I was injured on another world, a misstep that caused a minor wound. I ignored it and it grew into infection, into breach. In my sickness, I believed I was close to the Fortress, and would not rest. I would have died, if not for your ministrations."

"We ask for nothing," Opaka said honestly, her sadness for Raiq tempered now by caution. She silently thanked the Prophets for her earlier reserve, thinking that an explanation of the Celestial Temple would only have confused matters. "We are glad to help you."

Raiq tilted her head, a curious expression on her delicate features. "The True are all-powerful and all-seeing, and someday, if I am vigilant, I will join them. Why . . . why do you worship these prophets?"

Opaka spoke carefully, but with conviction. "On my world, we believe the Prophets watch over us. They are like . . . mother and father to me, to all the people of my planet, providing as a good parent provides—showing each of us the potential we carry within, to be fulfilled as beings, and to build peaceful communities in which to live, and grow, and care for one another."

Raiq nestled back against the cushion she was propped against, blinking slowly. "I need to rest. Tomorrow, I will begin deciding upon your reward."

Opaka studied her a moment, not sure what, if anything, she should say, but already Raiq's eyes were closing. It seemed that the interview was over.

After a moment, Opaka rose and left the chamber, to tell the others what little she'd learned, and to ask that she be informed the moment that Raiq awoke. It was unfortunate, that Raiq had been raised with such severe beliefs, but the alien was also dangerous, and Opaka meant to stay close until she was ready to leave them.

In the days it took for Raiq to recover her strength, she mostly slept and ate and sat silently, her eyes closed in meditation, often for hours at a time. Opaka took to sitting with her, using the time for her own prayers. When Raiq did speak, she asked questions about the Sen Ennis, about their moon and their war, though she told Opaka little more about the Ascendants. Opaka did manage to find out that they were long-lived—Raiq, at one hundred and twelve, wasn't half through her life—and that about every fifty years, gatherings were arranged among them, where information and technology were exchanged, and matings were orchestrated to perpetuate the species. Raiq asked no more about the Prophets, and Opaka didn't offer . . . nor did Raiq express interest in speaking to anyone but Opaka, about anything. She treated Tadia and Korin like servants in their own home, and during her few public recuperative walks with Opaka, she openly ignored the people they encountered. The Sen Ennis, in turn, were relieved when Opaka suggested that they leave Raiq to her.

After nine days of lucid recovery, twenty-five days since she'd blasted her way to the surface, Raiq and Opaka walked to Raiq's ship for the second time in as many days, Opaka waiting outside the small, bladelike vessel as Raiq ran another systems check.

It was a cool, windy afternoon, the desolate landscape—towering cliff walls and cracked earth—painted in stark shades of gray. Opaka sat cross-legged on the ground, leaning against the small vessel, enjoying the brisk air and demanding scenery, so different from Bajor. There truly was beauty in everything.

"I'm prepared to leave," Raiq said from behind her, "and I've decided on your reward. When I depart, I will destroy the rest of the network that keeps you here."

Opaka turned to look at her, wanting to tell her again

that no reward was necessary, also feeling her heart jump at the thought. No more satellites meant no more crashes, no more innocent victims.

"Raiq, that would be very kind of you," she said, smiling.

"You are aware, the artificial organisms here that relate to cellular function will also be deactivated," Raiq added.

Opaka pushed to her feet and stared up at Raiq, not sure she'd heard correctly. "I don't understand," she said, her voice barely audible to her own ears.

"From what my vessel's sensory data suggests, the energy fields that perpetuate the microbes' environment-specific mechanism are manufactured by the satellite network," Raiq continued. "By destroying the network, the mechanism will fall dormant. You will be free to leave this moon."

"But . . . I thought we were dependent on these microbes for cellular functions," Opaka said.

"You are. If your bodies were to be flushed of the microbes, you would die. What I propose is deactivation. Death will again become an option, but your people should also be able to procreate."

Babies! That alone . . . Opaka was so thankful that she could hardly breathe. She instinctively stepped forward to embrace Raiq, her heart full . . . and Raiq stepped back, her expression blank.

"This is the reward," she said coolly. "Once this is done, the Ascendants owe you nothing."

Opaka lowered her arms, her happiness faltering, tainted with pity for Raiq. If only she could accept another's friendship, or comfort of any kind. Opaka might have felt differently if Raiq had seemed fulfilled, if she'd been content to pursue her indifferent gods alone, to feel nothing but contempt for others . . . but Opaka had seen her sick, crying from fear and loneliness, afraid that she would be left behind.

And those things are so deeply hidden that if she had seen herself then, she wouldn't recognize herself as the same person.

"I . . . understand," Opaka said, for that was all there was to say.

"I will go now," Raiq said, and without another word or gesture, she turned and reentered her ship. Opaka stepped back and away, watching as the narrow vessel powered up and then lifted from the surface. An instant later, Raiq was gone.

Opaka silently wished her well, asking the Prophets to keep safe those who encountered her . . . and then turned away from the empty cliffs, back toward the settlement. She walked a few steps, smiling, wondering how best to tell the Sen Ennis of Raiq's reward . . . and as the full import of the implications hit her—free, the Sen Ennis were *free*—she suddenly found herself feeling so light, so young, that she lifted her skirts and broke into a run, laughing with sheer delight at the joy in her old bones, running like a schoolgirl to spread the news.

14

ALTHOUGH THE STORY wasn't a long one, Jake found it hard to concentrate, not as much from the alcohol as from who was telling it. Kai Opaka. He couldn't believe it.

The prophecy, your *prophecy,* his brain kept saying, refusing to leave it alone. *"A Herald, unforgotten but lost to time and removed from sight, a Seer of Visions to whom the Teacher Prophets sing, will return from the Temple. . . . The first child, a son, enters the Temple alone. With the Herald, he returns, and soon after, the Avatar is born."*

It was true, after all. But not his father. *Kai Opaka all along.* Kai Opaka, who had heralded the Emissary.

". . . and so we were free to leave," Opaka was saying. "Over the years, the tribes had salvaged enough from the crashed ships that they were able to set up a transmitting station, and a month or so after Raiq had gone, a survey ship's crew happened upon us. They were able to help the Sen Ennis repair the ships they had originally landed in. There was room for us all."

Opaka smiled, the expression soft and amused. "And most of the Sen Ennis are still on the moon, raising their children. The last I heard, there were twenty-three. They worked so hard to build a life there, you see. It had become home."

"But you and about thirty of your followers moved on," Wex said. "And went to the Ool'sp hospice on Syll8, where you helped care for the last of the *hevgin* test victims. And then to the colonies at Arshiv and Arshiv Prime, where you established their first civil-war orphanages. Before you came, many of the children starved to death."

"We were also at the Beras for a few months," Opaka said, her eyebrows raised slightly. "To pray with the refugees. And now we're here, on Ee, and we've just managed to get a government doctor to come to the camp, twice a week. When we got here, there were people actually dying from untreated infections. . . ."

She trailed off, then smiled slightly at Wex. "You must have heard about my healing powers, if you know all that. I've only recently heard about them myself. I'm sorry to say, I haven't any magic. Only a little determination, and a willingness to help."

Jake finally found his voice. "You said you knew about the Dominion War . . . why didn't you go home?"

Opaka turned to him, her own voice gentle, almost apologetic. "Because I always knew that the Prophets would send for me, when They were ready."

Jake looked away, not sure how he felt, only that it was messy and confusing. The Prophets, of course. Why had he even bothered to ask? They had it all organized, They knew who was going to do what from the beginning of time to the end of it. *Why bother to make any decisions? It's all taken care of, isn't it?*

Opaka had turned her attention to Tosk, who had remained silent throughout. "Is there something you have to tell me, Tosk?"

Tosk stared at her a moment, his eyes bright, and then blurted it out. "You are the Other, Oh-paka," he said, in a rush, "and you have to come with me, back to the star system nearest the Anomaly, to the planet where I touched the crystal. I don't know why, or what will happen, but I will take you back to your home afterward if you come with me."

Jake shot a glance at Wex, who only watched with a neutral expression. *Kai Opaka is his new purpose?* The only thing that could have been more surprising was her reaction to Tosk's excited declaration.

"All right," she said evenly. "I just have to speak with Zlangco and the others, to be sure they understand what's left to be done here . . . and to say good-bye. I can be ready by tomorrow afternoon."

Jake was speechless. She hadn't heard Tosk's story, she had no idea what he was talking about, he *sounded* crazy, and yet she hadn't even blinked.

"I will have to get a new ship," Tosk said, almost to himself. "If it were only a few hours, mine would suffice, but it will take three, perhaps four weeks. . . ."

How long before Kas has the baby? Six weeks? Jake felt a flash of bitterness. If Opaka didn't make it back in time, would the Prophets hold the Avatar back?

"I would like to go with you," Wex said suddenly, addressing Opaka. "I know that you have no reason to allow it, but I feel strongly that I should accompany you . . ." Wex nodded at Tosk. ". . . if that's agreeable to you both, of course. I have no ship." Tosk nodded back at her, apparently agreeable to anything, now that he'd found his Other.

Opaka motioned for Wex to approach, to kneel at her side . . . and when the Trelian had complied, Opaka reached out to touch her left ear, grasping it firmly. Startled, Wex started to pull away, but Opaka shook her head. The aging Bajoran closed her eyes while Wex blinked rapidly, an expression almost like guilt on her young face. After a few seconds, Opaka let go, and Wex immediately stood and backed away, reaching up to touch her ear with one nervous hand.

"Of course you must come," Opaka said, and turned her mild gaze toward Jake again. "Will we all be traveling together?"

Jake stared at her, feeling like everything was happening way too fast, feeling a terrific headache settling in. His first impulse was to tell her no, they would *not* be traveling together, the prophecy was crap and the Prophets were wrong . . .

. . . but she's Kai Opaka. She's been lost for seven years, but she belongs on Bajor . . . and the Even *is going back toward the wormhole anyway. . . .* The tentative plan was for Facity to pilot him through on the dropship, so that he could get some things together and say his good-byes. So that he could have something of his own, away from DS9 and Bajor.

Forget it, let the Prophets take care of her, a part of him spat, and that same part wanted to tell her as much, to thank her for naming his father the Emissary, he couldn't forget *that,* and he hadn't even recognized her, he didn't *know* her . . .

. . . but he knew himself. He couldn't leave Kai

Opaka with strangers, not without at least trying to see her home.

"I . . . I'm not sure," he said, and then sighed. "Let me talk to the captain of the ship I'm on. It's not up to me, but I'll try."

Opaka gazed at him with such kindness that he glanced away, embarrassed by his thoughts. Why was this happening to him? Why couldn't he just walk away?

"You're so much like your father," Opaka said warmly, and Jake felt his cheeks flush, with dull anger and shame. He wasn't at *all,* his father wouldn't have wavered, his father would do the right thing without thinking twice about it.

Yeah. But he's the Emissary of the Prophets. I'm just . . . Jake.

Jake stood up, wanting to get out and get it over with, hoping that Dez would tell them no . . . knowing deep down that if he did, Jake would try to change his mind. It wasn't fair. He'd been out with friends, having fun, having a *life,* and things had changed. Now he was faced with a responsibility that he didn't want, and couldn't ignore.

"Why don't Tosk and I go with you, to talk with your captain," Wex offered, and Jake nodded. *Why not?* He didn't trust himself to speak.

Opaka said good night and they left her, Jake thinking that it didn't matter, whatever he wanted. One way or another, he would be taking the Kai back through the wormhole. After all, it had been foreseen.

". . . and it just makes sense, we could take Tosk's ship with us," Jake said. "That system Tosk described—it has to be Idran, three light-years from the wormhole.

We could drop them off, and they could make it back to Bajor on their own from there."

Beneath the bright lights of the transporter room, Facity could see that his eyes were bloodshot but not bleary. *He's sober, all right.* Hard as it was to believe.

"So . . . what do you think?" Jake asked.

It was silent, Dez frowning thoughtfully, Facity hoping that he'd break the answer to Jake gently, and quickly. Pri'ak and Pif had already dragged Coamis off to bed, where everyone else was, having returned hours before. Where she should be, where she *had* been, dozing next to Dez after a satisfying dinner and several hours of quality time, a good portion of it active. It was late and she was tired, and not a little unnerved by Jake's decision to bring strangers back to the ship. His new acquaintances, the Tosk and the Trelian girl, still stood on the transporter pad behind them, both having added bits and pieces of their individual stories where Jake had faltered.

Dez jerked his chin toward the door, and Jake and Facity walked with him to stand in front of it, hopefully out of earshot of the other two.

"I think you're right, it makes sense," Dez said. "We'll call it our good deed for the day."

What?

Jake seemed to relax, though he didn't smile. "Okay, good. Thanks, Dez."

"Dez, are you—" Facity started, but Dez wasn't finished. He nodded toward the Trelian girl, Wex, with a frown, still addressing Jake in a low voice.

"Except it seems to me that Wex could find her own ride. I'm not worried about having a Tosk know that we're retrievers, and this Opaka person obviously won't be a problem, but why does she want to come, again?"

Dez shook his head. "I know Trelians are into self-discovery, but it seems a little suspect, to be honest—"

"I agree," Wex said loudly, calling out across the room. "Which is why—I'm sorry, may I . . . ?"

She had nerve, Facity had to give her that. *And damned good hearing,* she thought, as Wex stepped off the transporter pad and approached them.

"I apologize for interrupting," Wex said. "I just wanted to tell you that my family is extremely wealthy, I can pay you for passage."

"We're not a transport ship," Dez said, frowning.

"Please," Wex said. She seemed deeply uncomfortable asking, which struck Facity as a bit odd. Trelians were generally a humble species. "I just . . . wish to spend time with Opaka. Trelians only seek the experiences of self-enlightenment—I promise you, I have no wish to interfere with your business."

Dez hesitated, and Wex pressed the point. "And like I said, I can pay. Quite well."

Dez sighed, and nodded. "Fine."

He's lost his mind. Facity couldn't stand another minute. "Dez, may I have a word?"

Before he could answer, she turned and walked out, and Dez followed. It was all she could do not to start shouting as the door slid closed behind them. Jake might be a favorite, but a crazy Tosk, and some mad mission with passengers they knew nothing about. . . . It was too much.

"Explain," she said simply.

Dez grinned, his eyes glittering. "You weren't listening, my sweet. Replay what the Tosk told us, why don't you?"

"He told us he's *insane,*" Facity said, shaking her head. "What's gotten into you? I know you care about

Jake, fine, but you're taking this father-figure business much too far."

Dez placed his hands on her shoulders. "Facity, he touched a crystal that disappeared, that *melted.* But first, it implanted something in his mind."

"So? I think he *damaged* his mind, he—" Facity abruptly shut up, felt her eyes go wide. The Eav-oq.

It was a retrieval myth, like the one about the women who wept gems. Every few years, somebody somewhere claimed to have found one of the Eav-oq vanishing crystals, on which the millennia-dead race had recorded aspects of their culture. The problem was, touching the crystal released the information into the mind of the person who touched it, which made it impossible to actually verify whether or not one of the artifacts was real. If it was real, the crystal itself disappeared.

"You think he found the Eav-oq planet?" Facity asked, her voice low. "You think it was one of the crystals?"

"I think he found *something,*" Dez said. "And I think you're right, it did damage his mind. Think about it—he's a Tosk, and Tosk only do one thing. It makes sense that a piece of technology like that could warp his program."

"But . . . the Eav-oq disappeared something like fifty millennia ago," Facity said. "How could he have found an Eav-oq crystal that told him to find this Opaka person? And how could it have guided him to her?"

Dez shrugged. "No idea. But I want to be there when he takes her back, to see what happens. And if she wants this Wex person to tag along, fine by me."

He grinned again. "At the very least, maybe we'll find a few more of those crystals."

He kissed her, briefly but with passion, and she responded in kind, as excited as he was at the prospect of the new adventure. The Eav-oq world! They would be living legends in the retrieval business if they managed to find it.

"Let's go welcome our new friends aboard, and then get some rest, we've got a big day tomorrow," Dez said. "We should leave as soon as we sell the Giani'aga box. We don't want the Hunters to come looking for our map."

He paused, cocking one brow at her. "We should keep all this to ourselves, though . . . we can tell the crew in private that Wex is financing this thing, and that it's a secret, they shouldn't ask her about it, or talk about it. If they get excited about the Eav-oq, they might let something slip to our passengers about the specifics of our business."

And there's no reason Jake has to know why I really decided to help, Facity silently finished for him, understanding more than Dez probably did himself, remembering his "beggars are fine" foray from earlier. She hoped that nothing hurtful would come of Dez's misguided need to impress Jake. Besides being a sweet kid, between the box and the Tosk, Jake had turned out to be very good luck, indeed. She'd hate to lose him.

"Right, of course," she said, taking his arm as he turned back to the transporter-room door. She pasted on a glazed expression and her *chula* eyes, not wanting to seem too happy, her heart skipping gleefully in denial. *The Eav-oq,* as she lived and breathed. It had been well worth getting out of bed.

15

Day 121, morning. We left Ee a few days ago, and things are strange. We're hurrying, for one thing; Dez says we'll be at Idran in less than a month. And I guess our basotile contract fell through. . . . We were going to take care of that on the way, but it seems we've got a clean agenda now, nothing to do but drop off Tosk and Wex and the Kai and then take me home.

So. I've been sticking around my quarters, mostly keeping to myself since we left, claiming the hangover (which was bad, by the way—remind me not to drink again, ever), but I think it's mostly because of this whole prophecy business. I feel . . . strange again, that's a good word. Lost. Angry at being used. Tired of caring. I don't know where to go with it, or how I'm supposed to feel, that everything that's happened to me over the last four months has apparently been about taking Opaka home. It makes everything seem so . . . I don't know, pointless. It makes me feel pointless. I keep trying to work out the specifics, too—if it's true, I'll be going back through the wormhole with Opaka, which I guess means that she'll be coming with me and Facity . . . or I'll be going through with her and Tosk. Or who knows. The Prophets, apparently.

Part of me says so what, I'm free to make my own decisions, I can do whatever I want—and if it just so happens to coincide with some religious writing somewhere about the Emissary's son, big deal. It doesn't mean my life has been plotted out, or that I'm helpless to decide my own fate . . . but there's another part of me that feels totally helpless, and frustrated to the point of screaming. It makes me sorry that I asked Dez to help the Kai, like I'm this willing pawn, participating in my own puppetry, if that's the word. I really wish I could talk to Kas about it, I know she'd understand. And I finally understand a little more about her, I think . . . and maybe Dad, too. When I think back to how it was for him, from the beginning, from the very moment that Kai Opaka told him he was Bajor's Emissary . . . he went through denial, and anger, and even periods of depression, I think, over years. Maybe he finally embraced it not only because it was true, but because he just got tired of worrying about what it all meant, in terms of fate and free will. I don't know, maybe that's stupid. Maybe not.

Anyway, I don't really feel like I can talk about any of this . . . maybe to Dez, but he's been sort of unavailable since we left. Even when I do see him, he seems distant. I wonder if he's angry that I asked him to take on passengers . . . I mean, he's still Dez, he's glad to see me and all, but I can see that there's something on his mind that he doesn't want to discuss, or at least not with me.

And I know that Pif or Facity or Coamis would be happy to listen, but . . .

I know this is going to sound dumb, but I don't want to talk about it to anyone here, because I don't want them to think less of me. I don't even think that they would, it's just . . . it's hard to explain. They're my friends, I know that, but they're new *friends, forged under kind of extraordinary circumstances—Drang, and Stessie dying. Drang was so exciting, it was a very big deal for me, and it's been meaningful* for *me, to be around people who were there, who experienced the same things I did. And then when Stessie died . . . I suddenly felt very close to everyone, because we all had this terrible thing in common, we could all talk about it. What I'm dealing with now, it's not big, it's not exciting or tragic, it's just . . . me. Which isn't embarrassing, I don't mean that. . . .*

What do I mean? It's like—when I think about my relationship with Nog, about some of the boring, stupid things he's seen me through, I'm not self-conscious, I think because it's an entirely reciprocal situation. For all the times he had to sit and listen to me talking about Mardah, or writing, or what I thought about politics or whatever, I had to listen to him complaining about his uncle, or going on about Starfleet. Not big stuff, just stuff. I guess what I'm getting around to is that I don't want my exciting new friends to find out that I'm boring, sometimes. That's going to have to change, I know . . . but at the moment, I think I'll stick to writing.

I should go check on the Kai, make sure she's comfortable and everything; I've put it off as long as I could, and she's probably starting to wonder why I haven't dropped by. She seems like a nice lady, too, so I can't even tell myself that I'm dreading her personally—truth is, I haven't wanted to get drawn into a conversation about Dad, or the Prophets, or my prophecy (which she doesn't even know about, yet, and I'm not sure if I'm going to tell her; as far as she knows, I was caught in a storm and saved by the Even, which is *the truth. Just not all of it). Now that I think of it, I should probably see how Wex and Tosk are doing, too. Wex came by twice yesterday, and once the day before, but I told her I was busy. . . . I'm not being much of a host, am I?*

I'm not much of anything, at the moment, but things will get better, I know that. I wish . . . I wish I knew everything, how about that? That's all.

16

In the days following Ee, as the *Even Odds* traveled to the Idran system, Opaka spent a lot of time walking B Deck and meditating, trying to digest the things Jake had told her about Bajor. So much had happened since she'd left, so many things she never would have expected: Minister Jaro Essa and his failed attempt to seize power and isolate Bajor; the rescue and heroic death of Li Nalas; Winn Adami elected Kai, and her recent disappearance; the resistance fighter, Shakaar Edon, becoming First Minister; Bareil Antos's death; the brief stir created by the return of Akorem Laan and his claim to title of Emissary; the rediscovery of B'hala; the foretold but incomplete Reckoning; Benjamin Sisko's marriage and the conception of his second child, shortly before his disappearance; contact with the Dominion, who for a time had successfully pitted the major powers of the Alpha Quadrant against one another, leading to years of conflict and death on a scale Opaka could scarcely bring herself to contemplate, culminating with the near-genocide of the Cardassian people. . . .

It was a lot to think about, to celebrate and mourn, and as eager as she was to see about the Tosk's strange mission, to go home again, it was also a relief that the journey was to take almost a month. She was thankful for the time, to accept the things that had come to pass for Bajor.

When Jake signaled at her door, Opaka had just returned from a walk, her second of the day though it was barely midmorning. She was coming to realize that while her heart was relatively calm, she was already feeling physically restless after only a short time on the ship. In the years since she'd left Bajor, particularly the last few, she'd become accustomed to a fairly active lifestyle. As Kai, she'd walked in gardens; on the Sen Ennis moon, she'd tended them. Since leaving the moon, she'd dealt with everything from caring for the sick to watching large groups of children, and though she certainly felt it in her joints and muscles at night, she'd come to enjoy the exercise. And miss it, it seemed.

"Jake, come in," Opaka said warmly, pleased to see his reluctant face at her door . . . and guessing, from his expression, that he was finally ready to talk to her about the one topic he'd carefully avoided since they'd left Ee, twelve days earlier.

Jake sat, and accepted a cup of tea, and politely asked after her comfort. Opaka reassured him that she was well, that everyone she'd met had been remarkably pleasant . . . and waited. After a few moments, Jake cleared his throat softly, his pleasant brown face a study of tension.

"Why haven't you asked me about my father?" he

asked, holding her gaze for only a second before dropping his own. "About what happened to him?"

Opaka took a deep breath, hoping that she would be able to comfort him. "I thought it might be a painful subject for you," she said gently.

Jake seemed surprised. "But he's in the Temple. He's with the Prophets, and everybody's been telling me how wonderful that is. For a Bajoran . . . I mean, isn't that a good thing?"

"For him, yes, I believe so," Opaka said. "And I rejoice for him. But for you . . ." She shook her head. "Your feelings are your own. If I were in your stead, the last thing I'd want to hear is how someone else feels positively affected by my personal loss, or what the religious significance is."

"But I thought . . . you're the *Kai*," Jake said, as though that explained something, and Opaka had to smile.

"And so I don't care that you miss him?" she asked lightly. "To me, to Bajor, he is the Emissary. But he's your father."

"I didn't mean . . ." he began, then shook his head, smiling self-consciously. After a few seconds, his smile faded. "Actually, I guess I did. I thought that you'd want to tell me how blessed he is, about what the Prophets have planned for him, about the great tapestry of life."

"You overestimate my awareness of Their plans," Opaka said, aching for the scarcely disguised bitterness in his voice.

"But . . . I thought you had visions," Jake said. "You said you've dreamed things . . . and you told my father that he was the Emissary."

Again, the barely restrained distress . . . and she thought of her own son, and how it must have been for him during his all-too-brief life, to be the child of someone driven to seek a spiritual truth. Had he privately experienced feelings of jealousy, fears of being left behind? He was Bajoran, his faith had been strong, but had that mattered, when she had been in retreat, when he had wanted his mother?

You can only be honest, she thought, feeling regrets of her own, wondering if any parents really knew how to balance their own lives with the lives of their children . . . and if any child understood the depths of such struggling.

"The Prophets do have ways of letting Their will be known," Opaka said. "For me, there have been visions, and dreams . . . but those are rare, indeed, and not always specific. To walk with the Prophets . . . it's about truth, about finding the things that are meant to be . . . and we find the truth inside our own *pagh,* the vast majority of the time. I'm afraid that faith in Them is usually quite undramatic."

Jake nodded noncommittally, his expression carefully blank, and Opaka quickly continued, tempering her feeling for the Prophets with empathy for the young man in front of her.

"But as I said, my feelings are my own, and yours are surely different. And I'm sorry for your pain, Jake. You didn't ask for your father to be the Emissary, and I regret the unfairness of it to you."

As Jake dropped his gaze again, working to control the hurt that showed so clearly on his face, Opaka felt a touch of wonder at her words, at her feelings, at the changes implied. Seven years earlier she would have been determined to at least say that the Prophets had plans for him, too, that Their love extended to everyone who wanted it . . . but she was no longer the same person she had been. As Kai, she had been responsible for the spiritual guidance of Bajor. Since leaving home, she had learned only to be responsible for herself, and for the touch of her hand or the kind word she expressed to the individuals she encountered. How had it taken her so very long, to understand that truth was a matter of perspective?

"I . . ." Jake began, then began again. "I was looking for him, in the wormhole. I read this prophecy, that I would go into the wormhole, and come back out with . . . with one of the Chosen. I thought it was going to be him."

At the naked longing in his voice, Opaka felt her eyes well with tears. "I'm sorry," she said again. "I'm so sorry."

"It's not your fault," he said, after a moment. "It's just how things are, I guess."

They sat for a moment, silent. As much as she wanted to go to him, to embrace him, Opaka held back, respectful of his private reckoning and his space. After a moment, he managed a faint smile.

"If the prophecy is correct, at least we'll be home in time for my little brother or sister's birthday," he said lightly, and while there was no real humor in his face, in his voice, she could see that it was what he needed to do. A distancing from a lost hope, a recognition that life went ever onward. The questions that she had about the prophecy would wait.

"That will be lovely," Opaka said, smiling back at him. "Tell me, has Kasidy chosen names?"

She could see the relief in his eyes as he answered, and was glad that she could do at least that much for him.

They were only a few days from their goal, according to Tosk, and Dez sat on the bridge, staring at the passing stars on the viewscreen, thinking about Jake. Once they were done with the Eav-oq world—Dez couldn't help thinking of it that way—Jake and Facity would be heading back through the wormhole, to pick up his things . . . and Dez was thinking that he ought to go with them, to meet Jake's friends, to reconnect with Jake. Keeping quiet about the Eav-oq had put something of a strain on their relationship, and he figured that going with Jake to the station would be a good way to fix things . . . but he didn't really *want* to go, and he wasn't sure why. He'd been thinking about it a lot, and the best he could come up with was that he knew that he should, and he hated having to do things he was supposed to do.

And . . . the vague resentment he'd been feeling toward Jake wasn't helping. Why did the boy have to be so insistent about the charity thing? Dez had tossed off a comment about it weeks before, to assure Jake's interest in staying on, and he just kept bringing it up.

What does he want? I offer him an exciting future, a position on one of the best crews in the quadrant doing anything he wants, and he puts me in a position where I have no choice but to pretend, to lie. All I've ever wanted was to help, and look where it's gotten me; I can't even tell my own crew what we're doing.

And yet . . . he couldn't really blame Jake, not entirely. He'd played his part. Dez could still so clearly remember finding Jake on his broken shuttle, freezing, still clutching the pitiful words that had almost been his last. All Jake had wanted was his father, and Dez knew how that felt, he *understood.* He'd wanted to provide that security for Jake, to step in where Jake's father had failed, where his own father had failed. He still wanted that . . . so why was it so hard? What was he doing wrong?

"Srral, could you take a look at something for me?"

Dez looked up at the slight concern he heard in Facity's voice. It was just the two of them on the bridge; Fac had been killing time listening to random communications, but she'd apparently walked over to the sensor array at some point.

"What is it?" Dez asked, standing. There hadn't been any alert signals.

"What is it?" Srral echoed, a half second later.

Facity shrugged as Dez moved to lean over her shoulder. "It's probably nothing. I just looked up, and I thought I saw a slight subspace variance in the prox scan, but it seems to be gone, now."

"You are correct," Srral said. *"For point eight seven seconds, there was a temporal shift in subspace density, at approximately 1630 kilometers port, bearing—"*

"We see that," Dez said, frowning at the freeze that Srral had pulled up to Fac's screen. The panels wouldn't sound an alert on anything singular under a second, they passed too much random debris . . . but the sensors had picked up a flash of something big, that appeared to be moving at warp. "What does it mean?"

"Insufficient data to be certain," Srral said.

"Reflection?" Facity asked. "It's either that, or . . . do the Hunters use cloaking tech?"

"No," Dez said. They were advanced enough, but they didn't bother with it. The same with the Dominion, and they wouldn't stalk the *Even,* they'd probably just open fire . . .

. . . except hadn't he heard that Thijmen was looking into buying a cloak ship? Rym Thijmen, probably the *Even*'s main rival, ran an aggressive retrieval crew, they'd snatched a number of jobs away from the *Even . . .*

. . . and how many people did that Tosk go spilling his story to before he told it to Jake? Was it possible that Thijmen had heard about the Tosk's experience, and was following the *Even* to get to the Eav-oq crystals?

Dez looked at the scan another moment, then sighed, shaking his head. It was about a thousand times more likely that they'd caught a reflection, a bounced signal. He was digging for trouble where there was none, tired of his own boring self-analysis, tired of hassling with the whole Jake equation.

"Reflection," he said. "Srral, tune the scans up to alert at two-tenths of a second, at least until we hit Tosk's planet."

He smiled at Fac, then returned to his chair, sinking back into his silent reverie. It occurred to him, not for the first time, that things would have to change once they reached the Eav-oq world. Although he hadn't announced it directly, everyone knew by now that he was planning to head down to the surface with a team . . . and if they found what Dez was hoping to find—evidence that it was the Eav-oq world—Jake would figure out in about a heartbeat why he'd been so willing to transport the Tosk.

Dez shifted in his chair, irritated that the thought bothered him, suddenly glad that Eav-oq was only a few days away. It was time to stop pretending, it was time for Jake to accept how things were going to be, to accept *him.* And if Jake was disappointed . . . well, Dez wasn't his father, it wasn't his job to be Jake's role model, or to keep Jake from being disillusioned by the universe.

Besides, he'll get over it, Dez thought, watching the stars slip past. *We all do.*

17

TOSK STEPPED OFF of his ship and breathed deeply, feeling the slick rocks beneath his feet, smelling the wet-soil smell of the morning air. He was relieved beyond measure to be back at the small and empty planet, to be looking out across the gentle rifts and peaks of stone. On the way down through the ice storms, his vessel had suffered a terrible beating, he'd even taken a possibly serious hit to his warp drive that he'd have to see about before leaving, but his relief had nothing to do with having survived the trip. He'd lost grasp of his original purpose here, but it was almost over . . . and then he would be Hunted again, only Hunted.

It will be my time once more.

His pursuers need never even know that he had faltered from his duty. Though not ideal, it was not unheard-of for Hunters to lose track of Tosk for months at a time. The crystal had made him act unpredictably; he was certain that once the Other matter was settled, he would revert to patterns he wasn't even aware of, and the Hunters would once again find his trail.

Behind him, the roar of the second vessel. He turned to watch the *Even Odds*'s dropship settle to the ground, and he hurried to greet them as soon as the engines rumbled to a stop, as the doors opened and the crew members began departing the ship.

Captain Dezavrim had insisted on escorting Opaka Sulan to the surface, and had brought a number of the crew, as well, presumably to conduct a salvage survey. Besides the captain and first officer there were Jake, Pifko, Brad-ahk'la, Glessin, Neane, and Coamis, each of them wearing equipment belts. Tosk didn't care, he only cared that Opaka, too, was departing the vessel, Wex at her side, that she had agreed to come and was now standing on the surface of the unnamed planet, brushing a tendril of silvery hair behind one ear as she looked around. The others filed out, talking among themselves about the fierce ice storms and the planet's apparent emptiness, gradually falling silent as they turned their collective attention to Tosk's approach.

Excited, ready to be relieved of his second purpose, Tosk stopped in front of Opaka . . . and didn't know what to do next. There was something else, there had to be something else because he still felt it, but he didn't know what it was. Opaka looked up at him, smiling slightly, waiting.

I brought her back. I brought her, what else is there?

A full minute passed, Tosk staring at Opaka, waiting, his desperation growing . . . and still, nothing.

"Well, that's anticlimactic," the Aarruri stated dryly, and someone told him to be quiet.

"I don't *know,*" Tosk said pleadingly, looking down

into her kind face, dreading that it might not yet be over . . . and he saw her eyes widen. She turned away, closing her eyes, one hand pressed to her chest, the other reaching out. She took a few steps, and a few deep breaths. After a moment, she opened her eyes again, smiling a slightly puzzled smile.

"I . . . It's that way," she said, gesturing vaguely west, looking at Tosk again. "Do you feel it?"

"What?" the captain asked quickly.

Opaka shook her head. "I really couldn't say. I sense . . . *pagh.* It's a kind of spiritual energy, but I've never . . . I've never in my life had such a strong sense of it."

Tosk walked several steps to the west as she spoke, and *did* feel something, but he would not have known it as a spiritual energy. It was more like a . . . lessening, similar to what he'd felt on Ee . . . as though a vast noise in his head was becoming softer, an anxiety falling away.

The first officer was holding up a reader, frowning at the sensory device's readings. "Nothing, same as on the ship. According to this, there's nothing out there."

"Can we walk to it?" the captain asked Opaka, and again she shook her head.

"I don't know how far it is, but it's so powerful . . . it can't be far," she said.

She turned back to Tosk, smiling up at him. "Shall we see?"

He nodded, and together, they started walking, picking their way across the algae-wet rocks beneath the cool sky. After a moment, the others followed.

The *pagh* was like a river, flowing over them from somewhere ahead, an invisible outpouring of spiritual energy unlike any Opaka had ever known. It reminded her of the monastery, before she'd left Bajor, the feel in the air at the weekly mass meditations . . . but even then she'd felt only a fraction of what she now sensed. Her whole body tingled as she walked, flushed with the subtle but distinctive rush of life.

She occasionally leaned on Tosk for support as they navigated their way over and through the rocks, Opaka letting her feelings guide them. Wex caught up to them and did what she could to help, but the going was unsteady, the rocks treacherous with moist algae.

Behind them, she could hear Jake trying to explain his understanding of *pagh* to his friends, and a few skeptical whispers and jokes in response. Opaka liked the *Even*'s crew, overall, particularly Glessin and Neane, who had each privately expressed to her a personal interest in spiritual seeking during their journey . . . but she had not found them to be the most patient people she'd ever met.

No matter, no matter . . . She could feel the *pagh* getting stronger, its source very close, but there seemed to be nothing in sight to account for it. The landscape was an endless expanse of stone, and while there were rises and dips in the rocky sea, there were no buildings, nothing large enough to contain the life it would take to create such an outpouring. *Unless* . . .

Could they, whoever they were, be underground? Because of the environment's sameness, it was hard to see, but she thought they were walking toward the edge of a low cliff, a drop-off, really, only a few meters high. A few stumbling steps later, she was sure . . . but again, because of the conformity of the stones, she couldn't see a way to get down without jumping.

She looked back, and was surprised to see that they'd

already lost sight of the ships among the stones, the small Tosk vessel and the larger dropship. The crew of the *Even Odds* were all watching her, their expressions ranging from polite interest to curiosity to hunger, the hunger coming from the captain and his first officer. They were searching for something salvageable, she understood, and hadn't yet found it.

"We have to find a way down," Opaka said, and gestured at the drop-off, still fifty meters away. "I think there must be a cave opening, or—"

"Pif, why don't you see—" Dez said, before she had finished, and before *he* had finished the Aarruri had darted away to the south, angling toward the drop-off at a scrambling run. His feet danced and skittered across the slippery rock, but he made excellent progress; in seconds, he angled downward and then seemed to disappear, dropping out of sight.

"Quite the runner," Wex said, her eyebrow ridges arched, and Tosk silently nodded agreement. Wex was an unusual, solitary girl. Opaka had still not decided what to make of her, but she sensed a strong and gentle spirit in the young Trelian; she was not unhappy that Wex would be returning with her to Bajor.

Less than a minute after he'd disappeared, Pifko reappeared, north of where Opaka and the others were standing, and close enough for her to hear him panting lightly.

"You're right, there's a cave down there," he said, grinning. "There's a gradual slope to the south, but this path is a lot faster."

"Not as fast as you," Dez said, smiling, and Pif grinned impossibly wider. "Let's do it."

* * *

The path was only a tumble of slick stones, but they managed to get down without anyone falling, much to Jake's relief . . . and there was the cave, a long, dark, narrow fissure in the frozen flow of rock, a dozen meters from where the "path" leveled out.

As the last of the crew carefully made their way down, Jake noticed that Facity and Dez were immersed in some private conversation, standing away from everyone else. It was the third time he'd witnessed one of their huddles in less than an hour; they'd done it back on the *Even* while the crew got ready, and again after landing, as everyone was getting off. They were both wound up about something, and the whole crew knew it, and still, they weren't telling.

Jake looked away as everyone reassembled outside the cave, reminding himself that he was just one of the crew, that no one else knew, either, that there was no reason to feel slighted. Whatever they were up to, he'd just have to wait along with everyone else until they decided to share.

Facity started to take a reading on the cave . . . and Opaka simply walked inside, Tosk right behind her. Wex glanced back at the others and then hurriedly followed.

"No screaming," Pif said, a beat later. "Guess it's safe."

Jake glared at him, but Facity was nodding, looking at the reader.

"Small and empty," she said, and sighed, looking at Dez with an expression Jake couldn't read.

"Glessin, Brad, stay out here," Dez said, turning on his light as he stepped through the narrow opening. The others fell in behind him, the cold damp of the cave making Jake shiver as he turned on his own light.

Though the opening was tight, the natural cave opened up on the other side, a tall, narrow room defined by the bobbing lights of the *Even*'s crew, and by the sliver of natural light that crept in through the entrance. Opaka had walked to the point farthest from the opening and had her hands pressed against the stone wall, her eyes closed. Tosk and Wex both stood close by, watching her.

As the last of the crew filed inside, Opaka dropped her hands and turned, looking confused and exhilarated at once. "I still feel it, I can feel it, but . . . there's no one here."

"False wall?" Dez asked. Facity held up her reader, but Opaka answered him first.

"No, I don't think so," she said. "The energy is unfocused . . . but this is where we're supposed to be, this place is where it's all coming from."

Dez looked frustrated. "All right, let's have a look around. Everybody pick a piece of a wall, look for anything unusual, anything that doesn't belong."

The crew spread out. Jake turned his own light toward the back wall and started looking, focusing on the tiny sphere of light as he worked it up and down, seeing nothing but plain rock. A few scratches, a few cracks, a lot of dust, but nothing he'd call unusual.

"There are some rocks sticking out over here," Neane said. "I can't quite reach them. . . ."

"Rocks?" Pif's voice came out of the dark. "That's *amazing!* I haven't seen anything like that—"

"Quiet, Pif," Dez snapped. "Just keep looking."

They worked in silence for a moment, Jake going over the same places, wondering what it was Dez expected to find . . . and how long he'd been expecting it. It would explain a few things. Dez had been so quick to invite Tosk aboard, had talked Facity into it without a struggle, even though Jake knew they'd fought about his coming aboard . . . he'd been avoiding talking to Jake ever since, and now, today, he and Facity were both acting like they'd planned on finding something—

"What about the writing?" Tosk asked.

Jake turned, saw that everyone else's lights were suddenly trained on Tosk. Tosk squinted against the brightness, and pointed to where wall met floor.

They all turned their lights to where he was pointing. Dez crouched next to the wall, putting one hand out to support himself, shining his own light along the base of the wall. As the lights spread out, searching for the writing Tosk had seen, Jake saw nothing but scuffed and scratched rock. There did seem to be a lot of scratches, some of them even shaped oddly. . . . Struggling to make something out of them, Jake saw what looked like a symbol in ancient Bajoran, three crossed lines with another line on top. It meant "bird," he thought, and immediately felt stupid. *That's* not *ancient Bajoran.*

"It's not writing," Dez said. "Trust me, I know. It's much too random."

"Yes, it is," Tosk said, leaning over. "There, it says, 'and from the now to the beginning, in order touch the eras—' You must move the light, I can't . . ."

Tosk trailed off, straightening abruptly. "Tosk only know *ochshea-hos,* the Hunter's word."

He turned to Opaka, an expression on his face that Jake hadn't seen, didn't know he was capable of. Tosk was overwhelmed with excitement, his eyes shining, even bulging with it, his mouth curved into a tiny "o" of shock and understanding.

"That is it!" he said, looking from Opaka back to the rock floor again. "I know the language there, that is what I was supposed to do, that's the last part of my purpose! To bring you to see it, to know what it says!"

Opaka touched his arm, smiling. "Then you've fulfilled your purpose," she said gently.

"What else does it say?" Dez asked eagerly, turning his light back to the wall—

—and Glessin's sharp voice filled the small cave, a single word that stopped everything.

"Hunters."

18

THE QUAD OF *Ochshea* had been forced to circle around the small and stormy planetoid, away from the ship that had carried their quarry, using the time to mask their own ship's outer hull signature. Their shields now projected a series of readings that mimicked a cloud of icy debris, allowing the quad to draw close; not a perfect cover, but near enough, provided the Tosk's comrades did not notice that the cloud's drift patterns repeated every five cycles. It would not do to tip the Tosk to their presence, not now, when they were so close after so long. It had been many weeks since they'd last spotted the prey, the days barren and uninteresting by the end in spite of an extremely promising beginning.

No matter, thought Elshada, as they stepped to the particulate transmitters on their hidden ship. Elshada was leader, and felt a great pride that they had tracked the Tosk so successfully. It had been difficult, tracing rumors on the trader's planet, scanning the dark, silent seas for traces of the ships that had docked there when their quarry had last been seen—it had been mere chance that they had stumbled across an acquaintance to the wise woman, who told them that she had left for the Alpha Quadrant with their Tosk at her side—but today was their day, he could feel it, and he knew that the others could feel it, too. Their visors were polished and in place, their bows charged and missiled, the victory shroud packed. It would be today.

Elshada nodded at the others, secure in the knowledge that they were ready. Bryn and Halada would transport closer to the Tosk ship, while he and Yimis tracked from the last clear read, a small cave. It was unfortunate that the small planet offered so little cover, but perhaps an unhindered kill was for the best. Elshada knew his team, knew that their frustrations—as well as his own—could be sustained no longer. This Tosk had been away from their sight for too long.

Together, the quad stepped into the beams of transmission, stepping again onto the surface of the planet in two groups. Elshada took in the environment at a glance, and was pleased. Prime target distance.

"Stand ready," Elshada said, his heart thumping with pleasure, his senses alive and alert. Yimis raised his bow. In front of them was a rock ridge, two beings standing near a dark fissure in the rock, neither armed. At the sight of the Hunters, the smaller of the two spoke into an earpiece. Elshada couldn't hear his words, but they were close enough that he could see their expressions of shock, their faces telling the story of the Tosk inside the cave. His visor's sensory read told the same story.

Excellent! Elshada raised his own bow, smiling

tightly, feeling the glory of life as he waited for Tosk to emerge.

Tosk spun and ran. Behind him, someone shouted, but he was gone, through the fissure, invisible before the light of day touched him.

Two of them, southwest at fifty meters, *others must be at my ship* but he had no choice, he had to get off the planet. He turned north and ran faster.

"Tosk! I have him!"

They wore their visors, they had their weapons drawn, and Tosk could hear the excitement in the lead Hunter's voice, and was proud . . . but they knew he was present, and there was nowhere to hide.

Tosk sprinted, parallel to the line of the cave, wishing there were a way to mask the sound of his feet against the wet rock, that there were real cover to be had. With their visors on, they only had to scan for heat.

"Wait!" someone shouted. It was the captain. "You don't understand, we need him—"

Tosk leapt, came down four meters away, using the cover of voice to conceal his landing and was running again—

—and saw a dancing green light sweep the stones in front of him, a visor scope. They were closing in. Tosk leapt again, *won't make it—*

—and heard the sharp, electrical *cra-ack* of a Hunter's bow firing, and saw the blinding light, and felt most of his lower left leg disintegrate.

Tosk came down on his right and immediately tried to leap again, the pain bearable, the damage too great. He fell, and heard a Hunter laugh, and heard the most glorious, most wonderful words he could imagine.

"You die with honor, Tosk!"

Tosk just had time to smile, to feel whole.

Cra-ack—

They all watched in numb silence as the Hunters gathered, four of them, and carefully approached the Tosk. He was very much dead; Facity had made it out of the cave just in time to see the second shot burn a fist-sized hole through his chest.

Two of the four Hunters solemnly wrapped the blasted body in ceremonial red, the same red as their uniforms. All four bowed their heads for a moment, and one of them spoke a few words—and then they were carrying the Tosk away, chatting agreeably, congratulating the Hunter who had dealt the final blow. One of them stopped long enough to tell the stunned watchers that the first half of the Hunt had been excellent, though it had fallen off until the very end, and to ask if they knew anything about that. Dez had snarled a furious negative, the rest of the crew too shaken or angry to respond. The Hunter had expressed indifference to his emotion, and gone to catch up to his group, their red-clad bodies sharply defined against the blue-green rocks as they walked away.

Facity watched the last Hunter hurrying to join his fellow killers, watched with the others as the red finally disappeared behind a curve of rocks and didn't reappear. She had to resist an urge to scream. She couldn't believe it, it was like a joke; just as the Tosk was going to tell them what the impossible writing actually said, was going to offer up some proof that the empty rock had once belonged to the Eav-oq, the Hunters had arrived.

"That's just great," Dez said, a look of disgust on his face. "Could the timing have been any better?"

Jake stared at him, his gaze wounded and disbelieving, but Dez didn't seem to notice, turning and stalking back into the cave. Facity saw that while the entire crew was unhappy, Opaka and Jake both seemed particularly upset, or were at least having a harder time disguising their feelings. Alphies. It was a sad business, but the Tosk were bred for it, after all.

"Brad, Glessin, if you could keep watch for another minute," Facity said, and sighed. "The rest of you, let's see if we can find anything else." They'd have to go back to the ship, see if the text translator could figure out what the scratches meant . . . and she was already dreading what would certainly be a long, drawn-out, and probably pointless production. They'd have to take casts of the scratches for depth as well as shape . . . and she was willing to bet that there was no real writing on the wall, or at least nothing that they'd be able to prove. It had been something the Tosk had seen because of the crystal he'd inadvertently touched.

And I don't see any more of those lying around, she thought sourly, as the silent crew moved back into the cave, Wex and Opaka following. Except for the Tosk's "writing," she hadn't seen anything at all to suggest that they were on a planet that had ever been inhabited, by anyone. The only good news so far was that Dez wouldn't have to admit to Jake that he'd helped the Tosk for less than altruistic reasons . . . though considering the look Jake had given him after his timing comment, Facity thought that there was already a little disillusionment going on there. Dez had only said what everyone had probably been thinking, anyway, but Jake was a sensitive young man . . . and unfortunately for them all, it didn't look like he was planning to toughen up any time soon.

Facity stepped back through the opening after Wex, working to let her own disappointment go, finding that it wasn't too difficult. It wasn't in the Wadi nature to take such things too seriously; not every gamble paid off, it was a fact of life. The *Even* had canceled their contract with the Rodulans to clear their schedule, but that wasn't so great a loss. Witnessing the death of a Tosk might be the worst of it.

"What are those?" Pif asked, bringing her attention back to the job at hand. He was shining his light on some protruding rocks high on the wall.

"Rocks," Neane said lightly, "the ones I saw earlier. Amazing, aren't they?"

Before Pif could retort, Dez shushed him, training his own light on the rocks. There were eight, nine of them, small and almost flat, set at about eye level for Dez in two curved, vertical lines. Each stuck out only a few centimeters, was roughly the size and shape of a smashed ferment-grape; if not for the loose formation, too symmetrical for a random occurrence, Facity doubted that anyone would have noticed them at all.

Dez walked over and brushed at them . . . and came away with a handful of dust. The stones beneath were different colors.

"Get Brad in here," Dez said, as the rest of the crew gathered around. Facity leaned back outside and asked Brad to come in, wondering if the rocks were actually jewels, wondering if they'd found something worthwhile, after all.

"That one's kejelious," Jake was saying, as Facity and Brad stepped back inside. Opaka was nodding.

"And that pink one's temonis," she said. "I had a box made from it when I was a child."

Facity didn't know geology, but neither sounded expensive. Brad stepped in to look, touching a few of them before shaking her head.

"Most of these aren't stone," she rumbled.

Jake was nodding. "Kejelious is a kind of clay," he said. "So's, ah, grem. That greenish one. I think the red one is, too . . . I forget the name."

"How do you know all these?" Pif asked.

"B'hala," Jake said, still squinting at the lines. "It looks like they're all materials the ancient Bajorans used. I spent a lot of time cataloguing fragments."

Brad pointed at a dark blue stone, at the bottom of the second line. "That one's semiprecious, it's called dezomin. But the grade . . . it's not worth prying out of the wall."

Facity sighed. So much for walking away with a handful of gems. She turned to Opaka, who hadn't said anything since before Tosk's discovery of the scratch writing.

"Are you getting any kind of, ah, feeling about this?" she asked.

"I still feel the *pagh*," Opaka said, "but nothing new or different. Though I think it quite unusual that these pieces apparently coincide with materials once used on Bajor . . . don't you?"

Facity nodded, repressing another sigh. Except for feeling her way to the cave, Opaka didn't seem to have much use. And the connection to her homeworld—ninety thousand light-years away—*was* unusual, but not bizarre. Considering the Anomaly was only three light years away, Idran and Bajor weren't all that far apart.

"What's that one?" Brad asked Jake.

"Not sure, but I can tell you it's from the end of the Sh'dama Age," Jake said . . . and as he spoke, Facity started to get an idea, thinking of what Tosk had said, and Opaka . . . and she looked at Dez, and saw that he'd already gotten it.

". . . and from the now to the beginning, in order touch the eras . . ." Ages?

Instructions. The wording was strange, but not even particularly cryptic, telling them to touch the materials in reverse chronological order, dating from the present—or the present when the device had been built—to the beginning, presumably the beginning of time, or culture.

"Jake," Dez said urgently, and when Jake turned away from the lines of stones, Facity could see that he had exactly the same idea.

"Now to the beginning, isn't that what he said?" Jake asked, his eyes bright with dawning, and Facity started to grin. It seemed that Tosk had told them just enough.

"Before Aclim was Sh'dama . . . and before that was Eyisla . . ."

"Wait," Jake said, staring at the stones, frowning in concentration. "That's . . . kejelious, then dezomin, *then* grem . . ."

Opaka waited, filled with wonder at what they'd found, still flushed and tingling from the overwhelming sensation of so much energy in one place. Even the terrible death of poor Tosk hadn't wiped away the physical excitement, much as it saddened her. Such a brutal death for such a simple creature, who had harmed no one. She prayed that the Hunters would someday learn to respect life . . . and she hoped very much that Tosk had heard the Hunter say that his death would be honorable. Opaka didn't believe in such things, but knew that it had been important to Tosk.

The others in the small cave had fallen silent, obviously wanting to let her and Jake concentrate. She knew the Ages by heart, but had never seen some of the materials that Jake had seen, working at B'hala.

"And the, ah, Tumika Age was first, right?" Jake asked, and Opaka nodded.

"Okay," he said. "Then we're ready."

He turned and looked at Dez. "There's one here I don't know, but I'm going to guess it predates the others, whatever it is." He smiled a little. "If I'm wrong, I guess I can do it over again, put it somewhere else."

The captain nodded, and Opaka felt a shiver of anticipation. What would happen when all the pieces were touched? Jake, Wex, Tosk, herself . . . they'd been brought together to do this one thing, to solve this puzzle in a place that felt full of life, but was lifeless. So many others had been affected by the undertaking, from the Sen Ennis to the *Even*'s crew, all to do as the Tosk had been directed, as the Prophets had foreseen.

Jake touched the first stone, then the second and third, naming them in a whisper. Opaka and the others watched, no one seeming to breathe as Jake hesitated, touched and hesitated again.

". . . grem . . . ashflake . . ." He sighed, reaching for the last stone. ". . . and whatever this one is."

Jake touched the last piece, a soft, white rock . . . and then everything changed, in the blink of an eye. Somebody gasped, and somebody else let out a short, sharp yelp of sound, but Opaka didn't, couldn't see who. Her senses were flooded, the *pagh* exploding in intensity, so much of it washing over and through her that she felt like she was floating.

And oh, the singing!

The tiny, dark cave was gone, just like that. There was luminous white light, coming from everywhere, and they were standing in a great chamber, towering and massive, with rows and rows of strange beings lining the walls, sitting or standing on wide ascending steps, the beings hunched over and pink, long arms wrapped around long bodies. There were hundreds, perhaps thousands of them, all of them perfectly still, and making a beautiful sound. The sound should have been overwhelming with so many of them but it wasn't, it was soft and lilting, a hum, serene and yet exultant, that went on and on.

Opaka turned, saw that that the front of the chamber was glassed, that it looked out upon a small but beautiful city stretching out to the west. There were paths of flowers and stones twining around a number of tall, curved buildings, a few of them shaped like stars, multi-limbed like the creatures who sat in the rows, singing. She saw that Glessin was inside the chamber now, that he was both frightened and excited, and she saw that the others around her wore similar expressions of awe and amazement and fear.

How can they fear? Can't they feel it? The creatures were meditating, they were joined in spirit, and radiating such wondrous peace. . . . She'd never felt anything remotely like it.

Opaka turned again, saw that one of the singing creatures closest to them had ceased its tuneful chant. It unfolded itself, standing, stretching out long, willowy pink limbs, seven that Opaka could see. Its body was slender and tubelike, and very tall, half a meter taller than the captain. It opened a single eye that stretched across its narrow face, a soft gray, which it blinked slowly, which curved upward like a smile as it saw them. With a last sinewy stretch, it broke away from the singers, propelling itself forward over a dancing tangle of limbs, its eye curving even more as it approached.

It stopped in front of them and started to speak, a beautiful language that the translators didn't know, the creature's voice deep and calm, the sound it made seemingly continuous. It spread its upper limbs wide, and Opaka stepped forward, ignoring Wex's warning hand on her shoulder, ignoring the sound of a signaling communicator and Dez's soft conversation. The translators picked up the very last words as she, too, opened her arms, and embraced the radiant creature.

". . . welcome to you, my sister," it said, and its flesh was warm, and smelled like the sea.

Two things had happened, simultaneously, both basically impossible. Prees and Srral were on the bridge when the two things occurred . . . and they happened so suddenly, and constituted so immense a change, that Prees could only stare mutely at the viewing screen while Srral offered up statistics, as everyone on the ship called at once to report that the Wa had leaked out of the subdeck. Feg said there were a number of small birdlike animals laughing in his bathroom, Aslylgof had been showered with drops of something like honey, the Wadi art appraisers were calling to say that a small panel of the bulkhead wall on C had turned into a mouth and was chanting. Triv and Pri'ak were both reporting strange tastes and smells . . . and still, Prees was dumbstruck, could only stare at the planet below, and at the stars all around.

"Repeat, Srral," she said finally, feeling breathless.

"We are now less than thirty light-minutes from the Anomaly," Srral said calmly. *"Using this ship as a point of reference, a vast region of space, including all celestial objects therein, has rotated thirty-eight degrees bearing two-seven-two on an axis approximately five light-years away. We are now three-point-three light-years from our previous position."*

Not possible. Space didn't just move like that . . . but it had, and all at once. They were still orbiting the planet, but both they and it had traveled, apparently along with the entire Idran system and who knew what else. And it had happened in the blink of an eye.

"And the planet?" she asked, studying the drifting ice that still swirled around it, *not at* all *possible, their atmosphere would have been ripped away and we'd all be dead, everyone should be dead. . . .*

"Is now showing over a thousand living beings, no matching biosignature on file, concentrated at the landing site," Srral said. As it spoke, a smell like freshly baked bread filled the bridge. *"There are a series of buildinglike structures surrounding the area."*

A city appearing, beings included, as a huge region of space shifted from one place to another, as the Wa erupted. Prees reached for the com unit on the arm of her seat as one of the bridge walls changed color and the switches on the science-station monitor began to sing.

"Are you sure?" Dez asked, keeping his voice low. Opaka was hugging the pink creature.

"Fairly," Prees said, her tone mild, a bit shocked. *"Srral says the sensor arrays are all functioning prop-*

erly . . . and I can see it, Dez. We've moved. And the Anomaly is now inside the system."

"What about the Wa? Are you in any danger?"

There was a pause. *"Negative,"* Prees said. *"The internal sensors say the Wa is starting to recede, drawing back to the subdeck."*

That was something. "Keep me posted," Dez said. "I'll get back to you when we can talk." Now was definitely not the time. As intriguing, as insane as the concept of shifting space was, Dez had no doubt that the source of it was standing in front of him, hugging the elderly Bajoran . . . and Dez's sights were set on making friends.

When Opaka finally released the pink creature, it stepped back and Dez immediately stepped in, smiling, explaining that the translators hadn't worked for most of its brief speech. The language was apparently entirely too strange. Pretty, though, Dez thought, almost like singing.

"I will tell you again," the creature said pleasantly, curling its long, tentacle-like limbs around itself. "My name is Itu, and I welcome you, and thank you for bringing the Eav'oq back into the living time. The Eav'oq are my people, and they share my undying gratitude. We are young in the care of the Siblings, who watch over us all with Their Eyes of Light. We have been waiting for one of the Siblings' Chosen to be found, to come to us and tell us that the persecution is no more."

Itu curved its eye at Opaka. "You are Chosen, my sister beneath the Siblings, I feel Their sight upon you. We are united."

Dez couldn't stop smiling. Not only had they found the lost world of the Eav'oq—not the Eav-oq, as it turned out, but the Eav'oq—they had found the whole damned species, and the leader of said species was extremely grateful to the crew of the *Even Odds* for waking them up.

Well, sort of waking them up, Dez thought, looking around the giant chamber at the motionless, humming creatures. Unbelievable. And what Prees had told him . . . he had more questions than he could count.

"The Siblings," Opaka said, nodding as if she understood. "I . . . we call them the Prophets."

"They are surely as one," Itu said, and though Opaka seemed somewhat unnerved by the statement, she only nodded, managing a smile. Itu turned its curved eye to look at the crew. "Is the one who found the search key among you? The crystal?"

"No," Opaka said, her smile fading. "He has passed, Itu. He was killed after translating the instructions you left."

"Killed?" Itu asked, his eye seeming to expand slightly. "How is this?"

"His death . . ." Opaka seemed to search for words. "Representatives from his culture came to claim him in a ritual of hunting," she said finally. "We are saddened . . . but he passed as he would have wished."

Itu's voice was sympathetic. "I mourn with you. And I regret not being able to meet him, to extend our recognition of his help."

"You say 'him,' " Pif spoke up. "Do the Eav'oq have, ah, sexes?"

Facity shot a death-look at the Aarruri, but Itu's eye curved slightly. "Yes. The males have eyes the color of mine. The females . . . do not."

Itu was a male, then, and seemed to have at least a little bit of a sense of humor. Good. Dez wanted very much to stay on his good side.

Opaka introduced everybody, and Itu welcomed each

of them before suggesting that they move outside, so as not to disturb the other singers. He said that the meditation would end for each of them individually, when they were ready to wake, and Dez added another handful of questions to his list.

Itu led them through a carved opening in the front of the chamber, nothing like the fissure that they'd originally walked through, out onto a leveled path of stones, entirely free of algae. Where had the cave gone? Were there slime-covered rocks underneath the path? Dez looked around at the giant, silent buildings, obviously empty, entirely awed by it all. An instant city, back after half an eternity because a Tosk had picked up a crystal . . . and the Gamma Quadrant itself had been affected.

Itu seemed to breathe deeply, two of his lower, thicker limbs expanding and then deflating.

"The air is different," he said.

"It's been a long time since you were, ah, in the living time," Dez said. "Something like fifty millennia."

"That is a long time," Itu agreed, not seeming overly bothered by it.

"If I might ask . . . where have you been?" Dez asked. "And why?"

"We have been hiding," Itu said. "For a hundred years, our cities burned, and our people were killed, by a race of fanatical beings who believed our devotion to the Siblings to be blasphemous. The Eav'oq have always been a peaceful people, we do not, will not end sentient life. We could only turn to our trust in the Siblings for comfort and guidance . . . and They sent us a vision, and told us to go away from the sight of these beings."

"So, you've been in . . . subspace?" Facity asked.

"Of a kind," Itu said. "Folded space, undiluted space. We had been experimenting with such transformations, physically and spiritually. We built this city, our new capital, in a fold of this space to save it from destruction—and the Siblings showed us that we could save ourselves if we went to our city, if we could manage a perfect unity of idea to remain with it."

Itu gestured back at the great chamber, at all the hunched figures behind the glass. "We achieved it, but it was difficult, and not something any of us could wake from on our own. We have been together with the same vision for so long, it may take many days for some of them to let it go."

So they left out an alarm crystal to wake them up, Dez thought, amazed. Tosk had found it, and it had guided him to Opaka, somehow. . . .

"We set out a number of keys, that would tune the finder to the power of *res,* spiritual energy," Itu explained. "Of a kind similar to ours. In each one there was also a request for aid, and an understanding of the Siblings' gift, the era stones."

"The stones are of my planet," Opaka said.

"Prophets and Siblings," Itu said happily.

"And these era stones just . . . tore you out of subspace, when we touched them?" Dez asked.

Itu seemed amused. "I'm not sure how the gift works, but I believe that when you touched them, my eye itched. The unity was broken when I thought of relieving the itch."

Amazing. Fifty thousand years of a meditational trance, broken by a need to scratch. It seemed the Siblings had a sense of humor, too.

"Are you aware that the space around this planet has

moved?" Dez asked, drawing the stares of his crew. "That there's been a . . . rotation of matter?"

"I am aware," Itu said simply. "It is no concern. No life will have been harmed."

But how, why? Before he could ask, Facity had jumped in.

"Where . . . We were in a cave," Facity said. "What happened to it? What happened to the planet's surface that we saw, before you appeared?"

"It is still here," Itu said. "Just as the stars shifted, but did not shift. The reality is other."

Dez didn't understand, but it seemed to be all the explanation Itu meant to give. He had turned to Opaka again.

"Would you care to walk with me? Soon, the others will be waking, and we will be engaged in reestablishing an existence for ourselves . . . but I'd like to know about your world, and the Prophets. You're all welcome, of course."

Dez remembered what they were there for, and shook the amazement. There was business to be done. "Actually, I was hoping to explore your city, with some of my crew," he said.

"Our homes are open to you," Itu said.

Dez smiled. "Thank you, Itu."

Jake, who'd been watching Itu and Opaka with an expression that Dez couldn't read, cleared his throat.

"If it's all right, I'd like to stay for a few moments," he said. His face, usually so easy for Dez to read, was perfectly neutral.

"Sure, right," Dez said. Of course Jake would want to stay, with his personal connection to the Bajoran religion . . . but Dez was disappointed, too. He wanted Jake with him, he wanted to explain about the last few weeks, why he'd kept so quiet.

He'll understand, once he realizes what's going to come of this, Dez reassured himself. The return of such an advanced species, one in which the members had actually been alive for fifty millennia, accompanied by an actual change in the Gamma Quadrant's delineation . . . it was going to be huge, and the *Even Odds* was going to be right in the middle of it.

He nodded at Facity, and at the rest of the crew, and as Opaka and Itu turned and started to walk away, trailed after by Jake and Wex, the team turned and went in the opposite direction.

19

WALKING ALONG the silent, empty paths of the beautiful city, Jake listened to Itu and Opaka talk, but only half heard them, only just registered the grand, strange buildings that they were passing, that made up the Eav'oq's capital city. He'd only asked to stay behind because he needed to be able to think for a moment, and what he was thinking about was the retrieval myth that Dez had told him, back on that day not so long after Drang, the day that Facity had made the bet about the Iconians.

He said that every GQ retriever who'd ever lived would trade a limb to get a line on one of the lost worlds, the Luw, the Eav-oq . . . with their vanishing crystals, that implanted information in the minds of those who touched them.

Jake still couldn't believe that he hadn't seen it himself, after listening to Tosk's story . . . and Dez had known all along, of course. It was why he'd agreed to take Tosk and Opaka and Wex aboard—not because it was the right thing to do, or because Jake had asked, but because he was hoping for a payoff. He almost certainly had the team looking around right now, trying to decide on what they'd ask for as a reward. Which, in and of itself, Jake could understand, whether or not he liked it; the *Even* worked retrieval. What he couldn't understand was why Dez had felt the need to keep it a secret.

You do understand, though. Think about it.

It required a minimum of thought. Jake also remembered how happy and relieved he'd been, the day that Dez had suggested that they skip the last Dominion salvages . . . and how happy that had made Dez.

It's me. For whatever reason, since the very beginning, Dez has wanted to keep me on board. He's been telling me what I want to hear, and keeping quiet about things he thinks I won't like. Why, though? Why would he do all that?

Again, it hardly took any thought. It was because Dez liked him, and wanted Jake to like him in turn, to respect him. It was sweet and desperately immature . . . and it was so like Dez that Jake realized it could only be the truth.

". . . and when I left, they had just begun to rebuild," Opaka was saying. Jake looked around, saw that they had stopped near some kind of ornamental fountain. Wex was still intently listening to the two "Chosen" talk . . . and watching Opaka smile at Itu, her new spirit mate, thinking of how surprised Bajor was going to be, that the Prophets had a connection to another species, when Jake suddenly remembered the prophecy again. Now that Tosk was gone, Opaka would be coming with Jake and Fac back through the wormhole.

Tosk probably died just so she'd need a lift, Jake thought bitterly, not believing it but sourly sure of it, anyway. He was suddenly incredibly tired of the Prophets and Siblings and prophecies, he was tired of being used for reasons that no one could be bothered to explain. He wasn't shocked that the Prophets didn't care about his feelings, but he'd expected more from Dez.

Jake waited for a break in the conversation, and then excused himself, wanting to be alone for a few minutes. Itu and Opaka smiled benignly as he fumbled an apology, and then he was free.

He started back for the dropship, hoping it was still where they'd left it, that the city hadn't "shifted" over it. He could see, though, as he walked through the shadows of the tall, curving buildings, that the chamber where they'd met Itu seemed to mark the easternmost edge. Beyond lay the familiar plain of algaed rock.

Jake was just stepping off the city's last path, back onto the slippery rock, when Wex caught up to him.

"I hope you don't mind if I walk with you," Wex said. "I thought . . . I thought you might want the company."

Jake did mind, but couldn't see a polite way of saying so. He forced a smile. "I'm just going back to the dropship."

Wex nodded, and said nothing. Jake supposed he should be happy about that much; with as much as Wex talked, it would be almost like being alone.

They started walking, the wet, rocky ground sloping gently upward. Jake hadn't realized that they'd been walking downhill before, everything had been so gradual, but he felt it, now. It was a struggle to keep his balance . . . and it was a relief, to have something to do besides feel sorry for himself. He turned to help Wex over some of the more difficult spots, but she didn't seem to need any help, her balance much better than his.

They teetered on in silence for a moment, which Wex finally broke.

"You seem unhappy," she said. "Is it . . . Tosk?"

Jake felt a flash of shame. Wrapped up in his own petty misery, he'd barely spared a thought for Tosk.

"Because I think he was . . . happy, at the end," Wex went on. "I could see that he heard the Hunter's words, that his death would be an honorable one."

Jake nodded noncommittally, feeling some small measure of consolation. He hadn't seen that, but he couldn't think of any reason that Wex might have to lie about it. It was good to know.

"I thought I might take Opaka back to Bajor, in the Tosk vessel," Wex said. "If you don't think your crew will salvage it."

Jake stopped walking for a beat, vaguely surprised. "You know how to pilot his ship?"

Wex nodded. "Well enough, I think. And I thought . . . you might choose to go with us. It would be crowded, but it's not a long trip. Shorter now, it seems. I heard Prees tell the captain that we are now much closer to the Anomaly."

That was so strange, he couldn't even begin to consider it. Jake started walking again. Up ahead, he could see the bow of the Tosk's ship peeking out from behind a rim of rocks. The dropship was still hidden.

Go with Wex and Opaka . . . yet another interpretation of the prophecy's logistics, one that meant he wouldn't be leaving with the *Even*'s crew. He was upset with Dez, he thought they had a serious problem to talk about, but did he really want to part company over it? No . . . and he couldn't imagine not even trying to work it out.

"I don't think so," he said, and was about to say more

when he heard a patter of wet footsteps behind them. He and Wex both turned, and there was Pif, panting, apparently running on three legs because he held what looked like a blue glass goblet in his front right hand.

"Hey," Pif said, shooting a sidelong glance at Wex. "Good deal, I was going to have to come find you, pretty soon; Dez wants to get gone."

"Why?" Jake asked.

Pif smiled nervously and ignored the question. "Anyway, Dez was going to ask you, Wex, if you wanted the Tosk's ship."

"Where did you get that?" Jake asked, nodding at the goblet.

Pif glanced again at Wex, and again ignored Jake. "Everyone's already at the ship, I think. I'll meet you back there."

Pif hurried past them. Even on three legs, he was remarkably fast, though Jake only saw that glint of blue glass, and what it meant . . . not just about Dez and what he'd done, but what it meant for him.

There was nothing to work out.

He stood watching the Aarruri hop away, waiting for it to hit—anger, or depression, or something stronger, something more than what he did feel . . . but there was only a kind of melancholy acceptance.

"Tell Opaka that we'll be escorting her home in the Tosk ship, whenever she's ready," Jake said, turning to Wex. "I'll be back in a little while." For once, he was glad for her tacit nature. She nodded mutely, and left him.

Sighing, Jake continued to walk back to the ship.

Pif told Dez that Jake was on his way, so Dez was ready. The fourteen certainly priceless pieces they'd taken were already stored, back by the transporters . . . and though he suspected that Jake might be unhappy about it, Dez was prepared to have it out, to point out a few facts of life to his reluctant young friend.

It's time he grows up a little, stops being such a child, Dez thought, watching as Jake crested the last hill. Dez walked out a little ways to meet him, he didn't want to embarrass Jake in front of everyone . . . but as he stopped and waited, as Jake carefully stepped across the last few meters that separated them, he was struck by how grown Jake suddenly seemed to him. There was something in his face, or in the way he was walking . . . he didn't seem like a child at all.

Jake stopped in front of him, looking evenly into Dez's eyes. "I don't guess I can talk you into putting it back," he said mildly. "Whatever you've taken."

Dez grinned, shaking his head. "Jake, you've got to understand. The run on this one is going to be short-lived. In another few months, they'll probably be selling it themselves, the market will be flooded . . . but right now, this is a big opportunity for us. We found them, don't you see?"

Jake only looked at him, an expression of vague sadness in his gaze. "I'll take that as a no."

Dez felt a stir of guilt, the way Jake was looking at him, irritation quickly taking its place.

"You honestly think they'd begrudge us a few dishes, a few urns?" he snapped. "You heard Itu. They're grateful to us, Jake. And we didn't take anything important, they probably won't even miss it. It's not like . . ."

He trailed off, realizing what he was doing. Realizing that he was trying to justify himself, to rationalize retrieving a handful of trifles, nothing the Eav'oq would care about but that would make the *Even* a tremendous lot of money. And once the story got out, how they were there when the stars changed and the Eav'oq appeared, how they had been responsible for making it happen, they'd be overrun with eager clients. Why wasn't that reason enough for Jake?

"It's our job," he said, sighing. "This is what we do, Jake, it's what we've always done."

"I know," Jake said, and smiled a little. "I do. But it's not for me, Dez. Wex is going to take Opaka home in Tosk's ship, and I'm going to go with them."

Dez stared at him in disbelief. "Because of this?"

"No," Jake said. "I just . . . I don't belong on the *Even.*"

"Look, we can ask them for this, all right?" Dez said, feeling a kind of desperation settling around his heart. He'd worked so hard . . . and he'd felt so good, knowing that he was helping Jake out, that he was doing the right thing by him. He was such a naive kid, too, he *needed* someone to watch out for him. "I'll talk to Itu myself, you can go with me."

"That's not it," Jake said. "Think about it, Dez. I know you know why."

"Don't patronize me," Dez snapped, angry, angry that he felt angry. "And you're right, I *do* know why. It's your father, you still want to go chasing after your perfect father. It's a dream, don't you get that? Do you really think that he's going to drop whatever he's doing to be with you, that he's going to give up his life for you? Because let me tell you, it's not going to happen. He's a grown man, Jake, and it's time *you* started to act like one, it's time that you give up this absurd notion that it's the two of you against the rest of existence."

At Jake's hurt expression, Dez felt his anger dwindle,

felt an inkling of shame. He stepped closer to Jake, reaching out to touch his shoulder. Jake didn't move.

"I'm trying to help you wake up, Jake. You don't have to be what your father is, you don't have to do what he does . . . and you don't have to waste your time running after something that you can't have. It's time for you to make your own life."

Jake stared at him a moment longer, his gaze again so careful, so hard to read . . . and then nodded. His voice, when he spoke, was calm and sure.

"That's what I'm doing. I'm going back to a place I feel strong, where I have friends, and history . . . and family. You say you're trying to help me, and in a lot of ways, you've been a good friend to me . . . but I'm awake, Dez. Whether or not my father ever returns, this is my life, my decision. And I'm leaving."

Dez opened his mouth to tell him that he was wrong, that he was being ridiculous . . . and instead thought of how he'd felt about himself over the last weeks. How ridiculous *he'd* felt, not talking to the crew about business, and avoiding Jake. How guilty he'd felt, every time Jake brought up the idea of working charity. How ready he'd been only a minute ago, to tell Jake that he had to grow up, that he wasn't going to pretend anymore.

So stop pretending.

He looked into Jake's youthful eyes, and saw a universe of possibilities . . . and the assured, steady gaze of a capable young man who knew his own mind.

"We're going to miss you," Dez said, and though he felt his throat locking up, he managed a smile.

Dez and Jake talked for a minute or two, and hugged, and then talked for another minute. Standing next to

Coamis and Brad, Pif stretched, cooling down from his second run into the city, watching as Dez called Facity over . . . and a second later, *she* was hugging Jake.

"What's *that* all about," Coamis asked, leaning against the ship.

"Maybe he found another Giani'aga box," Pif said idly, and then grinned. "Hey, how much do you figure we'll get for that black vase?"

Coamis shrugged, but was also smiling. "A lot."

"Yeah, that was my estimate," Pif said. Brad tittered her strangely deep giggle, seemed about to say something . . . and then Jake, Fac, and Dez were walking toward them, and from the look on the first officer's face, Pif just knew that something was wrong.

"What is it? What happened?" Pif asked. At the alarm in his voice, Neane and Glessin, who'd been sitting together a half-dozen meters away, stood up and came to join them.

"Relax, Pif," Jake said, smiling. "It's, ah . . . I'm leaving, that's all. I'm not going back with you."

"What? Why!" Pif demanded, as the others shifted about in surprise.

"I've got things to do back home," Jake said. "And honestly, I just don't think I'm cut out for the retrieval business."

"That's crazy," Pif said. "You're great at it. Dez, tell him."

"I think his mind is made up, Pif," Dez said, and Jake nodded.

There was a brief, unhappy silence and then Glessin stepped forward, and bowed his head formally, a single, low nod. "It's been a pleasure to know you," he said. "I mean that very sincerely."

"Thanks, Glessin," Jake said, smiling. "I feel the same way."

Before anyone else could speak, Brad promptly burst into tears.

"Hey, none of that," Jake said, and Brad stumbled over to him, embracing him tightly as she wept. He was buried in her.

"I will miss you," she intoned, and Jake patted what he could reach of her back. After a moment she let go, sniffling mightily.

Neane only hugged him, and Coamis promised to say good-bye to the others on the ship for him, and then Jake was crouching down next to Pif, who still couldn't believe it.

"Thanks for everything, Pif," Jake said.

"You don't really want to go," Pif said, his brow furrowing. "I like you, Jake. I don't want you to leave."

Jake nodded. "I like you, too, Pif. I'm sorry. But you can come visit me any time you want . . . and whenever I'm in the Gamma Quadrant, I'll stay in touch."

"You won't, though," Pif said. "You'll forget about us."

"Never, Pif," Jake said. "How could I forget you? You're the fastest Aarruri I've ever met."

"I'm the only Aarruri you've ever met," Pif said moodily, but was glad Jake had said it, anyway. And he *was* fast.

"Hey, do me a favor . . . tell Feg and Triv that my closest friend back home is Nog, son of Rom. Can you remember that?"

Pif nodded, felt a slow grin building at the sparkle in Jake's eyes. "They're going to hate that, aren't they?"

"Oh, yeah," Jake confirmed with a wicked grin, and leaned forward to nuzzle his head against Pif. Pif laid his furry cheek against Jake's smooth one for a second, then stepped back, deeply touched that Jake had remembered the Aarruri good-bye. The only person he'd ever said good-bye to in front of Jake had been Stessie.

There was another minute or two of conversation, Facity promising to beam down Jake's things, Jake and Dez exchanging a few more private, obviously heartfelt words, and then it was over. The crew boarded the dropship, and Jake watched through the open door, smiling and waving, and then the door closed and he was gone.

As the ship lifted away, Dez's face was carefully, stonily still . . . and though their hold was full of treasure, no one spoke or laughed. Pif wanted to break the silence, to lighten the mood . . . but while he could think of plenty to say, anecdotes to share, he didn't really feel like talking.

After a moment, Brad started to sniffle again, and Pif scooted across to where she sat, and laid his head in her lap, telling himself that she needed the comfort, not minding at all when she rested one massive hand against his brow.

20

THEY STAYED with Itu for three peaceful, lovely days, and on the third day, it was time to leave. The Eav'oq were waking, returning, and though their visitors were offered an indefinite stay, Opaka could see that Itu's people needed time to renew their lives.

After promising to be in contact again soon, after another long, warm embrace between Opaka and Itu, they left the Eav'oq at the edge of his beautiful city and started for Tosk's ship. Wex and Jake flanked Opaka silently, steadying her as they moved across the unstable rock surface. Opaka let herself be steadied, let herself be led, her mind full of other things.

Raiq, for one. The Ascendants were who had persecuted Itu's people; after listening to his descriptions, Opaka no longer had any doubt. What Itu called Eyes of Light, Raiq had called Eyes of Fire . . . and the Bajoran people knew them as Tears of the Prophets. It seemed obvious to her now, the "fortress" in the stars, the all-seeing gods—but was it any wonder that she hadn't recognized Raiq's frightening religious views as related to her own? She hadn't told Itu about meeting Raiq, hadn't wanted to worry him overmuch, but wondered what it would mean for the Eav'oq in the future . . . and what it might mean for Bajor. That a being from the race that chased the Eav'oq into hiding had been responsible for her freedom . . . it was too great a coincidence. Will of the Prophets.

As it must be Their will for Bajor and Eav'oq to stand together, if Raiq's people should come this way, Opaka affirmed to herself. Whatever happened now, the Eav'oq wouldn't be alone.

As happy as she was to have met Itu, to have learned of the Siblings, Opaka felt more than a little overwhelmed by the implications . . . and wasn't sure how the existence of a "sister" planet would sit with the Vedek Assembly, or the Chamber . . . or the people. Having met Itu, having felt his radiant *pagh,* she believed that it could only lead to an expansion of awareness for Bajor . . . but even after seven years abroad, learning to loosen her definition of what it meant to love and be loved by the Prophets, she still found it difficult to accept that the relationship between the Prophets and Bajor was not a singular one. It was one of the first tenets of the faith, one of the first things taught to children—that the Prophets were for Bajor, that Bajor was for the Prophets.

And yet . . . the Emissary was an alien. She'd known and accepted from the beginning that he was connected to the Prophets in a way deeper than any Bajoran. Had that itself not been a sign that They saw more than Bajor only?

Now there are the Eav'oq, Opaka thought, leaning against Wex as she helped her over a slick patch, smiling absently, gratefully at the girl. Only fifty years ago, an awareness of the Eav'oq would have been welcomed, she thought. But as she'd told Itu, the Cardassian Occupation had changed things. The Bajor she'd left behind had barely touched upon the healing process, and though it had pained her to tell Itu, to admit as much to herself, the systematic abuse and degradation of her people had left them with wounds and suspicions that seven years would not, could not have erased.

To complicate matters, there were a few fundamental differences in the way the Eav'oq worshipped . . . primarily, that they didn't. There were no rituals to their meditations, no holy days, no . . . separateness. Itu and his people believed that the *pagh*—or the *res*—inside each of them wasn't just *from* the Siblings, they believed it was their own Siblinghood, developing. They believed in reincarnation of spirit . . . and that each Eav'oq spirit would one day transcend to the Temple, to become a new Sibling, to watch over the young Eav'oq still on their planet.

It was a lovely faith, and there were things in it that Opaka felt strongly could only further Bajor's understanding of the Prophets . . . but it was different, very different, and sometimes—particularly in matters of faith—that could be a difficult thing.

But to know that the Prophets have reached out to others, Opaka thought, feeling renewed hope. It was an example to be admired and followed. The Bajoran people were more than capable of opening themselves to experiences beyond the realms of their own lives.

She put the thoughts aside and glanced at Jake as they approached the Tosk ship. He wore his carry bag slung over one shoulder, his young face still and a bit sad. He'd said very little since the departure of his friends.

She still wasn't sure why he'd decided not to go with the *Even Odds,* but she was glad for it; prophecy or no, it seemed right that they should return to the Alpha Quadrant together.

Wex opened a hatch at the front of the Tosk ship and looked inside, turning an apologetic gaze to both Opaka and Jake.

"It's going to be very tight," she said, and Opaka smiled at Jake, and shrugged.

"I take up very little room," she said. "How about you?"

She won a smile from the tall boy, who gestured grandly for her to crawl into the ship first. With a last look back at the still and shining buildings of the Eav'oq people, Opaka obliged.

The Tosk's ship wasn't unbearably cramped, but it was close. Jake's knees were pressed against the back of the pilot's seat. Opaka was right next to him, the two of them sharing the one tiny bench directly behind Wex's seat, their few belongings shoved underneath next to an entirely foreign tool kit.

At least it's fast, Jake thought, smiling resignedly at Opaka as Wex powered up the vessel, as they lifted away. The Hunters had equipped the ship with hardly room enough for one, but with a warp drive unlike anything Jake had ever seen. They'd be back in the Alpha Quadrant in moments; in the shuttle Jake had traveled over in, even with the system shift, it would have taken hours.

The ride through the ice storm was jerking and uncomfortable, but Wex was a surprisingly good pilot, taking the small ship through its paces as she dodged through the spinning fields. They were hit a few times, but Wex managed to avoid anything really big, and they were clear in a matter of moments.

"Nice flying," Jake said, impressed. Wex nodded, but said nothing. Jake wondered if Dez would have been impressed, seeing the tiny vessel clear the hazard so deftly . . . and decided probably not; Dez was a terrible pilot, if the stories were to be believed. Jake smiled inwardly, and found that it hurt, a little, but not nearly as bad as he would have thought.

Except . . .

What Dez had said about Jake's father, about Jake never having the relationship he wanted. For a few seconds, he felt an all too familiar panic creep up in his gut. *What if he never comes back? What will I do?*

"Are you all right?" Opaka asked gently.

Jake nodded again, not sure if he meant it . . . and Opaka smiled, shaking her head slightly.

"You've done a wondrous thing today, Jake. You should be proud."

Jake waited, certain that she meant to tell him that his father would also be proud . . . but it didn't come. She only continued smiling at him, and it occurred to him that he *had* done a wondrous thing, or at least been involved in it. He'd found a lost world of myth and moved it—a whole star system, apparently—light-years away from where it had been, waking a sleeping race of mystics to a new universe.

And being Ben Sisko's son had nothing to do with it. Or maybe it did . . . but it felt good, anyway.

He smiled back at Opaka. "Thanks. I guess I am."

"Going to full sublight," Wex said, touching a button—

—and a loud, high-pitched whine filled the tiny

space, getting louder and higher, and the vessel trembled violently all around them.

"Shut it down," Jake said automatically, saw that Wex was already doing it—and though the trembling immediately stopped, the whine continued to grow in pitch and volume, fast. After only a few seconds it was a piercing shriek, and the ship began to shake again, worse than before.

"What is it?" Jake shouted, saw that Wex's hands were flying over the controls, that nothing was making any difference at all.

"I don't know!" Wex shouted back, and he could barely hear her.

Jake looked at Opaka, saw her eyes closed, saw her lips moving in prayer as the mechanical shriek drowned out everything, even his own scream at Wex to do something, to do *anything*. It was happening too fast, the vessel was going to come apart, and Jake tried to reach for the tool kit, helpless to do anything else, and couldn't manage that, the space too tight.

We're going to die, Jake thought, and there was a light, and it was over.

It was silent, she could move . . . and she was on a floor. Opaka opened her eyes, and saw that she was on a transporter pad, Jake sprawled next to her, Wex in front of them.

"What happened?" Opaka asked, disoriented.

Jake carefully climbed to his feet, and helped Opaka to hers. Wex stood up and joined them.

"Don't make any sudden movements," Jake said, his voice tense. He moved so that he was in a position to shield Wex and Opaka, presumably from the two creatures who watched them from the shadows of the sparse, low-lit room.

Across from them was a control stand manned by a tall, reptilian being, another standing at the room's door, loosely holding a weapon across his chest. They were reptilian, but not at all like Tosk. Where Tosk's face had been wide-eyed and rounded, these beings had angular heads, beaded with blunt spines. Their eyes were small and dark and hooded, the casts of their faces fierce, angry. Each wore a clear, slender tube in its throat, sputtering with a white substance. Opaka had never seen one before, but had heard many stories . . . and had little doubt that she was looking at Jem'Hadar, the Dominion's soldiers.

The door to the room slid open, and in walked a small, well-dressed man, very pale with black hair and wide, innocent violet eyes, and a kind of flesh collar that surrounded his smiling face. At the sight of him, Jake's entire demeanor changed. His mouth dropped open, his shoulders sagging in surprise.

"Weyoun!"

Weyoun bowed his head. His voice, when he spoke, was strangely breathy, his manner simpering and insincere.

"Jake, my dear friend," he said, his eyes shining. "It's been too long! And who are *your* friends, if I may ask?"

Jake wasn't over his shock. "But . . . I thought you were dead!"

Weyoun clasped his hands together. "An interesting and educational story, my dearest friend, but we have so little time. Suffice it to say, some things serve too well to let rest. I so very much hope that you and your companions weren't injured . . . ?"

Jake's expression darkened. "Did you do something to our ship?"

Weyoun looked deeply wounded. "We merely saved you from it, its engines exploded scant seconds after we transported you out." He smiled again, the wound forgotten. "But you still haven't introduced me . . ."

"And how did you just happen to come across our ship, when it was on the verge of exploding?" Jake asked.

Weyoun's smile barely faltered. "We've . . . been pursuing another ship, a ship of thieves and smugglers, with which the Dominion holds legitimate grievances," he said. "Just as we were preparing to apprehend these criminals only a few days ago, circumstances changed, quite suddenly. It seems the planet you were on, the planet that was uninhabited until quite recently, has . . . altered things, to say the least." Weyoun's gaze flickered nervously over Opaka and Wex. "Even as we were preparing to leave, we saw your vessel, saw that it was in dire straits . . . and saw that it had a Bajoran and a human aboard . . ."

Jake was watching him closely, as was Wex. They obviously didn't trust the little man . . . and though Opaka was not one to judge lightly, neither did she. He seemed most disingenuous.

Weyoun smiled, showing small square teeth. "Well, we had no choice, did we? We were forced to set our own business, our *legitimate* business aside, to let those . . . *terrorists* loose. For how could we disregard a chance to lend needed assistance to old friends from the Alpha Quadrant? To do the decent, the honorable thing, even in times of crisis and change? And as luck would have it, we've detected the approach of the *Defiant*, and are presently moving to intercept it."

"The *Defiant?"* Jake asked. "They're in the Gamma Quadrant?"

"As I said," Weyoun said. "A fortunate coincidence, is it not?"

"Yeah, right," Jake snorted.

The wounded look was back. "After all the times we shared on your station, Jake, you doubt me. Such wonderful times! Tell me, do you still write? I remember your stylistic flair so fondly, those superior articles you wrote for the Federation News Service . . ."

"You—your *clone* said they were biased," Jake said. "You intercepted them before they ever left the station."

"Truly a joy to read," Weyoun said, as though Jake hadn't spoken.

"The *Defiant* is in range," the Jem'Hadar behind the control stand said. "Sensors indicate there is a Founder aboard."

For an instant, a flash of suspicion crossed Weyoun's face . . . and then it was gone, and he was smiling again, the consummate host.

"I'll handle the call from the bridge," he said, nodding again at Wex and Opaka before turning his attention back to Jake. "A delicate touch is necessary for these matters, don't you agree? If you'll remain on the transporter pad, I assure you that you'll be back in familiar territory very soon."

Weyoun backed toward the door, clasping his hands to his chest once more. "It's my misfortune, not to have more time to spend with you and your friends. I . . . I hope that we shall all meet again, soon, under the best of circumstances. And please . . . extend my warmest personal regards to your father, if you see him again."

With that, Weyoun bowed his way out of the room, the door closing on his beaming, sentimental face.

"Who was that man?" Opaka asked.

Jake stared at the closed door. "That's a tough question."

"The *Defiant* . . . these are friends of yours?" Wex asked.

Jake smiled suddenly, as if surprised into it by Wex's question, a purely happy smile. "Yes. They'll take us back to the station, to DS9. You can get a transport to Bajor from there."

Opaka, too, was surprised into a sudden smile. Bajor. She was going home.

EPILOGUE

As they waited for Weyoun—Weyoun!—to arrange for transport, it occurred to Jake for the first time that he'd lost his bag, that it had burnt up along with the Tosk ship. The prophecy had been in it, a few books, some clothes . . . and his journal, which he'd started the day he'd left DS9. Everything that had happened to him in the Gamma Quadrant was in it.

No, everything that happened is in you. *Never forget, it's about the experience . . . and having a good story to tell when you've been drinking.*

Dez's voice. Jake smiled a little, thinking about some of the stories he had to tell. He'd have a little half brother or sister soon, very soon . . . and he suddenly envisioned sitting with the child someday, telling them all about the time he'd tried to raid the underground lair of the Drang, or about the secret subdeck of the Wa, or maybe cautioning them against the perils of too much spinewater. By the time the child was old enough to listen, who knew what else he might have to say? Helping alter the face of the Gamma Quadrant was definitely a promising start to a whole series of good stories.

"Prepare for transport," the Jem'Hadar at the controls said, and Jake straightened his shoulders, and took a deep breath.

THE DEEP SPACE NINE SAGA
CONTINUES IN
UNITY

ABOUT THE AUTHOR

S. D. (Stephani Danelle) Perry writes multimedia novelizations in the fantasy/science fiction/horror realms for love and money, occasionally in that order. She's worked in the universes of *Resident Evil, Aliens, Xena,* and most recently *Star Trek;* she had also written a few short stories, and translated a couple of movie scripts into books. Danelle, as she prefers to be called, lives in Portland with an incredibly patient husband and their two ridiculous dogs.

Look for STAR TREK fiction from Pocket Books

Star Trek®

Enterprise: The First Adventure • Vonda N. McIntyre
Strangers From the Sky • Margaret Wander Bonanno
Final Frontier • Diane Carey
Spock's World • Diane Duane
The Lost Years • J.M. Dillard
Prime Directive • Judith and Garfield Reeves-Stevens
Probe • Margaret Wander Bonanno
Best Destiny • Diane Carey
Shadows on the Sun • Michael Jan Friedman
Sarek • A.C. Crispin
Federation • Judith and Garfield Reeves-Stevens
Vulcan's Forge • Josepha Sherman & Susan Shwartz
Mission to Horatius • Mack Reynolds
Vulcan's Heart • Josepha Sherman & Susan Shwartz
The Eugenics Wars: The Rise and Fall of Khan Noonien Singh, Books One and *Two* • Greg Cox
The Last Round-Up • Christie Golden

Novelizations

Star Trek: The Motion Picture • Gene Roddenberry
Star Trek II: The Wrath of Khan • Vonda N. McIntyre
Star Trek III: The Search for Spock • Vonda N. McIntyre
Star Trek IV: The Voyage Home • Vonda N. McIntyre
Star Trek V: The Final Frontier • J.M. Dillard
Star Trek VI: The Undiscovered Country • J.M. Dillard
Star Trek Generations • J.M. Dillard
Starfleet Academy • Diane Carey

Star Trek books by William Shatner with Judith and Garfield Reeves-Stevens

The Ashes of Eden
The Return
Avenger
Star Trek: Odyssey (contains *The Ashes of Eden*, *The Return*, and *Avenger)*
Spectre
Dark Victory
Preserver
Captain's Peril

#1 • *Star Trek: The Motion Picture* • Gene Roddenberry
#2 • *The Entropy Effect* • Vonda N. McIntyre
#3 • *The Klingon Gambit* • Robert E. Vardeman
#4 • *The Covenant of the Crown* • Howard Weinstein
#5 • *The Prometheus Design* • Sondra Marshak & Myrna Culbreath

#6 • *The Abode of Life* • Lee Correy
#7 • *Star Trek II: The Wrath of Khan* • Vonda N. McIntyre
#8 • *Black Fire* • Sonni Cooper
#9 • *Triangle* • Sondra Marshak & Myrna Culbreath
#10 • *Web of the Romulans* • M.S. Murdock
#11 • *Yesterday's Son* • A.C. Crispin
#12 • *Mutiny on the Enterprise* • Robert E. Vardeman
#13 • *The Wounded Sky* • Diane Duane
#14 • *The Trellisane Confrontation* • David Dvorkin
#15 • *Corona* • Greg Bear
#16 • *The Final Reflection* • John M. Ford
#17 • *Star Trek III: The Search for Spock* • Vonda N. McIntyre
#18 • *My Enemy, My Ally* • Diane Duane
#19 • *The Tears of the Singers* • Melinda Snodgrass
#20 • *The Vulcan Academy Murders* • Jean Lorrah
#21 • *Uhura's Song* • Janet Kagan
#22 • *Shadow Lord* • Laurence Yep
#23 • *Ishmael* • Barbara Hambly
#24 • *Killing Time* • Della Van Hise
#25 • *Dwellers in the Crucible* • Margaret Wander Bonanno
#26 • *Pawns and Symbols* • Majliss Larson
#27 • *Mindshadow* • J.M. Dillard
#28 • *Crisis on Centaurus* • Brad Ferguson
#29 • *Dreadnought!* • Diane Carey
#30 • *Demons* • J.M. Dillard
#31 • *Battlestations!* • Diane Carey
#32 • *Chain of Attack* • Gene DeWeese
#33 • *Deep Domain* • Howard Weinstein
#34 • *Dreams of the Raven* • Carmen Carter
#35 • *The Romulan Way* • Diane Duane & Peter Morwood
#36 • *How Much for Just the Planet?* • John M. Ford
#37 • *Bloodthirst* • J.M. Dillard
#38 • *The IDIC Epidemic* • Jean Lorrah
#39 • *Time for Yesterday* • A.C. Crispin
#40 • *Timetrap* • David Dvorkin
#41 • *The Three-Minute Universe* • Barbara Paul
#42 • *Memory Prime* • Judith and Garfield Reeves-Stevens
#43 • *The Final Nexus* • Gene DeWeese
#44 • *Vulcan's Glory* • D.C. Fontana
#45 • *Double, Double* • Michael Jan Friedman
#46 • *The Cry of the Onlies* • Judy Klass
#47 • *The Kobayashi Maru* • Julia Ecklar
#48 • *Rules of Engagement* • Peter Morwood
#49 • *The Pandora Principle* • Carolyn Clowes
#50 • *Doctor's Orders* • Diane Duane

#51 • *Enemy Unseen* • V.E. Mitchell
#52 • *Home Is the Hunter* • Dana Kramer-Rolls
#53 • *Ghost-Walker* • Barbara Hambly
#54 • *A Flag Full of Stars* • Brad Ferguson
#55 • *Renegade* • Gene DeWeese
#56 • *Legacy* • Michael Jan Friedman
#57 • *The Rift* • Peter David
#58 • *Faces of Fire* • Michael Jan Friedman
#59 • *The Disinherited* • Peter David, Michael Jan Friedman, Robert Greenberger
#60 • *Ice Trap* • L.A. Graf
#61 • *Sanctuary* • John Vornholt
#62 • *Death Count* • L.A. Graf
#63 • *Shell Game* • Melissa Crandall
#64 • *The Starship Trap* • Mel Gilden
#65 • *Windows on a Lost World* • V.E. Mitchell
#66 • *From the Depths* • Victor Milan
#67 • *The Great Starship Race* • Diane Carey
#68 • *Firestorm* • L.A. Graf
#69 • *The Patrian Transgression* • Simon Hawke
#70 • *Traitor Winds* • L.A. Graf
#71 • *Crossroad* • Barbara Hambly
#72 • *The Better Man* • Howard Weinstein
#73 • *Recovery* • J.M. Dillard
#74 • *The Fearful Summons* • Denny Martin Flinn
#75 • *First Frontier* • Diane Carey & Dr. James I. Kirkland
#76 • *The Captain's Daughter* • Peter David
#77 • *Twilight's End* • Jerry Oltion
#78 • *The Rings of Tautee* • Dean Wesley Smith & Kristine Kathryn Rusch
#79 • *Invasion!* #1: *First Strike* • Diane Carey
#80 • *The Joy Machine* • James Gunn
#81 • *Mudd in Your Eye* • Jerry Oltion
#82 • *Mind Meld* • John Vornholt
#83 • *Heart of the Sun* • Pamela Sargent & George Zebrowski
#84 • *Assignment: Eternity* • Greg Cox
#85-87 • *My Brother's Keeper* • Michael Jan Friedman
    #85 • *Republic*
    #86 • *Constitution*
    #87 • *Enterprise*
#88 • *Across the Universe* • Pamela Sargent & George Zebrowski
#89-94 • *New Earth*
    #89 • *Wagon Train to the Stars* • Diane Carey
    #90 • *Belle Terre* • Dean Wesley Smith with Diane Carey
    #91 • *Rough Trails* • L.A. Graf
    #92 • *The Flaming Arrow* • Kathy and Jerry Oltion

#93 • *Thin Air* • Kristine Kathryn Rusch & Dean Wesley Smith
#94 • *Challenger* • Diane Carey
#95-96 • *Rihannsu* • Diane Duane
#95 • *Swordhunt*
#96 • *Honor Blade*
#97 • *In the Name of Honor* • Dayton Ward

Star Trek®: The Original Series

The Janus Gate • L.A. Graf
#1 • *Present Tense*
#2 • *Future Imperfect*
#3 • *Past Prologue*
Errand of Vengeance • Kevin Ryan
#1 • *The Edge of the Sword*
#2 • *Killing Blow*
#3 • *River of Blood*

Star Trek: The Next Generation®

Metamorphosis • Jean Lorrah
Vendetta • Peter David
Reunion • Michael Jan Friedman
Imzadi • Peter David
The Devil's Heart • Carmen Carter
Dark Mirror • Diane Duane
Q-Squared • Peter David
Crossover • Michael Jan Friedman
Kahless • Michael Jan Friedman
Ship of the Line • Diane Carey
The Best and the Brightest • Susan Wright
Planet X • Michael Jan Friedman
Imzadi II: Triangle • Peter David
I, Q • John de Lancie & Peter David
The Valiant • Michael Jan Friedman
The Genesis Wave, Books One, Two, and *Three* • John Vornholt
Immortal Coil • Jeffrey Lang
A Hard Rain • Dean Wesley Smith
The Battle of Betazed • Charlotte Douglas & Susan Kearney
Novelizations
Encounter at Farpoint • David Gerrold
Unification • Jeri Taylor
Relics • Michael Jan Friedman
Descent • Diane Carey
All Good Things... • Michael Jan Friedman

Star Trek: Klingon • Dean Wesley Smith & Kristine Kathryn Rusch
Star Trek Generations • J.M. Dillard
Star Trek: First Contact • J.M. Dillard
Star Trek: Insurrection • J.M. Dillard
Star Trek: Nemesis • J.M. Dillard

#1 • *Ghost Ship* • Diane Carey
#2 • *The Peacekeepers* • Gene DeWeese
#3 • *The Children of Hamlin* • Carmen Carter
#4 • *Survivors* • Jean Lorrah
#5 • *Strike Zone* • Peter David
#6 • *Power Hungry* • Howard Weinstein
#7 • *Masks* • John Vornholt
#8 • *The Captain's Honor* • David & Daniel Dvorkin
#9 • *A Call to Darkness* • Michael Jan Friedman
#10 • *A Rock and a Hard Place* • Peter David
#11 • *Gulliver's Fugitives* • Keith Sharee
#12 • *Doomsday World* • Carter, David, Friedman & Greenberger
#13 • *The Eyes of the Beholders* • A.C. Crispin
#14 • *Exiles* • Howard Weinstein
#15 • *Fortune's Light* • Michael Jan Friedman
#16 • *Contamination* • John Vornholt
#17 • *Boogeymen* • Mel Gilden
#18 • *Q-in-Law* • Peter David
#19 • *Perchance to Dream* • Howard Weinstein
#20 • *Spartacus* • T.L. Mancour
#21 • *Chains of Command* • W.A. McCay & E.L. Flood
#22 • *Imbalance* • V.E. Mitchell
#23 • *War Drums* • John Vornholt
#24 • *Nightshade* • Laurell K. Hamilton
#25 • *Grounded* • David Bischoff
#26 • *The Romulan Prize* • Simon Hawke
#27 • *Guises of the Mind* • Rebecca Neason
#28 • *Here There Be Dragons* • John Peel
#29 • *Sins of Commission* • Susan Wright
#30 • *Debtor's Planet* • W.R. Thompson
#31 • *Foreign Foes* • Dave Galanter & Greg Brodeur
#32 • *Requiem* • Michael Jan Friedman & Kevin Ryan
#33 • *Balance of Power* • Dafydd ab Hugh
#34 • *Blaze of Glory* • Simon Hawke
#35 • *The Romulan Stratagem* • Robert Greenberger
#36 • *Into the Nebula* • Gene DeWeese
#37 • *The Last Stand* • Brad Ferguson
#38 • *Dragon's Honor* • Kij Johnson & Greg Cox

#39 • *Rogue Saucer* • John Vornholt
#40 • *Possession* • J.M. Dillard & Kathleen O'Malley
#41 • *Invasion! #2: The Soldiers of Fear* • Dean Wesley Smith & Kristine Kathryn Rusch
#42 • *Infiltrator* • W.R. Thompson
#43 • *A Fury Scorned* • Pamela Sargent & George Zebrowski
#44 • *The Death of Princes* • John Peel
#45 • *Intellivore* • Diane Duane
#46 • *To Storm Heaven* • Esther Friesner
#47-49 • *The Q Continuum* • Greg Cox
    #47 • *Q-Space*
    #48 • *Q-Zone*
    #49 • *Q-Strike*
#50 • *Dyson Sphere* • Charles Pellegrino & George Zebrowski
#51-56 • *Double Helix*
    #51 • *Infection* • John Gregory Betancourt
    #52 • *Vectors* • Dean Wesley Smith & Kristine Kathryn Rusch
    #53 • *Red Sector* • Diane Carey
    #54 • *Quarantine* • John Vornholt
    #55 • *Double or Nothing* • Peter David
    #56 • *The First Virtue* • Michael Jan Friedman & Christie Golden
#57 • *The Forgotten War* • William R. Forstchen
#58-59 • *Gemworld* • John Vornholt
    #58 • *Gemworld #1*
    #59 • *Gemworld #2*
#60 • *Tooth and Claw* • Doranna Durgin
#61 • *Diplomatic Implausibility* • Keith R.A. DeCandido
#62-63 • *Maximum Warp* • Dave Galanter & Greg Brodeur
    #62 • *Dead Zone*
    #63 • *Forever Dark*

Star Trek: Deep Space Nine®

Warped • K.W. Jeter
Legends of the Ferengi • Ira Steven Behr & Robert Hewitt Wolfe

Novelizations

Emissary • J.M. Dillard
The Search • Diane Carey
The Way of the Warrior • Diane Carey
Star Trek: Klingon • Dean Wesley Smith & Kristine Kathryn Rusch
Trials and Tribble-ations • Diane Carey
Far Beyond the Stars • Steve Barnes
What You Leave Behind • Diane Carey

#1 • *Emissary* • J.M. Dillard

#2 • *The Siege* • Peter David
#3 • *Bloodletter* • K.W. Jeter
#4 • *The Big Game* • Sandy Schofield
#5 • *Fallen Heroes* • Dafydd ab Hugh
#6 • *Betrayal* • Lois Tilton
#7 • *Warchild* • Esther Friesner
#8 • *Antimatter* • John Vornholt
#9 • *Proud Helios* • Melissa Scott
#10 • *Valhalla* • Nathan Archer
#11 • *Devil in the Sky* • Greg Cox & John Gregory Betancourt
#12 • *The Laertian Gamble* • Robert Sheckley
#13 • *Station Rage* • Diane Carey
#14 • *The Long Night* • Dean Wesley Smith & Kristine Kathryn Rusch
#15 • *Objective: Bajor* • John Peel
#16 • *Invasion!* #3: *Time's Enemy* • L.A. Graf
#17 • *The Heart of the Warrior* • John Gregory Betancourt
#18 • *Saratoga* • Michael Jan Friedman
#19 • *The Tempest* • Susan Wright
#20 • *Wrath of the Prophets* • David, Friedman & Greenberger
#21 • *Trial by Error* • Mark Garland
#22 • *Vengeance* • Dafydd ab Hugh
#23 • *The 34th Rule* • Armin Shimerman & David R. George III
#24-26 • *Rebels* • Dafydd ab Hugh
  #24 • *The Conquered*
  #25 • *The Courageous*
  #26 • *The Liberated*

Books set after the series
  The Lives of Dax • Marco Palmieri, ed.
  Millennium Omnibus • Judith and Garfield Reeves-Stevens
    #1 • *The Fall of Terok Nor*
    #2 • *The War of the Prophets*
    #3 • *Inferno*
  A Stitch in Time • Andrew J. Robinson
  Avatar, Book One • S.D. Perry
  Avatar, Book Two • S.D. Perry
  Section 31: Abyss • David Weddle & Jeffrey Lang
  Gateways #4: Demons of Air and Darkness • Keith R.A. DeCandido
  Gateways #7: What Lay Beyond: "Horn and Ivory" • Keith R.A. DeCandido
  Mission: Gamma
    #1 • *Twilight* • David R. George III
    #2 • *This Gray Spirit* • Heather Jarman
    #3 • *Cathedral* • Michael A. Martin & Andy Mangels
    #4 • *Lesser Evil* • Robert Simpson

Star Trek: Voyager®

Mosaic • Jeri Taylor
Pathways • Jeri Taylor
Captain Proton: Defender of the Earth • D.W. "Prof" Smith
The Nanotech War • Steven Piziks

Novelizations

Caretaker • L.A. Graf
Flashback • Diane Carey
Day of Honor • Michael Jan Friedman
Equinox • Diane Carey
Endgame • Diane Carey & Christie Golden

#1 • *Caretaker* • L.A. Graf
#2 • *The Escape* • Dean Wesley Smith & Kristine Kathryn Rusch
#3 • *Ragnarok* • Nathan Archer
#4 • *Violations* • Susan Wright
#5 • *Incident at Arbuk* • John Gregory Betancourt
#6 • *The Murdered Sun* • Christie Golden
#7 • *Ghost of a Chance* • Mark A. Garland & Charles G. McGraw
#8 • *Cybersong* • S.N. Lewitt
#9 • *Invasion! #4: The Final Fury* • Dafydd ab Hugh
#10 • *Bless the Beasts* • Karen Haber
#11 • *The Garden* • Melissa Scott
#12 • *Chrysalis* • David Niall Wilson
#13 • *The Black Shore* • Greg Cox
#14 • *Marooned* • Christie Golden
#15 • *Echoes* • Dean Wesley Smith, Kristine Kathryn Rusch & Nina Kiriki Hoffman
#16 • *Seven of Nine* • Christie Golden
#17 • *Death of a Neutron Star* • Eric Kotani
#18 • *Battle Lines* • Dave Galanter & Greg Brodeur
#19-21 • *Dark Matters* • Christie Golden
#19 • *Cloak and Dagger*
#20 • *Ghost Dance*
#21 • *Shadow of Heaven*

Enterprise®

Broken Bow • Diane Carey
Shockwave • Paul Ruditis
By the Book • Dean Wesley Smith & Kristine Kathryn Rusch
What Price Honor? • Dave Stern

Star Trek®: New Frontier

New Frontier #1-4 Collector's Edition • Peter David
#1 • *House of Cards*

#2 • *Into the Void*
#3 • *The Two-Front War*
#4 • *End Game*
#5 • *Martyr* • Peter David
#6 • *Fire on High* • Peter David
The Captain's Table #5 • *Once Burned* • Peter David
Double Helix #5 • *Double or Nothing* • Peter David
#7 • *The Quiet Place* • Peter David
#8 • *Dark Allies* • Peter David
#9-11 • *Excalibur* • Peter David
#9 • *Requiem*
#10 • *Renaissance*
#11 • *Restoration*
Gateways #6: *Cold Wars* • Peter David
Gateways #7: *What Lay Beyond:* "Death After Life" • Peter David
#12 • *Being Human* • Peter David

Star Trek®: Stargazer

The Valiant • Michael Jan Friedman
Double Helix #6: *The First Virtue* • Michael Jan Friedman and Christie Golden
Gauntlet • Michael Jan Friedman
Progenitor • Michael Jan Friedman

Star Trek®: Starfleet Corps of Engineers (eBooks)

Have Tech, Will Travel (paperback) • various
#1 • *The Belly of the Beast* • Dean Wesley Smith
#2 • *Fatal Error* • Keith R.A. DeCandido
#3 • *Hard Crash* • Christie Golden
#4 • *Interphase, Book One* • Dayton Ward & Kevin Dilmore
Miracle Workers (paperback) • various
#5 • *Interphase, Book Two* • Dayton Ward & Kevin Dilmore
#6 • *Cold Fusion* • Keith R.A. DeCandido
#7 • *Invincible, Book One* • David Mack & Keith R.A. DeCandido
#8 • *Invincible, Book Two* • David Mack & Keith R.A. DeCandido
#9 • *The Riddled Post* • Aaron Rosenberg
#10 • *Gateways Epilogue: Here There Be Monsters* • Keith R.A. DeCandido
#11 • *Ambush* • Dave Galanter & Greg Brodeur
#12 • *Some Assembly Required* • Scott Ciencin & Dan Jolley
#13 • *No Surrender* • Jeff Mariotte
#14 • *Caveat Emptor* • Ian Edginton & Michael Collins
#15 • *Past Life* • Robert Greenberger
#16 • *Oaths* • Glenn Hauman

#17 • *Foundations, Book One* • Dayton Ward & Kevin Dilmore
#18 • *Foundations, Book Two* • Dayton Ward & Kevin Dilmore
#19 • *Foundations, Book Three* • Dayton Ward & Kevin Dilmore
#20 • *Enigma Ship* • J. Steven and Christina F. York
#21 • *War Stories, Book One* • Keith R.A. DeCandido
#22 • *War Stories, Book Two* • Keith R.A. DeCandido

Star Trek®: Invasion!

#1 • *First Strike* • Diane Carey
#2 • *The Soldiers of Fear* • Dean Wesley Smith & Kristine Kathryn Rusch
#3 • *Time's Enemy* • L.A. Graf
#4 • *The Final Fury* • Dafydd ab Hugh
Invasion! Omnibus • various

Star Trek®: Day of Honor

#1 • *Ancient Blood* • Diane Carey
#2 • *Armageddon Sky* • L.A. Graf
#3 • *Her Klingon Soul* • Michael Jan Friedman
#4 • *Treaty's Law* • Dean Wesley Smith & Kristine Kathryn Rusch
The Television Episode • Michael Jan Friedman
Day of Honor Omnibus • various

Star Trek®: The Captain's Table

#1 • *War Dragons* • L.A. Graf
#2 • *Dujonian's Hoard* • Michael Jan Friedman
#3 • *The Mist* • Dean Wesley Smith & Kristine Kathryn Rusch
#4 • *Fire Ship* • Diane Carey
#5 • *Once Burned* • Peter David
#6 • *Where Sea Meets Sky* • Jerry Oltion
The Captain's Table Omnibus • various

Star Trek®: The Dominion War

#1 • *Behind Enemy Lines* • John Vornholt
#2 • *Call to Arms...* • Diane Carey
#3 • *Tunnel Through the Stars* • John Vornholt
#4 • *...Sacrifice of Angels* • Diane Carey

Star Trek®: Section 31™

Rogue • Andy Mangels & Michael A. Martin
Shadow • Dean Wesley Smith & Kristine Kathryn Rusch
Cloak • S.D. Perry
Abyss • David Weddle & Jeffrey Lang

Star Trek®: Gateways

#1 • *One Small Step* • Susan Wright
#2 • *Chainmail* • Diane Carey
#3 • *Doors Into Chaos* • Robert Greenberger
#4 • *Demons of Air and Darkness* • Keith R.A. DeCandido
#5 • *No Man's Land* • Christie Golden
#6 • *Cold Wars* • Peter David
#7 • *What Lay Beyond* • various
Epilogue: Here There Be Monsters • Keith R.A. DeCandido

Star Trek®: The Badlands

#1 • Susan Wright
#2 • Susan Wright

Star Trek®: Dark Passions

#1 • Susan Wright
#2 • Susan Wright

Star Trek®: The Brave and the Bold

#1 • Keith R.A. DeCandido
#2 • Keith R.A. DeCandido

Star Trek® Omnibus Editions

Invasion! Omnibus • various
Day of Honor Omnibus • various
The Captain's Table Omnibus • various
Star Trek: Odyssey • William Shatner with Judith and Garfield Reeves-Stevens
Millennium Omnibus • Judith and Garfield Reeves-Stevens
Starfleet: Year One • Michael Jan Friedman

Other Star Trek® Fiction

Legends of the Ferengi • Ira Steven Behr & Robert Hewitt Wolfe
Strange New Worlds, vol. I, II, III, IV, and V • Dean Wesley Smith, ed.
Adventures in Time and Space • Mary P. Taylor, ed.
Captain Proton: Defender of the Earth • D.W. "Prof" Smith
New Worlds, New Civilizations • Michael Jan Friedman
The Lives of Dax • Marco Palmieri, ed.
The Klingon Hamlet • Wil'yam Shex'pir
Enterprise Logs • Carol Greenburg, ed.
The Amazing Stories • various

UNLOCK THE SECRETS OF TEROK NOR
STAR TREK
DEEP SPACE NINE®
TECHNICALMANUAL
TECHNOLOGY FROM THE EDGE OF THE FINAL FRONTIER
AVAILABLE NOW FROM POCKET BOOKS

ds9T